Excessively Attentive

Jessica Schlenker

Excessively Attentive

ISBN 978-1-943801-09-1

Evening Primrose Press

press@firehazel.com

To my children, Cassandra and Alexander.

You were but a distant hope and a wish when this story first started. I am grateful for you every day.

Other Works by Jessica Schlenker

So Gradually: A Pride & Prejudice Tale

Solitude – *Freehold: Defiance*
Spider's Web – *Freehold: Resistance*

The First Magic – *Imagine THAT!*
All That is Gold

with Michael Williamson:

Skjaldmóðir – *Fantastic Hope*
Fire in the Grass – *Crucible (Valdemar)*
Medley – *Tempest (Valdemar)*

Chapters

One

"My dear Mrs. Collins!" Mr. Collins cried as he entered the house. "The wondrous Lady Catherine de Bourgh has seen fit to notice our family and Miss Bennet on only their second day in the area!"

"And how has she done so, Mr. Collins?" asked Mrs. Collins.

"She has expressly invited us all to tea, in an hour's time!" Mariah Lucas' response was to squeak and fan herself, while Sir William made comments about being so greatly honoured and his eldest's most fortunate alliance.

Mr. Collins urged the guests to retire and change, but to not be shamed for their lack of finery, for Lady Catherine "preferred the distinctions of class to be preserved."

Elizabeth was unsure how Mr. Collins construed this as a positive trait, but the turn of phrase recalled a moment in Meryton Assembly, with Mr. Darcy declaring to Mr. Bingley that he would not give notice to young women slighted by other men. She wished to judge the aunt without reference to the nephew, but her cousin's pronouncements certainly made that difficult when they seemed a piece of Mr. Darcy's behaviour. She firmly closed the door behind her, though it did little to silence her cousin's commentary.

Privately, Elizabeth owned she felt a strong curiosity about the great lady, as described by her cousin. Mr. Collins would likely be put out that she was certainly not experiencing the trepidation he was

7

loudly assuming. Her cousin's behaviour varied little from his visits to Hertfordshire, although he was, perhaps, not *quite* as marked in his attentions towards her. He had followed his guests up the stairs to share his inane proclamations as to how she *should* feel by his reckoning, interspersing admonishments to hurry her dressing. She forwent response to all of it, and continued to hold her tongue for Charlotte's sake. It gave her no small pleasure to perceive that his comments increasingly sounded frustrated that she was not in a dismayed state over her "failure" to make *this* "fortunate alliance." But she was desperate to be out of *his* house for at least a few hours. It was a small house, made smaller by the company of certain individuals.

The walk down the lane to Rosings Park showed plenty of evidence of early spring's touch stirring from its winter's slumber. She and Mariah pointed out several lovely specimens with new buds starting.

"Are these not the loveliest gardens in all of England?" Mr. Collins queried.

"They are certainly beautiful," Elizabeth acceded, "for gardens still waking up from winter." She thought of Hyde Park, a week into May, and the expansive roses there. Little could compare to *that* sight. "I suppose Lady Catherine prefers strict order, for I see no wilderness near this area," she continued. "It all seems quite regimented. I would hate to be the flower who grows out of bounds *here.*" Even the arboretum in London tolerated more deviance than could be seen within Rosings' front gardens, at least.

She nodded along as her cousin, once again, enumerated the cost of the glazing on the front windows, much as he had in her Aunt Phillips' parlour before Charlotte's wedding, nearly word for word. She agreed the house was indeed grand. She chose to restrain her commentary, as she felt it unwise to antagonize her cousin so early in her visit by actually *voicing* that she felt it too grand. Charlotte's willing amusement would suffice until later.

Mr. Collins and party were greeted by the doorman. Servants escorted the party to the little ante-room where Lady Catherine and her daughter Miss de Bourgh awaited their company. Elizabeth preferred a more brightly lit room herself, and she wondered at the dimness before recollecting Charlotte's comments about Miss de Bourgh's weak health. Mr. Collins began the introductions, Charlotte's father and sister being introduced first. Elizabeth stayed a little behind the rest of the party, waiting for her turn, while taking in the room itself. Of Lady Catherine herself, she felt the tug of remembrance, but after consideration, felt it must be the resemblance to Mr. Darcy.

"Cousin Elizabeth?" Mr. Collins queried, motioning her forward. She complied, stepping into direct light for the first time since she entered the room. Lady Catherine, at first, did not exactly look at her, appearing quite bored with the proceedings taking place in front of her. "And this is my cousin, Miss Elizabeth Bennet." Lady Catherine finally deigned to look Elizabeth full in the face, and with a half-strangled gasp, such a look of shock and surprise crossed her expression that Elizabeth was taken aback. Lady Catherine half rose from her chair, a hand stretching out to the girl before her. Miss de Bourgh, equally startled, grasped her mother's other arm.

"Elizabeth?" the great lady whispered. "Have you come back to us?"

Two

Half an hour after a startled Elizabeth replied with a reflexive "I beg your pardon?" the commotion in the ante-room quieted down, due in no small part to the ever-present practicality of Mrs. Charlotte Collins. While often practical herself, Elizabeth felt herself to be excused from such considerations after having been the target of hugs and tears from two women she honestly could not recall, but who were certain she was "their" Elizabeth. Mr. Collins did little other than attempt to admonish Elizabeth for upsetting her ladyship, at least until Lady Catherine rounded on him and told him in no uncertain terms to hold his tongue. He was currently seated in mute shock, slightly removed from the rest of the group.

Charlotte finally peeled Lady Catherine off of Elizabeth, although Miss de Bourgh proved, for all her slender sickliness, to be the more challenging of the two. And it was Charlotte, again, who finally asked the question, "What did you mean, 'come back to you?' To my knowledge, Elizabeth has never been in Kent before."

Miss de Bourgh spoke, after sharing a glance with her mother. "I was six, going on seven, the day my sister was born. I had barely turned ten the day she disappeared."

"Disappeared?" Elizabeth asked.

Lady Catherine rose from her chair again, pacing to the window. She reminded Elizabeth of Mr. Darcy again. "I never did discover how my second born disappeared, nor did we find any trace of her. Not a servant was missing. The nanny had just taken her for a nap, and had

10

come to tell me she might be a little feverish, and was certainly restless. Ten minutes later, when I followed her to the nursery, my Elizabeth was gone." Lady Catherine pressed a tightly clenched fist to her mouth, visibly attempting to force back sobs. "Sir Lewis roused the household to find her, and the search finally spilled out into the night." This time the sob broke through, though it was quickly stifled. "I remember it was a new moon, with so very little to see by outside. The searchers did not return until daylight, nor did my husband. At first, I was preoccupied with searching and re-searching the house for Elizabeth, but when Sir Lewis did not appear by midday, I had a few of the servants also looking for him. They found him and his horse, but …" Lady Catherine's voice trailed off.

Miss de Bourgh had closed her eyes in pain before picking up the story. "I remember Father as an excellent horseman. No one thought he would be thrown from a horse, but that appeared to be what happened. The party that found him brought him back to the house, but the injuries he sustained from the horse rolling over him were too much for him. Combined with the grief of losing Elizabeth, he lost his battle to survive not a week later."

Elizabeth felt it would be right to say something, anything, but the only things she could come up with sounded trite and uncaring. Still, the effort should be made. "A double blow, then," she said softly. "It must have been very difficult. My condolences." She hesitated, searching for the politest way to phrase her objection, "But I fail to see what this has to do with me."

Lady Catherine turned from the window. "Yes, it was. And as for what it has to do with you, Elizabeth – forgive me, but I cannot make myself call you 'Miss Bennet,' not now, not yet – it has quite a bit. But I think you should see what I mean. Anne?"

Miss de Bourgh concurred, and her companion immediately came to her assistance as she rose. Miss de Bourgh motioned her away.

"Miss Elizabeth? Would you mind very much lending me your assistance?"

Elizabeth could not think of a polite way to decline. She did not want to foster false hopes within Lady Catherine or her daughter that she was the missing Elizabeth. Miss de Bourgh took her arm, and Lady Catherine motioned for the party to follow. Sir William and Maria had been remarkably quiet throughout the conversation. Elizabeth hoped it would last at least a little bit longer. Miss de Bourgh, a wayward part of Elizabeth's mind noted, was actually almost of a size with her, although general ill-health kept her from being of the same weight, and from this particular angle, she could almost see a resemblance to her more awkward years, just a few years past.

Lady Catherine led them to the family portrait gallery, and they ended up in front of one of Lady Catherine some twenty years prior, seated with Sir Lewis de Bourgh, who had been shorter than his wife. Somewhere behind Elizabeth, Charlotte gasped in recognition. Elizabeth felt disconcerted as she looked up at a masculine face that so resembled her own. Her features were softer, with her cheek bones a fraction higher, but the slightly crooked nose she had always despaired at after a night of being compared to Jane was certainly the same as the one painted in front of her.

"You see now, why our reaction was so… marked," Lady Catherine said quietly. "I do apologize for that. We must have startled you terribly, Elizabeth. But I would not have my daughter frightened or scared of me."

"There is no saying for sure, Lady Catherine," Elizabeth responded after wrenching her attention from the portrait, "that I am indeed your lost daughter. Surely, Charlotte, *you* can remember hearing my birth be announced to your parents? Sir William, do you not recall anything?"

Sir William floundered, this not being a situation where civility could solve everything. "I ... cannot recall anything specific. It was, after all, nigh twenty years ago."

"Charlotte?"

Charlotte shook her head, frowning. "We had not yet moved to Lucas Lodge when you would have been born, Lizzy, not until you were six. And it was not until that point that our households became so close."

"Then, with your leave, Elizabeth, I would like to send an express to Mr. Bennet, to attend us here. My nephews, as well, as I believe Mrs. Collins has mentioned one of them, Mr. Darcy, is acquainted with your family?" Lady Catherine replied.

"Yes, we are, indeed, acquainted with Mr. Darcy, madam. But I am not certain my father will respond. He is… not fond of correspondence, or I should say more precisely, he is not fond of *responding.*"

A curious expression flashed across Lady Catherine's face when Elizabeth said 'my father.' If she had to name it anything, she would have said it was a mix of pain, wistfulness and fury, but it was so quick, she would not swear to seeing it. "Then, if he will not come *here,* on a matter of utmost urgency such as this, we will have to go *there.*" Lady Catherine's tone brooked no disagreement.

Elizabeth, not knowing what she should think, or what she wanted to think, actually had no disagreements with the plan at this moment. *Some*thing had to convince her ladyship that she was not the missing daughter. But, as she found herself involuntarily looking back up at the portrait, she admitted to herself that she less certain than she had been, not ten minutes ago.

Three

During the ensuing dinner and discussion, Lady Catherine broached the idea of Elizabeth removing to Rosings, to stay in one of the family rooms. Elizabeth prevailed after pointing out that she was still Charlotte's invited guest, and it would certainly cause talk amongst the servants and villagers. Lady Catherine finally agreed that it was proper for Elizabeth to remain at the parsonage, at least until they had more information from Mr. Bennet. "After all, since certain events, I have learned to be excessively attentive to such things." Her words echoed Mr. Wickham's descriptions of the lady, but her tone sketched a different picture than words alone.

Elizabeth spent the rest of the visit in a vain attempt to keep the de Bourghs' hopes from being brought too high. Her birthday somehow was brought up by a comment of Charlotte's, and it corresponded to their Elizabeth's. According to Lady Catherine, her daughter had been a bright, precocious child, with a fondness for and knack with animals of all sorts by the age of three. Her father had doted on her, already beginning to teach her how to read and simple mathematics, something that Miss de Bourgh laughed (interrupted by a cough) at, as she recounted her Cousin Darcy's astonishment at his then-youngest cousin's achievements. "I believe," Miss de Bourgh said, "he nudged our cousin Richard Fitzwilliam, who is slightly younger than either Darcy or me, and told him that he'd best be getting on with his reading as a three-year-old was beating him at it. The look on Richard's face was quite a sight to be seen."

During this entire time, Maria and Sir William spoke and participated in the discussion. To Elizabeth's embarrassment, some of her less genteel escapades were being shared with someone she did not know, and in front of her cousin, who, however silent he may be at the moment, would doubtlessly scold her later. Still, one bright spot in her day: should she indeed turn out to be a de Bourgh, then at least she would no longer be Mr. Collins' cousin!

But how would it affect poor Jane? Jane would always be her sister, she decided in the privacy of her mind, regardless of her bloodlines. And if Jane's *connections* were to include Mr. Darcy's own aunt, then surely Miss Bingley and Mr. Darcy would not be able to use that argument against Mr. Bingley any longer. She would do almost anything to further Jane's happiness, even be related to Mr. Darcy!

This thought encouraged her to exert herself over the remainder of the visit. Lady Catherine wanted to know all about her life… Then Lady Catherine was going to know about all of Jane's virtues and strengths, for without *those,* Elizabeth would have been condemned to Bedlam years ago.

To Elizabeth's private astonishment, Lady Catherine *did* seem to want to know all about her life, and she also seemed inclined to be interested in Jane's prospects and talents. "You speak so warmly of her, my dear," Lady Catherine added at one point, "that I cannot but believe you are very firmly attached to her. I would certainly not force you to give up anyone in your current life you did not want to: they may not be your real family, but they own the credit of taking you in and raising you as their own, as a gentlewoman. For that I could not praise and thank them enough."

Lady Catherine's gratitude almost broke at one point. "No governess? Five daughters and no governess?"

"You forget, ma'am," Elizabeth replied with as much civility as she could muster, reminding herself again that this entire situation was a very grey area in the realms of propriety, "that Longbourn is a modest, entailed estate, however old it may be. My fa–" Elizabeth caught herself, as she had already noticed Lady Catherine responded poorly to hearing him spoken of by that title, "Such of us as wished to learn, never wanted the means. We were always encouraged to read, and had all the masters that were necessary."

"Your education sounds like it has been neglected," Lady Catherine fretted, for lack of a better word, a worried frown creasing her brow for a moment.

Elizabeth felt a ripple of amusement as she found herself reassuring Lady Catherine. "Perhaps compared with some families, I believe we were, and those who chose to be idle, certainly might. But while I must confess my accomplishments do not include the ability to draw, it is because Mr. Bennet's library held a greater attraction for me than did charcoal and paper."

Lady Catherine seemed quite astonished at such an answer, and hardly knew how to respond. Therefore, she redirected the conversation towards Charlotte, asking her how the poultry got on. And after instructing Charlotte on a few more particulars, she turned her attention to Mr. Collins, asking after the general parish.

Finally, Mr. Collins could shine and speak, and speak he did. The flattery and anxiousness to please his patroness Elizabeth had previously noticed in Hertfordshire reappeared. He seemed to not know what to call Elizabeth; he stumbled over 'Cousin Elizabeth' a few times. The simultaneous displeasure of the de Bourgh ladies dissuaded him quickly, but he was not in the habit of referring to her as 'Miss Elizabeth'. He praised Elizabeth as completely as he praised Lady Catherine and Miss de Bourgh. Elizabeth ruefully resigned herself to having her abilities and attributes distorted by such an ineffectual lens. She could only hope that Lady Catherine and Miss de Bourgh were capable of filtering out Mr. Collins' more ridiculous comments about herself.

After a long, trying evening, the hour finally turned late enough that Lady Catherine could not detain the Hunsford party without being overly impolite. The carriage was offered to Mrs. Collins, who accepted it gratefully, and it was ordered around directly. Mr. Collins took the opportunity to alternate between thanking and re-thanking Lady Catherine for her evening's hospitality, and promising to take extremely good care of Elizabeth while she remained under his protection.

This reminded Lady Catherine, and she spoke to Elizabeth. "I shall send the express to Mr. Bennet on the morrow; I dare say it will take that long to compose. If you wish to have a letter sent along, do have a servant bring it over as early as possible."

Elizabeth thanked her ladyship for her offer, wondering if she did dare send a note to her father, and what she would write if she did. A laughing account of the spectacle made of her resemblance? It seemed too heartless to the de Bourghs to write such a thing, and she truly did want her father to respond, preferably with a sound negative. Perhaps she would simply entreat him to respond to Lady Catherine's letter as it merited, and not let it sit idle. Yes, that seemed like an appropriate option.

The carriage was announced, and Lady Catherine walked with the party to the door. She instructed Elizabeth on what to wear should she choose to venture out the next day, as surely Elizabeth would be caught in the spring storms on the morrow, and cautioned her to stay near the Park where she might be easily found. It occurred to Lady Catherine to suggest that a footman be made available for Elizabeth's walks, for betwixt Charlotte, Maria, and Mr. Collins, Lady Catherine had been apprised of Elizabeth's habit in all its dreary detail. However, Elizabeth firmly, but politely, pointed out that she had been walking on her own for several years now, and that it might give rise to gossip if she were found to be walking with a liveried servant of Rosings. She compromised: if Mrs. Collins could spare a servant, one would accompany her. A glance at Mrs. Collins revealed that she would definitely *not* be able to spare a servant at any point Elizabeth might be wanting to walk, and she felt relieved that her friend was willing to go along with a little misdirection.

Four

Mr. Collins' raptures were scattered even worse than normal as the carriage pulled away from the great house. "To think that you might be a de Bourgh, Miss Elizabeth! Such connections to so great a family as the de Bourghs could only benefit the Bennets and Mrs. Collins and myself."

Mrs. Collins attempted to stifle her husband's commentary. "While I am sure that Lizzy would not turn her back on either us or the Bennets, it truly is too early to start speculating how this might affect anyone." She gave Elizabeth an uneasy look as her husband completely missed the point.

"You are correct, my dear Charlotte. But Cousin Elizabeth must surely make use of this time to try to ensure that Lady Catherine takes her on, even if Mr. Bennet can positively state that Elizabeth is not her daughter, such a striking resemblance! Indeed, it may be for my Bennet cousins' benefit if Mr. Bennet and Miss Elizabeth do *not* dissuade Lady Catherine from her belief. Surely the dowry that Lady Catherine would settle on her would make what my cousin can offer her pale in comparison!" Elizabeth and Charlotte both reproved him for speaking so lightly of 'giving up' her family for such material concerns. Mr. Collins sputtered an attempt to say he had not *meant* that, but surely, they could see the benefits for all involved? Thankfully, the carriage arrived at the parsonage a moment later, providing Elizabeth the relief of escaping the carriage's close confines and she hid in her room.

Still, her thoughts would not rest, and she listened to the quiet murmurings of an occupied household slow and settle into a night's rest. She found herself in her nightclothes, sitting at the window, vaguely looking up at the moon. Her thoughts were in complete disarray, and she contemplated what she ought to write to her father. What about dear Jane and the Gardiners? Should she send them a letter as well, or wait to hear back from her father?

But here at long last, she had an answer to the enigma of Mr. Darcy's constant watching of her back in Hertfordshire. Despite her being only tolerable, he must have recognized her subconsciously, for even if she was not his relation, she looked much like she *could* be. She guessed he was very close to Miss de Bourgh in age. He most likely would have met his uncle Sir Lewis enough to have a vague recollection of his appearance, even if he did not remember it directly.

A quiet knock was followed by Charlotte's voice. "Lizzy?"

Elizabeth rose from her spot at the window and went to open the door for her friend. Charlotte held a tray of tea things, and Elizabeth bid her to enter. "I thought," said Charlotte, "that after this evening, you might benefit from a bit of tea to soothe you."

Elizabeth smiled. "It may help," she conceded, as Charlotte poured out a cup for her and added her preferred amount of sugar. Elizabeth took it from her and sipped it, her eyes closing as she luxuriated in the warmth.

"Do you wish to talk about it?" came the predictable question.

"I do not suppose there really is that much to talk about," Elizabeth sighed. "You heard everything that I did, and you would remember more than I would, regardless. Even your father was not able to recall anything. Then there is the portrait ..." her voice trailed off and then she shrugged.

Charlotte sighed as well. "Until today, I had not known that Lady Catherine had a second child, let alone that the child had been lost. I also had never seen the portrait of Sir Lewis. Lady Catherine has always subtly, for her, discouraged visitors from the portrait gallery."

Elizabeth frowned into her tea before taking another sip. "I suppose in a way that is reasonable. Unable to take the portraits down for fear of forgetting, but unwilling to be reminded of her losses." She glanced up at her friend. "Although I must admit I am shocked that Mr. Collins had not found out such a grave matter, given how *fond* of his patroness he is."

Charlotte, caught unawares by the comment, choked slightly on her tea when she laughed. A little anxious, but amused, Elizabeth started to rise to help, but Charlotte waved her back down. "How many times do I need to warn you, Lizzy, to not say things like that when my mouth is full?"

Elizabeth felt like laughing out loud, but did not wish to disturb their current solitude. "Oh, at least since my eighth birthday when you had convinced your parents to give me one of the pups from your father's prized hunting dogs to raise."

Charlotte giggled, albeit quietly. "Aye. I can see you now, as solemn as you ever got, swearing to your mother you would not let the puppy play in the mud then sleep in your bed, and finding out two days later that you'd meant it, because you intended for the two of you to be sleeping outside."

Elizabeth chuckled. "Well, it did get Mama to back down from *that* particular ultimatum."

Charlotte grinned. "Indeed, it did, although she complained to my mother for at least a week, until something distracted her from it." They lapsed into a companionable silence for a few moments, and then Charlotte put her cup down on the little table. "Lizzy?"

"Hmm?"

"What is your letter to your father going to say?"

Elizabeth grimaced. "I am not sure what to write. 'Dear Father, Lady Catherine wants to know if your favourite daughter might have been a foundling that happens to be her daughter. Please come rescue me, or find a knight in shining armour to save me from the dragon? – Lizzy'. That just does not sound quite right."

Charlotte chuckled at the 'knight in shining armour' comment before sobering a bit. "Something along those lines might not be out of place; but it may be exceedingly prudent that Jane is brought here as well. With that in mind, please note in your letter that I am extending an invitation to both your father and Jane to visit here for a few days, so as not to impose upon Rosings Park."

"But Charlotte –"

Charlotte raised a hand, forestalling her. "Lizzy, I have loved you like a sister since we first met, but right now, the two *you* need are your father and Jane. Mr. Collins unfortunately takes too much of my time to be as much use to you as I would like to be. Your father would need to stay in our smallest room, I fear, but you and Jane would not oppose to sharing?"

"Indeed, we would not. We do so at the Gardiners' when we stay there at the same time."

"Then it is settled," Charlotte nodded firmly, and then changed the subject before Elizabeth could protest again. "What do you think of Lady Catherine having her nephews attend her sooner than anticipated?"

Elizabeth sighed again. "I know nothing of Colonel Fitzwilliam. Mr. Darcy, however, almost certainly saw the resemblance, even if he did not know it himself. But, while I am aware that Mr. Darcy is intelligent, I must confess I am not eager to meet him again."

Charlotte nodded, looking off into the distance. "Lady Catherine," she started, "has frequently mentioned her hope that Mr. Darcy wed Miss de Bourgh." Here she glanced at her friend. "Given the frequency with which he looked at you in Hertfordshire, it would not be untoward to hope she may be persuaded to convince Mr. Darcy to make an offer to you instead, so that both of her daughters are well provided for."

"Untoward to hope Mr. Darcy would offer for me?" Elizabeth was aghast. She set the teacup down on its saucer. "Charlotte, do you not recall he said I was not tolerable enough to tempt him? That he was cold and arrogant to nearly all of Hertfordshire?"

Charlotte leaned over the small table and gripped Elizabeth's hand. "He is sensible, Eliza, more so than… certain other of your prospects. Lady Catherine speaks of him a great deal. Even in Hertfordshire, he never struck me as a *bad* man."

"But you heard what he did to Mr. Wickham as surely as I did," Elizabeth protested.

Charlotte pursed her lips and tilted her head, watching Elizabeth for a moment. "And, I know I have little room to speak, with Mr. Collins for my husband and Lady Catherine for my patroness, but does that not give you a pause at all?"

Elizabeth blinked at Charlotte, startled. "I… never thought of that," she admitted.

Charlotte nodded. "Neither did I," she agreed, "until these past few months. But it did occur to me earlier today, that… even if your father soundly denies you could be Lady Catherine's daughter, she still may consider you to be her responsibility. You *could* happen to mention Mr. Wickham in the next day or so, as a new acquaintance, and see how Lady Catherine responds."

Elizabeth bit her lip before nodding. "That is reasonable, I suppose. I guess…" she stopped and Charlotte raised an eyebrow to prompt her to continue. Elizabeth finished sheepishly. "I suppose I never really did get Mr. Darcy's side of the story, did I?"

"No, and nor did anyone else. Perhaps it is time to change that," Charlotte added, rising with the tea tray. "And now I shall quit talking your ears off and let you sleep. You need it."

"I have missed you, Charlotte," Elizabeth said, as she opened the door for her friend.

Charlotte flashed her a smile. "Not, I dare say, quite as I have missed *you,* Lizzy." With that, Charlotte was down the hallway and stepping down the little staircase. Elizabeth shut the door before returning to the windowsill. The late-night talk had taken an hour or so, she guessed, and she did not feel terribly less conflicted. But at least, she mused, the tea seemed to have done the trick, for at least she was considering her bed as a stop for the night.

Five

Elizabeth awoke the next morning to the same thoughts and meditations which had at length closed her eyes. Her mind was still awhirl, and she felt quite indisposed for writing to her father. But she knew that if she did not add her own entreaty to it, Lady Catherine's express might be read with indifference and not acted upon, or perhaps worse, not read at all. She assured herself that his answer would be in the negative, of course, for certainly he would have told her something, or the Gardiners or the Phillipses would have let it slip. Even Mrs. Bennet could not be trusted to not speak of it, and here Elizabeth came to a pause. She *was* her mother's least favourite daughter, which very well could be the foundation of her dislike. Elizabeth consoled herself as she finally gathered pen and paper to begin her note. As soon as she found a suitor she would accept, she would be Mrs. Bennet's favourite daughter, at least until one of the others managed the same feat.

Still, her pen hovered over her bottle of ink, as she frowned at the blank piece of paper. She dare not be flippant or risk her father not responding to Lady Catherine.

Hunsford Parsonage
March 13th

Dear Papa,

An interesting occurrence has arisen during my visit here at Hunsford. I assure you, I remain in the same good health that you saw me off in, and neither Charlotte nor my cousin are indisposed. Lady Catherine's express should detail the nature of the occurrence. I know not what to think of it.

Charlotte has requested that I extend her offer of hospitality to both you and Jane. She is under the belief that I would benefit from having the two of you here for the next few days while this is sorted out with Lady Catherine. I confess, my mind would be eased knowing that two of my dearest are close at hand. I beg you to please respond, be it by letter or in person.

Ever your loving daughter,

Elizabeth

She read it back over before nodding at it. Once she blotted and closed it, she addressed as proper. As she exited her room, she met Charlotte.

"Did you get your letter written, Lizzy?" Charlotte asked.

Elizabeth nodded, waving it. "I should deliver it to Rosings now, I suppose. Would you mind horribly if I did not sit down for breakfast immediately?"

Charlotte smiled and shook her head. "Of course not, Lizzy. Do as you need. I will simply inform Mr. Collins that you have gone to Rosings, and try to convince him not to follow."

Elizabeth laughed. "You are the best of friends, my dear Charlotte."

Charlotte disclaimed all praise and threw it back at her friend. "Be gone with you now. However tame Lady Catherine's behaviour was last night, I would not expect her to hold back the express any longer than she must."

Elizabeth nodded, and gathered her bonnet and other articles. She admitted to herself that while it may have been more proper for her to send a servant, she could not pass up the opportunity to forgo a morning of her cousin's company. Were it not for the events of last night and the letter in her, the beautiful weather alone would have ensured she had naught but enjoyment in her walk to the great house.

Upon approaching, a servant opened the door for her, and after she gave her name, took the letter, begging that she wait in the entryway. Apparently, Lady Catherine had given orders if Miss Elizabeth arrived, she was to be informed. The same servant hurried back with a second, who was carrying several letters to be dispatched. "Pardon me, ma'am, but her ladyship has offered you breakfast if you wish it." Elizabeth actually did *not* wish it, but felt it would be polite to sit a few moments before continuing her walk.

The breakfast nook was as grand as the rest of the house, and in her opinion, the setting did not lend itself to a comfortable meal. Still, Lady Catherine set as fine a breakfast table as she did a dinner table, and not even Elizabeth could resist her favourite dish when it smelled as divinely as it did at that moment. She made the necessary polite comments while Lady Catherine talked of nothing but how she had predicted but the night before such a clear and beautiful day. Elizabeth kept her countenance although she knew not how. Lady Catherine's opinion on the matter was finally exhausted as breakfast drew to a close. "We should, my dear," said she, "speak of what your dowry and entitlement will be."

Elizabeth coloured and spoke to forestall such a discussion. "Ma'am, I beg you recall we have not spoken with m- Mr. Bennet. Certainly, such a topic of discussion need not take place until that time, if at all?"

Lady Catherine pursed her lips. "Even if you were not my daughter, you are a gentlewoman, and in the last day, despite a tendency to voice a decided opinion, you have shown discretion." She tilted her head slightly. "But I agree to defer on details; those will require a solicitor regardless. But the general knowledge of the *Ton* has been that should my missing daughter be recovered, there is a small estate and a fortune of fifteen thousand pounds settled on her. There have been … attempts … at persuading us of false identities before, although it has been some years."

Miss de Bourgh glowered at her mother's reminder, and said nothing. The sharp clink of her fork into her breakfast plate as she stabbed at her meal spoke for her. Elizabeth surmised she had not forgiven the transgressor, and sympathized with such a position.

Lady Catherine rose, signalling the end of breakfast. "Indeed, Elizabeth, I do believe you can be trusted." Lady Catherine inclined her head towards Elizabeth and then Anne. "I have some matters of business to discuss with the steward. I have little doubt, Elizabeth, that you will insist on continuing your morning constitutional now that you have broken your fast. I suggest you wander to the East Garden; it is most attractive in the morning sun."

Elizabeth managed to formulate a polite response, and took her leave of both Lady Catherine and Miss de Bourgh. An oppressive weight seemed to lift off of her shoulders as she exited the house. If Lady Catherine remained this… overbearing, even *if* she was her daughter, how would she remain in such a household? Her opinion of the lady, as of yesterday, had been far more favourable. Charlotte *had* said Lady Catherine's behaviour had been tame in comparison to her usual self. As Elizabeth made for a path that she had already established a preference for in the past few days, studiously avoiding the garden on the morning-side of the house, she wondered how she would make it through the next few days. Her father could not be expected to be here much before the day after tomorrow, and that would only be if it was possible for him to leave the estate on such short notice with neither Jane nor herself there to stay in his stead.

Eventually, Elizabeth's thoughts turned towards her might-be-cousins. The Fitzwilliams she knew little of, other than Mr. Darcy's mother had been a Fitzwilliam, the daughter of an earl, which made Mr. Darcy the grandson of an earl. Laughter bubbled up inside of her as she imagined the look on Mr. Darcy's face if Lady Catherine announced they, after all, were cousins. She wondered if he would remark that he could not be related to someone who was not handsome enough to tempt him, but she reminded herself, Miss de Bourgh was too ill to be handsome. However, had she been healthy, that may have been a different case altogether.

But even these thoughts gave way as she contemplated Jane's situation. How would she stand being parted from the one person she loved as much as her father? Her younger sisters, as much as she loved them, being parted from them would in all honesty not be a bad thing. Should the idea be true, it was entirely possible that Lady Catherine and her father *would* agree to place her within the de Bourgh household. It would be a fine connection for the Bennet girls, and one less split of their meagre fortune. She was unsure whether to trust Lady Catherine's previous statement of not wishing to part her from her beloveds after her officiousness this morning. Which was the true Lady Catherine?

Mr. Wickham's comments offered little help, although she could see some of the same behaviour Mr. Darcy exhibited under duress in Lady Catherine. Proud and condescending, she could well believe, but even when she had suggested the East Garden, Elizabeth now felt Lady Catherine's motives had been to try to give Elizabeth a chance to familiarize herself with Rosings on as much of her own terms as Lady Catherine could give her room to do so. She felt a prickling of shame and guilt she had so rebelliously avoided the garden. The older woman must be as terribly confused as Elizabeth herself was: here she had the girl she believed to be her daughter, yet was a stranger to her. Her maternal feelings must surely be at war with her more normal behaviour, and it was clear she was a woman who considered herself to be in charge of all matters within her realm, even if they were not *actually* within her control.

Elizabeth found herself looking at a small pond with a log bench beside it. She sat and tried to lose herself in the quiet whispers of the breeze in the trees, the chatter of the birds, the sounds of the insects and frogs. But to no avail, not even here was there respite from her confusion. She sighed and took in a slow deep breath, much like she would when trying to combat her embarrassment at her mother's behaviour, exhaling just as slowly. And then she began to list the pros and cons of each possibility. Better to be prepared, she supposed, than caught unawares, if Mr. Bennet told them she *had* been a foundling.

Elizabeth started off with the problems: being related to a family who was prideful, arrogant and condescending was certainly a con in her books. Still, Elizabeth had to admit, even Mr. Darcy's pride was not entirely undeserved; he was easily one of the most intelligent men Elizabeth had had the displeasure of meeting. Strength of mind and character were two traits that Elizabeth herself prized and prided herself on, something she certainly had in common with Mr. Darcy and the de Bourghs, from her current observation.

In Lady Catherine's favour, Elizabeth had to start off with the fact that Lady Catherine seemed to be endeavouring to remember all of Elizabeth's preferences, that she preferred to walk for long periods of time, even how much sugar she took in her tea. Charlotte had mentioned some time that Elizabeth favoured strawberry jam to honey on her toast, and Elizabeth distinctly recalled that Lady Catherine noted how little she and Anne liked strawberries. Apparently, it had been their Elizabeth's favourite food, and they never did understand why. Yet this morning, there had been strawberry jam on the table for her use. When compared with the mother who had raised her, Lady Catherine's behaviour seemed far more concerned with *her* than with Lady Catherine's own wishes. The oft-repressed desire for a mother more like herself in temperament attempted to raise its head for a moment before Elizabeth promptly pushed it back down under the proverbial table.

She came to the conclusion she was in the same situation she was before she settled down to think about it: she had no idea what to think. She could only hope that Mr. Bennet would arrive sooner rather than later, and that he would have the answer to put this entire incident to rest. Then she could go home in five weeks, and in ten years look back at this and laugh at her confusion. She started back for the parsonage. She certainly was not doing anyone, including herself, any good out here contemplating something that could not possibly be true

Six

"Lizzy!" Miss Lucas cried, when she returned. "Come help us!" She had been waiting in the hallway for her, apparently, and began tugging Elizabeth towards the kitchen.

Elizabeth frowned, removing her outdoor garments quickly. "Of course, Maria. With what, may I ask?" Maria pulled her into the kitchen and gestured at the main preparation table.

Mrs. Collins hovered over a basket, looking up as Maria pushed open the door. "Oh, thank goodness, Lizzy, you are here. *You* know what to do in these situations."

"In what –" Elizabeth broke off, for the basket had answered her question with a hungry, tired little mewling. "Ah." Elizabeth felt amused. Surely Charlotte should know this by *now*. Still, she moved over the basket to peer down into it. A little black and white kitten blearily peered back up at her, then mewled again. "And who might you be?" she asked the kitten, already reaching to pet the tiny, bony creature. "An egg yolk, milk and a little bit of sugar, well mixed and warmed up. A clean rag. Goat's milk, if you have any, would be best, or sheep's milk," she added as an aside to Charlotte and the kitchen maid who hurried to find what she requested.

The kitten was hungry, and immediately began to investigate her hand to see if it could nurse on her fingers. "Shh, little one. In due time," Elizabeth cooed at the baby. She glanced at Maria. "I take it there are no other kittens?"

Maria shook her head, large brown eyes filling with tears. "I found him in with a couple of other kittens, but they were not ..." Maria glanced away from Elizabeth, trying to stifle herself. "I saw no signs of the queen."

Elizabeth nodded, and patted Maria on the shoulder with her unclaimed hand. "Sometimes it happens that way. At least this one has a chance."

"Does he?" Maria asked hopefully.

"That mostly depends on it," Elizabeth replied. "It seems hungry enough – that is a good sign. It is a little young to be motherless, but not so young it definitely will not make it. I think it is four or five weeks old. We may even be able to get it eating some of the leftovers from the meat dishes in the next couple of days."

Maria nodded, and reached into the basket to pet the kitten. "I have never had a queen abandon her kittens before."

Elizabeth could only shrug helplessly. "She may not have abandoned them by choice. I wonder if there are any nursing cats nearby who might take this one on. That might be for the best."

Charlotte and the kitchen maid appeared with her requisitions. "Shall I show you how to feed the kitten, Maria?" Elizabeth asked.

Maria's eyes lit up. "Do you think I can help then?"

Elizabeth laughed. "Of course. Just because your older sister has problems with taking care of kittens, it does not necessarily follow that you should."

"Lizzy!" Charlotte protested. Elizabeth merely grinned at her friend before showing Maria how to test to make sure the milk was not too warm, and how to soak up just a small amount to give to the kitten at a time. Soon, the kitten's belly was full, and Maria was ecstatic that the kitten had fallen asleep in her arms.

Maria refused to relinquish the kitten, still cuddling it in the sitting room when Mr. Collins returned to the house half an hour later, Sir William in tow. Mr. Collins was taken aback when he had three women shush him upon loudly coming into the room. "You will wake the kitten, my dear," Charlotte told him.

"A kitten?" Mr. Collins repeated stupidly.

"Maria found an abandoned kitten," she explained.

"Is he not adorable, brother? See, father?" Maria piped up, still protectively cradling the leggy ball of fur.

Sir William, well used to random creatures being dragged into his or a neighbour's house by anyone close to Elizabeth, nodded and wisely agreed with his daughter. Mr. Collins simply shook it off much like a dog shakes water, and continued to relay to Elizabeth what he had intended to in the first place. "Cousin, Lady Catherine has invited us to dinner again tonight; she thinks it is not unlikely that her nephews may arrive, and she wishes to see if they see the resemblance before she tells them of her beliefs."

Maria, surprisingly, protested. "But if we go to Rosings, who will tend the kitten?"

"The kitten could be left with the servants," Charlotte responded, "unless you wish to stay at home to tend to him."

Maria looked divided – the glories of a dinner at Rosings, and the chance for more gossip, versus the lure of caring for an abandoned kitten. Elizabeth solved it. "Maria, if you leave the kitten with the staff this evening, you could simply care for him overnight. The kitten will surely get hungry in the middle of the night."

"Oh." Maria considered the idea. "That would keep me from being impolite, would it not?"

"Indeed, it would," Elizabeth concurred. To herself, she could only hope that Maria's chattering about the kitten may help prevent Lady Catherine from divulging any other family information. If the remainder of the day was any indicator, Elizabeth felt there was a good chance this would hold true. Maria, having never cared for a kitten or even an older cat all on her own, spent the day peppering Elizabeth with questions of all sorts. Elizabeth finally managed to talk to Charlotte alone for a moment, and she asked, "I do hope Sir William will not mind another mouth to feed? I do not think Maria is going to give up the kitten easily."

Charlotte smiled in the direction of her younger sister, seated across the room, quite engrossed by the baby. "Oh, after having lived around you for all this time, my dear Lizzy, I doubt anyone in Hertfordshire would have the gall to deny a kitten admittance into their household."

"Charlotte!" Charlotte merely grinned and went back to her sewing.

When it came time to dress, Maria startled Charlotte and Elizabeth both, by hurrying and barely caring how she looked. She wanted to stay with the kitten as long as possible. Elizabeth, on the other hand, discovered she felt a little bit of trepidation at the idea of meeting the forbidding Mr. Darcy and the unknown Fitzwilliam cousin under such circumstances. She did her best to not dress up any more than she would have a day ago, but she suspected she failed. She could only hope that no one would interpret it as her attempting to catch either one's eye, particularly after Charlotte's comments from the night before.

Even after the kitchen maid swore faithfully to wait on the kitten's every demand while she was gone, Maria was fretful about leaving the little one behind, and could barely make herself walk from the parsonage to Rosings. Elizabeth and Charlotte kept their countenances at Maria's constant turning around to look at the parsonage, even after it was not easily in sight, but Elizabeth knew not how she did it. When finally, they reached Rosings, Maria remembered herself, mostly, and began to attend to what was going on around her.

They attended Lady Catherine in the parlour, and both she and Miss de Bourgh greeted the party more civilly than Elizabeth would have suspected from this morning's interactions. Thankfully, when asked how she was doing, instead of giving the normal politely positive answer, Maria launched into a retelling of the day's events, and not even Lady Catherine's astonishment could slow her words. She was quite oblivious to anything except talking about the kitten, even though shortly she had repeated herself at least twice. The only thing Elizabeth regretted about the situation was how often she was praised by Maria for knowing how to take care of the kitten and for showing *her* how to do it as well.

It was in the middle of the third, or was it fifth? Seventh? Elizabeth had lost track at least a repetition ago, recital of Maria's kitten-filled day that the sound of newly arrived guests broke into the room. Even as it was apparent that the guests were not going to immediately enter the parlour, almost certainly going up to their rooms to refresh themselves prior to being seen, there was no question that Elizabeth was going to have to face Colonel Fitzwilliam and Mr. Darcy today, after all.

Seven

Lady Catherine sent messages up to her guests, requesting their presence as soon as may be, on the matter of grave importance she had mentioned, but not specified, in her express that morning. Elizabeth hoped Lady Catherine had been more specific in the letter to her father, else Mr. Bennet would never come, even with Elizabeth's own entreaty.

As it was, Elizabeth sat in Lady Catherine's sitting room, feeling as if she were on tenterhooks with the morrow's meal. Searching for some sort of employment until she had to face Mr. Darcy again, she asked if Lady Catherine minded over-much if she availed herself of the pianoforte for the next few moments. Lady Catherine, anxious to hear her capabilities, agreed.

Thus, Mr. Darcy found himself walking head-on into a situation that, during waking hours, he avowed to himself was his worst possible nightmare: Elizabeth Bennet seated at a piano, singing. However, one must also add that for a "worst possible nightmare," Mr. Darcy had regularly found himself lingering abed to recall those dreams a time or three, these past few months.

He stopped. He stared. And Colonel Fitzwilliam ran smack into him, while he stood dumb in the doorway. "I say, Darcy, what is the matter with you?" the colonel exclaimed. Elizabeth, startled by the unknown and somewhat unexpected voice, missed a few notes and then stopped playing. She had nearly forgotten why she had retired herself to the pianoforte. Mr. Darcy had, by this point, roused himself from his momentary stupefaction, and come into the room, bowing as he greeted the occupants, the colonel coming up behind.

"Come here, Elizabeth," Lady Catherine beckoned. "I should introduce you to Colonel Fitzwilliam." Elizabeth duly came to Lady Catherine and Miss de Bourgh's side, and it was then that both Mr. Darcy and Colonel Fitzwilliam stiffened in recognition.

"But –" Mr. Darcy started.

"How –" the Colonel sputtered.

Lady Catherine nodded, a triumphant expression on her face. "You see what I do, then. I can only suppose," she nodded at Darcy, "that the resemblance to Anne was something you would not have seen without them side by side."

"I –" Mr. Darcy was at a loss. He could not very well admit he had been looking at Elizabeth for months, although something in Elizabeth's expression made him believe she had been quite aware of his attention. An emotion he hesitated to call "hope" began to rise in him. If she *was*... but there was still much to be discussed and analysed, he reminded himself before he could finish that thought.

Elizabeth, on the other hand, was surveying both the men in front of her. Colonel Fitzwilliam had the air of a generally genial man, an almost convivial attitude that Elizabeth would have thought at odds with someone in the regulars. He was not as handsome as his cousin, but not unpleasant either. Mr. Darcy, on the other hand... she almost suspected he was more *relieved* by this possible revelation than horrified, as she had privately believed he would be. Perhaps, she reasoned, it was that now he had the answer as to why he had been unable to stop watching her.

Mr. Darcy started again. "I readily admit, Aunt Catherine, I never even thought to consider such a possibility." He shrugged slightly. "We had, after all, given up on finding my cousin Elizabeth years ago." He glanced between Miss de Bourgh and Elizabeth again. "But the resemblance is… striking."

Mrs. Collins agreed. "The portrait of Sir Lewis looks much like her, although one can see the Fitzwilliam influence."

Mr. Darcy became grave again. "Has Mr. Bennet been asked about Miss Elizabeth's history?"

Lady Catherine nodded. "I sent an express to him at the same time I sent the one to you."

"Then, with any luck, he may be here as soon as tomorrow," Mr. Darcy half-asked, glancing at Elizabeth.

She smiled mirthlessly, before moving back in the direction of the pianoforte. "Only, Mr. Darcy, if he does not treat this as a grand joke." Ordinarily, she would not be so interested in the pianoforte, but she preferred the option of music to talk about something she still refused to believe was a possibility, even with the growing consensus among the also growing party at Rosings that she did indeed favour the de Bourghs in appearance.

Mrs. Collins observed Mr. Darcy as he watched her friend return to the pianoforte. He was as inscrutable as he had ever been in Hertfordshire, but the intensity with which he watched Elizabeth gave Charlotte a great deal of hope for Elizabeth's future. However, she retrained her attention to Elizabeth's performance when she realized that Lady Catherine had noticed her watching Mr. Darcy watching Elizabeth. Lady Catherine bore a thoughtful frown as she glanced between Mr. Darcy, Elizabeth, and Anne. Mr. Darcy compounded the problem himself, however, when he attended Elizabeth to the pianoforte, ostensibly to turn the pages for her. Elizabeth had little choice but to be polite and accept his assistance.

Thankfully, to Elizabeth's mind, dinner was announced 'ere long, and she rose quickly from the pianoforte to escape Mr. Darcy, believing he would be relieved to not have to escort her to the dining room. He forestalled her by requesting exactly that, and Elizabeth had to stifle an impulse to glance around for someone else to lay prior claim to that office. Elizabeth acquiesced with as much grace as she could muster. She hoped she would be able to escape to the far end of the table once in the dining room, but to no avail. As soon as they entered, Lady Catherine asked, "Elizabeth, I should like it if you sat on my left, across from Anne. Darcy can sit beside you." Elizabeth once again found herself caught by politeness.

The only saving grace remained that Maria was in easy speaking distance, and after the servants had withdrawn for the moment, Elizabeth forestalled direct conversation with herself with a single question. "Maria, have you given thought as to what you will name the kitten?" And Maria was off, talking of nothing but the kitten.

Mr. Darcy was quiet and grave as usual, to Elizabeth's experience, although she did detect at least a slight amusement at Maria's single-mindedness. Still, he did ask some pertinent questions of Maria regarding the kitten, and the colonel made a few suggestions for a name. Mr. Darcy cautioned against naming the kitten anything too *suggestive,* thereby shutting down one of the colonel's suggestions of "Loki." Mr. Darcy carefully worked around to asking how the kitten was found, and the recital of the morning's events began once again. Elizabeth felt the tiniest bit of relief, surely if Lady Catherine had been unable to turn Maria's attention away from the kitten directly, Mr. Darcy would meet with the same failure.

To Elizabeth's dismay, alas, she was proven wrong. Mr. Darcy, for all his sullen graveness in Hertfordshire, proved quite adept at getting a young girl on to the topic he wanted, which involved Elizabeth and her habit of rescuing kittens and puppies and anything else, except horses, that came with four legs. Elizabeth reminded herself that Mr. Darcy did have a younger sister about Maria's age. "You do not like horses, Miss Elizabeth?" the colonel asked in astonishment.

"For as long as I can remember, I have trusted my own two feet more than four feet under the control of another," she replied.

Mr. Darcy looked thoughtful. "Do you remember, Fitzwilliam, during our last visit to Rosings before our cousin disappeared, how enthralled she was with the horses?"

The colonel laughed. "Indeed. She did little but beg us for a ride on the pony your father bought for you and Wick—" here the Colonel abruptly stopped, and Mr. Darcy and he turned simultaneously grave and quiet for a few minutes. Lady Catherine glowered and Miss de Bourgh drummed her fingers on the table for a moment.

Elizabeth longed to ask what Wickham had been doing at Rosings with the Darcy and Fitzwilliam families, or even to mention she had met him, and thought him amiable, but from the expressions of the four seated closest to her, she thought that may be foolhardy.

Charlotte had other ideas.

"We met Mr. Wickham in Hertfordshire, when he joined the regiment there," she said nonchalantly into the lull. "I and several others thought him quite amiable. Although he had told us there was a… falling out, between himself and you, Mr. Darcy."

Lady Catherine spoke, her expression exceedingly grim. "Mr. Wickham is no longer acquainted with this family, Mrs. Collins. And for the time being, this will be the last time his name is brought up in a conversation." Mr. Darcy had turned exceptionally pensive and withdrawn, even for a normally quiet and taciturn man.

Elizabeth was astonished. Such a baldly stated disassociation was worse than the cut direct, and she could not help but wonder what could have affected such a thing. Even a steward's son could be a useful connection, for properly trained stewards were fiendishly difficult to come by, and as rare a commodity as a rich single man of marriageable age. A sullen air hung heavily over the remainder of the meal, and extended into the visiting hours.

At last, Lady Catherine offered the use of her carriage again, and Mrs. Collins accepted. Lady Catherine spoke to Elizabeth while they waited. "The moment Mr. Bennet arrives, do send me word, for I should like to speak to him as soon as may be."

Elizabeth nodded. The sooner her father arrived and put an end to this flight of fancy on behalf of the de Bourghs, the sooner her life could go back to normal.

* * *

Thomas Bennet read and re-read the express from his cousin's patroness with rising disbelief. After seventeen years, he had long since stopped fearing this day would come. He required all of his composure to keep himself from crying. Fanny… she would need to be told. Fortunately, Kitty and Lydia were walking into Meryton. Even Mary had bestirred herself to accompany them, and he knew where to find his wife at this time of day.

He stood outside of her bedroom door, steeling himself for the conversation to come. He knocked. "Fanny?"

She opened the door. "Yes?"

"May I come in?" She was perplexed, he could see, for it had been several years since he had willingly stepped foot in here, for all too often it had reminded him of his multiple failures, but she opened the door further for him to enter.

Once inside, he felt his resolve start to crack. He took Fanny's arm and led her to a chair. He kneeled beside it, holding her hands. "My dear, I have an express from Lady Catherine de Bourgh."

Mrs. Bennet was all astonishment. "What could her ladyship have to say? Oh, I hope my dear Lizzy is well, even if she is an entirely ungrateful daughter."

Mr. Bennet swallowed hard. "It is, indeed, about Lizzy." He stayed her as she began to rise in a fret. "She is well. But..." he closed his eyes, and then pulled Lady Catherine's letter from his pocket. "I think it best if you read this."

Mrs. Bennet took the letter from him and began to read. She sat in mute shock for a moment, and then began to protest its contents. "This cannot – She is *our* Lizzy." Mrs. Bennet started to cry, reaching for her husband. "Please, do not let her take our Lizzy away from me! Not a second time!"

Mr. Bennet drew his wife to him, his own tears dampening her hair, but said nothing, for he knew not what to say.

Eight

When Madeline Gardiner heard her brother-in-law's voice at her door, so late in the day, she was instantly worried something grievous had happened at Longbourn. Mr. Bennet disliked travel intensely, and would often go to great lengths to avoid it. To find him *here...* she would not complete the thought until she knew more of the situation. The maid announced him to the room, just as Jane turned around and saw her father.

"Papa!" Jane was clearly pleased to see him, until concern flashed across her face. "This is unexpected; how fares my mother?"

"Jane, it is good to see you looking tolerably well. Your mother is... well enough." Mr. Bennet rarely temporized, and this heightened both Mrs. Gardiner's suspicions as well as her niece's. "My dear sister Gardiner, it is good to see you as well."

"Brother Bennet, the same. What brings you to London then?" she asked. There was no sense in beating around the bush about the unusual situation.

An expression Mrs. Gardiner recalled from the earliest days of her acquaintance with her now-brother flashed across his face so quickly, she could not be sure she had seen it. "There is a matter that I need to speak with both of you and Mr. Gardiner about, prior to my travelling to see Lizzy. Jane will be accompanying me, and it may be best for all of us if you came with us, sister."

Jane gasped. "Is Lizzy ill? Injured?"

44

This time the expression could be nothing other than what Mrs. Gardiner had suspected originally. "She is in health. This… does concern her, and by extension, the entire family."

Mrs. Gardiner watched her brother-in-law for a few minutes more. "It has been discovered then, has it?"

Mr. Bennet looked away from Mrs. Gardiner and drew in a deep breath before nodding, still not looking at either of the women. "Indeed, it has, although only a part of the story is known."

Jane looked between her father and her aunt, clearly bewildered. "I do not understand. What is going on with Lizzy?"

Mrs. Gardiner patted her niece's hand. "In due time, my love," she said. "I doubt either your father or your uncle will have the strength to tell the tale twice, much less three times."

"You share part of it, Madeline," Mr. Bennet observed quietly.

"Yes," she sighed. "Indeed, I do."

* * *

Elizabeth escaped the next morning, as early as she was able. She did not wish to speak to anyone; she only wanted Jane or her father. She resolved to avoid the party at Rosings Park, and even her dear friend if she must, to avoid the discussions about her possible parentage. She hoped, desperately, that her father was able to arrive today, tomorrow at the latest, because it was increasingly difficult to force everyone around her to recall they had not verified *anything* yet, had not established *anything* apart from a likeness to a portrait and Anne de Bourgh.

Everyone, except Maria, who only partook partially, as the kitten absorbed most of her attention, discussed, without reference to any wishes of Elizabeth's, how her future should be handled. Mr. Darcy had even intoned, "But of course she must come to Pemberley after she has gotten comfortable at Rosings. I have been looking after Brandywine for Aunt Catherine since I took over the management of Pemberley. It would allow me a chance to introduce you to your own estate, Miss Elizabeth, and to show you the paperwork and books."

Frustration was not an unknown emotion to Elizabeth, but it had always before been related to her mother and her younger sisters, and the occasional gentleman who attempted to court her, or Mr. Darcy, but he was his own category in more ways than one. Now she felt frustrated at everyone, Lady Catherine, Mr. Collins (that was not unexpected), Mr. Darcy (again, not unexpected), Miss de Bourgh, herself, Charlotte, her father and even Jane. The latter two had become a source of frustration the longer the day wore on without news they were to arrive or had arrived.

She found herself seated on the log bench once again after a couple hours of restless walking up and down the paths around the parsonage and Rosings Park. With a conscious effort, she focused on the sights and sounds around her, attempting to lose herself in more pleasant reflections. Such a plan proceeded with difficulty, but she persevered, settling on recitation of multiplication tables as a method of distraction when her mind would not quiet of its own accord. Diverted by the cool logic of the activity, she became properly inattentive to her surroundings, as one ought, when seeking solace outside.

"Six times three," she started.

"Is eighteen," supplied a most unwelcome voice.

"Mr. Darcy!" she exclaimed, rising. "Forgive me, I did not notice you."

"It is of little matter, Miss Elizabeth," he replied. With a slight smile, he continued, moving to stand by the bench looking at the lake, "Although I had thought your enjoyment of nature to be such as to not need mathematical recitations to enhance it."

Elizabeth coloured but spoke with composure. "I was always fond of mathematics, multiplication in particular. I enjoyed watching the patterns evolve. Mathematics, at least, follows a clear logic, and does not vary based on one's mood."

"It is good to know I am not the only soul in the world who resorts to numbers as a way to quiet my thoughts," Mr. Darcy replied. "And I suppose situations like the one we are currently experiencing are so unnatural as to need greater measures to be employed to act as one ought."

"Just so," Elizabeth concurred and lapsed into silence. She had truly nothing she felt like discussing with Mr. Darcy.

Mr. Darcy continued to stand for a moment longer before asking, "May I join you on the bench?"

"Oh, excuse me, of course." Elizabeth started to rise, "But I should likely return to the parsonage; Charlotte is sure to have missed me these last few hours."

Mr. Darcy prevented her. "Mrs. Collins is aware of your discomfort, Miss Elizabeth. When she sent me in the correct direction to look for you, she also said you were perfectly welcome to stay out as you felt necessary."

"She sent you to look for me?" Elizabeth's expression showed her doubt.

Mr. Darcy looked mildly abashed. "I offered to find you, after Mr. Collins professed concern about you being out so long and started to suggest he look for you himself. I thought… you may wish to avoid his company a bit longer."

Elizabeth could not help but laugh at such an astute observation. "You are forgiven, then, for interrupting me. But I should still return."

"I…" Mr. Darcy paused, searching for words. "I did not just come to find you. I wanted to discuss a mutual acquaintance of ours."

Elizabeth felt a rush of sudden anger, and rose abruptly. "There is little regarding either Mr. Bingley or his damage to my sister that I wish to discuss."

Mr. Darcy looked startled. "I was not speaking of my friend, but of another person, the one touched upon last night."

"I am sure there is even less regarding your and this family's treatment of Mr. Wickham I care to hear, Mr. Darcy," she responded coldly. For the moment, she could not be neutrally rational, as she had the last three days. "From all that I have seen, even if I *am* Lady Catherine's missing daughter, I am not sure I could force myself to associate with such a family."

Mr. Darcy flushed with anger himself, before going pale. "Force yourself to associate with your own family?"

"Indeed, sir," she replied. "Even *if* this wild hare of an idea is true, do you think I would give up the family who raised me, give up my father or Jane, who is as much an angel as any mere mortal could be, for one that is cold and unfeeling of those outside of their immediate circle? For a family that can be so heartless to one raised as their own? Be cousin to one of my own enemies?"

"You speak, I suppose, of Mr. Wickham's supposed problems caused by my hand?"

"Supposed?!"

"Yes, supposed." Mr. Darcy had risen himself, and would not look at her, his hands clasped so tightly behind his back that his knuckles had turned white. "It is a story that must be kept within the family, Miss Elizabeth, and I do mean the Bennets as well as the Darcys and Fitzwilliams." He finally looked at her. "Because they *are* your family, even if you belong to us, even as degrading as such connections might be for us, gratitude and respect for raising you as they have must take precedence over everything else."

"Degrading!" Elizabeth snorted. "At least my mother does not offend every person she meets the moment she meets them, unlike yourself."

"Lady Catherine is your mother," Mr. Darcy replied quietly, ignoring the rest of her comment.

"You are mistaken. Mrs. Bennet is my mother."

Mr. Darcy closed his eyes for a moment, and then opened them to look at Elizabeth. She was startled, for she had thought he was furious with her, but his expression… was something else, something she could not define. "Yes, she is," he finally agreed. "But so is Lady Catherine. And here and now is not the place to discuss what we need to regarding Mr. Wickham, and I do not wish to have to repeat it to Mr. Bennet when he arrives. I should much rather we say it only once."

Elizabeth gritted her teeth. "And what of Mr. Bingley and his toying with my sister?"

"That…" Mr. Darcy looked torn asunder. "I am sorry, Miss Elizabeth. Mr. Bingley is his own man. I had not realized Miss Bennet was so attached to him as you seem to indicate; else I would have counselled him more strongly to return to Netherfield."

"You… counselled him to return?" Elizabeth was startled. She had felt sure he had helped keep Mr. Bingley from Jane.

"His… sisters wished for me to do otherwise," he confessed, once again not looking at her. "At first I thought the same, but the more I thought upon it, on the ride into London, the more I felt his honour had been engaged, after such marked attentions. I told him both my concerns for such a match, as I believed Miss Bennet to only be but slightly touched, and my concerns for *him* if he did not make an offer.

And when he settled upon returning only a week after he had originally meant to, to weigh his options, in a distinctly non-Bingley fashion, Mr. and Mrs. Hurst left Miss Bingley while they travelled to visit Mr. Hurst's family."

Elizabeth was not sure if she was angrier he had originally set out from Netherfield to dissuade Mr. Bingley, or that Miss Bingley had apparently forced her brother into remaining in London. "But she has been in town these last three months," she finally settled on saying.

Mr. Darcy's head snapped around. "I had not heard a word of it, and I know Mr. Bingley has not; surely she has corresponded with Miss Bingley?"

"Miss Bingley stated that her brother had been much engaged with visits to you and your sister, and that she had informed her brother of Jane's stay. She spoke of her certainty of calling Miss Darcy her sister at some point in the near future." She could not quite bring herself to tell Mr. Darcy how injured Jane truly was, not yet.

"My sister is not yet out, and will not be for another two years at least," Mr. Darcy replied. He glowered at the pond a few more moments, while Elizabeth once again thought of several punishments for Miss Bingley and Mrs. Hurst. He broke the silence. "I had not realized your opinion of me," he said quietly. "I am sorry to have… misinterpreted things. In the name of… familial harmony, I should like to propose that you and I call a truce, Miss Elizabeth, at least until we know of more from Mr. Bennet. I have never wanted to quarrel with you."

Elizabeth felt disoriented once again. Politeness forced an answer from her. "I cannot promise to not quarrel with you, Mr. Darcy. Forgive me for assuming you had anything to do with my sister's pain, but until I have the particulars regarding Mr. Wickham, knowing what I do of his misfortunes, I do not know that I can be more than coldly polite. Forgive me for being frank."

"His misfortunes?" Mr. Darcy sighed and shook his head. "That will suffice for now, Miss Elizabeth. I can but hope that once you have heard of what his misfortunes truly entail, you will think differently of both of us."

Something in Mr. Darcy's tone prompted a wry comment from Elizabeth. "You make it sound like you actually *care* what my opinion is. If I am *not* your cousin, then surely my *degrading* connections will be as much a factor in our mutual behaviour as it ever was in Hertfordshire. You shall be arrogant and aloof, provided you ever again sully your shoes with our soil, and I shall be irritated with you for being so."

"Did I truly call them degrading?" he asked with a flinch.

Elizabeth felt another flicker of wry amusement. "Even if you had not, just a few minutes ago, your behaviour has been such that there are few in Hertfordshire who would think differently than I."

Mr. Darcy looked abashed. "I have to admit, Miss Elizabeth, that I was... I was not myself, in Hertfordshire, for more than one reason. Even I know I can be taciturn and unsociable, but I promise I am not normally quite *so* bad. I apologize for the comment I made just now, however; it was inexcusable."

She did not acknowledge his apology, not quite yet. "May I ask why?"

"I should like to defer that conversation until Mr. Bennet arrives, for it is part-and-parcel of the conversation I should dearly like to only have once, not twice."

Elizabeth sighed. "Then I shall attempt to stay my irritation and curiosity until my father arrives." She glanced at her watch. "I suppose I truly should return to the parsonage now. Perhaps I can find some form of meaningful employment with which to distract myself until my father and Jane arrive."

Mr. Darcy started to reply, then shook his head as he thought better of it. "I think it is time I returned myself. May I escort you back to the parsonage, so that Mr. Collins may be assured you were kept safe?"

Elizabeth hesitated. She had not agreed to a truce, but he seemed sincere enough in the wish for it. She accepted his arm for the walk back, something completed in near-silence. At the parsonage gate, he released her arm, and she started into the house. "Miss Elizabeth?" She turned. "Thank you for the honour. And I am… I apologize, for having spoken so freely the last day, of things we should not assume until we know more."

Elizabeth curtseyed in farewell. "Apology accepted, Mr. Darcy. Please tell Lady Catherine that when my father arrives, I shall have her informed."

"As you wish." That look she had not been able to define earlier was back, but she could no more decipher its meaning now than she had half an hour before.

Nine

Early the next day, while Elizabeth attempted to be usefully employed indoors, Mr. Darcy and the colonel arrived at the parsonage. After being announced and seated, the gentlemen spoke with Mrs. Collins and Maria; Mr. Darcy asked Elizabeth if she had news yet of her father or his plans. Even as she regretfully denied such hopes, the rumbling of an approaching carriage was heard, followed by the distant sound of Mr. Collins, excited by the visitors. "With any luck," she added to Mr. Darcy, "that is my father now."

The party adjourned to the front door, even as Mr. Collins, still in his gardening clothes, nearly danced with impatience for the passengers to descend. Elizabeth caught the same expression on Mr. Darcy's face that she hoped she was not expressing herself. *At least we are one mind regarding* him, Elizabeth mused to herself.

The carriage door opened, and Mr. Bennet swung out. "Papa!" she cried, running up to him.

He caught her in a hug, in an unusually fervent display of emotion, and even kissed her on the forehead. "Ah, my Lizzy."

She was startled, however, when Mr. Gardiner stepped down from the carriage as well, and handed out her Aunt Gardiner as well as Jane. Jane hugged her sister with a nearly desperate strength, but Elizabeth had barely a moment to register that Jane had been crying; the appearance of her uncle as well as her father rattled her composure, and she glanced between them with an unspoken question. Mr.

Gardiner explained, "'Tis a tad complicated, my dear. My brother Bennet will have to explain at least part of it to you himself."

Mr. Collins greeted Mr. Bennet and Jane, and Mrs. Collins greeted Elizabeth's aunt and uncle, then introduced them to her husband. Mrs. Collins conferred with Mrs. Gardiner, "Alas, ma'am, the parsonage does not have enough room for *all* of you."

"Not to fret, Mrs. Collins. Mr. Gardiner and I are only here for a short period; he cannot be spared from his business for long, even for this," Mrs. Gardiner replied.

The meeting between Mr. Darcy and her father, Elizabeth noted, was not quite as cool as she would have expected; Mr. Darcy was endeavouring to be as open as he could be, with Mr. Collins flitting about like a hummingbird, no doubt in search of gossip already.

"Come, let us go into the house," Mrs. Collins beckoned the group. As soon as she had them settled, she directed her husband to change and to inform Lady Catherine of their arrival, and asked her father go with her husband. She pulled Maria into the kitchen to assist her and the kitchen maid with making refreshments for the unexpectedly large group.

Mr. Darcy glanced at the colonel before asking, "Shall my cousin and I leave to also inform Lady Catherine of your arrival?"

Mr. Bennet shook his head. "You may as well hear this out. It may be better for you to relay it to Lady Catherine than for me to repeat it again." Mr. Darcy nodded, and shut the door.

Mr. Bennet waited until the door was closed. "I am sorry, Lizzy, for this situation. I should have told you something, anything, a long time ago." In too much shock at such a beginning, Elizabeth could not feel any emotions of her own in particular. She noted, however, that Jane looked exceedingly distressed; indeed, she had not yet relinquished her spot by her sister. Her father looked as if he had aged a few years in a matter of days. "You have heard, I believe, of talk about the only Bennet son that survived past infancy?" her father began.

Elizabeth nodded. The eldest child, Thomas Jr., had taken ill when he was sent to London during his mother's confinement with Catherine. The heir of Longbourn had not survived. Jane had accompanied her brother and nearly succumbed to the same fever. Elizabeth had always assumed she had been kept at home along with Mary, for her name never came up during the very few times it was mentioned.

"What we never told *you,* and what Jane never remembered, is that there was a third child who was sent to London. Mrs. Bennet could not bear to be separated from Mary, who was two at that time, but the eldest three were deemed to be 'in the way,' and my mother Gardiner had politely offered to host her grandchildren until the newest one was born." Jane reached out and gripped Elizabeth's hand tightly. "The third was Elizabeth Anne."

Elizabeth felt light-headed. She did not, to the best of her knowledge, even *have* a middle name.

Mrs. Gardiner took up the story. "My father, Dr. Hollsworth, had been the physician in Lambton – "

"Lambton? That's but five miles from Pemberley. Was it your father who attended my mother, then?" Mr. Darcy broke in.

Mrs. Gardiner smiled, a tight, strained smile. "It is indeed possible, Mr. Darcy. But my father rarely spoke to us of his clients; we moved from Lambton to London when I was fourteen." Mr. Darcy nodded and murmured a vague apology for interrupting.

"My own mother volunteered her services with an orphan's shelter. I often assisted her, as it gave me something beyond my studies with which to occupy myself, instead of missing old friends."

Elizabeth knew that much of her aunt's history, and wondered how it applied. "The summer I was sixteen, there was a sickness that flew through both the orphans of the city, and most of the families as well. My father was kept busy attending his clients' children, including those staying in the Gardiner house. Mother and I spent many of our waking hours in an attempt to ease the suffering of those at the orphanage."

Mr. Gardiner picked up the thread. "Dr. Hollsworth had told us it was a children's fever, a vicious, fast acting illness that there was little to be done to stop. Most of his patients, he told us, lived or died with little input from his treatments, but he would attempt to control the fever of the children – that much seemed to help. So, I, along with mother and the nurse, and several of the staff, did everything we could to save my nephew and nieces. We could only save one, Jane." Jane's grip on Elizabeth's hand had gotten almost painful, but she was barely able to feel it.

"But –" Elizabeth started.

"The orphanage had recently picked up another girl – dark haired, bright, precocious," Mrs. Gardiner overrode her niece's interruption. "Her clothes were far too fine to be anything but a gentleman's daughter, and my mother and I paid for a notice to be put into the paper, hoping her family would come and claim her. She had not yet fallen ill, so my mother brought her home, in the hopes of minimizing her chances of infection. My father, although much taken with the child, knew of a family who had just lost a girl by the same given name, although their daughter had been fair haired like the elder sister. He knew the children's father would be arriving that day, having gotten the express that they had fallen ill. He thought, perhaps, the family would be open to taking the girl on, at least until her family could claim her, as something to ease their grief."

"No," Elizabeth whispered in disbelief, shaking her head to clear the information, hoping it would help. She could not be hearing this.

Mr. Bennet picked up the tale. "I arrived not a day after the express came to me, which had been sent only two days after the children had fallen ill. By then, my son and my daughter were no longer of this world, and Jane was failing," Elizabeth gripped Jane's hand tightly, stricken at the thought of how close she had come – beyond disbelief, that was the only emotion she could yet feel, "My brother Gardiner introduced me to the doctor, who explained how rapid and merciless the fever was for those under ten, and then told me of the child his wife had found at the orphanage. I was... mad with grief, and anxious to grasp at any straws; when he told me the girl said her name was Elizabeth, like my daughter, what else could I do, but agree to at least meet her?"

Mr. Bennet broke off, and knelt in front of Elizabeth, taking both of her hands in his – Jane had not wanted to relinquish her hold, but did so, instead wrapping an arm around Elizabeth's shoulders. "Do you know what she did when I met her?" Elizabeth mutely shook her head. "She crawled up into my lap, patted my cheeks, told me not to cry, and asked me if I wanted one of the kittens that had just been born. She said there were five to choose from, and that she had counted them all herself. And she asked if there were any books to be read from." Mr. Bennet was crying, albeit softly, now. "I love you. And I swear, Lizzy, I have loved you as my own from the moment I laid eyes on you. It matters not to me that you were three instead of newly born. You have always been my daughter in your own right, not as a replacement for a loss." He looked up at her. "That's why we called you 'Lizzy' – you were not our Elizabeth, but you were still a bright, sparkling jewel of a child, and neither I nor Mrs. Bennet could do anything but love you."

He looked away again, not yet giving up her hands. "I took you home to Longbourn; Dr. Hollsworth said that you had been but barely exposed to others who were sick, and to keep you in health we should remove you from London immediately. Miss Hollsworth – now your aunt Gardiner – offered to stay to assist with Jane until she recovered. Jane did not recover enough to remove from London for another fortnight."

Mrs. Gardiner laid a hand on Elizabeth's. "In a way, as much tragedy as there was that summer, it permitted me to meet your uncle, and to find you, Elizabeth, and those are two things I cannot but be grateful for."

Elizabeth's brain kicked into gear finally. "You expect me to believe… all this?" She wrenched her hands from her fa – Mr. Bennet's. "If it is the truth, how have I not heard this before?" She pulled away from Jane and Mrs. Gardiner. "How could you?"

"Lizzy?" Jane said quietly. She was silently weeping; Elizabeth recalled the silent tears from the day that Grandma Bennet had passed. Her heart twisted, and she could do nothing but reach out to Jane, who held on to her tightly. "You are my sister. No one is going to take you away from me. I promise." Jane, dear, sweet, gentle Jane, sounded as fierce and possessive as Lydia ever could about a bonnet of Kitty's.

Mr. Gardiner spoke. "Even after Jane recovered, Dr. Hollsworth kept in touch with us, but no response was ever made to the notice in the paper. After a while, we mostly chose to forget you had not been born to our family, Lizzy. We never told you, because we never expected it to be necessary information; it was not like we knew where you had come from. I promise, if any of us had, we would have returned you to your proper family."

"*We* are her proper family; we have been her family these last seventeen years." Jane was still fierce and protective. "If she remembers no other, then *we* are her family."

"Miss Bennet?" Mr. Darcy broke in. He looked quite affected himself. "I assure you; it is not my aunt's intention to take Elizabeth away from the Bennets. She has already told both Fitzwilliam and myself," he nodded to his cousin, "repeatedly, that she intends to give Elizabeth all her rightful dues, and hopes to be part of her life from now on; but she will not demand to be the only family Elizabeth recognizes." Jane could only nod at such a truce. He looked at Mr. Bennet. "And for my part, you *are* her family as much as we are, if not more so. As such, Mr. Bennet, I hope you and Lady Catherine will agree to share joint custody of Elizabeth until she is of age; and even after, that you will acknowledge our family as yours, as well."

Mr. Bennet nodded. "I will admit, Mr. Darcy, that my only concern is for Lizzy and my other daughters. I care little what the de Bourghs, Darcys and Fitzwilliams think on the matter, other than that they know that Lizzy will always be *my* daughter." Here he glanced at her, and added softly, "Even if she chooses to remove herself from us, as punishment for being too cowardly to tell her before necessity required it."

Elizabeth – still angry, still hurt – could not withstand the fear and trepidation in his expression and voice. "Oh, papa." She pulled away from Jane, and hugged her father. "We have never finished Virgil's *Aeneid*; certainly I cannot disassociate from you until then!"

Mr. Bennet laughed, as did most everyone in the room, albeit most of them sounded strained. "Then I shall endeavour to misplace that book once again, my dear; for I had just found it, in hopes I could convince you home a few weeks sooner – but now I see it shall have to disappear again."

A light note to end the conversation; that was all Elizabeth wanted at this point. She was nearly on the point of excusing herself for a walk, so that she may be able to hide and think on everything. Mr. Collins and Sir William, however, returned, and their news forestalled her departure. "Lady Catherine, in her benevolence, has asked that Mr. Bennet and the Gardiners stay at Rosings for the night."

Mr. and Mrs. Gardiner glanced at each other. "I am afraid," Mr. Gardiner responded, "we shall have to decline such an invitation. We only came to tell Lizzy our parts of her story – what we know of it – before returning to London." He glanced at Elizabeth. "We also thought to offer you a trip with us to the Lake Country this summer before anyone else can claim a month of your time then; but we will understand if you feel you must decline."

Elizabeth shook her head. "It sounds beautiful and wonderful," she smiled at them. "Of course I will go."

"What about travelling to Lambton, so that Mrs. Gardiner can see her old friends?" Mr. Darcy broke in.

"Oh?" Mrs. Gardiner replied.

"As a de Bourgh, your niece was left a small estate; I have been managing it on Lady Catherine's behalf since I took over the management of Pemberley. I had already offered to let her come to Pemberley this summer, so that I may show her the estate and the books for it. You could come as well, and make a family party of it, and stay at Pemberley." Here he glanced at Jane. "Mr. and Mrs. Hurst will have returned from visiting his family at that point, and intend to join Mr. Bingley and Miss Bingley at my estate." He looked at Elizabeth. "I am sure you would prefer to have Miss Bennet with you, for a second opinion on the estate."

Elizabeth could not help but beam at him for such a suggestion, which elicited that same expression she had now seen on Mr. Darcy's face directed at her twice, but she barely thought of it. *Two birds – or more? – with one stone,* she thought to herself. "Indeed, such a plan would do nicely. I believe I speak for both Jane and myself, that we should like to meet Mr. and Miss Bingley as well as the Hursts again." She looked at Mr. and Mrs. Gardiner, who were looking between herself and Jane, who looked both relieved Elizabeth was determined to include her in such plans, and slightly anxious at the thought of meeting Mr. Bingley again.

"I do believe that would be a fine idea," Mr. Gardiner declared after a glance at his wife. "We shall have to determine the particulars later, as I truly must return to London; I must be at the warehouse on the morrow."

"Then you should leave," Mr. Bennet answered. "We will see you off before we go to Rosings as Lady Catherine requests."

Mr. Collins was ecstatic that they would call on her directly, for he would be able to see his patroness at least twice today! After the Gardiners departed, he chattered non-stop about the beauties of 'Miss Elizabeth's ancestral home.'

Elizabeth, on the other hand, had to consider much deeper subjects, and she could tell that Mr. Bennet and Jane both were likewise occupied.

Ten

Lady Catherine met the party as close to the door as she dared. She could not be accused of loitering in her own house, but anywhere else, it would have been a different story. The sight of Lady Catherine hurriedly straightening herself from leaning against a wall was almost enough to elicit a laugh from Elizabeth. Almost, but the stifled, abortive movement of Elizabeth's, so familiar to her, was enough to let the slightest bit of tension slip out of Jane's body. Elizabeth was dealing better than she would have expected.

In her impatience, Lady Catherine made an educated guess as to the identity of those she did not know. "Mr. Bennet, Miss Bennet. Welcome to Rosings. I trust your journey from Hertfordshire and London was no more eventful than required?"

Mr. Bennet sketched a bow, even as the party moved further into the parlour. "If an express from one such as yourself, madam, can be called uneventful, then that is true." Jane said nothing but curtseyed in greeting.

Lady Catherine waved a hand at the girl already seated in the room. "This is my elder daughter, Anne." Miss de Bourgh seemed nearly fretful in her anxiousness to cut to the heart of the matter, but her mother stilled her with a stern glance.

"I shall not sport with your impatience," Mr. Bennet launched into the topic at hand. "But before we go any further, I should like to see this portrait you wrote about."

Lady Catherine and Miss de Bourgh seemed disappointed Mr. Bennet would not speak of it immediately, but Lady Catherine agreed, and the party once again journeyed to the gallery to view the portrait. Mr. Bennet had pointedly taken Elizabeth's arm before Mr. Darcy had the opportunity; Mr. Darcy was forced to content himself with escorting Jane. Jane, torn between worried possessiveness for Elizabeth, and amusement with how inattentive Mr. Darcy was without Elizabeth on his arm, did not attempt to distract her escort from his thoughts, mostly because of how obviously his attention was focused on Elizabeth.

A few bruised toes, Jane thought to herself, were well worth the chance at seeing just how school-boy lovesick the quiet Mr. Darcy could be. Charlotte always maintained to Jane that Mr. Darcy was fair on the way to being in love with Elizabeth. It seemed the belief that she was now properly of his sphere had been all that was required to tip the man head over heels for her most beloved sister. The look of affection on her escort's face predictably brought up a painful wave of memory: how Mr. Bingley had looked at her in such a way as well! Jane vowed to herself that Elizabeth would not be jilted as she had been, and the moment she got a chance to tell this to Mr. Darcy in no uncertain terms, she would. Lizzy was *her* little sister, and by G-d she was going to take care of her.

A gasp from her father abruptly pulled Jane out of her mediations. She looked up at the portrait, pulling her arm away from Mr. Darcy, barely knowing what she did. She looked between the portrait and Elizabeth, once, twice, thrice. She wavered, feeling a tad faint; she had put so much hope into the idea that, even if Elizabeth was adopted into the Bennet family, as seemed to be the case, with no way for her to argue out of it, she would still have only *her* as an elder sister, that her family was long gone and not looking for her. Elizabeth was looking between her father and Jane, anxiously waiting for a more substantive reaction. With her free hand, Elizabeth timidly reached out to Jane, whose immediate reaction was to step close and hold her tightly as Mr. Bennet released her, and she coaxed Elizabeth's head to her shoulder, whispering in her ear. "Still my little sister, Lizzy. Still my little sister." Elizabeth sagged slightly, as if she had been terrified that, regardless of what Jane had said only half an hour earlier, Jane would suddenly want nothing to do with her. She suspected that, had they been the only two in the room, Elizabeth would have been crying from relief. She happened to catch sight of Anne de Bourgh's face as she half-cradled Elizabeth; it was a mix of wistfulness, grief, and longing, and for just a moment, Jane felt guilty for being so possessive of Elizabeth.

Mr. Bennet's voice broke the silence, and cracked while doing so. "I cannot tell you for sure if my Lizzy is your Elizabeth, Lady Catherine, Miss de Bourgh. She was a foundling from an orphanage; the rest of the story, your nephews have heard, what little is known of her past stems from that point." Elizabeth stiffened in Jane's arms, but Jane kept whispering soothing nothings. Perhaps, Jane thought, Elizabeth was putting on a good show; but she still felt an irrational twinge of anger at Charlotte for inviting Elizabeth to Hunsford, and at her cousin for having taken Lady Catherine's living, for surely if neither of those two things had happened, Lizzy would not have had to confront this – well, not for several more months, Jane amended to herself, with a glance at Mr. Darcy, whose attention was quite fixed on Elizabeth's reaction to the seeming capitulation of Mr. Bennet.

With a shuddering breath, Elizabeth pulled away from Jane, supporting her own weight again. She stepped a little bit away from the group as a whole, and Jane half-smiled at the involuntary step Mr. Darcy took in her direction. She had no idea if Elizabeth's opinion of the man had changed, but there was little that she could do to determine that at this moment. She wondered if Mr. Darcy realized how obvious he was being in front of his own family. But, then, she reminded herself, it appeared *Elizabeth* was his own family now.

"Elizabeth?" Lady Catherine asked quietly.

Jane watched as her sister, normally so quick with words and ideas, struggle for words. Elizabeth half-turned towards Mr. Bennet. "I do not know what to think or what to say or what to believe," Elizabeth answered haphazardly. "I do not want this to… *adversely affect* Jane or my other sisters." She gave Mr. Bennet a desperate glance. "What if Lady Catherine and you announce my 'astounding' recovery, and they blame *you,* sir, for my going missing? Even if everything was documented correctly and completely, surely there will be talk that you had kidnapped me in your grief, or commissioned someone to do so on your behalf, Papa." The words seemed to trip heedlessly on their own. "I cannot bear the thought of sacrificing you and Mama and Jane and all the rest for material comforts."

Lady Catherine and Mr. Bennet alike seemed stunned by the suggestion. Lady Catherine narrowed her eyes. "If – when – we announce it to the world at large, Elizabeth, I will do everything in my power to ensure the Bennets are not adversely affected by such talk."

"But do you not see?" Elizabeth pleaded. "We do not know how or why I went missing. It is entirely possible there is no one still alive who does. I myself cannot recall. A kidnapping of some sort would be just the sort of… *romantic* idea that would take root heedless of any remonstrance, even from you or Mr. Darcy. And the Bennets' prospects are too few and frail to survive such scandal."

Jane listened in growing astonishment as she realized Elizabeth was arguing to remain a Bennet. She knew how distasteful Lizzy often found Mrs. Bennet, Lydia, and Kitty's behaviour. She would have thought that on some level, Lizzy would be thrilled to no longer be associated by blood.

Mr. Collins, on the other hand, took great offence that Elizabeth would think that his patroness could not sway the opinion of all of London, and he began to almost-scold her.

"Then you agree that the evidence points to you being a de Bourgh?" Mr. Darcy interjected. Mr. Collins almost swallowed his tongue to keep from talking over him.

Elizabeth's countenance became mask-like, even as her back straightened and her chin came up defiantly, a reaction Jane had not seen in years. "I cannot argue with my being a foundling, if my father insists it to be the truth. And I cannot argue against the fact that I could be almost the sister of the man in that portrait in looks."

"That does not sound like an agreement to me, Lizzy," her father gave her a pointed look.

Elizabeth shrugged, the mask breaking a little. "I do not know what to think, Papa. The only thing I know for sure is that, even if *I* can be convinced beyond a shadow of a doubt, there are those who will not be, and who will either think me a fortune hunter preying on Lady Catherine's past, or think *you* a criminal, a kidnapper." She finally looked Lady Catherine in the face. "I am not convinced that the benefits of claiming me as your lost daughter, Lady Catherine, will outweigh the damage to everyone I care about."

"Then I believe a strategy must be devised," Mr. Darcy said, before Lady Catherine could respond.

Elizabeth paused, her head tilted slightly as she looked at Mr. Darcy. "And do you have any immediate suggestions?"

Mr. Darcy did not answer instantly. "None that would work, not yet. It will have to be something to be meditated upon." He glanced at Elizabeth then Mr. Bennet. "And while we wait for ideas to simmer and thicken to usefulness, I suggest we tend to the *other* matter." His glance back at Elizabeth was expressive enough for her to understand. She inclined her head in agreement. "A smaller party for that discussion, I think," he added to Lady Catherine who pursed her lips in agreement.

Mrs. Collins picked up the cue immediately. "My husband and I should be returning to the parsonage. We have left my father and Maria there alone for long enough." Mr. Collins looked downcast at being removed from Lady Catherine's presence so soon, but nothing he said to her encouraged an invitation to stay longer.

Lady Catherine, instead of encouraging her parson, led the group to the library, and bade a servant to return with minor refreshments. The conversation in the room was light banter, mostly between Mr. Bennet and Colonel Fitzwilliam, regarding the books on the shelves, until the servant withdrew for good. Colonel Fitzwilliam's demeanour abruptly changed.

"How did you meet Wickham?" The normally genial man was scowling now.

"He took a lieutenantship in the militia quartering in Hertfordshire shortly after I arrived in the neighbourhood myself," Mr. Darcy supplied.

"Do we know this was not on purpose?" Fitzwilliam asked.

Mr. Darcy shrugged. "Impossible to tell with Wickham, but I doubt it. I do not bandy my affairs about to be seen. I certainly had not spoken to anyone but my host, my sister, and my steward as to where I was going."

The colonel drummed his fingers on the table in front of him. "Does not mean that sister of Bingley's did not crow it about her cronies, though." Jane's eyes went wide at such a rude description of Miss Bingley's behaviour. Elizabeth, on the other hand, stifled a derisive snort of her own. Mr. Bennet did not feel the need to stifle it, and the colonel looked amused when he finally noticed Jane's expression.

"May I ask what this discussion is regarding, if not Elizabeth's heritage?" Mr. Bennet asked.

Fitzwilliam and Darcy exchanged quick glances, and Darcy inclined his head towards his cousin. Fitzwilliam bared his teeth in a non-grin for just a second. "Mrs. Collins mentioned that an... old acquaintance of ours, a Mr. George Wickham, had made himself quite pleasant to the populace of Hertfordshire."

"And given that I have had some confirmation of his usual ways when he and I are in near residence, namely, yarning, I thought it would be prudent to tell my cousin," Mr. Darcy glanced at Elizabeth sharply, "and her father the real history of Mr. Wickham."

"He is an amusing fellow, to be sure," Mr. Bennet replied dryly, "but my daughters are too poor to be objects of prey to anyone."

Mr. Darcy's response was sardonic. "If one is shopping the horse market to buy, perhaps. But not if one is just... trying out the stock."

Mr. Bennet's eyes narrowed, even as Jane gasped. "And if that be the case, why were at least your closest neighbours not warned when you knew of his arrival?"

Mr. Darcy flinched. "I... felt it beneath me, to open my private affairs up to the general public. Additionally, the worst of it, from my point of view, at least, *cannot* be known to the public, not without damaging someone very close to me." He looked quite agitated, and Jane felt sorry for him.

Colonel Fitzwilliam touched Mr. Darcy's shoulder lightly. "Let me tell the story, Darce." Darcy nodded his agreement, and Fitzwilliam sighed, picking up his glass, and leaned back in his chair a bit. "Mr. Wickham was the son of my Uncle Darcy's steward. Old Wickham was a right smart man, a good steward. My father even tried to hire him away, but Old Wickham was loyal to a fault to my uncle. His son, however, was a failure.

"My uncle was Wickham's godfather, and he took the responsibility seriously. Darcy, Wickham, myself, and several of the

Fitzwilliam cousins played together as children. Somewhere along the way, Wickham... strayed."

"I was never certain if he grew jealous, while my father and his father groomed the lot of us for running estates *properly*. He was grooming Wickham to take his father's place when the old man died, and thus he learned what I did about estate management. Perhaps he thought he was being treated in such a way because he was going to inherit one of the satellite estates." Darcy interjected.

"I know at one point he had alluded to an idea that he was your father's natural son," Anne sighed.

"He what?" Darcy replied, startled.

"The last time he came here," Anne explained, "with your party, he must have been very bored, to flirt with me. He tried to convince me he was higher-born than a steward's son, and that your father must have had *some* reason for treating him like one of his own."

Darcy glowered, and Fitzwilliam sighed. "I should have expected as much," Fitzwilliam said, "but somehow I had hoped he would not go that far."

"If he really believes that, instead of just using that to try to convince Anne to marry him," Darcy added, "then it makes some of his offences even graver."

"Indeed," Fitzwilliam replied.

"His... offences?" Elizabeth asked.

"My uncle died five years ago, and left Wickham a legacy of one thousand pounds; Wickham's own father followed shortly thereafter. Uncle Darcy recommended it in his will that Wickham be giving a particularly valuable living should he go into the church."

"Thankfully for us," Lady Catherine added, "that boy decided he was too good for the church. The stories I heard in Lambton of him did *not* indicate someone who should have been allowed in the church to begin with." Jane caught an amused expression on both Elizabeth's and Mr. Bennet's faces. Even she had to admit, only to herself, that was a bit of an outlandish statement coming from the patroness of Mr. Collins. Not that Mr. Collins was a *bad* man, just a foolish one.

"Indeed," Fitzwilliam agreed. "He asked Darcy for three thousand pounds, and made some squawking about wanting to study the law, which a thousand pounds would not be enough to support him for. In return, he relinquished support in the church."

"I wished, rather than believed him to be sincere in the idea," Mr. Darcy sighed. "He did not study the law. When the living became open, he came to me, hoping to be granted the living the second time around. He said he had found the law to be quite unprofitable, and now hoped to make his future within the church. He assured me his circumstances were quite bad, and *that* I could well believe."

"Can we not all believe *that?*" Anne muttered.

"He was quite abusive when we turned him down," Fitzwilliam added. "I have to admit, some of his invective was quite inspired."

"We?" Mr. Bennet asked.

"Fitzwilliam and I share custody of my sister, and he was one of the executors of my father's will," Darcy replied.

"*That* was a somewhat unexpected honour," Fitzwilliam said, seemingly to himself. "But it means," he added with a glance at Darcy, "I have been acquainted with the particulars of the transactions.

"Obviously, after such a situation, Darcy dropped all appearance of acquaintance with Wickham. The Fitzwilliam clan, at least, was spared Wickham attempting to latch on to one of *us* instead."

"Last summer, however, he returned, in a most painful manner," Darcy said.

"We never should have let her go," Fitzwilliam muttered. "I failed her, there."

"If you did, I did as well, Richard," Darcy replied. He looked at Elizabeth. "Regardless of what Miss Bingley says about her, my sister is a shy creature, the fault, I believe, of being the youngest in the extended family and no playmates to have grown up with. She also bore the brunt of, shall we say, increased attentiveness to matters of security after certain events before she was born. She was excited by the idea of going to Ramsgate for a summer, on holiday. We let her go with a companion by the name of Mrs. Younge, in whose character we were cruelly deceived.

"She only had warm childhood memories of Mr. Wickham. It never occurred to me to tell her the truth about him. With Mrs. Younge's aid and active assistance, he was able to recommend himself to my sister, convince her she was in love, and agree to an elopement. She was then but fifteen."

Here Mr. Bennet, who had been following but disinterestedly, shot straight up in his seat. Jane felt faint. Elizabeth whispered something to herself; Jane could not be sure what it was, but she thought it was "Lydia!"

"Darcy had the greatest luck, that day. He left the group he was with, which included myself, quite suddenly, wanting to visit Georgiana, quite out of the blue." Fitzwilliam sighed. "I had actually attempted to talk him out of it. However, he prevailed and it is certainly one instance I have never begrudged him."

Darcy and Fitzwilliam exchanged ironic half-bows. "I arrived but two days before the intended elopement, and Georgiana, unable to support the idea of grieving and offending a brother whom she almost looks up to as a father, acknowledged the whole to me. I do not have words for my reaction."

"I can certainly imagine what it was," Mr. Bennet said. "What of Wickham?"

"I could not publicly denounce him, of course, for my sister's sake, but I wrote to him, and he left immediately. Mrs. Younge was removed from her charge," he replied.

Mr. Bennet nodded, before leaning back in his chair, fixing a firm eye on Darcy. "Then may I ask, why now? Some of this could have been communicated to me months ago, particularly given the age of my youngest. At least enough to put me on my guard."

Darcy flinched again. "You are my cousin's adopted father. Perforce, I consider you family, and, despite how much I would rather ignore Wickham's existence, family must at least be told some of the worst."

"Then it was avoidance? Not the most responsible of actions," Mr. Bennet replied.

Mr. Darcy flushed, with anger or embarrassment, Jane could not tell, but she felt his discomfort acutely. Jane looked at her father beseechingly. Mr. Darcy did not have to tell them anything, and *he* was not responsible for Wickham. "Perhaps Mr. Darcy was attempting to let Mr. Wickham re-establish himself with some measure of credit, so he would not be in such desperate circumstances," she offered.

Mr. Darcy sighed. "Thank you for trying to give me more credit than I am due, Miss Bennet. But the reality was… I was too selfish, hoping if I ignored the problem, it would go away, and if I did not speak to him directly, I could pretend he was not there."

"And instead, you risked letting another girl fall into his trap. One who may not be as *fortunate* as your sister," Mr. Bennet replied.

Darcy turned one hand palm up and opened it, a gesture of defeat and acknowledgment, but he could say nothing else.

"I hope that the intelligence still comes in time to prevent that, Mr. Bennet," Anne offered. "I knew enough of his ways to dislike him quite heartily, even before he attempted to hurt Georgiana."

"It is believed he will be engaged to a Miss King, within the next week or two," Mr. Bennet responded. He frowned. "She inherited ten thousand pounds a month or two ago, when her grandfather died, and I believe that was when he began to court her." Mr. Bennet's eyes flicked towards Elizabeth for confirmation.

She shrugged, trying to hide her uneasiness that *she* would be the one to confirm such behaviour. "I would say he gave her a week after the event." *Why had I not noticed this before?* she wondered to herself. At the time, it had seemed innocently enough done and rational enough.

The de Bourghs and Fitzwilliam glanced at Darcy in concert. Darcy looked torn. "Is it possible," he ventured, "that the most… minor of his crimes would be enough to persuade her family to prevent such an event?"

"If you have, say, the documents to prove he left Lambton's merchants in debt? I am going to assume, given the responsibility for his actions the Darcy family seems to have taken on, you discharged those. That may be enough," Mr. Bennet conceded. "Miss King's uncle owns the bookshop, although few realize it is his. As a matter of fact, it may be *more* than enough, if it seems to be jibing with his shop's books."

Jane was the only one who noticed Anne de Bourgh's sudden distraction, the frown of concentration and narrowing eyes flicking, as if trying to recall some faded fragment of memory, at least at first. Elizabeth soon saw it, and her attention focused Darcy's as well. It was Fitzwilliam who asked gently, "Anne, what is it?"

She startled, and her attention focused outward on her cousin. "All this talk of Wickham has… almost reminded me of something. And I am trying to place *what*." Abruptly, she sat up straight, excitement in her face. "The pony! Richard, William, *the pony!* The one your father bought, William. George had stayed here a week longer than you had, remember? He had been supposed to stay longer to acquaint himself with the local families, because father thought if he did not become a steward, he could take the living at Rosings instead of Pemberley. *Your* father took him home, after he came to help us after Papa died. We never thought to ask *him* about what happened to Elizabeth!"

Eleven

Later, Elizabeth would think to describe the behaviour of Mr. Darcy and Colonel Fitzwilliam as that of bloodhounds given a whiff of something interesting. It took the combined efforts of all the ladies and Mr. Bennet's obvious exhaustion to rein in their enthusiasm about going to Hertfordshire to 'ask' Mr. Wickham about that day at Rosings, seventeen years ago. Elizabeth particularly exerted herself in the persuasion. While she did not doubt they were both well-bred gentlemen, there was something in each man's expression that made her feel distinctly uneasy. She pointed out that however horrible his behaviour in the *recent* past, it was highly doubtful that even *if* he had anything to do with the situation, it had been done so with malicious intent. She did not notice that Darcy had capitulated into agreeing to delay such an action at least until the morrow only after she had specifically asked him to do so. Perhaps, she reasoned, something could be done to summon Wickham here, to Rosings, if he had been involved, being in the house should surely jar his memory. She *did* notice that even as Darcy, well, *William,* as Anne had pointed out in the midst of the semi-debate, she was Darcy's cousin, and could address him by his given name, and demanded the same for herself (as her sister) and Richard as well, capitulated, Lady Catherine had a very thoughtful expression on her face, and kept glancing between her and Dar – *William.* Whatever *that* may be about.

Accordingly, the party had broken up into its pieces; Lady Catherine pressed Mr. Bennet and Miss Bennet to stay at Rosings, but both demurred, stating that Mrs. Collins had offered them lodgings at least for the night.

"Then," Lady Catherine sniffed, "I shall send a note to Mrs. Collins to see if she can do without her guests for the time being, so that my daughter can move into her proper household, even if for a short duration. I will invite them to dinner tonight, and you all must stay; surely Mr. Collins will not wish to miss an evening at Rosings."

Elizabeth wanted to argue with this course of action, and even opened her mouth to do so, but Mr. Bennet shot her a look and she subsided. He responded, "For now, madam, I should dearly enjoy a few hours to rest myself. I believe that Lizzy and Jane have had an emotional day, and at least one of them needs a turn or four out-of-doors." Elizabeth could wholeheartedly agree to *that* statement, and it was decided that while Lady Catherine dispatched her note to the parsonage, Elizabeth and Jane would go walking, with William and Richard escorting them. Elizabeth was not terribly pleased with the arrangement, but she would not gainsay her father, Jane *and* Lady Catherine all at once. One would almost think that they were frightened someone would kidnap her *now*. Mr. Bennet would be shown to a guest room in the family wing. Lady Catherine set about picking a room for Elizabeth, and Jane as well, should Mrs. Collins agree to her wishes.

Thankfully, Anne, who must have realized Elizabeth truly needed time to think alone, interceded a little and convinced Richard that Elizabeth would be safe enough with both William and Jane with her. As an aside, Anne asked Jane's permission to call her by her given name, saying that they were sisters in an odd, roundabout way, due to Elizabeth being a sister to them both. Jane's little flicker of guilt over being so possessive as to want Elizabeth to only have the Bennets as her sisters made itself known again, and she agreed with Anne.

Elizabeth, thus found herself able to stroll along the lane, as Dar–*William* and Jane walked a few steps behind her, and as much as she could, she gave way to consideration.

It seemed what she had said earlier was true. As long as Mr. Bennet insisted on her history of being a foundling, as much as she would like to argue against it, she could not. And, with that information, she also could not disagree that she *did* favour the de Bourghs in appearance, abnormally so. Then there were all the little titbits Lady Catherine and Anne had mentioned about their Elizabeth; for a personality not yet formed, she *did* show quite a few of the same little preferences and tendencies as that child of three.

She felt divided. She loved her family, even when she despaired of them. Yet she could not be untouched by the insistence of the de Bourghs, William and Richard about claiming her as their own. William's previous offer of a truce underscored her suspicion that Anne, Richard, and Lady Catherine were quite desperate to approve of her; that they were willing to love her as family, while still so barely knowing her. But what of Richard's family? Would the earl be so willing to welcome her open-armed as his son? And would *he* welcome the Bennets as extended family, by their relationship to her? She did not know if there were more Darcys to consider beyond Georgiana; perhaps they, too, may be unwilling to accept her into the fold, as it were. She made a note to herself to mention to Richard and William that the earl's opinion should be canvassed as well, perhaps even prior to the long-overdue discussion with Wickham.

She could acknowledge that Wickham's character had sunk upon every review of the information provided to her. She had no reason to doubt Anne or Richard's parts of the tale, even if she could still find it in her to doubt William's role in the matter. But the concern for his sister, the guilt in his expression as he admitted his failures to his neighbours in Hertfordshire, that, if nothing else, convinced her he spoke the truth as he saw it. Guilt did not ride upon those who lied easily. Selfish, then, she could see both Wickham and Darcy sharing that trait. She pondered for a moment, the similarities between the men. Was it possible Wickham believed, or even knew, he was William's half-brother? They did seem to share a few traits, but those could be discounted to a degree by being raised in the same household.

Would not Mr. Darcy have told his son, if that were the case, or taken greater care to ensure his illegitimate son was brought up to be a good, wholesome sort of man?

Her mind digressed further. Richard had said something about Wickham *straying,* and now she wondered when that occurred. If it had only happened after her disappearance, then perhaps it was as Anne hypothesized. Wickham knew some of those happenings, and if he had started out a good, honest sort of boy, such a terrible secret could easily turn his entire character bad as he sought to either divest himself of the guilt, or to do something just to be *caught* and forced into a confession he could not make on his own. And if that were the case, could the restoration of Elizabeth de Bourgh cause the redemption of George Wickham? She was Christian enough to hope he was not beyond amendment, although she had not Jane's goodness to trust in it.

Not all the questions that crowded in on her consciousness could be answered yet. Some would have to remain deferred until more information was gathered. Still, she felt more at ease, her equilibrium restored as much as it could be under such circumstances. She glanced back to William and Jane, who seemed to be discussing something intently. She slowed her pace for them to catch up, but as soon as Jane noticed she had paused, the discussion ended. She narrowed her eyes at her sister, who returned the look with an expression of utmost innocence. *That* she did not believe, but she did not feel it appropriate, badgering her sister for the contents of their discussion. One or the other would tell her… eventually, at least.

Jane was quietly relieved that Elizabeth did not press the issue – she still did not know her sister's feelings on the subject, but it would certainly not further the gentleman's suit for Lizzy to know that Jane had just roundly, pre-emptively scolded him, if he dared tried to trifle with Elizabeth. On the other hand, Jane reflected, it might arouse her sympathies for Mr. Darcy; that may not be such a bad thing.

When Mr. Darcy had offered Jane his arm as they set out, she had accepted, knowing that Elizabeth would not, and this would give her the ability to slow his pace enough that Elizabeth could at least pretend she was alone and could sink into her own thoughts. Indeed, when Jane did lag behind, at first Darcy had frowned and made to disengage his arm to catch up with Elizabeth. "No, Mr. Darcy. Give her some room. If she is half as conflicted and confused as I am, she needs it. She always did work things out better on her own, out on a walk," Jane spoke as quietly as she could, hoping Elizabeth would not hear her.

Mr. Darcy's expression had showed his doubt of the wisdom of such an idea plainly, but he did not entirely gainsay her. "If you think, Miss Bennet, that is the best idea ..." his voice trailed off on a note of disbelief.

"It is," she assured him, even as more distance opened up. "It is something you should learn about her now, if you intend to pursue her."

That got his attention, and he nearly stopped dead in his tracks, his expression vulnerable and open for a moment. He recovered quickly. "What makes you think I have any interest besides cousinly concern for Elizabeth?"

Jane smiled sadly. "Mr. Darcy, if Mr. Bingley's attentions to me had raised my hopes so easily, I dare say Elizabeth would be in a similar danger of disappointment, based on your actions these past hours, should they continue. If she did not actively dislike you, as I know she did at least of last week."

He flinched. "I... discovered, just yesterday actually, that her opinion of me was far worse than I had imagined." He glanced at Jane in chagrin. "I had thought she was aware of my interest in Hertfordshire, and was at least welcoming of our acquaintance."

"Then perhaps you ought to be more guarded in what you say in a public assembly," Jane replied.

His expression was blank for a moment, then he flushed. "That – I –" he stumbled for words. "I was not in a mood for even being in public; my uncle, the earl, had almost forced me to leave Georgiana in his care for a few months, to give us time to recuperate from Wickham's actions apart. My uncle appeared to be of the belief that we were feeding each other's anxiety over the situation, and some time apart with friends or family might put a damper on the reactions. Bingley had all but demanded I attend; I could not insult my host by keeping to my rooms."

Jane felt herself flinch ever so slightly at such a casual mention of Bingley. Mr. Darcy's frown of concern showed it had not gone unnoticed. "Miss Bennet, are you well?"

"I am well enough," she replied. "I am torn between treating you as a cousin of my own, or simply an acquaintance."

"I would that you treat me as a cousin," Mr. Darcy replied. "Elizabeth is of a concern to us both. Surely with such a point of mutual commonality, we cannot be merely acquaintances?"

Jane inclined her head in agreement. "How… *easily* her name falls from your tongue, Mr. Darcy. You sound as if you have been practicing calling her by her given name for quite some time." He blushed and looked away from her. Yes, now was the time, Jane decided. "I suspect you would not be averse to becoming my brother."

His voice was low. "Am I so obvious, Miss Bennet?"

"Perhaps not to Elizabeth, but I suspect that more than myself have noticed, just since I have arrived in Kent. I am particularly sure that Lady Catherine has noticed your focus," she replied. He winced, but she continued, her voice becoming as stern as it did when she attempted to scold Lydia. "I was not jesting when I said what I did about Mr. Bingley raising hopes. But I swear, by all that is holy, if you *dare* trifle with Elizabeth –"

He raised a hand to stop her. "I have no such intentions, I promise. I –" he stopped.

"Yes?" she prodded.

Still he hesitated. "I had already decided, should I meet her again, I would offer for her," he admitted. "Her *active* intelligence alone would make her a valuable asset to the Darcy estates, certainly more so than most women of my acquaintance."

Jane could not help but smile, even as she felt a twinge of heartache for herself. Why had not Mr. Bingley come to the same decision?

"I have a confession to make," Mr. Darcy added.

"Yes?"

"When I left Hertfordshire in November, I spoke to Bingley about you." She flinched and steeled herself for something terrible indeed, remembering the way Caroline Bingley had treated her. "I told him then that I thought you were but slightly touched, but I feared his honour could be considered to be engaged from the obviousness of his actions."

Jane felt both hurt and soothed. At least Mr. Darcy had even noticed she was touched at all. Charlotte had always told her she should be more forward to Bingley. "And what did he say?"

"I told him my reasons for thinking the match was not good for *him.* I swear, I thought only of his happiness, but counselled him to consider his options." Here Darcy flinched yet again. "He agreed to think on it for a week, but then Mr. and Mrs. Hurst went to visit *his* relations, and Miss Bingley was determined her brother must be her escort to the various goings-on in London." He glanced down at her. "My sister is *not* out, I will add."

Jane no longer knew how she felt, a rueful, bitter elation, perhaps, may be the description to use. "Does he… does he ever talk about me?" her voice trembled slightly.

"Not recently," she noticed he sounded regretful at relaying that information, "but his spirits are as depressed as they have been since the end of November." They walked in silence for a few more moments, before Darcy spoke again. "If we remove the entire Rosings party to Hertfordshire, perhaps I can convince Bingley to reopen Netherfield so that my aunt and cousins will be more at ease. If I am not mistaken, Longbourn cannot hold quite such a large party."

"No, indeed, particularly not if your uncle, the earl, also journeys to Hertfordshire," Jane replied, trying to keep the little ember of hope in her heart from turning into something greater.

"Hmm," was Darcy's only reply, for Jane had just realized Elizabeth had stopped her private ruminations and was waiting for them to join her. *This* time, when Darcy offered his arm to Elizabeth, she hesitated only a moment before taking it, and Darcy nearly beamed.

"What will the earl say?" Elizabeth asked Darcy.

"About?" he replied.

"About my recovery… about my intention to retain my relations with the Bennets," she clarified.

Darcy could only shrug. "I cannot say for sure. We will know when we apply to him."

"Should he be contacted now?" Jane asked.

"Perhaps," Darcy conceded. "I will speak to Lady Catherine, Mr. Bennet, and Richard when we return to the main house. We will see what the consensus is. Richard should be able to give us an idea what to expect, I would think." He glanced down at Elizabeth. "What will you choose if he demands that you give them up?"

Jane stiffened, and Elizabeth gave her a worried glance. "*My* intentions and wishes have not changed; the Bennets are my family. If Lady Catherine –"

"She would like you to call her 'mother', I am sure," Darcy interjected.

Elizabeth frowned slightly. "'Mother' remains Mrs. Bennet to my mind, I shall … I shall have to think on what to call Lady Catherine. Formality remains a safe option." She shrugged. "But if Lady Catherine chooses to agree with her brother, I shall not agree to be recognized as her daughter. Even if she disagrees with him, I may try to convince her to do so. At least publicly. I would hate to disrupt the family in such a way, but the lot of you have gotten along without me for seventeen years. Continuing on without me will not destroy you all."

"*We* shall not give you up any more than you wish to give up the Bennets," Darcy's countenance had clouded in dismay, but his determination was clear. "And I know I do not speak solely for myself."

Elizabeth shrugged, her eyes worried. "It may have to be kept quiet, then, although if your and Richard's reaction to seeing me beside Anne is any indication, some explanation would be required for the general public."

"That would be a minor concern," Darcy sighed. "Her health is such that she has but rarely been in public."

Jane felt even sorrier for her semi-cousin/rival for Elizabeth's sisterly affection. "Is she truly so ill?"

"As a child, she was not, but she was… extremely attached to her little sister, more so than perhaps even Sir Lewis was," Darcy replied, his eyes flicking at Elizabeth. "*She* has never recovered from the blow. I suspect the resulting depression made her susceptible to catching the most trifling of illnesses, but in her, they were magnified to something much worse."

Elizabeth frowned, her expression troubled, but she said nothing. For herself, Jane felt terrible about being so possessive of Elizabeth, but she could no more imagine stepping aside and letting Anne take her place in Elizabeth's heart than she could imagine not protecting Elizabeth to the best of her ability.

Twelve

Rosings, Kent

Friday, March 15

Dear Father,

You are, of course, aware that my aunt summoned Darcy and me to Rosings early this year, but did not provide us with a reason for doing so, only that it was a matter of utmost importance.

For once, she was not exaggerating: my cousin Elizabeth has been found.

Her story is an odd one; her discovery a coincidence. She is now known as Miss Elizabeth Bennet of the Longbourn estate in Hertfordshire. Her adoptive father, Mr. Bennet, has confirmed for Darcy and me (and Elizabeth) that she was a foundling – in London. His cousin is my aunt's new parson, Mr. Collins, and Mrs. Collins is a great friend to our Elizabeth. Mrs. Collins invited Elizabeth to Hunsford, and my aunt recognized her as soon as she was introduced. Indeed, when beside Darcy and Anne, she looks like the finest mixture of the de Bourghs and Fitzwilliams. There is little mistaking her for anything but a de Bourgh, although I can well understand how Darcy, who met her around Michaelmas, did not recognize her until he saw her beside Anne.

Elizabeth is, naturally, very confused and upset at this point, for until this occurrence, she had not known anything of her history. She is handling the situation with aplomb worthy of a Fitzwilliam. She apparently has no recollection of any life but that at Longbourn. As such, they are the only family she knows, and she is very insistent that, as the 'price' of her agreeing to be recognized as Lady Catherine's lost daughter, she must not be forced to give up the Bennets. She – Elizabeth, that is – has requested to know what your opinion and outlook on this subject will be. She is quite determined, and while I know little of the other Bennets, both Mr. Bennet and Miss Bennet are well mannered gentlefolk, even if below our normal sphere. Darcy will not describe the younger sisters or their mother to me; he says it is immaterial to the question at hand.

Lady Catherine is all willing to acknowledge the Bennets, sight unseen, because she is quite desperate to reclaim her daughter. My aunt begs that you agree with her on the subject. The Bennets raised Elizabeth as a gentlewoman, and as such, should be held in some esteem for having done so.

As a further note, I must ask, despite it bringing up a shunned name – did you or my uncle Darcy ever speak to Wickham about Elizabeth's disappearance? I know he was naught but a boy when it occurred, the same as Darcy and I, but Anne and my aunt cannot recall ever speaking to him about it. If not, Darcy and I intend to travel to Hertfordshire, where Wickham is currently posted with the militia. He is already acquainted with the Bennet family, so there should be little difficulty in engineering a meeting with him for the purpose of discussing that day with him.

I hope to hear from you soon, but before I close out this letter, I wish to make my own personal plea. Today is the Ides of March – the day that we lost Elizabeth seventeen years ago. Pray, Father, do not let this year be known to the family as the year we lost Elizabeth a second time. We have had enough heartache to last all of us a lifetime. Recognize her as Lady Catherine's daughter – and the

Bennets as our friends and almost-family for their part in
protecting and raising her.

Yours, etc,

Richard Fitzwilliam

Richard signed his name with a flourish and blotted the letter. He
had told Darcy, Elizabeth and Jane he doubted his father would
disapprove of Elizabeth's desire to retain the Bennets as family; but the
reality was, he could not be sure himself. The earl, by virtue of his
position, was well aware of the clout he held in society, and both he
and the countess wielded that influence with devastating accuracy.
Based on a few comments Lady Catherine had let slip, information
gleaned from her interrogations of Mrs. Collins and Elizabeth, the
younger Bennet sisters would need a bit of firm control and schooling
before they would be presentable in Society as Miss Elizabeth de
Bourgh's adoptive sisters. It still may not help them to garner better
matches, not with the small fortunes Richard suspected they possessed,
but at least it would not damage the Fitzwilliam clan.

As for Elizabeth … oh, but she was a treat. A lively disposition
mixed in equal parts with pert intelligence, grace, affection and
compassion. He had long known what Elizabeth's inheritance had been
deemed to be, should she ever be recovered. Comfortable
independence was the phrase that sprang to mind. Indeed, she was the
sort of woman he had searched for alongside Darcy since the two of
them came of age. But he knew his cousin well – being the nearest
age-mates growing up, and with Wickham increasingly being
distanced from them due to the combined force of their displeasure
with his activities, they were nearly brothers – and he had never had
the fortune of seeing his dearest friend in love… until now.

He could well see how it would have happened – an unconscious
familiarity that would have encouraged more attention than Darcy was
wont to give *anyone,* combined with a conscious recognition of wit

and intelligence. Her incandescence made it nearly impossible for her to enter a room unnoticed. Such a fountain of warmth and vitality spilling heedlessly over everyone in her vicinity would have thawed the defences Darcy had erected around himself these past years faster than a midsummer's sun could melt a snowball.

He still wished, in the envious, twisting pain of happiness to see Darcy in such a state, he had met the grown-up Elizabeth first. The past could not be changed, he reminded himself, and he tried to distract himself from his cousin – either of them – with thoughts of Miss Bennet – of Jane, his quasi-cousin. *She* was beautiful, no doubt, although her expression when watching Darcy watch Elizabeth held more joy than sadness, the pain was there, lingering like an ominous storm cloud on an otherwise clear day. No, even if he was drawn to the steel-wrought lily type, her heart was held elsewhere, and he briefly wondered who would have had the insanity to jilt her. Her devout affection for Elizabeth meant, however, he could not help but love her as much as he loved Elizabeth.

He wondered, yet again, if Elizabeth realized how precious she was to him – to Darcy – to them. His reference to the Ides of March had not been idle rhetoric. His elder brother, the viscount, and his wife had yet to bring a living child into the world; Georgiana's bruised heart and broken innocent joy weighed upon the entire family. Darcy and he had not found a reason to hope for founding families of their own; Anne's unending despair had mellowed with age into a withdrawn cynicism and quiet resignation to a pale fate. Wickham – who Richard still, in his heart of hearts, loved as a brother even when he hated him with a murderous passion – had strayed beyond redemption, a cut as deep as any other. Elizabeth… it was not just Darcy who needed to be thawed and protected from himself, it was their entire family who needed her. They needed a second chance, a way to break the curse that had descended upon them with her loss.

He meditated upon the letter a moment longer before sealing it. There was naught else for him to add or say, no more persuasions to exert – Darcy's stubbornness was a Fitzwilliam trait, and the earl himself proved it such, time and again. He could only hope his father, if he were indeed against accepting the Bennets, would be willing to be persuaded to not disagree outright, to give Elizabeth a chance to breathe life back into his fading family.

* * *

Charles Bingley morosely shuffled papers around on his desk, wishing he knew how long his friend was to be in Kent for the undisclosed familial emergency. He missed Darcy's company keenly. He had become quite accustomed to having company superior to his sisters on a daily basis, in London at Darcy's townhouse and at Netherfield. As was usual, the past few months, the thought – however brief and oblique – of Netherfield brought a wave of pain.

She does not love me, he reminded himself sternly. If she had, or did, Caroline would have passed along any sort of information – that Jane – Miss Bennet that is – had written to her to inquire about anything, or that they had exchanged visits. Indeed, Caroline had assured him, she had written to Jane thrice – the first and second letters had been given polite, but cold replies, and the third, sent a month and a half ago, never responded to at all.

Thankfully, before his thoughts could submerse themselves into well-worn habitual patterns again, a knock at his study door interrupted him. "Enter," he called.

One of the maids peered around the door. "The post is come, sir," she said.

"Ah, bring it here." He smiled at her, and she dutifully came into the room and deposited it in his hand. "Thank you." The girl curtsied, and after ascertaining that Bingley did not require anything else, quietly left the room.

He sorted through the various letters, pausing as he spied Darcy's handwriting. The other letters were set aside to be attended to later; his need for reassurance that there were people in the world without Caroline's cutting tongue overriding the need to tend to the more fiscally important letters in the stack. He cracked the seal and hoped it was nothing horrible that kept his friend in Kent.

"Rosings, Kent
Thursday, March 14th

Charles,

I am not yet at liberty to inform you the reason behind my aunt's unexpected summons to Rosings. I hope, by tomorrow or Saturday, I shall have the necessary agreements to do so. I do, however, wish to assure you that things are not as hopeless as I may have led you to believe, when I paced around my library muttering to myself after receiving it.

On a happier note, I wish to inform you that I have become… reacquainted with a neighbour of yours. Miss Elizabeth Bennet is currently in residence at Hunsford, the parsonage, visiting Mrs. Collins neé Lucas. We have come to a truce of sorts –"

Here, Bingley could naught but smile. He liked Jane's sister quite a lot, and had often thought she and Darcy would make a good match, if only she were not so stubbornly set against him.

"— but only after we quarrelled a little, namely in regards to yourself."

Bingley was startled. *That* was unexpected. They had quarrelled over him once, that memorable evening at Netherfield, but surely there were more interesting subjects than him!

"It seems I was wrong, and I wish to correct the oversight immediately. Miss Bennet was – is still, based on Miss Elizabeth's vehement defence of her sister – more attached to you than I had supposed in November. Moreover, she has been in London these last three months, and visited Miss Bingley shortly after her arrival there. Miss Bingley, Miss Elizabeth has been given to understand, was quite remiss in returning the visit, and did not do so until a month had passed."

Bingley repressed the desire to leap from his chair immediately to get the address from his sister, to pay a call immediately – Caroline's subterfuge could be dealt with later.

"I know you, Charles, and I know your first instinct will be to visit Miss Bennet right this very moment, as you read these words. However, there is more – much, much more – going on than your sister's behaviour, and I do not believe Miss Bennet will be in town for above another day or two at most. I believe – indeed, I hope – that she will be travelling to Kent, to visit her sister before the week is out.

"I wish I could tell you more; alas, as I wrote above, I am not yet at liberty to explain why I was summoned here, and I am only hoping that Miss Bennet will be arriving to visit her sister. For the time being, it may be prudent to look into reopening Netherfield, although I do not yet know if even that is necessary. The Hursts are returning soon, I believe, and they can easily escort Miss Bingley for the duration.

"I realize that this seems much like I am giving you hope only to snatch it away – but I assure you that is not my intent. I *will* inform you the moment I can about what is going on, for if you intend to pursue Miss Bennet – and, may I add, for the sake of preventing a repetition of my upbraiding by Miss Elizabeth, I do hope you do – you will need to be acquainted with the particulars, at least some of them, yourself. Consider the time between now and then an opportunity to deal with certain... situations closer to home, eh?

"Your friend, etc,

"Fitzwilliam Darcy"

Even as Bingley re-read the letter, Caroline's carrying voice broke the quiet solitude of his study. With an uncharacteristic frown, he set the letter down, tapping it just once, in staccato agreement, before moving to leave the room.

Certain situations, indeed.

Thirteen

Mrs. Collins quickly agreed to let her husband's patroness take over the pleasure of hosting her guests. Elizabeth owned she was somewhat disappointed in Charlotte's agreement with Lady Catherine, but while Richard wrote to his father, she, her father and Jane oversaw the removal of their belongings from Hunsford to Rosings. Anne had conjured some sort of excuse to keep William out of the way for the duration. Elizabeth knew not what it was, but she was grateful. She had begun to realize the look in William's eye was quite similar to the expression he granted her in Hertfordshire. Here, however, there could be no mistaking it for disapproval, not with the declaration he would not let the earl dictate the Darcys' response to her discovery.

He had even apologized, in an undertone, to Elizabeth. "I am sorry I have not summoned Georgiana here. Until I know what my uncle's response will be, I do not wish to subject her to conflicting arrangements. She will not quite understand what your recovery means to me – to our family, that is, for she was not born until after your disappearance. I do not wish her to see our uncle and myself at crossed purposes if I can help it."

She had been moved to compassion, and – oddly enough – affection. He was so intent on trying to protect Georgiana, but he was still willing to recognize her as his cousin, even if it meant exposing his sister to a break in some of her only family. She placed her hand on his arm, a comforting gesture between cousins and friends. "I can understand that, particularly if she still suffers from last summer. It would be best to show her a united front, even among the family, so that she does not doubt what she should do."

His eyes had been drawn to her hand on his arm, and he swallowed hard before glancing back up at her. His expression made her blush from embarrassment, although she knew not why, and she removed it. He shook himself lightly, like a cat trying to remove a single droplet of water from its fur. "There is another consideration," he admitted.

"Oh?" she hoped her voice had not wavered in her discomfort.

"Your mother," his lips twisted slightly, "had long desired a match between myself and Anne – a scheme that, for all she says, originated when we were babes in the cradle, did not occur to her until after your disappearance. That… *conflict*… of interests has not yet materialized during this visit. I presume it will, once she is assured of your place in the family."

Elizabeth affected indignation, although the long-suffering expression sparked her amusement and she could not repress an arch reply. "Conflict of interests? What, you have no desire to become my brother?"

"No, indeed," he replied, an amused smile breaking through. Elizabeth knew not what to make of the comment, but it was soon of no matter.

"Darcy?" Richard called, and William looked towards the door. A quiet murmur in the hall outside the door occurred, although Elizabeth could not place the second voice.

"It seems I am summoned – probably to the billiards room, if I know our cousin at all," William commented, and Elizabeth inclined her head in amused agreement. But before he quit the room, he glanced at Elizabeth, away, and back at her. "I have no desire to be *your* brother," he added quietly. "However, I find I have few reservations about being *Anne's*."

Elizabeth's jaw dropped in stunned astonishment, and William gave her a bright smile as he made his escape.

How so like the man, she thought, to drop something so stunning upon me, and then disappear. *Where is Jane? I need to talk to her.*

She was prevented from searching for Jane immediately. Anne entered the room not a moment after William had left.

"Elizabeth?" Anne asked uncertainly. "May we talk a while?"

"I… certainly," Elizabeth replied uncomfortably. "What did you want to talk about?"

Anne frowned, looking as if she were deliberating, then taking Elizabeth's hand, led her to a chair closer to the window. "Richard and I heard William's last comment to you just now."

Elizabeth blushed scarlet. "I am… sorry if –"

Anne shook her head, laughter echoing in her eyes. "Our mother is who wanted the connection. For years she has not listened to either my protestations, or William's, that we did not want to marry each other." She tilted her head, a smile tugging at her lips. "I would, however, much like to have him for a brother."

Elizabeth blushed even more furiously. "I…"

Anne's expression suddenly became solemn. "You did not like him, when you first came to Kent, did you?" Elizabeth mutely shook her head. "What do you think of him now?"

A helpless shrug – this is the conversation she had thought she would have with her sister – and then she realized, she was, just not the one she had thought of originally. It occurred to her, all of a sudden, she had done a disservice to Anne since coming to agree she was most probably a de Bourgh. At least Anne did not seem to be holding it against her.

"Elizabeth?" Anne interrupted quietly. She glanced up at her. "I... would like – I should so greatly *wish* – that we be sisters in truth, and not just blood. I... have no intention of coming between you and Jane – nor you and the other Bennets."

Elizabeth looked back down at her hands, now twisting in her confusion. "I... think I should like that, as well," she admitted. "But I am quite confused, even without William's... unexpected declaration a moment ago."

"Of course you are," Anne said, as she took Elizabeth's hands in her own, leaning forward. "I promise you – we *all* are, Mr. Bennet and Jane not excepted. But the one thing all of *us* have in common, is that we love *you,* in various strengths and forms. That is what is binding us together right now – but only you can decide if you can love all of us."

"I am scared of hurting Jane," Elizabeth's voice was quiet, downcast. "We have been not just the closest of sisters, but the best of friends."

Anne sighed. "Jane... loves you so very much, Elizabeth. She sees me as a threat, I think." Elizabeth winced, and Anne shook her head. "It is not your fault, sister. I will... talk with her myself. I would not have any wounds festering between the three of us. I would not mind gaining a bevy of sisters in one fell swoop."

Elizabeth nodded in relief, before Anne continued. "And what of William?"

Elizabeth smiled ruefully. "He is proud, obstinate, and," she swallowed, "strangely gentle and supportive." She glanced at Anne. "You were quite correct that my opinion of him was quite low when I came to Kent, but – at his request – we came to a truce the day after his arrival, after we… cleared the air in regards to a… misunderstanding or three. He has… been helpful, since."

"Were some of those misunderstandings based on Wickham's story?" Anne asked, and Elizabeth nodded. She sighed, half laughing. "I had wondered why he had been… *so*… insistent on ensuring you and Mr. Bennet were told exactly what happened. But it makes sense now."

"What should I do?" Elizabeth asked quietly.

"I disagree with William. I think Mother will *not* be championing a match between him and me," Anne said. Elizabeth gave her a sharp look, and Anne shrugged, with a slight smile. "William has been blindingly obvious in his attentions to you, Elizabeth, and I think our mother is so grateful to recover you, she will do anything that forwards your happiness."

"I do not know if that could be found with William," Elizabeth replied.

"You have only known and seen his true character for a matter of days," Anne answered. "Give yourselves more time to really get to know each other. Richard and I will speak to him about… not forcing you into an uncomfortable position at this juncture. But," she added with a hint of laughter, "at least you cannot think he believes you merely *tolerable,* now."

Elizabeth's jaw dropped for a second time in the space of half an hour, and Anne laughed. "He told me that himself, while, may I add, he was roundly scolding himself for being a pompous twit that day."

Betwixt Anne's laughter, the way she phrased her explanation and the image of William pacing about a library scolding himself out loud, Elizabeth could not help but giggle, herself. The giggle turned to laughter, and before she knew what had happened, Elizabeth realized she would most probably be able to love her new sister with tolerable ease.

* * *

Lord Randall Fitzwilliam, Earl of Matlock, was uncomfortably ensconced in his library, rubbing his temples in a vain attempt to soothe back the headache forming. The letter from his younger son, Richard, sat open, at an angle that would have an observer believe it had been tossed down as the reader paced away from it in a fit of… undefined emotion.

Thus, when his wife Sarah slipped into the room, her first question was "Does the letter from our son bring *bad* news, darling?"

He looked up and shook his head, paused, then with a shrug, replied, "No… and perhaps yes. He is well, at least."

Lady Matlock gave her husband a tolerant, amused look. "Do make up your mind."

"I cannot," he replied with a sigh, and she frowned, coming around the desk to rub his neck.

"What does our wayward son write?"

"My sister's lost daughter has been found."

Sarah gasped. "Elizabeth? It cannot be! After all this time?" She leaned over her husband's shoulder to peer at the letter – alas, her eyesight was not as keen as it had been, and she could not read it. Her husband did not need her request to enlighten her. He teased her about the need for reading spectacles often enough.

"It seems, somehow, she was transplanted from Kent to London. Even if we discover how she left Rosings, I doubt we will ever know how *that* happened. A Mr. Bennet of Longbourn in Hertfordshire brought her into his family and raised her as his own daughter; she recalls nothing of Rosings."

Sarah frowned. "I suppose her inability to remember is the bad news, then?"

Randall shook his head. "No, indeed… between her adoptive father's information and my sister's persuasion – and apparently her own looks mark her distinctly as a de Bourgh – she has been convinced to allow she may be Catherine's daughter… but she will not agree to be recognized unless she is allowed to retain the Bennets as her family as well."

His wife's voice was gentle. "Then, my love, I fail to see what the problem is. They cannot be wholly bad if they raised her to be someone admirable. There are not many women in the world who would think twice about walking away from the family they've known for years, for the chance at instant social promotion and fortune."

His fingers paused in their circling on his temples. "I had not quite thought of it from that light," he allowed. "I had only thought that the Bennets may be an… embarrassment to the Fitzwilliam clan. Darcy – who has met them – will not describe the younger siblings or the mother to our son. Richard writes he says it is immaterial."

"William has always had a knack for being correct," she replied. "If the younger siblings are indeed a bit wild, as one would be led to suspect by such circumspection, we may be able to offer some assistance in placing them in situations outside of the household, where they may gather decorum and schooling. The mother – well, I certainly doubt William would make a moment's hesitation of informing Richard if the lady's behaviour was *malicious.* She may just be like many society wives: vapid and of mean understanding."

He sighed, his hands moving to capture his wife's over his shoulders. She leaned against him, arms encircling him in a loose embrace, and he kissed one of her hands. "Richard spoke of the Ides of March," he said quietly, sadly.

"We have suffered unduly, these past years," she replied. "I suspect Richard is desperate for anything he can take to be an omen of a change in luck."

"Are you willing to take on the task then, of taming our niece's wild adoptive family, if it comes to that?" His acceptance hinged entirely upon her answer, and she knew it.

"If it returns Elizabeth to her rightful family," Sarah answered, "I would be hard-pressed to think of something I would not be willing to do."

"Such as accepting Wickham as a Darcy?"

"No. I think I would even do that, particularly if it meant we could finally bring the boy under control. We erred, I think, in not telling the boys the truth, once they were of an age to understand."

Fourteen

The evening passed at Rosings with little indication any major upheavals had or were occurring within the de Bourgh family circle. Mr. Collins praised and ate, ate and praised, while Sir William followed his son-in-law's lead readily. Quiet conversation found itself scattered amongst those around the table, and to Mr. Bennet and Richard's obvious amusement, Elizabeth and Darcy spent much of the evening affecting unconcern about the other's whereabouts, just so long as the other was looking in the primary's direction. Elizabeth knew her father and Richard were being entertained at her expense, but there was little she could do about it – even discussing it with Anne had done little to soothe the distraction caused by William's pronouncement. She intended to speak to Jane about it tonight – and, perhaps, invite Anne to her room for the nightly talk, as a way to show Jane that she had no intention of permitting anyone to usurp her place, but that Elizabeth was not so... shallow... as to be able to only love one elder sister strongly.

Still, a quiet end to a stressful day – such minor luxuries were to be treasured, as it had seemed a year since she had spent a dinner with such little vexation. Mr. Collins' voice droning on in the background was tolerable – she blushed as soon as that word crossed her mind, and she hoped desperately she would get over *that* soon – compared to the conversation of the last few nights.

She wondered if she was being too obliging, too accepting of the situation. Although her father's – and her aunt and uncle's – story could not be doubted, she still felt vaguely guilty for her partial agreement, as if it were a mark of disloyalty to her father, to not argue him out of the notion. But – for all her desire to marry for love – another blush at a remembrance of a very beautiful smile on a handsome face, vexingly, linked to such a phrase at the moment – she was a mostly practical creature; stubbornness could only do so much in the face of truth, earnestly spoken.

"Have you written to Mama?" she asked Mr. Bennet quietly.

He shook his head. "Not yet, my dear. She... knows that I will not do so, until it has been decided what will be done about you; we agreed to that before I left Longbourn."

She nodded, still slightly anxious. "And who is running the household?"

"Your younger sisters do not know why I left; they do not know that Jane is currently not in residence at London. We did not wish to... disturb them unnecessarily," Mr. Bennet replied, choosing his words carefully. "I presented the challenge of running the household to Mary. I told her it was time she learned yours and Jane's duties, should she find a household of her own at some point." He paused, reflectively. "She seemed quite pleased that I thought her capable of handling Longbourn for the week. She had not a phrase to say from her great friend Mr. Fordyce. Although should anything drastic occur, I will, of course, return instantly."

"With any luck," Elizabeth said, "she will be distracted enough in her nervousness at the duties, that she shall manage to make it the entire time without once looking at that book."

"I rue the day I read from it in jest, in her hearing," Mr. Bennet sighed. He picked at his plate for a moment. "What are your plans, Lizzy?"

"I... do not know. I would suppose that until we know how the earl will respond to finding himself connected to a modest gentleman's family, my plans are what they were," she replied. "I will remain another five weeks here in Kent – be it at Rosings or Hunsford, then return to Longbourn until we travel to Pemberley and Brandywine in the summer."

Mr. Bennet smiled briefly. "And how shall you like having your own estate?"

Elizabeth's eyes danced. "As long as there are walks aplenty, I believe I would like it just fine."

Darcy – who had been studiously not-looking (that is to say, he was the only one who thought his eyes *left* her) at Elizabeth, while Richard and Anne valiantly attempted to not snicker at his behaviour – perked up at Elizabeth's comment. "The estate is a pretty one," he interjected. "It is a bit south of Pemberley, but it is a comfortable distance."

"What do you know of its history, Darcy?" Mr. Bennet asked.

Darcy smiled softly, his eyes unfocusing slightly. "It is actually where my mother and father were first introduced, and although it was left to Aunt Catherine to augment the de Bourgh holdings, it has always been open to the Darcys."

"Why were they not introduced in London?" Elizabeth asked, curious.

"Mother never seemed to recall why they were staying there, actually," Darcy grinned. "She could barely ever speak of the estate – or that particular visit – with anything but the dreamiest expression."

"Your parents made a love match then, Mr. Darcy?" Jane asked innocently, flicking her eyes at Elizabeth in such a way as to give lie to such innocence. Elizabeth and Darcy were both suddenly blushing and looking at opposite ends of the room. Richard failed to hide the snigger sufficiently to avoid being the target of Darcy's embarrassed glare.

Mr. Bennet leaned over to his eldest daughter to say approvingly, but not quite *sotto voce*, "Good girl."

Darcy pretended to not hear Mr. Bennet's comment. "They did indeed," he finally answered. "The Fitzwilliam clan, for all its virtues, remains one of the few fashionable families of England to indulge in the unfashionable vice of forwarding love matches among its scions." He grinned slightly. "The Darcys, on the other hand, never cared for being fashionable." He started to say something else, turned a charming shade of scarlet (in Elizabeth's studied non-opinion), and could not be coaxed to say anything of substance for the remainder of the evening.

Eventually, the dinner broke up, and was followed by Elizabeth and Jane singing duets in the parlour. After a few songs, Elizabeth rose from the piano and went to Anne's side. "Come join us," she half-asked.

Anne looked askance at her mother and sister. "I have never learnt. I am sure our mother told you that."

"Then Jane and I shall teach you now," Elizabeth laughed. "Although I would caution you to learn more from her than from me!" Anne shook her head at Elizabeth in mock-displeasure, even as Elizabeth grasped her hand and tugged her towards the piano. Jane, to her father's eye, looked somewhat ill at ease, but he could but hope Elizabeth would be able to mend the bridge between her two elder sisters. Anne de Bourgh, he had decided, needed a few more people in her life.

Lady Catherine looked nonplussed for a moment. "Anne has always been so ill," she said to those remaining nearby. "I never thought her health sufficient to permit her the strength to practice with due diligence. That is why I never brought on a piano master for her."

Mr. Bennet laughed. "I assure you, madam, that Elizabeth – for all her healthfulness – does *not* practice with due diligence. If she did, her playing would be very well indeed, but as such, it remains she is a mere enthusiast."

"Why, then, knowing she could display superior skill, did you not hire on a governess or piano master yourself?" Lady Catherine still felt uneasy about this neglect of her daughter's education.

Mr. Bennet's expression lost most of its good humour. "My boy was eight when he died. We had… already established a pattern of spending that did not include having a worry as to our girls' futures. And I…" He frowned, before glancing at Darcy. "I should apologize to you, Darcy, for being so hypocritical. Much of my family's failures are because I chose the path of avoidance – of both memories and responsibilities."

Darcy, who had not actually been paying attention to anything but Elizabeth's laughter, was startled to hear his name, although he picked up the thread of the conversation easily. "There are some failures," he replied, "that can be forgiven. One hopes that the…" he hesitated delicately, "issues can be remedied."

Fitzwilliam's eyes narrowed. "I believe *my* mother can be… relied upon for advice, in the situation I presume we're discussing. She is much vaunted for her ability to assist members of the *Ton* with placing their scions in situations appropriate for each child."

Mr. Bennet gave him a meditative look. "Does she indeed?" At the younger man's nod, he tilted his head in consideration. "I believe the night grows late," he said, "and I should be finding my way to the room you were so courteous as to assign to me, madam," he added with a half-bow at Lady Catherine before he moved to the piano to interrupt the party there.

"Goodnight, girls," he said, kissing Elizabeth and Jane on the forehead. He smiled at Anne. "Do not let these two keep you from your rest," he advised, "Lizzy in particular is known for forgetting *others* in the world need sleep to function."

"Papa!" she laughingly protested. "And *he* will have you believe me without such considerations."

Anne smiled, and rose herself. "It is probably time for me to retire," she owned. "I do not normally stay in company so long," she added.

Mr. Bennet caught the look Elizabeth gave Jane – an entreaty, a request for permission. He felt quite proud of both of his girls, when Jane's only reaction was an acknowledging blink, and it was Jane who said to Anne – "I fear we should retire as well – would you mind showing us the way to our rooms? Are they far from yours?"

Anne nearly glowed at Jane's comment – Bennet felt his guess had been correct: Elizabeth, ever the peacemaker – for Jane was too sweet to be capable of the harshness sometimes required for the post – had spent the last few half hours attempting to ease the tension between her two elder sisters, and not, it appeared, without some measurable success. He escorted the girls out of the room, and shook his head in amusement when Elizabeth laughingly dismissed him to his room and books.

How was he to ever give her up? The question had plagued him frequently those first few months after he had brought her home to Longbourn. Fanny had been inconsolable with their loss – and while she came to love Elizabeth with the same sort of fierce unstable affection she had for all of her children, Bennet still felt that, on some level, Fanny blamed Elizabeth for the loss of two of their children. It was irrational and unreasonable, but so very much Fanny. Yet, had the Gardiners not had such obvious affection for Jane and Elizabeth, Fanny would never have let them leave Longbourn without her, for any reason. She had, in a surprisingly short time, come to his opinion of the matter – losing Elizabeth would be a blow that only losing another heir or Jane could surpass.

But years had passed, and the worry had faded, for a long while, until Jane was sixteen, and Bennet was suddenly confronted with the very real possibility he would lose his two eldest daughters to matrimony in the near future – that was, any time before they were forty would be far too soon for him. And he had once again had to confront the question – how was he to ever give her up?

After today, he felt that, even if she remained at Longbourn for the remainder of her unmarried life, time would pass by far quicker than he had ever dared fear. Darcy… he approved of the boy, in a roundabout way, if only for his good taste and sense in loving Elizabeth. He was smart, maybe even as smart as his Lizzy, and not as proud as perhaps Bennet had been led to believe. It was obvious something had been said betwixt the two of them, above and beyond what he had heard himself, and what Elizabeth had admitted to him while Darcy was being kept out of the way of moving arrangements.

How was he to give up the girl he had taught how to climb trees, and taught how to skip rocks properly? He could still remember boosting her up to reach the limb of an apple tree in the orchard so she could pick a few apples for them to munch on while they walked. How, on more than one occasion, as he started to set her back on the ground, she had flung her arms around his neck and told him how much she loved him. His darling, precious little girl; had it really been that long since she was too old for him to pick up like that? Could Darcy – or even Lady Catherine – appreciate her, as she ought to be appreciated? How could he possibly be expected to give her hand to Fitzwilliam Darcy, or anyone else, for that matter, some day in the not-distant-enough future?

It was Elizabeth's laughter that drew him from his slow, morose revere. She and Jane – and it sounded like Miss de Bourgh as well – were laughing behind one of the bedroom doors; he had no idea who had been given which rooms. How often had he heard such easy joy at Longbourn and thought nothing of it! More the fool he, apparently.

He stood still, trying to imprint the sound of her laughter perfectly on his memory. After a few moments, he became aware he was no longer the only man standing there in the hall, listening to the girls laughing. Darcy stood there as well, eyes closed, a slight bemused smile on his face. It was the smile that decided him.

"You will take care of her, will you not? No matter what happens during all of this mess?" He did not see a need to define which 'her.'

Darcy's eyes flew open, and he flushed, looking at the ground. "I…" he swallowed hard, and glanced back up to meet Bennet's eyes. "Whatever makes her happy, sir." He smiled ruefully, glancing at the door. "Although I will admit I am not sure I am qualified to know what that is."

The surprisingly honest answer – and the rueful tone – elicited a laugh from Bennet. He clapped Darcy on the shoulder, feeling more at ease than he had since he had agreed to let Elizabeth travel to Kent in the first place. Fanny was not the only one who was – in their own way – overly protective of Elizabeth. "No man does," he replied. "I am quite sure that women are a mystery even to their own Creator."

Darcy favoured him with an odd smile. "No less a mystery than their fathers could be."

Bennet inclined his head, feeling all the amusement of such a statement. "I am merely ensuring that my daughter has a more worthwhile cousin to take care of her, should certain eventualities occur, than I was able to provide her with."

Darcy's eyes wandered back to the door Elizabeth was beyond. "Whatever makes her happy," he repeated.

With such a reply, Bennet found he could be nearly content. It seemed Darcy, at least, was truly appreciative of what the joy Elizabeth brought to aught around her was worth.

He could live with that.

Fifteen

"----- House, London

March 16th

Dear Richard,

I was startled to receive the information contained in your letter, but it is welcome intelligence. Your mother and I look forward to meeting our rediscovered niece. She has promised to do her best by her niece's adoptive family. Thus you may reassure our Elizabeth, she is, indeed, welcomed back into the family with open arms and hearts. Your mother and I look forward to meeting her. When I informed your brother, he quite nearly made his first voluntary visit to Rosings in his life... without packing, might I add, and possibly even on foot. Georgiana has been told, although, naturally, she is uncertain and a little worried how her new cousin will like her. I will assume Darcy did not summon her to Rosings immediately for fear of exposing her to a break in the family. The excitement your information has given the family, however, seems to ease her spirits and apprehensions.

I admit I am disturbed by the fact there is little information known about Elizabeth's appearance in London, but I am at least reassured it would not have been by Mr. Bennet's hand, for else he would have ensured Elizabeth never came within twenty miles of Kent. Perhaps a word at the place she was discovered in London may bear fruit in the matter? We did not ask anything of Wickham, truth be told. The poor boy was traumatized severely by Elizabeth's disappearance and Lewis' extensive injuries and subsequent death. We could scarce get a word above a monosyllable from him for several weeks. Still, I suspect you are correct. He may indeed have information that would at least let us piece together that terrible night, that is, if he has not forced himself to forget more successfully than the rest of us had attempted.

However, you and Darcy are forbidden from bounding off to Hertfordshire immediately. It is the wish of your mother and me that Elizabeth be brought to London. I will summon Wickham, who should at least have sufficient deference as to come instead of leave, particularly if I word the 'request' in such a way as to hint at a possibility of money. We need to speak to you – all of you – about an only partially related topic, one we have avoided for years. It seems now would be the opportune time.

Your mother wishes to extend her hospitality to Elizabeth and Mr. Bennet. If we are correct in our reading of your letter, and Miss Bennet is also in residence at Rosings at this time, she is of course welcome to adjourn to London with Elizabeth. Your aunt and cousin Anne should come here as well. No sense in separating them from Elizabeth so soon. We expect to hear from you soon, detailing your travel arrangements.

Yours, etc,

Randall Fitzwilliam"

Darcy scowled as he handed the letter back to his cousin. "I should much rather ask the blackguard without your father's interference."

Richard smiled without amusement. "You are not the only one, William." He sighed dramatically as he reseated himself. "Still, father's ultimatum should be obeyed – by myself, at least. You have the relief of not being beholden beyond familial duty to him."

Darcy gave his cousin a pointed look. "Such talk of duty would not be required if you would settle upon a nicely dowered lady and be done with it." He handed a glass of port over to his cousin, and sipped his own.

Richard hid a grin behind his glass. "Do you think Elizabeth would do for me, then? She has money enough, now, as a de Bourgh, despite being only *tolerable*."

Darcy nearly choked on his drink in response. "Richard, if you *dare* –" he spluttered.

Richard laughed out loud; Darcy would forever be entirely too easy to tease. "No, William, you did find her first, and I am intelligent enough to know when the field of battle does not even exist!"

Darcy blushed and muttered something. Richard sobered slightly. "Truly, William, even if she were not our cousin, she would be a wonderful wife for you. Although you perhaps should be wary of her sisters – Jane and Anne, that is, specifically. They seem to be fiercely protective of her, in their own ways."

Darcy fiddled with his drink. "Jane already made her thoughts on the subject known, even before I attempted to gauge Elizabeth's reaction to my… interest."

Richard laughed. "Did she indeed? Pecked you right back into place like a mother hen ought to, then?"

"Quite," Darcy grinned. In a roundabout way, it *had* been terribly amusing to be subject to Jane's scolding. "I should send Bingley word when we have decided our travel arrangements; he will be anxious to see Jane again."

"Bingley?" Richard frowned. "Is he who has jilted her, then?"

Darcy glowered, although not, Richard felt, at him. "Nay – his sister did all the work in that regard."

"And poor Jane believed what that crone-to-be said?" Richard was somewhat astounded. Jane seemed entirely too intelligent to be taken in by Bingley's sister.

"She is entirely too inclined to think well of the world, I think, much like Georgiana," Darcy replied. "And, for Miss Bingley's part, all of her actions to her face, while insincere, were far more welcoming to *her* than to anyone else Miss Bingley interacted with."

Richard nodded. "How will the crone take it, knowing her brother has been reintroduced to Jane?"

"Probably by cutting remarks and double entendres," Darcy sighed. "At least until it is known that Elizabeth is *ours,* and Jane's status is improved by such a connection."

Richard picked his glass up again, and nonchalantly, said, "Not to mention how being your sister by marriage to her adoptive sister will help cement the Bennets in our sphere, eh?"

His companion flushed. "Her simultaneous pleasure in the connection and displeasure in its cause cannot be helped, I fear."

"Anne spoke to Elizabeth about what you said to her," Richard said, in all seriousness.

"How –?"

"We both heard you, and Anne felt she should take the opportunity to act sisterly – and find out what she could about Elizabeth's feelings on the subject," Richard explained. "Anne says that you will need to give Elizabeth more time – she disliked you quite heartedly before her arrival in Kent."

Darcy sighed and nodded. "That much I knew, but she has… softened, these past few days."

"Give her time, Darce, seriously."

"I intended to," Darcy replied. "I only said what I did so she would not be unaware of… what my future intentions are. But there is too much turmoil to expect rational choices be made at the moment." He shrugged. "So despite how desperately I wish to throw myself at her feet…" he half-grinned at Richard, who, realizing what he was about to say, repeated old Darcy's favourite saying in chorus with his cousin, "Discretion is the better part of valour."

"Sorry for forcing you to tell me that, William, but Anne promised Elizabeth we would make sure you did not force her into making a choice before she is ready," Richard apologized.

Darcy hid a smile of his own as he once again sipped his drink. "And when will Anne make you my brother?" Richard, in unconscious mimicry of Darcy earlier response, choked on his drink.

"I was not aware that Anne was your sister," Richard replied after he finished coughing the liquid out of his lungs.

"Not yet," Darcy agreed, "but I can hope and believe. And you still have not answered my question."

"You, William, are entirely too arrogant, did you know that?" Richard evaded.

"As I have been reminded frequently, these past few days," Darcy replied, all the humour evaporating from his tone. Something in his expression made Richard think Darcy had shut out all externals for the moment, and so, without so much as taking his leave, he left Darcy there.

He still had no answer to Darcy's question, anyway.

* * *

Richard found Lady Catherine and Mr. Bennet discussing estate matters fairly peaceably. "Aunt, Mr. Bennet, my father has responded."

"Fitzwilliam! And what does my brother say?"

"He writes that he and Aunt Sarah should like to meet Elizabeth, Jane and Mr. Bennet in London at our earliest convenience. He suggests that you and Anne travel with us," he responded.

"And what of our friend, Wickham?" Bennet replied.

"Father says that he shall try to summon him to London." Richard paused, and with a rueful smile, he admitted, "And William and I are expressly forbidden to chase Wickham down in Hertfordshire."

"I will suppose that shall remain true only if Wickham responds to the summons," Bennet half consoled.

"I suspect that my father *will* wish to visit Longbourn. My mother has offered her assistance," he expanded. "But I believe he wants to know Elizabeth first, to have a better idea of what our plan of battle with the *ton* shall be."

Mr. Bennet chuckled, and even Lady Catherine looked amused. "With what little interaction I have had with the *ton* myself," Bennet replied, "A 'plan of battle' is precisely what we shall need."

Lady Catherine concurred with such an insight. "Had my brother anything else to say?"

Richard frowned and unfolded the letter to glance at it again. "He asks if it may be possible to confer with where *you* – or, I suppose, Mrs. Gardiner, although he does not know that – found her, to see if there are any records of her arrival there."

Mr. Bennet frowned slightly. "I shall have to speak with my sister about that. I know that June was quite a disaster for the orphanage;

some of the records were hopelessly disarrayed in the panic of the epidemic."

Richard and Lady Catherine went still. "June?" he heard his aunt whisper in disbelief. "*June?* She disappeared in *March.*"

Mr. Bennet looked between the two of them – "Is that why there was never a response to my sister Gardiner's notice in the paper?"

Lady Catherine floundered. "I do not read the paper; my husband did. I cannot be bothered with the useless information that abounds there. What do I care of international affairs?" Lady Catherine's eyes closed and Richard swore she was trying to keep from crying. "June! A notice in a public paper. An orphanage – In London! Oh, my daughter, what happened to you?"

Mr. Bennet's face was grim. "That, madam, is a question I should dearly love answered myself. *When* in March did she disappear?"

"March 15th," Richard answered.

"Then there is a three month gap in her history, almost to the day," Mr. Bennet advised them. He drummed his fingers on the table in front of him. "At most, I expected a couple of days, perhaps a week." He glanced up at Richard, whose stunned brain was still not working properly. "I do not believe a young boy of the age Wickham would have been could have successfully hid her on his own for three *hours,* let alone three *months,* if he had anything to do with the matter. Elizabeth's *romantic* alternative may be a reality. Would you know if there were any tenants or nearby villagers who would have had a motive for ransom or revenge upon your uncle?"

Richard mutely shook his head, glancing at Lady Catherine. "Aunt?"

She shook herself back to the present. "I… cannot recall any," she answered. The normally forceful woman seemed shaken beyond anything Richard had witnessed before.

"I will write my sister Gardiner, then, and ask if she can inquire –
or if she recalls herself – how Elizabeth arrived at the orphanage," Mr.
Bennet declared. "I believe we should follow your uncle's request, and
remove to London. It seems likely our answers are to be found there
instead of here." He paused. "And if the persons responsible still
reside *here*..." he trailed off, meeting Richard's eyes. Richard nodded
in understanding.

"Yes, yes, we must get her to London, to my brother's," Lady
Catherine said. "I cannot think of where else might be safest for her at
the moment. Fitzwilliam, will you find Darcy and tell him of our
decision? I will find Anne and Elizabeth." Frantic was the word that
came to Richard's mind as he watched her hurry out the door, calling
for Elizabeth and Anne.

With a parting nod, Richard left Mr. Bennet to search for Darcy,
to relay the decision and new information. What a different spin this
put on matters!

Sixteen

"I do not understand why we are in such a rush to go to London," Elizabeth argued. Lady Catherine had readily found Anne and Jane in close conference; they reported Elizabeth had gone to walk in the grove. Darcy, upon hearing this, immediately offered to fetch her back to Rosings to pack for London.

Darcy sighed to himself. After Richard explained the newest information, something he had not thought to even ask himself, he had fully concurred. "Elizabeth, *please*," he begged. "I would rather not be the one to tell you this but – You were missing for three months; there is no telling who kept you for that length of time, nor what their motive for concealing you was. We wish to move you to London for your safety."

Elizabeth rolled her eyes. He truly wished she was not quite so enchanting when she was being stubborn and frustrated; it made it entirely too difficult to restrain a desire to soundly kiss sense into her. "Truly, William, would that not be the least safe place for me to be?"

"It must be safer than Rosings is for you now," Darcy argued. Even in his concern and impatience, he could not deny to himself the thrill it was to hear his name spoken by her, and how lovely she looked in the dappled shade of the grove. "Beyond that, it may indeed be necessary to remove you elsewhere; London is our first point of call, and from there, we will have to determine. Our uncle is most likely to have a solid recommendation. Please?" he offered his arm to her to escort her back, and with – he was amused to note – a somewhat

117

petulant sigh, she accepted. Given the longing glance she gave the path she had been walking down, he did not think the sigh was directed at *him,* per se.

They walked in silence for a few minutes before she spoke. "William?"

"Yes?" He wondered if Richard and Anne realized how difficult this notion of theirs was for him to go along with.

"I am… sorry, for having believed Wickham," she glanced up at him soberly then a mischievous expression flickered across her face. "Even if I was so mortified by being merely *tolerable,* it was quite inexcusable of me to believe him so readily."

Darcy blushed, and started to apologize. She shushed him quietly. "Jane told me some of what you said – about the earl making you leave Georgiana when you would rather not have – I have forgiven you, for what it is worth. I can well imagine what it must have been like, forced into society while mourning for a sister's broken heart; except in Jane's case, she has not had to despair over a mistaken faith in her chosen's character."

"I – thank you." He paused a moment, adding, "I told her that Bingley did not know of her presence in London, and hinted I would ask Bingley to open Netherfield for our family's use, should the earl wish to visit Longbourn."

Elizabeth looked up at him, eyes widening in surprise. "I thank you for that. Jane deserves to have a little hope."

Darcy swallowed and glanced away from her. "I hope you do not find me presumptuous – but I wrote Bingley that evening, after our… truce… and informed him of Jane's presence in London, although I did ask him to wait until… the situation *here* was more settled."

Elizabeth stopped in her astonishment. "You did? Then he knows?"

Darcy smiled ruefully. "Assuming he has read my letter by this point, then yes, he knows that Jane was in London – although I did not tell him what the situation was, as we did not yet have confirmation."

For a split second, Darcy thought Elizabeth was about to hug him – and heaven help him if she did – but she regained her composure and merely beamed at him. This course of action merely *almost* overcame his composure, instead of demolishing it completely. "I cannot thank you enough, then, William. While I realize this means it is now up to Mr. Bingley..." she trailed off with a shrug and a smile. He inclined his head in agreement, then – when she tugged on his arm in the direction of Rosings – gave her a quizzical expression. She replied with a grin. "Mr. Bingley is in London; that is where Jane should be now. And since I do not believe she will leave without me, I must go to London."

He could not help but laugh. Apparently, the trick to getting Elizabeth to agree to a course of action she disagreed with herself was to convince her it was in her beloveds' best interests. He hoped, one day, he would be included in that select group.

* * *

Tiny hands pressed against his waist while the pony methodically plodded along. Her excited murmurings had faded to quietness; perhaps she had fallen asleep. The light was failing fast, but he dared not say anything about the fact he was lost. To give voice to his concerns would make them that much more real, and he knew the only way to keep the little girl seated behind him calm was to remain calm himself. He glanced up at the sky as the sun set, trying to get his bearings. Rosings should be... *that* way. He still felt fairly sure of this, but despite this, they had been going in the same direction for what must be over an hour now – they had not been that far out when he had realized they *were* lost!

He cursed his failings fluidly in his mind. Despite his father's and godfather's attempts otherwise, with such a mother as his, his knowledge of vulgar language was quite extensive. William never had a problem with doing something on a whim; Richard could improvise without recrimination. *He,* however, attempted anything and quickly found himself in over his head. *There is no hope for this, George,* he told himself. If he were the only one out on the little grey dapple, he would just keep riding in this direction until he ran into a fence or a road. But he did not know if that was a sound plan, when one had one's father's patron's sister's three-year-old daughter out on an illicit pony ride. And it was getting darker very quickly, and he knew Elizabeth hated the dark; she had told him that herself. He could not see the moon rising; how would he find their way safely, without some kind light to see by?

He *never* should have agreed to Elizabeth's plea, there outside of her nursery door. "But George, I wanna ride the *pony.*" She still lisped his name a little, and her grammar was atrocious, but there was an undeniable charm to her begging. Her hands twisting on his jacket pulled him back to the immediate present. He could blame himself for their predicament, but he could never blame Elizabeth. He was the weak one, after all.

"George, I'm scared. It's getting dark," she lisped. He could hear her creeping fear, too, and he silently begged the moon to rise.

"It does that at night, Elizabeth, you know that," he replied gently.

"Are we going home soon?" she asked. "I want to go home now."

He swallowed, feeling a touch of panic. "We're on our way there now, dear."

"Oh," was her reply.

He felt a sudden inspiration. "Would you prefer it if I walked beside the pony, so you can ride by yourself?"

"Yes!" was the enthusiastic reply, the incipient darkness momentarily forgotten.

He brought the pony to a halt and slid down. He kept a tight grip on the reins, and adjusted her seating, surreptitiously attempting to ensure she would not slide off the pony while he could not see her. "There, you look like a big girl now," he said encouragingly.

"I am a big girl!" Elizabeth responded, predictably. "I'm three!"

He smiled at her. "Of course you are, only big girls can ride ponies by themselves." This encouragement did the trick. Even as the dusk deepened around them, Elizabeth was too proud of being told she was a 'big girl' to admit she was actually getting scared by the fading light. The situation bought him precious time to try to find his way.

Just as the gloom fell, he spotted movement that might just have been a carriage going past. A road? Dare he hope? He longed to bring the pony to a faster pace, but he dared not risk it with Elizabeth perched atop as she was. In the agonizingly slow moments it took to reach the road through the brush, the light disappeared altogether. He stood, reins in hand, at the edge of the road, trying to figure out where he was, so he could walk along the right direction. After a moment of deliberation, it was Elizabeth's stifled whimper which made him decide. He set off to the right, hoping against hope he was correct. After an indeterminate amount of time, but what he thought could not be more than half an hour, he walked – well, stumbled quite a bit – as he led the pony, his hopes rising that they were not far from the front gates of Rosings. He would take the licks – gratefully – and the scolding and the grounding too. All he wanted was to be back at Rosings, with Elizabeth safe in her nursery.

Hoof beats sounded up the road, and, suddenly fearful of whom they might encounter, he led the pony off the road a ways, considering for a moment to remount. The pony could run much faster than him, if it became necessary. But keeping the pony quiet and calm was paramount after Elizabeth. "Be quiet," he cautioned her softly. He thought he saw her nod in response. The sounds grew closer and Elizabeth began to tremble with the merest whimper. George whispered desperate calming words in her ear, trying to keep his own voice from trembling. In the next moment, as the horse and rider came close enough to be dimly seen, Elizabeth must have thought one of the night-terrors she had told him about had come for her, for she screamed in terror.

The reaction of the two equines dictated the result; the horse reared with a scream of its own, throwing its rider, who landed with a sickening crack, and the pony bolted, catching George unawares, and he tumbled, fractions of a second too late to secure his grasp on Elizabeth. Somehow, she did not topple off the racing pony, and before he was even able to scramble to his feet, all he could do was try to chase down the pony in the direction of her cries. He did not spare the figure sprawled out on the ground a second glance. *"Elizabeth!"*

George Wickham woke with her name in his throat and his heart racing. It had taken years of careful retelling in his mind to rid him of those dreams. He had, he assured himself, spent the evening in the library, and slept in his own room at Rosings, and had not known of Elizabeth's disappearance from the great house until the next morning, for no one had thought to inform him. It was pure fantasy to believe anything else. Except… ever since he had arrived in Hertfordshire and met *her,* the dreams had returned, and even though he had become able to believe his own stories after only a telling or two, he knew in the back of his mind that this story, the first one he had made himself believe, was about to unravel.

He painfully pulled himself out of bed – there was no point in trying to go back to sleep now – and methodically dressed. He did not know what it was about Elizabeth Bennet – besides her given name – that prompted the return of the dreams. He almost felt he knew her, from the moment he talked to her. He had watched Darcy's reaction to her like a hawk, interrogating his associates who saw them in company more frequently than he had, hoping to catch a cue that Darcy recognized her as well. All he saw and heard, however, was Darcy looked at her a great deal. She looked familiar, much like Anne de

Bourgh, but with Darcy's almost non-reaction, he could not trust himself. He found himself wishing Fitzwilliam was with Darcy, here in Meryton, for a confirmation as to whether he was losing his mind or not.

Like so many other events in his life, Wickham had never intended to repeat his Darcy-inflicted woe story to Miss Bennet. He had, obscurely, been acting on a protective instinct. Denny's comments about her had alerted him – one cad to another – where *his* interests lie with the lady. Wickham had wanted her sympathy and attention to shield her from Denny, who had been attempting to use his acquaintance with the younger Bennets as a method to break through to the elder Elizabeth. He, like Denny, cared nothing for the two younger girls; it was Elizabeth who was to be prized. But their reasons for it were different – Denny had fond ideas of being a conqueror of such a fiery spirit, and Wickham felt fiercely protective of her, much like Georgiana. His mind shied away from the younger Darcy; he was not yet ready to face the result of his actions *there*.

It was not without a certain sense of irony that he reflected his tongue had told her more truth intermixed with the story he had convinced himself of, than anyone had heard from him in years… and it was that very corrupted truth that made Elizabeth painfully angry with Darcy on his behalf. Wickham felt uneasy about this; to Wickham's mind, Elizabeth, much like Georgiana, was safest under Darcy's direct supervision and care. He was bitterly aware that his attempts to protect Anne's little sister and, later, William's little sister, had failed miserably. Thus, the only person *he* could trust with Elizabeth's safety – completely – was Fitzwilliam Darcy.

He had used his considerable charm to hear the story of the Bennets. He knew that the eldest child had been a boy who perished the same year Elizabeth de Bourgh disappeared, but no mention was made of Elizabeth. In other rooms and venues, chiefly amongst the officers, he spoke of her often, attempting to persuade the others his interest was of a serious nature, alternating with a bespoken belief that

Darcy favoured her himself. Thus far, it had worked, and her other admirers had subsided in their attentions, believing themselves out of the league of Wickham and Darcy combined. When he became concerned she may be *too* charmed by him, he half-randomly changed the directions of his attentions – Mary King was a nice enough girl, quiet like Georgiana, and obliging enough – knowing that the rest of the officers would not dare attempt anything with Elizabeth; he knew the betting pool had shifted to favour he would attempt to make Elizabeth his mistress after he married Miss King. Yet, he tried to downplay the, er, expectation of his colleagues for him making a move on either girl.

When he heard she was leaving for Kent, to visit the wife of Lady Catherine's parson, he was torn between deep seated terror and relief. Lady Catherine would know immediately if Elizabeth Bennet was the missing de Bourgh, and he would no longer feel responsible for trying to protect her in his unorthodox way, regardless of the outcome. Her fate would be out of his hands; Darcy would protect her if she was their Elizabeth.

When he heard Mr. Bennet had left Longbourn for Kent, quite unexpectedly – information passed on to him by the ever-obliging Lydia and Kitty Bennet – the relief he felt was nearly sensual. Lady Catherine most certainly had summoned him about Elizabeth – he had *not* lost his mind; it *was* her. He had done the right thing – perhaps not the most right of all right things, but *a* right thing – in trying, however haphazardly, to protect her. For the first time in seventeen years, he almost felt redeemed.

He finished dressing and made his way downstairs, where he discovered a letter awaited him from Lord Matlock. He hovered on the edge of opening the letter – torn between cowardice and hope – before breaking the seal. A ticket for the post carriage fell out; he caught it and read the letter.

"----- House, London

March 17th

Mr. Wickham,

While I vividly recall telling you in the not-distant-enough past you were never again welcome in my household, I find I need to extend an offer of hospitality to you at this time. The journey to London and a few days spent at my disposal will be made worth your while. Have no fear, I shall not harm a hair on your head, and as long as you do not purposely antagonize my nephew Darcy, Georgiana, or my sons, I will hold them to that promise as well. My reason for summoning you here is, as one once so intimately connected with this family, you, too, should be made party to the information that has been discovered.

I have sent a letter to your commanding officer – Richard's contacts with the military do prove so very useful, do they not? – explaining in as little detail as possible why you are being summoned. Do not bother attempting to glean information from him, however; he has less than you do.

Enclosed is a ticket for the post carriage; while I realize this is not the style to which you could be accustomed to, I felt it would not be fair to send my carriage to your encampment, as I do not know its exact location; I have little desire to treat my horses so ill. If your interest in horses remains what it was in years past, I have no doubt you will acquit me in this regard.

I expect to see you by the 20th, no later. Send word if there are unavoidable delays – but let me caution you that an attempt to flee will be frowned upon.

Randall Fitzwilliam, Earl of Matlock"

Flee? When the chances offered him an opportunity for confession which may be close at hand? – A confession for Elizabeth, a confession for Darcy, a confession for Georgiana – no, Wickham, despite everything, wanted nothing more than the forgiveness and love of his family, irrespective of how little he was deserving of it. As long as Elizabeth and Georgiana were safe – and he might have the opportunity of seeing them again – fleeing was the furthest thought from his mind.

He searched out Colonel Forster, who glowered at him slightly as he appeared before him. "I dislike having *requests* being made to me by earls," the man said, "and if you should want an excuse to avoid this *visit,* I can find a reason for why your presence is unavoidably required here."

Wickham shook his head. "Nay, sir. It would not do for me to offend Lord Matlock," *more than I already have,* his mind supplied, "for, you see, he was my godfather's brother by virtue of marriage."

"Family, in a roundabout way, then," Forster fixed a grim eye on Wickham. "I had wondered how a gambler like you had scraped together the money required for a commission."

Wickham felt no need to blush, although Forster was not far off from the reality. "Luck favours the prepared, sir," was all he was willing to offer.

"Very well, then," the colonel waved a hand at him. "If you are willing to go, you may as well leave now."

"Yes, sir," Wickham said, and left. He hovered a moment in his room before packing almost the entirety of his meagre belongings. The blessing of a uniform environment was that he could conceal how few clothes he owned. The trip to Ramsgate had cost him almost every farthing he had left of the settlement from Darcy. It had been worth it, until he realized that the situation had spiralled out of his control. He gathered from Darcy's reactions to him on the street in Meryton that the consequences had been at least as bad as he feared. At the end of it, he paid a bribe of a full pound, more than a month's pay, which he would never repine except for its necessity. He remembered with a sour smile how Georgiana's maid had looked at him askance as he mentioned to her it would be for the best that a word was dropped in her mistress's brother's ear that she was concerned about Georgiana. Darcy's arrival two days later proved it had been money well spent.

And now he was to see them all again – he longed for and feared this. How was he to explain everything, and regain some measure of credibility and forgiveness? It was too much, he knew, to hope to regain his brother's and cousin's affections. He would have to settle for their decreased animosity, although the thought tore at what remained of his heart.

Seventeen

The post carriage had not been the most comfortable he had ridden in, even without the uncomfortable swirling thoughts which accompanied him from Hertfordshire. He was grateful to find Lord Matlock had sent his own carriage to collect him from the station. One of the footmen who attended had been one of those who escorted him out of the Fitzwilliam townhouse after his last visit. Wickham noted the look of irritated disdain the man quickly masked. He did not blame him. "My lord will be pleased to see you so soon," the man said. Wickham well understood that meant Lord Matlock had suspected he would flee; with a meeting imminent, he felt a desire to do just that.

"I was most honoured to receive his lordship's request," Wickham replied. A flicker of surprise crossed the footman's face before Wickham entered the carriage.

He wondered what he would say when he arrived at the Fitzwilliam townhouse. Dare he ask after Georgiana? Should he tell his lordship he had suspected Elizabeth's identity before she left for Kent? Should he tell the real story of that night and throw himself at the earl's mercy? Questions such as these were dangerous. His courage was not his most plentiful virtue, else much in his life would have been better. Cowardly by nature, the easiest route had never been the full truth; that is, if any crossed his lips at all.

His musings came to a halt as the carriage slowed. He swallowed, and wondered again how he was to get through this. The disdainful footman opened the door and he got out. "I have been instructed to escort you to your room," he said. Wickham nodded in understanding – the earl would want him sequestered until he was apprised of his arrival – and followed the man up. He noted with dry amusement, in direct conflict with his fear of the earl, that the earl had bequeathed him a room at the very end of the guest wing, a room he had once heard Lady Catherine call a "wretched disgrace." There was no need for fearing anyone given this room in an otherwise empty wing could believe themselves *welcome* visitors. Still, it was several steps up from many places he had slept of late. He would not even begin to think of complaining.

His belongings were stored, and the footman fixed him with a firm eye. "I shall inform my lord of your arrival. His lordship has deemed that due to your unfamiliarity with the house" – a blatant lie, that, Wickham reflected, with him being as intimately familiar with the house as Darcy or the Fitzwilliam siblings could be – "you are to be accompanied by a servant should you need to leave the room. One shall be posted at your door for your… convenience. Have you any immediate requests?"

Wickham shook his head. "A few hours rest would be appreciated," he said. "That was perhaps the most wretched post-chaise I have ever known."

A touch of agreement flickered across the footman's face. Wickham could be relied upon to have a good eye for horses and carriages. That much was still widely accepted among those who served the Fitzwilliam family. "I shall convey that to my lord," the footman replied.

"If I have any other requests, I will inform my guard," he added, with an ironic smile. Perhaps the footman would mince words and be polite, but Wickham was too busy combating his innate cowardice to do so himself. The footman quirked an eyebrow, but did not correct him. Instead, he withdrew, presumably to do as he had said.

Wickham settled himself on the bed, swallowing against the rising nausea. This was going to be more difficult than he had anticipated.

* * *

Lord Matlock paced his library a couple of hours later. Dawson had faithfully relayed the entirety of everything Wickham had said or done since they met him at the station. After Dawson's scathing comment about the carriage – "One would believe we had not discovered sprung carriages" had been his exact words – Randall felt he could not demand Wickham's presence immediately, for that would be too cruel. Georgiana had been informed already of Wickham's coming presence in the house. Expecting his arrival today, she had petitioned Lady Matlock's company for shopping. It was a measure of the girl's dismay that she also expressed a wish to call on the Bingley sisters, one of the few families she could visit due to the brother's particular friendship to her own.

The letter that included the Rosings party's travel arrangements had included the most recently gleaned information, and it had thrown Lord Matlock more than he was willing to admit. He was assured that the person who was most likely able to find information from the orphanage Elizabeth had been found at had a letter of her own, requesting her assistance in the investigation, along with the address for the Fitzwilliam townhouse.

He reasonably expected to see Elizabeth with his own eyes in a few hours, but he was not sure he should speak to anyone else about the issue until he had spoken to Wickham. Extracting the information from Wickham was *his* job. He could not trust his sons or his nephew to do so without resorting to threats of violence. A knock sounded at the door. "Come in."

Andrews, the footman Dawson had assigned to guard Wickham's door, announced, "Mr. Wickham." Randall was startled. He had not expected to see the boy for at least an hour or two yet. He stepped into the room, and Randall actually felt remorse on the boy's behalf.

Wickham was obviously petrified and – for once in his life – trying to work through it instead of fleeing.

"Lord Matlock," Wickham bowed as the door closed. "I suspected you would wish to see me sooner rather than later."

Randall inclined his head in agreement, and gestured to a chair. "Before I start the inquisition, did you rest?"

Wickham shook his head convulsively. "I found that, even if I am weary, my mind is too discomposed to settle even for a nap."

An honest answer, Randall noted in surprise. "Then, perhaps, you can tell me why you have been so discomposed. I know my letter contained no particular information."

Wickham fidgeted, swallowing hard, and would not look at him. "I … is it …I know why you summoned me here." He shuddered, and brought his hands together in front of him, clasping them tightly. "I did what I could to protect Elizabeth, from the attentions of the other officers in the militia, before she travelled to Kent. I was not sure it was her, that she was *our* Elizabeth, for Darcy did not seem to recognize her, and I did not trust my own mind in the matter." He finally looked at Randall. "I swear, if I had been surer, I would have informed you immediately."

Randall was shocked. "How did you –?"

Wickham looked at the ground. "She looks like Anne, but even Anne has more of the Fitzwilliam features. Anne is the only one in the entire family she truly resembles. If you had not noticed," Wickham added with an ironic smile, "most of the family displays their kinship to the Fitzwilliams before their other family." Randall made an amused noise of agreement, but Wickham continued as if he had not heard. "I think I was the one to notice who she was, for I have for so long had to be content with seeing so little of my kinship in Darcy's face."

Lord Randall came to his feet and Wickham quailed. "What do you know of the matter?" Randall asked.

"Which matter?"

"Your parentage."

"I …" Wickham looked at the ground, biting his knuckles as he controlled himself. "When Georgiana was born …" he began, the memories as vivid as his nightmares, although he surely could not say *all* of it, not here, not now.

* * *

George Andrew Wickham, Jr. had come to speak to his father and Mr. Darcy. He wanted to see if he would be allowed to hold William's new sister, before he attempted to ask William or Lady Anne. Thus, he stood at Mr. Darcy's door, prepared to knock, when he heard slightly raised voices in the room. With a flicker of dismay at what he was about to do, he placed an ear to the door to hear more fully.

"Come, Richard," he heard his father say, "You cannot seriously mean to name the girl after me?"

"And why should I not choose to, George? Are you not my most stalwart friend?" George felt a flicker of pride in his father; to be spoken so highly by Mr. Darcy was a rare thing indeed.

"And no friend in any of our circle of acquaintances has two children named after him!" came the heated reply. George blinked – he knew William's name as well as his own, and neither 'George' nor 'Andrew' was in William's name anywhere.

"You know full well why we named the boy after you. There was no other way to pass him off as yours so completely." George felt the strength drain out of his body in horror. Surely, he did not hear what he thought he did.

"And *you* are fortunate enough that I had no interest in marrying at all, and was thus at liberty to… deal with that unfortunate situation you found yourself in," his father's voice replied sardonically.

"Quite," replied Mr. Darcy's cool tones, "and for that I can never repay you enough, old friend."

"You keep me supplied with books, conversation, and gave me a chance to raise a son, something I never expected to accomplish. That is repayment enough," Mr. Wickham replied.

Mr. Darcy answered, "But, still, to the world's knowledge, I only have *one* son, not two, and now I have a daughter, who I should like to legitimately name after you. No one will think it odd in the slightest. Humour me?"

In a voice filled with a tender defeat, tones George had never heard the man he had called father all these years use towards his mother, "As you wish, then, Richard. You know I could never gainsay you for long."

Mr. Darcy laughed. "Thankfully, you are easily persuaded to reason." A mirthless chuckle was the response, followed by footsteps moving towards the door.

George felt himself stagger back from the door, looking for a place to hide. A murmur of voices paused the footsteps, and he scurried away to hide and wallow in his confusion. He, the son of Mr. Darcy – brother to William! The man he had looked up to as his father, talking in such tender accents to Mr. Darcy! He felt vaguely thankful that Mr. Darcy did not appear to notice the emotions behind the older Wickham's words and actions. But what could he say – to either of them? What of Richard and William? And William's new sister – his sister! What of her?

He knew, obscurely, dimly, that his sense of honour and faith had been shaken severely, above and beyond the loss of – his mind shied away from those memories quickly. Had he not sworn to himself they were fevered memories, brought on by the stress of those dark days? But even as he stood there in that hall closet, secreted away from the world, for a breath of infinity, he promised he would do everything he could, to make his little sister happy, to make his brother – however little William may know him as such – proud of him. He was still proud of the man who had given him his name; such unrestrained and loyal friendship was rare, and he could not be but thankful for the legitimacy he had apparently gifted to his friend's illegitimate child.

But – oh! – how he wanted to be able to confide this to William. How was he to be strong enough to handle this secret – on top of the ones already concealed in his heart – on his own?

* * *

"You knew?" Randall hissed. "Yet you hurt Georgiana as you did? How *despicable* –"

"Sir, please," Wickham begged. "I never meant to hurt her. That was never my intent. Did not Darcy tell you I disappeared without a word contrary? Did he not tell you her maid had contacted him? *I* gave her maid money – as a bribe to do it, for I knew Mrs. Younge had forbidden any of the servants from telling Darcy of my presence – to send an express to Darcy." Wickham buried his face in his hands. "She is my *sister*. I wanted to see her – so badly. I knew Younge from my – " he coughed slightly "I knew her from before, and we had kept up correspondence. She had wished me to marry her, years ago, and after she was widowed, she wished it again. I had made some mention of needing a fortune to do so; her next letter said she had been hired as companion to Georgiana." Wickham fell silent for a moment.

"Continue, sir," Randall's voice had grown excessively icy, and Wickham flinched again.

"I – I confess, I thought nothing but how much I wished to see my younger sister, and I suggested that when Younge and Georgiana travelled to Ramsgate, I should meet up with them." He glanced up at Randall. "Younge mistook my intent as wishing to marry Georgiana," disgust flitted across Wickham's face, "so I could then keep *Younge* in a style to which she could be accustomed. I did not realize this at first," he sighed. "And once I did, I tried to downplay the idea – I suggested an elopement hoping it would dissuade her, and made mention of how little Darcy seemed to trust me. I said everything I could think of to discourage an attachment, except *that* which would have been most effective."

"Then why did you not *tell* her?" Randall glowered.

Wickham looked up at him, and Randall was hit by the vulnerability in his face. "I was too cowardly to do so, sir. I did not *know* until later that Younge had been actively encouraging an attachment to me. I had merely been enjoying the company of my most darling sister, who I do love very dearly, and treating her as I thought she should be treated. But – when I realized that Georgiana was serious – I found I could not say such things to her, when I had never been able to even breathe word of it to Darcy." He looked back down. "So I took the coward's way out. I bribed the maid to inform Darcy she was 'concerned' for her mistress, so he would visit Ramsgate and I knew – once she was confronted with him, she would confess, and I would be the villain, but I would not have to look in her face and see her heart break, nor see the result of the damage to her – our – father's memory."

Randall took a shaky breath. "I will have to confirm with her maid before I will trust your account of things."

Wickham nodded. "I expect nothing less, sir."

Randall fixed him with an ironic glance. "Lady Matlock and I have intended to inform you, Richard and William of your parentage – we thought it was long overdue intelligence. Seeing as you already know, we shall be informing them separately." He paused, recollecting his original reason for summoning Wickham to London in the first place. "Seeing as it appears to be your day for confessions – do you have any others to make?"

Wickham paled, closed his eyes, and took a steadying breath. "Sir… may I have your word, that I will be permitted to make my apologies to Darcy, Georgiana, and Elizabeth, before I am thrown from the house, regardless of what else I may say?"

Randall narrowed his eyes. "As long as you only have apologies – or confessions – to make, you have my word, regardless of how the rest of this conversation goes."

Wickham nodded. "Thank you, sir." He paused and took another deep breath. "I know how Elizabeth left Rosings that night."

Eighteen

Had this been any other day, Randall would have found it necessary to retire for a short rest prior to the next party's arrival. As it was, he was still exhausted – mind, body, and soul – at least some of it in empathetic echo of Wickham. He had given the boy a fortifying shot of brandy and sent him specifically to bed – just at the moment, he needed to be treated more like he was six, not six-and-twenty.

He knew Wickham to be a tolerable actor if he had reason to be assured of some success. He also knew Wickham could breathe in truth and breathe out a lie faster than the *ton* could affect sincerity. Tears and expressions of guilt – these were not the hallmark of the Wickham he had come to know. No – he firmly believed the boy was finally telling the truth, a truth he had long suppressed. He shuddered to think what they had done to him, not sitting him down and *making* him talk. He had blamed himself for Lewis' death on top of a childish thoughtlessness in regards to Elizabeth.

At least Randall now understood how Lewis – bloodied and battered by the fall as he was – had been so adamant that Elizabeth was alive and well. He could not remember the fall; they had asked him repeatedly, but he could only recall saddling the horse, not even leaving the front gates. Somewhere, Randall was now sure, Lewis had heard Wickham calling for Elizabeth, and even if he could not remember *why,* it had been enough to keep him alive through the night.

But a critical question remained unanswered – where had Elizabeth disappeared *to?* He hoped the person with the contacts at the orphanage was able to find the answers they needed. He glanced at the clock, rubbing his neck against the strain. The Rosings party would be arriving shortly. He had Georgiana's maid summoned – not that, after the last emotional hour, he doubted Wickham had done what he said he had – but it was better to verify than to simply believe.

The thought that the worst part of his day – informing Darcy, Richard, and Alexander of Wickham's parentage – had yet to come intruded upon his thoughts. The temptation to take a fortifying shot – or three perhaps – of brandy himself hovered on the edge of his thoughts. Perhaps, he decided, after he spoke with the maid, if the Rosings party had not yet arrived, he would yield – carefully, it would not do to appear in front of his niece anything less than sober – to that temptation.

* * *

Madeline Gardiner frowned as she read the letter from her brother. Three months was a decidedly long time for a little girl to be missing; more puzzling still was how her little gown had been only a little dirty and in good repair. After ensuring the children had settled down for their nap, she left them to the care of the nanny, and set off for the orphanage.

When she arrived, one of the carers was tending the little ones. "Oh, but you are here early," the woman said.

Madeline shook her head. "I am afraid I did not come to assist just at the moment, Natalie. Do you know where Frances is?"

Natalie nodded. "In her office, attending the correspondence that came in not long ago."

She gave her long-time acquaintance a smile. "Thank you." She departed to the back, up the stairs, and at the furthest end of the hall –

the stuffiest little room the building had, for it had been deemed nonsense to give a good room over to a mere office – she knocked on the door.

"Come in," called Frances. She entered, and Frances gave her a grateful smile. "Come to distract me from these accounts?"

Madeline laughed, albeit quietly. "Yes, if not for precisely what we would expect."

Frances raised an eyebrow at her old friend. "Oh? Do tell."

Madeline settled in the chair across from the desk. "We finally found Elizabeth's family – or they found her? I am not sure how one would phrase it. It is a tad complex."

Frances lit up. "Truly? That is astounding."

Madeline laughed. "Yes, indeed. I could not be more pleased. I always hoped we would stumble across them. However," she sobered, "I have been asked to search the records for Elizabeth's appearance here. It seems she disappeared for nigh on three months before arriving *here;* her original family and my brother are very concerned for her current welfare."

Frances frowned. "Three months? That is… troubling." Madeline nodded in agreement. "We can search the records, of course, but you know as well as I how disorganized this institution was under that particular head, even beyond the troubles placed upon us by that horrible epidemic."

"I know, but – if I am not mistaken, the women who would have been in charge of admittance are both deceased, and our only hope is that we have the paper records," Madeline replied.

"You are indeed correct," Frances answered. "And I, myself, was not even here that month, for my father had taken us on holiday." Madeline suppressed a grimace – Frances' memory was the most reliable she had ever witnessed. There went her first hope, that Frances would recall herself, for she had been unable to remember who had been at the orphanage during that time.

"Do I have your permission, then, to start searching?" Madeline asked.

Frances nodded. "With any luck, the information may even be in the proper location." Frances rose and beckoned Madeline to follow. "If nothing else, at least you can but say you tried."

"Indeed," Madeline agreed.

* * *

The records – such as they were – had not been as helpful as Madeline would have preferred. Elizabeth's name did appear on the rolls – "Elizabeth, age 3, family name unknown. Escorted by unrelated male, who did not wish to be named. Spoke of being unable to care for such a young waif." The date matched what Madeline had recalled, herself. She left to return to her children, disappointed. She did not a pen a reply to her brother's letter – he had stated he intended to return to London with Elizabeth and Jane in the next day or so, and as she had nothing further to add herself, it made little difference if she conveyed it immediately by letter or two days hence in person.

She had just settled back into the household, having freshened up after her excursion. Only her eldest daughter had woken from her nap; she was currently engrossed in the pianoforte. The length of time Elizabeth had been between known locations bothered her obscurely, and she wondered which of her acquaintances at the orphanage – the ones who did not go there daily or even weekly, but were seasonal, transitional – two or three tinkers among them, who fixed things for the orphanage for free – might have insight on the matter. Many knew one of her nieces had been adopted; only a handful knew which one it was, although, as long as Elizabeth had not known herself, it had not been spoken of in her presence.

Now that she thought about it, one of the tinkers had always known which niece was Elizabeth. He had always asked after her when he passed through. He had seen Elizabeth but a handful of times over the years; he generally drifted through London in August or September, when Elizabeth was in Hertfordshire. He had made mention, once, when Madeline wondered at his interest in Elizabeth, that he had met her prior to her being placed with Madeline's brother, and had been quite taken with the girl. She bit her lip in frustration – gypsies were difficult enough to pin down when one knew where they were! How was she to find him, now, and ask questions of him? Better yet, that her husband and brother asked the questions. It was only March now – should she mention the idea, so that they could all plan on converging on London in early August, in case he should pass through so early?

Even as she thought this, and began to move towards her writing desk – to jot down a note to herself, lest she forgot – when she heard unfamiliar footsteps in the hall, presumably being escorted to the parlour. Her housekeeper opened the door and announced – "Mr. and Miss Bingley, ma'am."

Madeline was astounded. After Miss Bingley's cold behaviour on her last visit to Gracechurch Street, she had been forced to gently convince Jane to not expect another visit – or even that a return visit would be welcomed. To find Miss Bingley here – with her brother, the man who had captured Jane's heart – she could not even begin to fathom what brought it on. Even as this flickered through her mind, however, she smiled charmingly at the two guests, and curtsied. "Miss Bingley, it is pleasant to see you again. I hope you are well?"

The lady's reply was cool and uncomfortable, her eyes glancing towards her brother anxiously. "Mrs. Gardiner; the pleasure is all mine. I am well, as is my brother." She nodded towards Mr. Bingley. "Charles, this is Mrs. Gardiner, the Bennets' aunt. Mrs. Gardiner, my brother Mr. Charles Bingley."

Mr. Bingley... glittered. That was the phrase that flickered through Madeline's mind. His personality was light and sparkling, much like his smile. "I am very pleased to meet you, Mrs. Gardiner. I hope you do not believe me overly forward, nor sorely lacking in manners – I only just recently was informed that some of my Hertfordshire acquaintances had lately passed time in town; your eldest nieces, that is."

Mrs. Gardiner smiled at him, quite unable to feel too dismayed with someone so cheerful. "Indeed, Jane has been in London with us since January. Her sister Elizabeth passed through on her way to Kent but a se'ennight ago, perhaps a few days longer."

"And how do they fare?" he asked. Miss Bingley – Madeline felt almost sorry for her, for this was not the arrogantly confident lady she had met previously – seated herself a little to the side, and was principally employed in toying with her bracelets.

"They are both well," she answered. "Jane travelled to Kent with her father at the end of last week, but we expect them both to return with Elizabeth to London before week's end."

Mr. Bingley nodded. "I confess, my friend, Mr. Darcy, did mention that possibility in his letter to me." Madeline noticed Miss Bingley looked up at this sharply and paled slightly, but she did not speak. The word 'possibility' indicated to Madeline that whatever information Mr. Bingley had from Mr. Darcy dated prior to her own trip to Kent. She wondered how much Mr. Darcy had passed on to his friend, although she did not suspect he had let on the truth of the situation. Mr. Bingley did not allude to anything about Elizabeth. This did, however, answer the question as to what prompted the current visit to Gracechurch Street.

"I met Mr. Darcy when Jane and Mr. Bennet journeyed to Kent, although it was exceedingly brief," Madeline replied.

"Oh?" Mr. Bingley asked, seeming to be more than politely interested.

"Yes," she smiled. "The Kent countryside is quite beautiful this time of year. He must be well pleased to be able to stay there – I understand it is a yearly occurrence."

"Indeed," Mr. Bingley replied. "He has visited his aunt, Lady Catherine, around Easter-tide for as long as I have known him."

Conversation lulled for a moment before Madeline asked if her guests would like some refreshments. Mr. Bingley smiled in reply. "I thank you, ma'am, but I do believe my sister has an appointment for this afternoon. I am sure she will agree with me that staying longer here would be pleasant, but prior arrangements ought to be kept, do you not agree?"

"Indeed," Madeline agreed. She did not take offence to the reply. She knew herself to not be the primary object of the meeting. "Dinner, then, perhaps in a few days' time, after Jane and Elizabeth return from Kent?"

"That would be lovely – would it not, Caroline?" Mr. Bingley glanced at his sister.

"Very," Miss Bingley replied.

"Then it is settled – do send 'round a note once you can fix a date, and we shall attend," he said to Madeline.

"You may count on it, sir," she replied. She saw her guests to the door – Miss Bingley said only the most basic of required civilities in farewell. Warmth remained for her brother to display. Even when Miss Bingley had called previously, she had spoken more than today – what had her brother said to her after receiving the intelligence from his friend to cause such a change?

Madeline recollected she had been about to go to her desk when the Bingleys arrived – to do what? A note to herself, yes, that was it, but about what? She had been fretting about Elizabeth's past... and... she had had a thought about a possible lead and... Oh! For the life of her, what had it been? She bit her lip in frustration, trying to recapture that thread of thought. It was like grasping air; only the barest tendrils of it remained, and she rued that the Bingleys had not arrived even but two minutes later. No matter how hard she tried, she could not remember. She could only hope that it would come back to her in due time.

* * *

The Rosings party had woken early enough to be ready to depart to make good time to London. Lady Catherine found herself in the library – a place she had rarely inclined to retreat to; it had been her husband's, and subsequently, her nephew's favourite haunt. She felt drawn, however, as she knew Elizabeth favoured books over more ladylike pursuits, and – even if she knew her second daughter to be above stairs, readying for the journey to London – she felt closer to her in here, than in the parlour where she had first recognized her.

Seventeen years of heartache, so close to being a thing of the past. It was not yet, however – for as much as she loved Elizabeth, and could not but rejoice at witnessing her daughters' attempt to work towards a common affection, she felt... distanced from Elizabeth still. Perhaps it was because no one ever thought to find themselves with two sets of parents, and siblings were already usually a multitude.

The pain had been worst that first year. Losing Lewis, whom she had loved from the moment she met him, and had jested to him she would prefer that he survive her so as to not live without him, *that* had been a blow she would never have been prepared for, even if she knew it was approaching. Losing Elizabeth, who looked so much like her father, had been a horrible blow, tempered only by an ever-fading hope of her recovery. Indeed, even while she refused to let go of that hope, she had slowly begun to let herself grieve for the child she believed had to have followed her father. To find Elizabeth – alive, hale, and still every inch her father's daughter – her joy was boundless, but she felt checked in her expression of it.

She wondered at the quiet in this room – was it the solitude that drew her nephew here? What of Elizabeth, who was a lively girl, and seemed to have a preference for company? But – she recollected – Elizabeth also sought solitary solace outside – perhaps she was more of a Fitzwilliam than she would have thought, just one who was able to balance her need for company and solitude better than most of the family. Perhaps – she hesitated to think this, but could not help it – it had been to Elizabeth's benefit to have grown up in a lively family, so far removed from the stately and formal Fitzwilliam clan.

Her musings were interrupted by the door opening and closing quickly. She turned to find Elizabeth standing there, her hands clasped behind her back. For the life of her, she looked like a child waiting to be scolded. "Yes, my dear?" Catherine asked.

Elizabeth bit her lip nervously. "I… I want to apologize."

Catherine raised an eyebrow in surprise. "Indeed? Whatever for?"

"I would not wish you to think I am… intentionally keeping my distance from you, Lady Catherine," she replied.

She thought – hoped at least – she kept from wincing at the title. "I have been trying to keep from smothering you," she admitted. "Some of the distance is undoubtedly my fault – I do not wish to scare you off."

Elizabeth smiled. "My courage rises at every attempt to intimidate me, your ladyship. I dare say it will not be the worse for a bit of maternal smothering."

"If that is the case…" Catherine paused until Elizabeth nodded encouragingly. "I should like it if you… did not address me so formally, my girl."

Elizabeth's eyes unfocused slightly as she nodded, then refocused on her. "I had decided that formality was… safe. Until I could think of *what* to call you," she answered.

Catherine felt a pang. "I would that you call me 'mother,'" she replied.

"I… I know you would," Elizabeth sounded extremely apologetic. "But when I say the word 'mother,' I think of Mrs. Bennet." Catherine winced. "But," Elizabeth continued, "I discussed this with my sister – Anne, that is, although Jane contributed – last night, and I believe I have come up with a… compromise."

"I should like to hear it," Catherine prodded.

Elizabeth smiled slightly. "I also had a question to ask, when I arrived in here – in which carriage would you prefer me to ride? My cousin William's or yours…" she paused very slightly "*mère?*"

Catherine had been nonplussed by the sudden change of subject – until the last word. She felt a sudden rush of tears, and moved to embrace her daughter, who returned it strongly. "Whichever you prefer, my girl. I am just glad for you to be home."

"I believe I am as well, *mère.*"

Nineteen

Lady Matlock assisted Georgiana in delaying her return to the Fitzwilliam townhouse for as long as she could. At length, however, their return was required. Sarah watched in sorrow as the glimmers of the girl who had begun to surface once again faded out the closer they came to arriving to Wickham's presence. She longed to say something, anything, to ease her niece's fears, but the words died before she could even begin to open her mouth.

When they arrived, Georgiana immediately attempted to plead fatigue from her long day, and to excuse herself from company. Dawson, ever the faithful man he was – one of the few servants even Georgiana felt at ease with – made an oblique comment to her ladyship. "Your husband's guest is currently resting at the master's orders, milady. He is not expected down until supper at the earliest." He pretended to not see Georgiana sag with relief, but the glance he gave Sarah spoke volumes.

"Where is milord?" she asked.

"In his study, milady," Dawson replied.

"Thank you," she nodded. "Come," she added to Georgiana, "let us tell him of our day." Georgiana followed docilely enough, her apprehension less with the assurances she would not be immediately in Wickham's company.

She knocked when they arrived, and heard a tired "Come in."

"We are back," she announced as she motioned for Georgiana to follow her.

"Welcome back, my loves," Lord Randall responded. He attempted to smile, but he was worn. He glanced at Georgiana. "Come to tell me how your day has gone?" he asked encouragingly.

Georgiana nodded, and at her aunt's careful prodding, gave a brief overview of what shops they had frequented, along with the news that they had only visited Louisa Hurst and her husband, as Mr. and Miss Bingley had been out visiting themselves. Randall asked open questions, carefully assisting Georgiana in expanding on her own sparse words. At length, however, the topic was exhausted, and Georgiana, in a fit of courage she did not know she possessed, asked, "Did you speak to Mr. Wickham already, uncle?"

Randall suppressed a start. Sarah surmised he had been intending to bring up the boy's past himself, and had only wanted an opening. "Yes, my dear, I have spoken with George." Georgiana and Sarah both looked askance at him for using Wickham's first name, and he gave them a wry smile. Taking Georgiana's hand, he led her to the only couch in this room of business. "Georgiana, I was not sure this was ever to be information for your ears, but my discussion with Wickham earlier has convinced me otherwise." Sarah felt herself stiffen – the boys, yes, but Georgiana would not survive the mortification! A quick, fierce glance from her husband quelled the protest on her lips. He obviously knew what he was about, and she reminded herself she had not been privy to the conversations going on in the past few hours.

"I realize some of this may confuse you at first, and I will hasten to add that, apart from George, myself, and your aunt, there is no one left alive who knows this information." Georgiana slowly nodded. "But first I must ask – had you known that Mrs. Younge had forbidden the staff at Ramsgate from contacting your brother, under threat of unemployment?"

Georgiana's eyes grew wide. "No, uncle, I heard not a word of that. How did you –"

"George told me, earlier today," he answered. "Do you remember that your maid gave you a small present, after your return from there?"

She nodded. "Yes – she had said she disliked seeing me so sad, and while I protested her spending her hard-earned money on *me*, when it ought to be the other way around, she insisted."

"It was not hard-earned money, Georgiana. When I spoke to her this afternoon, she said she felt she did not deserve the remainders, when the money had been given to her to help protect you." He paused. "Wickham had given her a bribe to convince her to send a note to your brother in defiance of Mrs. Younge's instructions."

"But –!" Sarah broke in herself. Randall glanced at her, and at her questioning expression nodded firmly.

Georgiana swallowed. "But he had suggested an elopement, and stressed I was not to tell my brother…" she trailed off, eyes tearing. "He could not even bear the thought of my *money?*" Sarah gripped her niece's hand tightly.

"Georgie?" her uncle asked softly. "Look at me." When she did not, he gently tilted her head up to look at him. "He never meant to marry you –" Georgiana winced, and Sarah stirred angrily. Randall narrowed his eyes at his wife for a fleeting second. "He never meant to, because that was an atrocity not even he could commit – Georgie, Wickham is your *brother.*"

Georgiana, who had been attempting to stifle the tears from what she believed to be a most complete rejection, jerked herself taut. "My *what?*"

"He is your half-brother, a Darcy by blood," Randall expanded.

"But he –" she floundered for a moment "William told me of his debts – his behaviour – he *courted* me in Ramsgate; Mrs. Younge *assured* me he was being so excessively attentive he could not but mean to marry me."

Randall frowned. "Wickham swears – and given how distraught he became during our interview, I see no reason to disbelieve him – he did not know Mrs. Younge had been encouraging an attachment. He *did* own he was lavishing you with attention, but he only meant to spoil you, as a brother ought to spoil his younger sister."

Georgiana, who never had the most robust complexion, paled to an astonishing shade of white. "What he must *think* of me! Such a simpleton I am!"

"*Never,*" her uncle responded fiercely, even as he drew her into an embrace, "call yourself a simpleton again. George does not hold you to blame – only himself for not being brave enough to tell you the truth. And *I* certainly could never hold you at fault, when I failed to tell you as well."

Georgiana, both mortified and relieved, could not repress her sobs completely, although she cried on her uncle's shoulder for but a minute. She did not lift her head from his shoulder, as Sarah stroked her hair. "Then he *did* love me?"

"As a brother loves his sister, yes, he did, and does," Randall answered.

He felt her nod slightly. "I do feel better," she said quietly. "That means I mistook his intent, but not his meaning."

Randall smiled into her hair as he pressed a kiss to it. "A reasonable misunderstanding without all the information at your disposal. We should have told you and William long ago."

"Why does William not know?" she asked, still quiet.

"Your father – did not like to own up to mistakes, not even those not entirely his fault. He never wished for the three of you to know," Sarah answered. "He thought it was painful enough for your mother to know he had failed her. He could not bear the thought of admitting to any of you he had failed you as well."

"Are you going to tell him?" she asked.

"Yes, that is one reason we requested your brother and Richard return to London with the de Bourghs and Bennets," Sarah responded.

Georgiana finally pulled herself away from her aunt and uncle. Her eyes were a little puffy and red from the tears, but she seemed to have regained her composure and was tolerably at ease. "I should like to speak with Mr. Wi – with my brother, George, before my brother William arrives, if he is willing."

"I do not know," Randall responded. "It has been a trying day for you, but *his* day has been past endurance. I shall see if he has rested enough to be tolerably fit for company."

Georgiana nodded. "I would like to retire now, for a short while, to refresh myself," she announced.

Sarah stood as well, intending to escort her niece, when her husband pressed her hand to stay. For a moment, she stood divided, but seeing Georgiana's composure, she said, "I shall see you shortly then, Georgiana, to help you."

Georgiana summoned a tepid smile and nodded before taking her leave. As soon as the door was shut, Sarah turned to her husband. "He knew?"

Randall sighed, moving back to his desk. "Yes. He overheard a conversation between his father – well, I suppose, father*s* – the day Georgiana was born." He paused, fiddling with the letter opener sitting on his desk. "I can only hope he is unaware *why* George agreed to take responsibility for him."

Sarah seated herself on the edge of his desk morosely. "I know that such things are to be an abomination," she said sadly, "but it always broke my heart, to see the way George would light up when Richard would enter the room, and how yet he never resented your sister for her marriage to him."

Randall smiled sadly. "George and Anne, I think, had long since established a friendship akin to that of siblings. I thought of him as the brother I never had, myself. It must have been a comfort to him, knowing he could entrust his heart's desire to her care. My father was quite shocked when George did not offer for her, but instead congratulated Richard so warmly."

"I always wanted to ask her if Richard ever knew," Sarah admitted. "I do not think Anne ever doubted."

Randall shrugged helplessly. "Would it have mattered? Such things are forbidden – and I know it tore at George, as devout a man as he was, that he was tainted in such a way. Richard was better *not* knowing, and George was correct in never saying anything. Richard would have broken off their friendship – and rightly so – had he ever suspected." He sighed again. "And yet when I offered him a chance of a life where he would not suffer the constant companionship of what he could not have…" he shrugged. "He made his choices – I can only hope he has been forgiven for them."

"I wish George the younger had followed in either of his fathers' footsteps," Sarah said. "With three sterling examples of adult behaviour around him, why did he have to follow his mother's?" The comment was not unexpected; she and Randall had both despaired in its repetition over the years.

"You know Richard was concerned with appearing too paternal towards the boy – and I think George was too concerned about punishing the boy harshly and angering Richard," Randall replied. "His mother certainly felt no such restraints in her treatment of him, and thus she was given a freer hand with his education than she should have."

"Do you think there is a chance to reform him, at this late date?" she asked.

He tilted his head in consideration. "I do not know. He has… suffered under the weight of many secrets – I will tell you the rest when the Rosings party arrives – since he was young." He paused. "I think there are two who may be able to affect his reformation – if he is willing, that is."

"Georgiana is one," Sarah half-asked, and Randall nodded.

"He *is* devoted to her – and I find myself grateful she has recovered as much as she has. If he had seen her those first few months, I do not think he would have survived the knowledge it was by his hand she suffered so."

Sarah pursed her lips. "And who is the other?"

Randall half-laughed, half-sighed. "Richard's hope – our Elizabeth."

* * *

The trip had been delayed. The road between Bromley and London suffered from the rain. Indeed, the party had been forced to linger there for over an hour longer than anticipated. At length, however, they returned to their carriages – Mr. Bennet impatient to return to his book, the women anxious to return to the tentative bonding still on-going, Darcy and Fitzwilliam anxious to ensure the trip's length did not cause undue alarm for those awaiting them in London.

At length, however, they arrived in the outskirts of London. The way was only slightly familiar to Elizabeth and Jane, for they had never travelled to the part of London where the Fitzwilliam townhouse resided. Anne – somewhat more familiar – pointed out salient locations, with Lady Catherine's assistance. Elizabeth had just commented on the handsome park they passed on the left, when Lady Catherine turned their attention to the right. "And there," she said, "is your uncle's – my brother's – house, Elizabeth."

"It is a handsome house, to be sure, *mère*," Elizabeth answered and Jane murmured concurrence. She hoped the inside was decidedly less *grand* than Rosings, even as she hoped to eventually offset her mother's taste in furnishings.

Although no one stood at the door when the carriages stopped, by the time Elizabeth had been handed out by William, an older man whose face bore kinship to her mother's stood at the top step with a handsome lady on his arm. They came down the steps in a flurry of movement. "Catherine!" the man exclaimed. "We had not expected your arrival to be so late."

"Brother," Lady Catherine answered, "indeed, we had not expected it ourselves; the road between Bromley and London was quite terrible – I cannot understand why they do not construct the roads like ours at Rosings, which can withstand the rain more effectively."

Elizabeth bit her lip at her mother's pronouncement – she was not sure she cared for such easy arrogance in her mother any more than the thoughtlessness of her adoptive mother. A flick of a glance at William showed her that he, at least, was mildly amused by her mother's comment.

"I am sure I do not know, sister," Lord Matlock replied. "Come, let us continue this in the house."

The party nigh swarmed up the steps. The rain seemed bent on following them to London, and was now making its presence known. Introductions did not yet take place – her mother's brother said that Georgiana was in the sitting room, and they were walking in that direction now. Indeed, even as they approached, Elizabeth could hear a quiet laugh as a random jumble of notes sounded on the pianoforte. A deeper laugh answered, and William – who still held her arm – started. She glanced up and was startled to see the same ferocious scowl on his face she had seen in Hertfordshire on occasion. He muttered an apology under his breath to her, and pulled away, deftly stepping around his uncle and aunt, even as they attempted to stay him. He burst into the room, where from her vantage point, Elizabeth could see a young fair-haired girl sitting at the piano, and beside her … Mr. Wickham. She sucked in a breath, fearful of her cousin's reaction.

"Remove yourself from my sister!" Darcy nearly bellowed, even as the earl attempted to stop him. Darcy took a few steps towards the piano when Wickham did not immediately move.

Surprisingly, it was Georgiana who responded by standing up and placing herself between William and Wickham. "George has been welcome company while we awaited your arrival, brother. There is no call for such behaviour."

The family had piled into the room behind the earl and Darcy, and the door was shut. Elizabeth glanced between her cousins in concern. This time, the earl had a fistful of Darcy's jacket, so when he moved towards Wickham again, he was pulled back. "Calm yourself, William. Things are not what you believe." Wickham, Elizabeth noted, was pale, but seemed to be aware of the wisdom of not goading William further by speaking himself.

"How can you let him in her presence?" Darcy growled to his uncle. "After everything?" An angry, agreeing murmur came from Richard.

"Because," Georgiana stepped forward to place one delicate hand on William's arm, looking up at him earnestly, as she responded quietly, "our brother means me no harm."

Twenty

Randall had never intended *Georgiana* to be the one to inform her brother – and certainly not in front of the Bennets or de Bourghs! This was, after all, a *Darcy* situation, not even a Fitzwilliam one. Yet, even as William stood there gaping at his sister, Randall felt relieved. Had *he* been the one to say it, he would be feeling the sharp edge of his nephew's tongue.

"Our *brother*?" finally came Darcy's strangled question. Georgiana nodded, her expression still earnest and intent. Darcy blinked twice, and with a slow deliberate turn of his head, trained his focus on Randall, who could but offer a wry smile. Darcy shook his head in denial.

At this, Elizabeth broke the tableau, leaving her sisters, Anne and Jane, and moving to Darcy's side. "William?" she asked softly. He barely glanced at her, but the look she exchanged with Georgiana – although they had just met and were not introduced – communicated their mutual concern, and with her younger cousin's assistance, they drew Darcy to a sofa and bade him to seat himself, then took a position on either side of him. Randall felt a wry amusement – Elizabeth had only accepted she was a part of this family within the past week, and already she handled Darcy better than his uncle and cousins could.

The party seemed reluctant to break the pause that Georgiana's words had caused – although now the entire party's focus was on the two girls and Darcy in close conference. Randall felt sure Georgiana was relating what *she* had been told – even as Darcy clenched one fist tightly, Elizabeth had placed her hand over it at the same time Georgiana had. The girls gave each other a quick, amused look.

Randall did not notice Wickham had drifted to his side. "I did tell you, did I not, that she is a de Bourgh in appearance?"

Randall tilted his head in consideration. "Indeed you had – and you are correct; it is readily apparent when one is looking for it."

Wickham smiled, still pale, and then, turning towards the Rosings party, said, "Please let me introduce you to the Bennets, my lord, milady. Mr. Bennet – Elizabeth's adopted father – and Miss Jane Bennet, the eldest daughter. Mr. Bennet, Miss Bennet, Lord Randall Fitzwilliam, Earl of Matlock, also known as Darcy's uncle, and Lady Sarah Fitzwilliam, Countess of Matlock."

A murmur of "delighted"s from the Bennets did not cover Richard Fitzwilliam's scowl, however. He refused to greet Wickham, and instead brushed past, headed for the sofa where Georgiana was relating her information to Darcy. Randall watched as Georgiana looked up at Richard. Elizabeth said something, and Richard abruptly moved of an ottoman in front of the sofa, seating himself. Randall assumed she had suggested he listen to the story as well.

After a moment longer, Lady Catherine turned her attention from her younger daughter to her brother. "Are you truly suggesting, brother, that the shades of Pemberley have been thus polluted? That our brother Richard connived *our* childhood friend into raising his bastard child?" Wickham stiffened, but at a look from Randall, did not say anything himself.

"George Wickham, Senior, did not require *conniving,* sister. It is true, Richard Darcy found himself in a particularly uncomfortable situation – quite unexpectedly, I might add – and would have done the same thing for our George Junior that countless other men of *rank* have done for their… unexpected additions. For that matter, our sister was willing to take him on as her own child as well. *George* offered his assistance, and Richard was not such a fool as to deny his and his wife's best friend the chance at raising a son."

"I assure you, madam," Wickham added himself, "I have nothing but pride for the father who gave me his name. I am only sorry to not have been worthy of it thus far."

"So you were not lying, that day at Rosings," Anne finally said, giving Wickham an appraising look.

It was odd to see a blush overlaying such paleness – he had not yet recovered his proper colour, and it was beginning to concern Randall – but Wickham responded with relative ease. "Nay, Miss de Bourgh, I was not. I had… accidentally come upon the truth myself, and I was a fool to have mentioned it to you in such a manner. I do hope you will forgive me my presumption."

She tilted her head in acknowledgement, but did not say anything else. At length, the party settled themselves down, while Elizabeth and Georgiana continued their attempts at keeping Darcy and Richard calm. Randall moved closer, and it seemed that Georgiana was only in the midst of convincing her brother and cousin her information had not come from Wickham, but Randall himself.

"But he tried to convince you to elope with him, Georgie – how can that be the act of someone who loves you as a brother?" Richard was intent on finding fault.

She sighed, and could not look at either of her guardians. "Mrs. Younge had convinced me he was courting me – and perhaps in a way he was. He had never felt permitted to treat me as a sister; we *all* know – now at least – he has long excelled in the courtship of women. It may have been his *actions,* but it was not his intent. Had I known of our kinship, I should never have been so horribly mistaken." She paused and looked up at William. "He told me – and our uncle – he had mentioned the elopement purely to dissuade me. How I wish Mrs. Younge had not been hovering just then! for it *did* give me pause, yet she assured me it was not unheard of and I – I believed her. You must see, William, it was never all *George's* fault. I was so desirous of being… *grown up*… I instead proved myself quite inept at the task."

Elizabeth smiled slightly. "Recognizing that now proves you are closer to it than you were then. And," she flicked her eyes at William, "even the best of us *backslide* on occasion." Randall marvelled to himself as he watched his self-assured, typically composed nephew *blush.* He chose this moment to inject himself into the conversation.

"Now that the drama for the initial hour's stay in London is almost over, may I secure an introduction to my niece?" he asked.

William started. "I, um, yes – of course, forgive me. Georgiana, uncle, this is Elizabeth Ben – de – um, my cousin Elizabeth. Elizabeth, my sister, Georgiana, and my uncle, Lord Randall."

Elizabeth laughed as William stumbled over what name to give her. She smiled up at her uncle. "I was thinking 'Bennet de Bourgh' has a nice ring to it, actually. A bit of a mouthful, but I should not wish to slight either of my families."

Randall tilted his head in amused agreement. "What says your mother?"

"*Mère* says as long as Mama and Papa do not complain, she will not either."

"*Mère*?" Georgiana asked. "Is that what you are calling my aunt?"

Elizabeth nodded. "'Mother' still remains Mrs. Bennet to me – and *her* command of French does not extend past pastries. I thought it appropriate that my mother de Bourgh should also be known to me as 'mother' – but calling her such in French removes the possibility of confusion."

Lord Randall nodded in understanding and agreement. "Elizabeth, if I may speak to you?"

Elizabeth looked up at him and nodded. She rose and followed him away from the rest of the party. "As you are the one *most* affected by the remaining information to be related, I wished to leave it for you to decide when it would be announced."

She eyed her uncle, and replied in lowered tones. "I am to suppose, then, that Mr. Wickham had information regarding my... disappearance?"

He arched an eyebrow at her and nodded. "Not complete information but... well... *something.*"

She nodded and bit her lip. "Dinner is soon, is it not?" At her uncle's nod, she sighed. "I... do not wish to delay the information any longer than necessary," she started, "but I do not see the point in not waiting until *after* the repast."

He smiled at her. "That is what I was thinking myself. Are we in agreement then?" She nodded. "Then I shall inform Wickham – he has requested the chance to relay the story *himself.*"

"Sir?" she asked as he was about to leave.

"Yes?"

"Is that... *wise?* Given William's reaction to him being in the same *room* as Georgiana – an hour or three is not enough to overcome such a reaction. I would not wish my cousin to... do something he may regret later."

"Earlier, when I made a similar argument, he insisted on the dubious honour." The earl shrugged. "Perhaps after having seen Darcy's temper today, he will reconsider."

Elizabeth nodded; that was obviously the best that could be hoped for currently. The earl drifted back to Wickham for a quiet conference. Elizabeth looked about the room, and could not be sure where she should settle herself back down. Her sisters and mother were seated with Lady Matlock; it seemed an animated conversation. Her father was reading the book he had brought with him in the carriage, although the quick glances about the room told her he was as much watching and analysing the behaviour of the party as he was his book. Georgiana still held earnest conversation with her guardians. Where did she fit at the moment? She did not wish to be... ill-judged, for making the wrong choice. So, instead, she let herself wander to a window, to look out on the street and wonder at being where she was.

"I thought I was the only one who looked out windows when uncomfortable," William's voice laughed a little behind her. She startled. She had not noticed his reflection in the window until just now.

"It is less feeling uncomfortable," she answered, "than wishing to not... make a mistake, at such a critical point in time."

A wry smile reflected back at her, as he looked down and over her shoulder out the window. "You forget that – despite everything – you are our *family,* Elizabeth. The only one among us who would have ever turned away from you, were you simply a Bennet, is the one who is your most staunch ally. *She* will see no flaw in you, not with her knowing who you are."

"'Were I simply a Bennet?'" she repeated with a laugh, however quiet they were speaking. "You cannot seriously mean that there is any reason I would have had purpose in caring for her opinion, were I not so closely related?"

A mischievous smile answered her. "Had you agreed to take another's name – mine, perhaps? – prior to being introduced to her – she would have descended upon Longbourn with all the fury of an avenging angel."

Elizabeth blushed. "You *are* quite forward, now that I am your cousin, I have noticed. But you despised the family who raised me." She shook her head as he winced. "No, there is no need to dissemble,

William. We both know I am only acceptable to you *now* because of *what* I am." Even as the words left her mouth, she wondered if that were true – and what on earth they were doing, having such a conversation in their aunt's parlour?

He took a step closer and made as if to point something out to her through the window. "I think your sister, Jane, did not tell you *all* of our conversation, if you believe that." He paused for a second. "But, indeed, even if you refused your share of the money to be split between the Bennet daughters, you would still be acceptable at *Pemberley.* And that," he added, "is all that a *Darcy* cares about."

There was naught to do in response but blush at such a comment, and she was thankful when dinner was announced. William offered her his arm with that distractingly charming smile he must have misplaced during his time in Hertfordshire. She had a momentary whim – after such a conversation, it was hardly surprising, really – to inform him his valet needed to be more careful in packing his smiles the next time he travelled to the wild countryside, for surely that package had been mislaid and left in London, but she checked herself in time.

Lady Matlock had seen no reason in assigning seats, thus Elizabeth found herself seated between William and Jane, while Georgiana sat on his other side, with Richard on her far side. Her father sat across from herself, and Wickham was to be found seated near Anne. The only seat left open was for Richard's elder brother, who was late. Richard advised Darcy, over Georgiana's head, that Alexander would be arriving without his wife tonight; she was feeling a bit ill, but would likely be 'round in the morning. Darcy, in turn, relayed this to Elizabeth.

"Alexander?" she asked.

"Oh – you did not know his name. The viscount," he clarified, "Richard's brother."

"Oh!" She tilted her head. "And who was he named after?"

Darcy laughed. "Lady Matlock's twin brother. She swore for the longest time that until her brother held his firstborn nephew, the babe did not quit screaming, not from the moment he came into the world. It was, she said, a sign he would be every bit the trouble to her that her brother had been."

Elizabeth grinned. "Was she proven prophetic?"

Richard – who had been listening to the conversation, as well as Georgiana – quipped, "Indeed, my mother underestimated my brother's capacity for trouble. Compared to him, I was surely an angel."

Darcy snorted. "Perhaps; until you kept the library well stocked with frogs that one particular summer."

Wickham, who had been listening intently, but not speaking himself, choked. "To this day," he said, after he quit coughing, "I remember the expression on our fathers' faces – yours too, Miss Elizabeth – when they went to open the cabinet where the port was stored, and five or six frogs leapt out at them, in an attempt to make a bid for freedom."

"And why, Mr. Wickham, were you able to see that?" Elizabeth asked.

"Well," he half-smiled, "I was always the smallest of us, being a couple of years younger, and not nearly so tall as Darcy or the colonel. I generally was the one tasked with witnessing the effects of our… games, as I could conceal myself more easily."

"Does that mean you were the one caught most often, as well?" she asked, flicking a glance up at William's expression. He looked… thoughtful, as if something had never before occurred to him. *That* was encouraging. Perhaps.

He gave her a diffident grin. "Well, in that incident at least, I managed to escape detection until nearly the last moment."

"Oh?" Jane asked, interested.

He grimaced. "I was perfectly capable of remaining silent. That is, alas, until a spider decided to crawl across my knee. I am… less than fond of spiders," he added. "So you can little doubt my reaction, just at that moment."

Jane smiled slightly. "Oh, indeed. Spiders do not bother me, in particular, but our sister Mary dislikes them intensely." Elizabeth smiled and concurred. William's expression, she noted, had become even more thoughtful.

Not a moment after the conversation had turned directions, as conversations are wont to do, particularly when childhood memories have been brought up, the viscount was announced. Lord Matlock rose from the table. "There you are, my boy! Come; sit; eat something."

Alexander Fitzwilliam, Elizabeth noted, was nearly as handsome as his cousin Darcy, and decidedly more so than his younger brother. At the moment, that face wore a slightly joking scowl. "Bah, father, you know I only came to meet my cousin Elizabeth – must you and mother force food at me at every opportunity?"

Lady Matlock spoke up. "Oh, Alexander. *Do* be careful to not give Elizabeth a poor opinion of you. We will never forgive you if you chase her off." She paused, eyeing him. "And do as your father says; sit down and eat something. You are entirely too thin, yet again. We will properly introduce you to her shortly. Now eat!" Good-natured laughter echoed around the table, and Elizabeth felt quite at home – such jibes and irreverent speech would not be out of place at the Bennet table, to be sure.

Yet, when she looked up at William – when had she acquired this habit of checking on his mood and temperament so constantly? – she was slightly disturbed to note he was not amused. "Is there something the matter?" she asked softly.

He glanced down at her and then at his plate, as he commenced to pick at it. "Wickham's story reminded me of something."

"And that would be?" she prodded slightly, when he did not continue.

He sighed. "Our fathers knew it had been done by all three of us, but Wickham would not turn against us and admit to that. It was… almost three hours, before we realized he was not going to say anything himself – Richard and I had hidden ourselves, believing we were to be punished for sure. When it did not happen… we went looking for Wickham, and discovered him in the kitchen, helping the cook, as his punishment." He paused and glanced up to meet her eyes. "When I realized he had lied for our sakes, I did the only thing I could – I dragged Richard to the library with me and confessed, and demanded the same punishment as Wickham had, so he would not be punished unfairly – it had been Richard's idea, and my planning, and it was not *fair*."

She nodded, even as she bit her lip. She wanted to continue the conversation but – not here. Not without the rest of the information Wickham held regarding her, either. "I think – perhaps tomorrow – we should continue this."

He gave her a sharp look which she met steadily. He nodded after a moment. "Another mind to bounce things off of – that would be beneficial."

She thought of what might be related tonight, and agreed. "For more than just yourself, possibly." With that, they consciously turned the conversation to something else, and ere long, Georgiana was nearly pushing her brother out of the way while Jane and Elizabeth spoke of music. He merely looked on in amusement.

At length, dinner came to a close, and Lord Matlock stood. "While I would normally wish to keep to convention, tonight is… abnormal. Thus, we will *all* depart for the sitting room." The party rose and began to filter out of the room; Darcy had once again offered his arm to Elizabeth, while Richard escorted Georgiana. "Darcy," the earl said; they paused. "I should like to escort Elizabeth myself, if only to introduce her to Alexander." Darcy smiled slightly, nodded, and released her.

Elizabeth took her uncle's arm, who then lagged behind the party, his eldest son at his side. "And this, Elizabeth, is my eldest son and heir, Viscount Alexander Fitzwilliam. Alexander, Elizabeth Bennet de Bourgh."

Alexander gave her an expressive smile. "You have *no* idea, cousin, how wonderfully thrilled I am to see you. In fact," he gave his father a sidelong glance, "if this old dotard would move out of my way, I should like to escort you myself."

The earl mock-scowled. "And you expect me to reward such insolence as this?" Neither man managed to hide the grins for long, and Elizabeth giggled. He affected an offended sniff. "Very well, I see I am unwanted at the moment." He moved out of the way, and Alexander wasted not a second in offering his arm to Elizabeth. The earl moved ahead towards the sitting room, but Alexander stayed Elizabeth a moment.

"I was not jesting about how much I am grateful to see you, Elizabeth," he said quietly. For the first time that evening, his face and eyes were solemn. "I – I was seventeen, myself, and the highlight of my family's visits to Rosings the last three years I went, was you." He paused and blinked hard. Elizabeth fancied she saw tears. "After you – disappeared, I could not face going back there. I tried, once, and was so haunted by you, by the terror of wondering what had happened, and if you were safe, or – if the unthinkable had happened – I – I could not even stay the night." His voice cracked. "I know it was wrong to treat my aunt and cousin Anne so but—" he swept her up into a hug unexpectedly – or perhaps not so unexpectedly, Elizabeth thought, her own eyes damp. "When I was courting my wife," he continued, speaking into her hair, "we somehow laughingly fell into a discussion of what we would name our children. I told her I wished my firstborn daughter to be named Elizabeth, after you. I – I hope you would not mind, if we can finally bring a daughter into the world, that we do so?"

Elizabeth drew back from her cousin, quite undone by such unreserved demonstration. Not even Anne or Darcy had been so unreserved in their determination and affection. "No, indeed. I should be honoured – I am honoured, to be held in such high regard."

He smiled down at her, like all the Fitzwilliam men did on account of their shared height. "You must think me a sentimental idiot."

She shook her head in denial. "No, I cannot, even if I cannot understand why you would have been so attached to a mere child. I certainly have done naught to earn it *now*."

He laughed, finally leading her to the sitting room. "And telling my aunt to her face that you would not take all the jewels the family can command if it meant harm to the Bennets is nothing? Nay, you were *never*, in anyone's heart, a mere child, like you are not a mere – what was the phrase I heard used – 'a country miss' now. Until the moment my aunt brought you into the world, I had held nothing but disdain for children younger than I – it was love at first sight, and my father had to tell me in no uncertain terms I was not allowed to bring you home to raise you as my own daughter."

She laughed. "At the age of fourteen? What does a boy of fourteen know of child-rearing, or should even want to have anything to do with it?"

He grinned. "What can I say? Besotted fools occur at any age." He paused, and added with a mischievous lilt to his voice, "Although I do recall, when you were but two years of age, and he a lad of ten, telling our cousin Darcy that he would be able to have the pick of any women he liked, when he was old enough – but if he dared settle his eye on you, he would not have to get just your *father's* permission, but mine, for I did not think he could ever be good enough for *you.*" He gave her a sly grin. "Shall I have to ask his intent towards you, do you think?"

Elizabeth blushed and did not even bother to keep from rolling her eyes. She knew Mr. Bennet believed they all lived to be made sport of by their neighbours and make sport in their own turn. But must the entire family make sport of William's attentions to her, now of all times? She felt the shiver of fear she had when Mrs. Bennet declared that she would never see her again if she did *not* marry Mr. Collins. Would she be placed into such a position again with William?

Twenty-One

Of all the news Alexander Fitzwilliam had expected to hear after a hurriedly scrawled note from his father, the recovery of his little cousin, Elizabeth, had certainly not been on the list. He had, of course, thought of her often, and his beloved Cassandra had learned that he only reached for the brandy on the days when the pain of the loss of Elizabeth or their unborn children haunted him. To have the grown-up Elizabeth on his arm at this moment – he had been unable to stop the tears, so profound was his relief. She could have been prematurely aged, haggard, and warty, and still he would think her one of the most beautiful sights he had ever seen in his life. He longed to tell her why Cassandra had been unable to join him tonight, but he was checked by the fear that there would be no news to give shortly. He only hoped she would not mind being a godmother in another six or seven months, should *this* pregnancy finally succeed. But – despite the information that his father had relayed in an undertone, to be barely heard over the click and clank of silverware – Wickham, his cousin Darcy's brother! – and Darcy's obvious attentions, as relayed by Richard, to Elizabeth – he was aware the evening's revelations had not been finished, and he reluctantly led Elizabeth towards the parlour. This time, she stayed him.

She glanced quickly around, ensuring the servants were not in earshot, he assumed. "Has my uncle informed you of Mr. Wickham's –" she hesitated.

"Peculiar connection?" he suggested, and at her nod and slight smile, nodded in affirmation.

169

"I am concerned for William," she added. "I do not know what Mr. Wickham is to relay tonight, but William's patience was sorely tested by merely finding Georgiana playing the piano with him."

Alexander grimaced. "You are asking me to keep William from… doing something he may regret?"

She glanced away and bit her lip, nodding. "It is not that I believe he will do anything intentionally, but this has been a particularly stressful situation."

"William has always been very temperate, very calm, despite having an implacable temper when finally goaded into anger," he replied. "My father related the events prior to dinner to me, and I can only agree that William is under an undue amount of stress. I will do what I can, Elizabeth." She gave him a brilliant smile, and he felt keenly, the injustice of having missed out on so much of her life. He smiled, trying to hide how much pain the realization of just how much time had been lost caused. "What of yourself?" he asked. "Are you concerned about what is to be learnt?"

Elizabeth glanced away from him sharply. "I have my suspicions, which Lord Matlock did not deny in general. I … I am afraid, yes, that what is to be shared may crush the fledgling relationships that I have admittedly been slow to embrace. So much turmoil in such a short time, not even a fortnight, and if this information suffocates it all under ill feelings and ill will, I and my whole family will have suffered such distress for … nothing." She paused before looking back up at him. "But this is the path my feet have been set on, and it is folly to hide from truth to avoid pain. I must see it through."

He nodded. "I cannot imagine any information that would provoke so dire a reaction, but I agree. Shall we see what else is to be learnt?" She nodded, and he led her to the parlour.

"We despaired of you, Elizabeth!" Lady Catherine cried, as they rejoined the group.

"We only delayed a few moments, *mère*," Elizabeth smiled. Alexander smiled to himself at the name – such an elegantly simple avoidance of what could have been an issue. "Alexander wished to speak to me, and as you see, we have followed in due time."

Lady Catherine looked as if she wished to scowl – and abruptly, Alexander realized his aunt was jealous that anyone else should wish for her daughter's company, as well as fearful for her welfare. "Go sit with her, Elizabeth," he whispered in her ear – no particular feat of skill given the disparity of their heights. "I think she is as worried as William is." He felt, more than saw Elizabeth's fractional nod, and she moved to sit beside her mother. Mr. Bennet promptly moved to sit near Elizabeth, and Darcy looked divided between keeping himself between Georgiana and Wickham – even though from what his father had told him, Alexander had few concerns there – and wanting to also be close to Elizabeth. Richard, apparently, was quite correct in his estimation of William's affections. As Elizabeth had requested of him, Alexander seated himself near William. Wickham had not taken a seat, nor had the earl; they stood in close conference near the fireplace.

After a moment, the earl apparently conceded defeat to whatever Wickham was demanding. He turned and addressed the group. "I believe we are all assembled?" A murmur of agreement answered. "Wickham has offered to tell us what he knows of the night of March 15th, seventeen years ago. I have heard it once already, and I warn you it only gives as many questions as it answers." He paused, and moved towards Elizabeth, kneeling. "I ask *you,* most in particular, if you are sure you wish to know what little he can tell us."

Alexander felt a trace of concern – his father would not be asking her a second time, if he were not concerned how the knowledge would impact her. But this Elizabeth was the Elizabeth he had known as a child – he saw an echo of fear in her eyes, in the set of her shoulders, but rarely was she intimidated by such things. She nodded. "I do, my lord." She looked towards Wickham, adding, "If naught else, I do not believe he deserves to carry the weight on his own."

His father nodded, for the merest moment looking defeated. He rose and glanced at Wickham. "Proceed, George, if you will." Alexander watched as his father settled himself beside Lady Sarah, then looked back at Wickham, who was pale but determined.

"I hardly know where to start," Wickham began, "but – *You* remember, Darcy, how Miss Elizabeth had wanted a ride on the pony your – our – father had bought for us?" Darcy nodded and exchanged a glance with Richard. Alexander, too, remembered. Wickham sighed, before looking at Elizabeth. "I had found you outside of your nursery, in your favourite dress, and you pleaded for me to take you on a pony ride. I did try to convince you to stay in the nursery, but, I own, I did not try overly hard. I, too, vividly remembered wishing to ride on a pony with Darcy and Richard, and being held back from it on account of being two years younger. I… thought I was doing you a favour." He grimaced, and swallowed, looking back at the fire. "I honestly expected to be stopped when we left the house and went to the stables. I had you sit down in the garden near the stables, so that the groom would not see you and put a premature end to our … adventure." Another grimace, at the word, and Alexander felt an echo of it. "I… did not wish to be caught, and so once I made sure you were seated securely on the saddle, I directed the pony outside of the park's main gates. Unfortunately, I had miscalculated both how far we had travelled, and how close to sunset it was, and by the time I realized we were lost – the sun was setting. Shortly after it became dark, we came to the road, and I frankly guessed which direction to go along it. After a while – I do not know how long – we heard another rider coming up in the dark, and I was fearful that it may not be a… friendly encounter." Alexander – while gritting his teeth at this bare-bones recital, was sharply reminding himself of Wickham's age at the time; just a boy, and his fear of a hostile rider was not unfounded. Rumours swirled about all sorts of horrors caused by the gypsies during their annual circuit through Kent in early spring. "I led the pony off the road – you, Elizabeth, on its back – and tried to keep the three of us quiet so we would not be discovered." Wickham paused, taking a deep breath.

The earl stirred uneasily, and Alexander gave his father a quick questioning glance, but only received a slight shake of the head in response. Wickham picked his story back up. "The horse and rider only came close enough for me to distinguish them faintly, before –" he hesitated, "something startled the pony." Alexander saw a flash of – relief? – fly across his father's face. "The pony reared, and I was knocked to the ground. The horse startled in reaction, and the rider was thrown, but my only concern was trying to capture the pony as it fled, you still on its back." By now, Wickham was speaking almost entirely to Elizabeth; Alexander had the impression that he only vaguely realized there was anyone else in the room. Wickham seated himself nearby Elizabeth and buried his head in his hands. When he looked up, his expression was haunted. "I ran for – I do not know for how long. Certainly long after I could no longer hear you calling for me. But I could not find any traces of you, in the dark. Somehow, I made my way back to Rosings, afoot – I cannot recall exactly. The house was in an uproar, and I… waited, for days it felt like, for someone to ask me what happened, but the questions were never asked."

"And did it never once occur to you to *tell* anyone, without being asked?" Alexander burst out. Wickham shook his head mutely. "Why ever *not?*"

Elizabeth broke in quietly – Alexander abruptly realized how pale she was. "It was my father, was it not? The rider thrown when the pony startled?"

Wickham hesitated. "I know of no other riders injured that night, but I also have no idea how far we were from Rosings." The earl murmured that he, too, knew of no other riders injured in the vicinity that night.

"My fault," Alexander thought he heard her whisper; he must have heard it, for Wickham was suddenly kneeling in front of her, pleading.

"Never your fault, Elizabeth. Mine, yes; I was old enough to have known better, to have said no, to have – done anything but risk your safety."

"My age was not an excuse," she replied, obviously fighting for composure, rising as if to flee so she could accuse herself in private.

Protestations from every party in the room arose, trying to convince her otherwise. Alexander was at a loss for words himself; she could not be blamed; she was far too young to have come even close to considering the ramifications of a fairly simple desire. Wickham – despite being old enough to have realized the initial action was wrong – could not have even begun to imagine such an outcome. But Elizabeth would not listen, and refused to even let Mr. Bennet, Jane or William comfort her. One person in the room, however, was just as stubborn, and when Elizabeth tried to pull away, Lady Catherine merely held her daughter tighter. Alexander could not hear the words his aunt whispered in his cousin's ear, but whatever it was, it broke Elizabeth's composure completely, and she sagged against her mother, crying. Anne came up hesitantly, glancing at her mother for permission, before she wrapped her arms around her little sister as well. Elizabeth's crying slowed as they cradled her.

Alexander found he could not keep watching. The pain in Elizabeth's posture tore at his heart, even as he realized Anne and her mother were convincing Elizabeth of her innocence. He met Mr. Bennet's eyes for just a moment, and felt grief for him, too. He looked as if he thought he was on the verge of losing his daughter, and Alexander moved to assure him otherwise. "You cannot think we would be so selfish a family as to keep her from you, even if she chose to move into our protection?" he asked quietly.

"I know not what to think," Bennet replied. "Her life – our lives – cannot go back to what it was before. I cannot help but think I am being supremely selfish by wishing to keep her at Longbourn for as long as I can."

Alexander was about to reply when he heard Darcy say uncertainly, "George?" He glanced towards his cousin's voice, and discovered that Wickham was dealing as well with relaying the story, as Elizabeth had to hearing it.

Wickham looked up at Darcy – he had not the Fitzwilliam advantage of height, although he was not short for a man by any means. "I had – hoped – she would not want to hear what happened. The relief of confession could never outweigh the grief of seeing her in so much pain – pain, to whit, that ought to be my burden only."

Darcy gritted his teeth – Alexander felt alarm – surely, he was not going to give into his temper *now* of all times. "I would that you had said something, anything," he replied.

"I do not know why I did not," Wickham answered. "After – a few days, I almost convinced myself it was a nightmarish flight of fancy, brought on by the horror of the situation, which even without being… particularly involved, was more than enough."

"You swear you tried to find her?" Darcy asked, even more quietly. Wickham nodded. Darcy closed his eyes for a moment. "And – you never meant Georgiana harm?"

Wickham shuddered. "All the treasures most sacred to me… The Ramsgate fiasco was another miscalculation on my part. I was in over my head before I knew what was happening."

Darcy gave him a long, measuring look. "I do not want to hear you have trifled with any more shopkeepers' daughters, nor run up any outstanding debts of either money or honour – brother."

Alexander felt himself take a startled breath, even as Wickham did the same. "It has been a long while since I did more than trifle with the heart of any daughter, and certainly not in Meryton. The protection of the Miss Bennets has occupied much of my spare time," he replied. "But I may need – assistance to right a few debts, but I – shall endeavour not to incur any more," Wickham hesitated, "brother." Darcy nodded and gripped Wickham's shoulder in acknowledgement, and then moved towards the de Bourgh ladies. Wickham watched him with a mixture of disbelief and hope in his expression, although Alexander felt almost complete disbelief. Still – Elizabeth's crying had subsided, and he, too, went to her side now, as did most of those in the room.

"Elizabeth?" Jane asked, her countenance worried.

Elizabeth slowly pulled back from Anne and her mother, seemingly more herself. "I am fine, Jane," she answered. At Jane's questioning expression, she half-smiled. "Truly, I will be fine. I – was not prepared for quite that information." Alexander noted – again – a fleeting expression of relief on his father's face, and determined to ask him about it. "I do think, however," she added, glancing around the group gathered close, "that I ought to retire for the night, if you all do not mind?"

Murmurs of "of course not, Elizabeth" echoed. Jane replied, "I shall retire with you, I think. I do not want you alone just now."

"And I," Anne added, as did Georgiana.

"Intent on protecting me from myself, are you?" Elizabeth half-laughed, and Alexander felt relief. She *would* be fine.

"Of course," Anne answered for the other girls, even as she drew Elizabeth towards the door. Lady Catherine elected to follow.

There was a lull as the men in the room stood, half-gathered around where Elizabeth had been standing. Richard broke the silence. "You know what startled the pony, Wickham, do you not?"

"Yes," Wickham replied quietly. "But I beg that you not ask for details. It was an accident, and could not have been prevented."

"Do you, father," Alexander asked, "know and approve of it not being spoken of?"

"I do," the earl replied. "It is as Wickham says – it is neither here nor there. We have Elizabeth back. The only things that should concern us at this point are – who found her, how did they find her, and why, by all the holies, they chose to keep her from us."

Alexander agreed, but saw Darcy's expression, and knew they were thinking the same thing. Elizabeth must have startled the pony somehow; not unexpected at such a young age. But she must be kept from knowing that as much as possible – she already felt the weight of guilt without knowing it. His poor Elizabeth!

* * *

When Jane woke the next morning, it was to find Elizabeth in her room, simply dressed, and sitting on the window sill, staring out. Her face was pensive as she traced designs into the dampness on the inside of the windows.

"Lizzy?" she asked quietly. Elizabeth started and swung around; Jane was hard-pressed to keep from gasping. "Oh, Lizzy – did you not sleep at all?"

Elizabeth shook her head. "I confess I could not – but I did not wish to wake you, either."

Jane held out her hand to her sister. Elizabeth readily came to the bed and took it, settling on the edge. Jane, however, could not be content, and drew her sister into an embrace. Elizabeth shuddered and sighed. "Is it wrong of me," she asked quietly, "to be both glad to know, and to – to wish none of this had ever come to light?"

Jane shook her head. "No, Lizzy, it is not. None of this was under your control; I cannot believe Wickham would have intentionally run a risk of causing injury to you or the Darcys."

Elizabeth was silent for a moment. "I think he knows what startled the pony," she said quietly. "And I – fear, greatly fear, that it was me, for whatever reason. If that is true – I *am* responsible for my birth father's death."

Jane shook her head. "No, you still are not. I am sure Sir Lewis would not wish you to think that; Lady Catherine certainly does not."

"Knowing that does not ease the feelings of guilt, Jane," she replied.

"Must you always be so quick to carry the weight of the world?" Jane asked with a sigh. Elizabeth blushed and Jane shook her head at her once again. "Suppose – and this *is* just supposition – you did startle the pony. There are… so many ways it could have come about, Lizzy. Did you not tell me Anne said her father was an excellent horseman? The worry he felt over your 'mysterious' disappearance from Rosings, and what I can only imagine would be frantic worry over finding you, played as much of a factor as anything *you* might have done. Perhaps, in his hurry to search, he neglected to tighten the cinch properly – or any number of other possibilities."

"For the want of a nail," Elizabeth murmured.

"Indeed," Jane replied. "It is unfair, to be sure," she paused before stroking a fallen lock of Elizabeth's hair back from her face, "but it brought me a most-cherished sister. I do not think *your* father would find fault with me being grateful for that much."

Elizabeth shook her head slightly in response, but Jane did not believe she was refuting her sister's claim. After a moment, Jane said she wished to ready for the day, and the two of them rose from the bed. Elizabeth began to assist her sister with her morning preparations; granted, it would have been appropriate to call for the ladies' maid, but the sisters had long since been accustomed to assisting each other, and this morning, Jane knew Elizabeth was finding solace in a quiet habit.

"William informed me Mr. Bingley should have a letter by now, inviting him here at his earliest convenience – he thought you should like to know, so as to not be caught unawares."

Jane blushed in pleased hope. "Do you really think Mr. Bingley will call?"

"I think wild horses could not keep him away, now that he knows *you* do not wish for him to be away," Elizabeth replied. "He has shown remarkable delicacy in refraining from beating down any door betwixt you and he, out of deference to my – our – situation."

Jane could not reply to that; she had only hopes and no answers. Darcy had been thus far invaluable, recounting everything he could remember of Bingley's actions and spirits these past few months. Her next meeting with Bingley was sure to be fraught with nervousness and awkwardness, no matter how much she should wish otherwise. "When did William tell you?"

"During dinner," Elizabeth replied, the faintest blush on her countenance. Jane arched an eyebrow in reply, and Elizabeth blushed more deeply. "Oh all right – he stopped by my room to check on Georgiana last night, after all of you left. He said he would leave Georgiana here with the Fitzwilliams, but he had to return to his townhouse. He had matters of business to attend to early this morning, ones he had left unfinished when *mère* summoned him to Rosings."

"Surely Mr. Bingley and I were not *all* you two spoke about last night," Jane teased. Elizabeth blushed and would not answer.

"What do you think of Wickham being William's brother?" Elizabeth asked finally.

"I think it is admirable that the elder Mr. Wickham willingly took responsibility for him," Jane responded, "despite the fact that – according to your uncle – the late Mr. Darcy would have ensured he was raised in a gentleman's household either way."

"I hope that Wickham is aware – now – that there is a possibility his actions could taint Georgiana, if the family acknowledges him to be a relation."

Jane felt amused that Elizabeth already fretted over Georgiana, but she did not reply for a few minutes. "I do hope – now that your cousin knows Wickham is his brother, that is – that Wickham may yet be salvaged. He at least seems to be aware he has faults – is that not a place to start? I should not want him to be desperate."

Elizabeth smiled at her sister in the mirror as she pulled the brush through her hair. "I remember thinking, the day you and William walked out with me, and then had this mysterious conversation you did not tell me all of, that *I* would be the one to hope my recovery would be enough to redeem him, and *you* would be the one to trust in it." Jane laughed, and Elizabeth began to set the pins to hold Jane's hair up in the style for the morning. "Now, perhaps you can tell me more of the conversation you had with William – he made a comment last night, before dinner, that he said something to you that you had not passed along to me."

Jane smiled slightly. "I am not sure I should tell you – it is not as if he seems to be afraid of pressing his suit."

"We did have a slight… argument. Or, more to the point, I accused him of something; I think more out of defensive reflex than any real belief it was true," Elizabeth admitted. "I told him I was aware he despised of our family, and that I believed I was only acceptable to him *now* because I am also a de Bourgh."

"What did he say?" Jane asked.

"That I would be acceptable at Pemberley, and that is all that a *Darcy* would care about."

Jane smiled. "Then, my love, he told you what he had already told me – all he said in addition, to me, is that he had already determined that if he crossed your path again, he would offer for you." She gave her sister a sly smile, as Elizabeth blushed. "I did scold him, you know, before he confessed to that, to ensure he knew better than to trifle with you."

"Jane! You did not!" Elizabeth protested, and Jane laughed. "You did?"

"He took it quite well, I must admit," Jane grinned. She sobered slightly. "Do you trust him? I should hate for you to find out too late that you do not."

"I…" Elizabeth searched for words. "I do not know. I want to – and that bothers me perversely because I do not know how *my* feelings transmuted as they did. I disliked him so frightfully much, not even two full weeks ago." Now that Jane's toilette was complete, Elizabeth sat herself on the edge of the bed again. "I worry that – in the mix of all this confusion – he has been something to remind me of what I have known previously, and that I am simply flattered by his attentiveness."

"Are you?" Jane asked. "Flattered, that is."

Elizabeth tilted her head as she looked at Jane. "You were flattered by Mr. Bingley asking you to dance a second time, Jane. How could I not be flattered by William all but declaring his intentions?"

"Well," her sister responded with a slow grin, "I do recall you were decidedly irritated with Mr. Collins' marked attentions."

"Oh! Decidedly indeed," Elizabeth laughed. "But William Darcy and William Collins are by no means comparing apples to apples. One is one of the most ridiculous personages in the land, even if he is my mother de Bourgh's parson, and the other is one of the most intelligent and prosperous personages, despite his tendency towards being taciturn."

"He has garnered your approval, has he not?" Jane marvelled. "My only advice, then, is to not let yourself agree to an engagement until perhaps after we have visited Pemberley and Brandywine come the summer."

Elizabeth smiled slightly. "Yes, but then how will I have my double wedding with you, my dearest Jane? I do not think Mr. Bingley will be pleased to wait nearly *nine months* to make you his bride."

Jane sobered and sat down beside Elizabeth. She took one of Elizabeth's hands in her own. "My place, right now, is at your side, Lizzy. Until I am sure you are comfortable and secure in your immediate future – as merely Elizabeth Bennet de Bourgh, or Elizabeth Darcy, or some other name – my future can wait – and if Mr. Bingley cannot wait that long, then he does not love me enough for it to be a marriage worth making."

Elizabeth smiled sadly before throwing her arms around her sister. "Oh, Jane. I do love you so very much. I do not wish you to be unhappy for my sake."

"Lizzy – you know I speak the truth. I remember you telling me of the discussion you had that day mama visited Netherfield while I was ill. Such an easy-going temperament may be well matched for mine – but if it does not come with enough resolve to wait through trying family times, then it is not enough."

"True," Elizabeth found herself agreeing again. "So – if I can keep my own head on straight, you will use this time to test Mr. Bingley's resolve?"

Jane hesitated. "If he seems inclined towards me still, I think my answer will be yes. If he is not… then the choice will be made for me."

Elizabeth nodded. "Then, I suppose, we shall see."

"Indeed we shall."

Twenty-Two

Although Darcy had been completely truthful when he told Elizabeth the night before he intended to finish out the business the abrupt trip to Rosings had interrupted, he found himself at his friend's home shortly after the time he knew Bingley to finally be up and readying for the day. He was, he reasoned to himself, only ensuring *Elizabeth's* happiness, by making sure Bingley did not have one of his infamous bouts of second guessing himself and his actions in regards to Jane. He did not let his mind consider the fact that, if he chivvied Bingley over to the Fitzwilliam townhouse this morning, he would *have* to go as well; it would only be politeness that he did so, after all.

As Darcy was conducted towards the morning sitting room, he and the servant both overheard Miss Bingley arguing with her brother, ostensibly to avoid going to meet acquaintances she wished him to give up. Although the Bennets were not named, precisely, Darcy felt convinced that was indeed who was under discussion. He had not spoken to anyone about how Elizabeth would be introduced to the Bingleys now – and even if it put Miss Bingley at a social disadvantage, her hatred of Elizabeth would not be enough to curb her tongue when presented with an opportunity to distribute such juicy gossip. He cautioned himself to watch his own tongue until he could speak to his aunt and uncle about it, and wondered if he should encourage Bingley to come alone, to ensure that the news remained from the *Ton* one more precious day.

"Mr. Darcy," announced the servant as he opened the door, Miss Bingley's mouth closing shut on her words with a snap.

Darcy found himself at a loss for words beyond the polite – not an uncommon occurrence, to be sure, but one he had long thought was in his past when in Bingley's company. He realized, however, that the only topic he wished to discuss – Elizabeth – was not the most… diplomatic of subjects. Bingley saved him, as he often had in the past.

"Did your trip to Rosings go well?" Bingley asked, motioning Darcy to a seat. "I hope the situation has been resolved to the satisfaction of all parties?"

Darcy smiled ruefully to himself. Bingley had only *partially* saved him this time. His tongue still yet may betray him. Miss Bingley did not even let him respond, however. "I thought, Mr. Darcy, you were not bound to visit your aunt for another fortnight at earliest?"

"Indeed, Miss Bingley," Darcy replied. "As I informed your brother, a situation arose at Rosings that required the attention of my cousin Fitzwilliam and me."

"I wonder Charles mentioned nothing of such a situation," Miss Bingley shot her brother a dark look.

"I asked he not speak of it, in terms of general discourse, Miss Bingley," Darcy replied with a shrug, "until such time as I could be assured of the exact nature of the situation." He paused, groping for the next words. "The situation is… not yet resolved, but the main parties are no longer in Kent. The entire party has returned to London, to be better able to conduct the necessary investigations."

"I did not speak of *Darcy's* situation, Caroline, because I was rather more concerned with *mine,*" Bingley answered. He glanced at Darcy. "And what of Miss Elizabeth?" Bingley asked. "I believe you mentioned meeting her at Rosings."

"She *was* staying at Hunsford with her cousin, Mr. Collins—" Darcy began to reply.

"*Was?*" Miss Bingley interjected. "Has she run off? She was always quite so wild and wilful, I should not be surprised."

"Caroline!" Bingley snapped, startling Darcy. Rarely had he heard the younger man speak in such accents. "Do I need to remind you the requirements for keeping your allowance?" Darcy was impressed – instead of avoiding the issue, as he had honestly suspected he would, Bingley had apparently called Caroline out on the topic of Jane. *Very* impressed, indeed. A mute, paler Miss Bingley shook her head. Bingley eyed his younger sister for a moment, then turned to his friend. "Are indeed *all* of the unexpected visitors at Rosings returned to London, as your letter last night indicated?"

Darcy replied affirmatively. "All but myself are currently hosted by the Matlocks, and given your prior acquaintance with members of the party, I thought you ought to be invited in person sooner, rather than later."

Miss Bingley apparently could not contain herself for long. "How can that be possible? Charles was insistent that we were to visit Miss Bennet this morning – her uncle resides in Gracechurch Street, and surely *you* would not have introduced them to an earl."

Darcy realized that – everything else aside, Miss Bingley – and indeed, Bingley as well – deserved to know what was awaiting them at the Matlocks'. "The necessity of introduction was decided upon by the family as a whole, Miss Bingley. The Bennets –" he paused, groping for words, thoroughly aware of how narrowly both Bingley and his sister were watching him. "Bingley, do you recall, once, me talking of the little cousin, the younger daughter of my aunt Catherine, who disappeared?"

Bingley frowned slightly, while he thought back. "I vaguely recall something of it, yes. You were but a child yourself, were you not?"

"Indeed, I was," Darcy agreed. "And my family had long since given up hope of her recovery." He paused, and took a steadying breath. "Imagine my surprise, upon being summoned to Rosings, to find that I have known her, under another name, for some months now." He met Bingley's eyes squarely. "Miss Elizabeth Bennet."

Darcy had not realized Miss Bingley had been holding on to anything – and by the sudden crash of breaking glass, she apparently forgot herself. "That cannot be!" Miss Bingley cried. "She is *nothing*. She is little more than a country nobody with *fine eyes*."

"Caroline!" Bingley called his sister to order again. "Darcy, is this true?"

Darcy, who had gritted his teeth against calling Miss Bingley to order, found himself replying to Bingley far more calmly than he thought could. "It is indeed – Wickham suspected it, almost from the moment of being introduced to her in Hertfordshire, and the resemblance to the portrait of my uncle, Sir Lewis, as well as to my cousin, Anne, cannot be coincidence. If Anne were more in health, I would have recognized her immediately; I dare say the ability to walk three miles to tend to an ill sister made me discount any suspicions I might have had. Mr. Bennet has also informed us – as well as Elizabeth – that she was taken in by the Bennets, a few months after her disappearance from Rosings. There can be little to doubt, except…" he trailed off. Miss Bingley could not be made aware of the possibility of danger to Elizabeth.

"Except?" Bingley prompted.

"The family has not yet decided when to announce her recovery to Society," he flicked a glance at Miss Bingley. "The information is to be kept *absolutely* secret, until my uncle can decide how this will be handled. I do hope I can rely upon you both?" Bingley's affirmative was swiftly given, but Miss Bingley hesitated just enough to make Darcy doubt how truthful the agreement was. "It should not be necessary to say," he added with a half-smile, "but if *I* can expect general displeasure from my family for relating the information to *you*, should the information make it out into general knowledge, I cannot vouch for the earl's temper against the offending party." Miss Bingley paled at that reminder of the social clout that could be brought against her. Darcy hoped it would be enough, but it was only fair *they* know.

"If Miss Elizabeth did not know – as you seem to indicate – did Miss Bennet know?" Bingley asked.

"Only Mr. and Mrs. Bennet knew; Miss Bennet had not been very old herself, at the time, and was very ill." Darcy winced. "*Our* Elizabeth was recommended to the care of the Bennets, to remove her from the children's fever that was rife in London at the time… the same fever that claimed both the Bennets' only son and *their* Elizabeth."

"How dreadful Mr. and Mrs. Bennet must feel," Bingley murmured, "to discover they might lose another child."

"They will not," Darcy replied, firmly. "The Bennets have been welcomed by the entire Fitzwilliam family with open arms, for had they not taken Elizabeth in, she likely would have succumbed to that same fever, nor are the chances great she would have been raised as a gentleman's daughter. We would never have found her, under any other circumstances. We owe them more than we can ever hope to repay." He paused, and glanced at Miss Bingley. "Mrs. Bennet and the younger daughters remain at Longbourn; Mr. Bennet returns there on the morrow." He looked back at Bingley. "I believe he would be pleased to see you, as would Miss Bennet – she will stay with Elizabeth for at least a month, until it is decided what steps need to be taken next."

Bingley almost smirked as he glanced at his sister. "Well, Miss Bennet still may be the relatively 'fortuneless daughter of a country gentleman,' but she does not lack in connections now, does she, Caroline?"

"Indeed not," Miss Bingley muttered in graceless reply. She toed the broken teacup at her feet – apparently it had been emptied prior to falling – in distaste. "If you are determined to pursue this folly, brother, I will need to retire to dress appropriately."

"As you wish," Bingley replied tolerantly, as he made his way to the door to request a servant clear the broken glass. Miss Bingley swept from the room, and Bingley's next comment was made with wry humour once the servant was gone. "I did not think it diplomatic to point out to her that she has worn that dress to *other* morning visits before; nor that she knew we were to be visiting acquaintances of mine this morning, and previously considered it acceptable."

Darcy laughed before he could catch himself. "She simply may need a few moments alone to compose herself, Bingley. She has never been fond of the Bennets – as we both know – and it must be difficult to hear that one is now known to be my cousin."

"That is why you told us now, when you would have rather not, eh?"

Darcy had long ago come to appreciate how insightful his friend could be, and this only reminded him. "Indeed, I would have rather not – nor did I think it polite to drop the information *until* you arrived there." He paused and admitted, "Although I likely would have enjoyed the dissemination of it at a later time – such as in the carriage in front of my uncle's townhouse, or in the parlour there."

"I think I am grateful," Bingley replied, "that your well-trained politeness usually trumps your wicked sense of humour." Bingley eyed his friend. "And how are *you* taking the information that Miss Elizabeth is your cousin?"

"Much like the rest of the Fitzwilliam family – grateful, relieved, desperately trying to keep from smothering her with overzealous caution." He shrugged. "I am not alone in being very concerned about her continued welfare, now that we have found her."

Bingley nodded. "I noticed you mentioned Wickham."

Darcy replied to the unstated question. "He has… made amends. I am not yet at liberty to discuss everything – perhaps I never will be. But he has been cleared of… the most grievous of offenses against me and my sister."

Miss Bingley's return forbade a continuation of the subject. She had indeed changed into something more formal, and perhaps overly so, but Darcy and Bingley both had long given up on attempting to understand the complexities and finer points of women's clothing – they could gauge the relative worth of the fabric and construction, but more than that was beyond their desire *to* understand. If Darcy was honest with himself, the only dress he truly cared to pay attention to was whichever one that Elizabeth happened to be wearing at the time. *That* dress – no matter what colour, formality, or design – never failed to please him. Miss Bingley happened to ask him his opinion of the one she wore now, and he managed to avoid telling her the only reason he liked it at all is because it meant he would be returning to Elizabeth's company sooner, rather than later.

For some reason, he thought to himself, as he entered the carriage behind Bingley, he did not think Miss Bingley would have overly appreciated that reply, anyhow.

Twenty-Three

Despite the combined efforts of Jane, Wickham, Anne, and even her mother de Bourgh, Elizabeth resisted retiring for an early morning nap. Perhaps, she replied to them all, later in the day, after luncheon. She had not slept well, this was true, but she did not feel completely unrefreshed either. She did believe that right now, despite Jane's words earlier, she was in dire need of reassurance that the father she could not remember would not have held her responsible for his fate. The father she knew and loved sought her out, in the library, where she was currently engaged in staring at the pages of a book, her mind still attempting to reconcile the information she had available. She tilted her head in greeting, but could not bring herself to speak.

"You should not brood over what you cannot change, my child," he said gently, sitting beside her.

"'Tis easier said than done, papa; you know this," she replied.

"True," he agreed. After a pause, he began again. "Jane spoke to me of your... feelings of responsibility." Elizabeth's only reply was an arched eyebrow, and he smiled slightly at her refusal to respond. "What I wanted you to know is that only the basest of parents would hold their child ultimately responsible for any action that might have had disastrous consequences, even if they were of an age to understand." He paused and glanced away for a moment; Elizabeth knew he was terribly uncomfortable with being completely open. "I... if I were the one, looking down on you now, I would only be grateful you had found your way back home, after all this time, that you were safe and sound, that you still had a chance at life and happiness. I cannot imagine Sir Lewis would be looking down on us now with any other thought than that."

"Do you really believe that, sir? Or are you trying to simply ease my worries?" she asked after a moment.

"I believe it. I am sure Jane has told you much the same; I doubt Lady Catherine believes anything else, either."

"I do not know what my mother de Bourgh believes," she replied softly. "We have not really spoken of it."

"I have watched Lord and Lady Matlock attempt to calm her fretfulness over you all morning, Lizzy. She does not want you to think she considers you responsible." He paused and eyed her. "Miss de Bourgh is nearly beside herself with concern, although she was not sure where you might be found."

"They worry excessively," Elizabeth said.

"Do they?" Mr. Bennet replied. "They do not know your character as I do, or even as Jane does. They only know what *they* would feel, in your place, and – we both know this – you are less inclined to brood than most. If Mr. Darcy is at all representative of the family, your… resiliency is not something they are familiar with."

"I do not feel like I even know who I am anymore," Elizabeth finally replied. "If the confusion *there* was not enough, now I have the weight of Sir Lewis' death on my shoulders, whether or not Wickham is inclined to share that burden."

"You are my most beloved daughter," Mr. Bennet replied. "And it is for your intelligence and your wit that you became my favourite; the same wit and intelligence that makes you at ease no matter where you go; that distinguishes you from the vast majority of silly girls that populate English drawing rooms. The only difference between the Elizabeth Bennet of a month ago, and the one sitting here now, is you can sketch the personalities of a much wider circle of acquaintances and family. You should never be without an easy moment of diversion, *now*."

Mr. Bennet had said this all with a straight face, only the twinkling in his eyes betraying his real purpose; Elizabeth, for her part, could not but laugh in reply and shake her head at him. She made to reply, but he continued. "Consider yourself fortunate in such a bounty! After all, *your* bounty of amusement is intent on depriving me of *mine*, by sending Kitty and Lydia to schools, so that they can come back prim and proper ladies."

Elizabeth laughed, and replied, "Come, papa, you know you find as much amusement in silliness as you do 'prim and proper' when taken to extremes."

Mr. Bennet grinned in response. "Indeed, I do," he agreed. "Even," he added with a sly look, "when it is one of my daughters' suitors, say, perhaps, Mr. Darcy?" Elizabeth blushed, and Mr. Bennet laughed. "I am less amazed by Lady Catherine recognizing you, than I am by discovering *Mr. Darcy* to have been long impressed with *you*. I did not think him capable of looking past his own pride to notice any pretty girls long enough to take an interest!"

"Papa!" Elizabeth scolded, even as she tried to keep from laughing. "William is perfectly respectable; you know much of our dislike was founded by Wickham's tale."

"And the fact that he insulted you, eh?" Mr. Bennet replied with a raised eyebrow, and Elizabeth blushed.

"I did express myself rather… more vehemently than necessary, did I not?" she replied.

"You always were rather more… *eloquent* about rights and wrongs, than I ever was, my dear," Mr. Bennet replied. "I have long been content to be merely amused or irritated by them, but nothing more." He frowned slightly, glancing around the library, and by extension, the Fitzwilliam family. "Having met your relatives, however, I wonder if I must reconsider my belief it was merely your youth that made you so; this is a particularly… *vehement* group, even if rather quieter than either of us are used to being around." He paused and gave her a significant look. "You may have to accustom yourself to not being the most stubborn one in the family."

"Papa!" she cried. "That is not fair!"

"No, indeed, it is not," he agreed, smilingly. "But it is an honest observation; regardless of their ties to you, you still do not *know* them. I have no desire to relinquish you to them any more than I am required, even if we *did* know them."

A knock on the library door interrupted the conversation, and a servant was bid to enter. The servant relayed the message that Mrs. Gardiner and Mr. and Miss Bingley, as well as Mr. Darcy, had arrived, and they were summoned to the morning parlour. After thanking the servant, Elizabeth and Mr. Bennet rose to attend the newly arrived (and re-arrived) guests. At the door, however, Mr. Bennet paused Elizabeth, with a hand on her arm. His voice was completely sober, much like it had been when he entered the library. "The one thing I want you to always remember, Lizzy, is that regardless of where you go, no matter what name you take, or what relatives you find or acquire… you are my daughter, and I love you prodigiously." With that, he kissed her forehead, and went ahead of her.

Elizabeth found herself discomposed; she was as unused to displaying her true emotions as Mr. Bennet, and even *less* used to being on the receiving end of genuine emotion, particularly from Mr. Bennet. She loved her father so dearly, and she realized how awfully afraid *he* was, that despite all of her insistence about the Bennets being welcomed by the Fitzwilliams, after being confronted with all the differences and changes in front of her, she would… forget them, perhaps, and leave them behind like so many forgotten flowers in a now-dry vase.

As much as she wished to see her Aunt Gardiner and William – and to sit beside Jane as she dealt with the conflicting emotions of seeing Mr. Bingley again – she found herself lingering there at the library doorway. She took two steps back into the room and closed the door. Leaning her head against the wall to the side of it, she closed her eyes, and reached to find her composure, as she had so many times when Mrs. Bennet had pushed it to the utmost limits. Then, remembering what her father had said about 'looking down', she looked up and said aloud, "I hope you *have* forgiven me, father. I hope you are not displeased by being displaced by papa; I truly never knew until lately, and he has done his best in raising me. You should not be displeased with *him*. I do not know that I love *you;* how can I? But perhaps you understand that part, and will forgive me, for I intend to ensure I love *mère* and Anne as much as I can. I am sure I *did* love you, when I knew you, and that you loved me, I do not doubt. Somehow, I suspect *you* would not wish me to forget the Bennets, either. I will do my best, to make you proud of me."

She felt silly, saying such things aloud, but she still felt better for it. It meant more, perhaps, to hear her voice taking the words and incoherent ideas that had been swirling inside her head since last night, and making them something akin to a vow. The thoughts lingered on her still, but their touch was not nearly so weighty. She felt herself to be calmer, and more ready to face the entire mass sitting in the drawing room now. Resolutely, she opened the door only to flush with embarrassment when she discovered William on the other side.

He flushed himself, and stammered slightly. "Mr. Bennet sent me to ensure you were not lost," he offered awkwardly. She did not reply and his blush deepened. "I – if you are concerned I overheard anything, I heard only vague sounds, although I can guess."

"How?" she asked, her discomfort at the possible eavesdropping warring with curiosity. He offered his arm and she accepted it unthinkingly. He led her towards the drawing room while offering an explanation.

"When... when *my* father died, five years ago, I blamed myself," Darcy replied, "although I certainly had no cause to do so. A fire broke out at one of the tenant houses, while I was at Cambridge. Two weeks later, I would have been home on break, to assist, but that did little to help *then*. My father, naturally, gathered everyone possible to help, and he himself was in the bucket line. A storm broke out, as it often does during that time of year, and while the rain should have helped, the winds simply waved the fire hotter and larger. My father... inhaled some of the smoke, while trying to pull some of the tenants away from the billowing flames. The damage done to his lungs was, the doctor tells me, almost instant, and beyond medicine's reach to cure." He paused, and glanced down to meet Elizabeth's eyes. "A messenger had been sent to me as soon as my father was alerted to the fire; I, of course, informed my professors – well, Richard did that, for me – and left instantly." He looked away, and his throat worked. "I arrived just in time to tell him how much I loved him, and to hold Georgiana during the first few moments of grief; Georgiana had stayed with him until the end, at her request and his."

"How could you blame yourself for *any* of that?" Elizabeth asked. "You reacted precisely as you ought; there was nothing else you could have done."

"Logically, rationally? I cannot," he shrugged in reply. "Logic... is not the only measurement by which reactions are judged. You, of all people, know *that*." He paused, and added, "Forgive me, that did not come out quite as I intended, perhaps." He shook his head. "What, perhaps, I truly need to say is that *your* guilt is as baseless as mine was. It does... take time, to come to terms with that." He gave her a wry smile. "Until you do, I fear you are in for a lot of comforting from all of us, so you do not forget that *we* do not blame you."

"A family inclined to take responsibility?" she asked wryly.

"Perhaps too much so," he agreed. He paused in the hallway near their destination. "Your sisters told me you did not sleep well last night."

"Is it so obvious?" she asked.

He smiled. "I am not the best one to judge *that*," he replied. "I think you are lovely regardless." She blushed and his smile widened. "Although I will admit that I rather do enjoy watching you blush." She made an abortive move, as if to pull away, or perhaps smack him for such cheek. He held on to her arm more tightly. "However, all I really wanted to say was – are you sure you are up for company now? I could easily make your excuses to the party, and inform them you have retired."

Elizabeth half-glowered at him for a moment, but then shook her head. "Nay, I *am* a little tired, to be sure, but not enough for retiring to be a worthwhile exercise. Perhaps, as I told my sisters and *mère* earlier, after luncheon, I will retire."

Darcy nodded and gestured towards the door. "Then a room only *slightly* more appealing (to me) than a dungeon awaits us." Elizabeth laughed. Only William could call a parlour analogous to a dungeon, and not be entirely jesting when doing so. With this thought in mind, she entered the room on Darcy's arm.

* * *

Just at that moment, and in that room, a second person would have likened the generally pleasant and well-humoured parlour to a dungeon. Caroline Bingley simmered in dissatisfaction. She had been outmanoeuvred and outwitted. The indignity of being called to order in front of Mr. Darcy earlier had not subsided, nor was the indignity of being so easily discounted among his illustrious relatives likely to pass easily. She had been greeted politely enough, and Mrs. Gardiner had indeed attempted to hold a conversation with her, but such pitying grace could only make Caroline more uncomfortable and displeased.

Her mood certainly did not experience a sudden brightening upon seeing Miss Eliza enter on Mr. Darcy's arm, laughing. Caroline noted with a critical eye that Miss Eliza seemed tired, and not any better dressed than she would have been in Hertfordshire. "Elizabeth!" cried Lady Catherine. "We thought perhaps you had retired after all."

"Nay, *mère,*" Miss Eliza replied with a smile. "I was hopeful there would be guests this morning, bringing news." She glanced at Mrs. Gardiner, who almost imperceptibly shook her head. A flash of disappointment flickered over Miss Eliza's face, and Caroline wondered at it. What information could the mere merchant's wife have, that the Matlocks could not gather themselves? Lady Catherine beckoned Miss Eliza to her side, although the latter paused near Caroline and greeted her politely.

Caroline, for her part, barely deigned to muster a coldly polite response; had she not been within sight of both the wife and sister to an earl, she may not have bothered. That Miss Eliza should be the daughter of Lady Catherine seemed laughable, back in her own comfortable parlour. Seeing her side by side with Miss de Bourgh, however, almost made Caroline believe it; she could certainly understand *now* how Miss Eliza was able to convince Lady Catherine of the relationship. Indeed, she felt the stirrings of respect for Miss Eliza's connivery, for she had not just convinced Lady Catherine, but she had managed to prevail upon the entire Fitzwilliam family – Mr. Darcy included – based upon the most coincidental of resemblances.

If anything, this trace of respect served to fuel Caroline's dislike of Miss Eliza further, instead of ease it. If Mr. Darcy's attraction to the girl – all of a year or year-and-a-half younger than Caroline herself – had been boarding on problematic in Hertfordshire, now that her connections were supposedly to his very own family, Caroline was very much aware how *strategic* an alliance with her might seem.

Undoubtedly, this had been part of Miss Eliza's plan to ingratiate herself with his family, in the hopes of usurping Caroline's previous, if unspoken, claim on the man and his name. Such schemes could do naught but fuel her ire.

However, on another front, Caroline found herself divided. She knew full well that Charles would sever her allowance – or worse, if there was such a possibility – if he detected any interference with Miss Bennet again, yet Miss Bennet's connections were such that she felt as if it was her duty as his sister to do so. Still, if Miss Eliza kept up her connections with Miss Bennet, even when Caroline foiled her attempts to steal Mr. Darcy away, the supposed relationship to Lady Catherine would be kept up to all appearances. Even as dubious a familial link as it would be, it *still* may serve the Bingleys as a whole to permit Charles' fancy with 'dear Jane' to progress as he wanted. It would, at the very least, give Caroline a slight edge in terms of Society, at least until Mr. Darcy came to his senses and married her. After all, it was highly unlikely that the younger de Bourgh daughter would have been left much, if anything, in the face of her disappearance; there, Caroline could have an absolute advantage over Miss Eliza.

She did like Miss Bennet, of course. Jane was such a considerate soul that many a more bitter spirit had failed to disapprove of her on her own merits. She could easily love her as a sister, and there certainly could be worse choices (for her own sake). *Jane,* after all, would never turn her out of Charles' house, to depend on Louisa's generosity or necessitate finding a husband of her own, as some spiteful women of the *Ton* might. While the slight increase in fortune that would occur if Lady Catherine fronted Miss Eliza's dowry versus the Bennets doing so would be nearly negligible, any increase would certainly be welcome. She could not help but notice that Jane favoured Charles with her attention far more than Colonel Fitzwilliam, who, for his connections and his own inheritance, small in comparison to the Viscount's, was not an ineligible match to someone of Jane's standing. For the first time, she wondered if perhaps it *was not* Mrs. Bennet's pushing that encouraged Jane towards Charles, but Jane's own inclination. The first stirrings of guilt gnawed at her – not for any unhappiness she may have caused Jane, but for the happiness Charles *might* have had, had she not interfered. But she could not be sure; Jane Bennet was too much like Mr. Darcy, whom, try as she might, she could not entirely read nor understand.

She wished Louisa was here. The eldest of the siblings, Louisa was long used to watching over Charles, and had particularly advised Caroline to guard their brother in her place when she was sent to school. Louisa would be better able to judge Jane's readjusted suitability for Charles – Caroline knew herself to lean towards excessive enthusiasm for protecting a brother she had been, due to the closeness in their ages, been nearly inseparable from until they were sent to separate schools on the same day. She truly did want the best for him, and as she would not willingly, happily leave his household unless she married or was forced into a position of no other recourse, it was best for *her* that she and he both be happy with his choice.

Perhaps, Caroline thought, it was indeed time to actually *ask* Jane her opinion of Charles, instead of assuming the eldest Bennet daughter was completely under her mother's power. But it would need to be done before Jane returned to her mother's *insistence.* Here, it was obvious there was little in the way of expectation of Jane acting in any particular matter, except to keep an eye on Miss Eliza. Caroline could not relish the idea of being connected to Miss Eliza, for her own sake, but – in deference to her supposed connections and strong affections for Jane – she would learn to temper her words towards the girl. But *only* if she decided Jane was suitable material for Charles. This did not mean, however, she intended to let Miss Eliza win the title of Mistress of Pemberley.

Such reflections soothed Caroline's temper such to the point that, when Mrs. Gardiner once again attempted to bring her into the conversation, Caroline found herself at least willing to make an attempt at participation. The approving smile from Charles, however, made her cringe inwardly. When did it happen that *she* should need to be the one being rewarded such? But she was grateful to see it nonetheless; perhaps he would forgive her, after all.

Twenty-Four

While Elizabeth had been relieved when Miss Bingley responded – and indeed kept up a conversation with – Mrs. Gardiner, Miss Bingley's subsequent renewed civility to Jane worried her. It did not seem to be the same sort of civility Elizabeth had seen in Hertfordshire, but she did not wish for Jane to be taken in by either Bingley sister again. Indeed, Miss Bingley *had* to know that they were aware of some measure of duplicity in her actions, if her brother also knew. Elizabeth may not think Mr. Bingley the steadiest of characters, but he seemed to prefer fairness, and given how smitten he seemed with her sister months later, she could not imagine him letting the transgression die a quiet death of pretended ignorance.

The most interesting thing about Miss Bingley's civility towards Jane was, unlike at Netherfield, where half of everything she said was directed towards Mr. Darcy, Miss Bingley seemed to be actually concentrating on analysing *Jane*. Perhaps, Elizabeth hoped, Miss Bingley was truly interested in her brother's happiness, and had previously believed herself to be working in his best interest. While Elizabeth could not but grieve such actions injured Jane as they had, it was not a trait she would be able to scorn. Had she not done her best to deflect unwanted suitors from Jane, herself? Granted, it had been with Jane's quiet, oblique agreement, which did not seem to be the case *here*. But William had resolved *that* part quite efficiently, and it had not even taken any demands or prompting on Elizabeth's part for him to decide on the matter.

There was, of course, now the matter of William, and her changing opinion of his character. Miss Bingley would undoubtedly still have her cap set for him, and she had not had the benefit of seeing William's persistence in his attentiveness towards Elizabeth this past fortnight. Elizabeth had been ill-inclined to be considered a rival for William's affections in Hertfordshire, when she could only hold him in a thinly-veiled contempt, but, despite Jane's advice earlier, Elizabeth now found she was even less inclined to permit Miss Bingley to pretend an intimacy with William like she had those few months.

Thankfully, it appeared that the first skirmish in that war would not yet be fought, for Mr. and Miss Bingley had already stayed past the polite visiting time, even if William had brought them along, and they rose to excuse themselves with polite adieus.

Elizabeth could barely contain her surprise when, unprompted, Miss Bingley invited both Jane and herself to tea a few days hence. She glanced at her mother, questioningly, as did Jane. Lady Catherine hesitated, but inclined her head ever so slightly. Jane politely accepted the invitation.

As the Bingleys' carriage had followed William's, William *could* have returned to his own townhouse to complete the business Elizabeth was fairly sure he had barely touched, but he did not. Lady Matlock had insisted he stay for lunch, after which Mr. Bennet and Wickham were to depart for Meryton and Longbourn, not that William had spoken more than a token protest. Elizabeth and Georgiana exchanged amused glances.

However relieved Elizabeth was to see Miss Bingley depart, she could not say the same about her Aunt Gardiner. But Mrs. Gardiner politely declined the lunch invitation, citing her own guests due later in the evening, and a need to attend to the related matters. With a fond hug and kiss on each girl's cheek, and a parting comment to Mr. Bennet, Mrs. Gardiner also departed.

With the guests removed from the expanded and extended family circle, however, another topic emerged: What to do about Elizabeth.

For her own sake, Elizabeth would have preferred to stick to the plans made during the beginning of the year, with the adjustment for her summer trip to Derbyshire to view "her" estate – as it was freely referred to during the difficult to follow conversation, even if it was still held in trust by Lady Catherine – and the incidental visit to Pemberley and Lambton. Mrs. Gardiner had passed on the message to William that Mr. Gardiner's business could not allow him that much time away; indeed, it would be better suited, he suspected, to ensuring the entirety of his vacation could indeed be spent in leisure.

Mr. Bennet seemed inclined to agree. "Mrs. Gardiner has not yet found any information of use from the orphanage, but I am still disinclined to believe Lizzy's safety is in jeopardy at Longbourn; she has been unharmed there for the past seventeen years."

"Yet," Lady Matlock replied, "her reappearance is bound to leak out sooner, rather than later. It cannot be supposed that the servants at Rosings are deaf and blind, or that any moment as emotional as Catherine has led me to believe that one was, completely escaped detection. All it would take is a careless word, and an innocent question, and Elizabeth de Bourgh is suddenly connected to Hertfordshire in gossip."

Elizabeth and Mr. Bennet grudgingly agreed with the possibility.

"Perhaps," William interjected, "we ought to retire to Pemberley, Matlock, and Brandywine. The main house at Brandywine has been kept closed for some time now; surely Elizabeth would like a chance to determine what is necessary for redecoration and comfort, at her leisure."

"That is, perhaps, something to consider," Elizabeth replied. "But surely the sudden departure during the beginning of the Season would increase any possible gossip related to our families."

Lord Matlock agreed. "There has not yet been any indication Elizabeth might be in actual danger; perhaps those responsible for the ... *delay* previously no longer have a reason to be interested. That being said, giving a *reason* to be interested is certainly not within our best interests."

"I wish to acknowledge Elizabeth formally, sooner, rather than later," Lady Catherine replied with a tone of finality. Yet so little had been finalized, it seemed out of place. It did serve, however, as encouragement for Lord Matlock.

"What say you, Bennet, to bringing your wife and other daughters to London for a short visit?" he asked. Mr. Bennet raised an eyebrow questioningly. "I only bring up the idea, for I am sure that Elizabeth would be uneasy at leaving her adopted sisters for so long of a time, so unexpectedly, and I believe that the best course of action is to keep Elizabeth in the country after the announcement. A few weeks remain before the opening events of the Season; by that time, your family will be able to return to Hertfordshire. It will give her time to select a few items she may wish to be forwarded from Longbourn to Brandywine, as well as select a few items that Brandywine might require. Darcy, the steward there can supply us an inventory, so we can assist her in choosing items as necessary?" Darcy nodded confirmation. "The announcement of Elizabeth's recovery will be made the day *after* our customary ball; Elizabeth will be introduced as a de Bourgh at the ball, but I see no reason to give advance warning regarding her appearance." He glanced around the room. "The response to the announcement will have to be judged; Darcy, send word ahead to Pemberley so that they will be prepared at a moment's notice. The moment we consider Elizabeth might be in danger, we repair to the north; Brandywine will be Elizabeth's destination. It is a small enough estate that few will have heard of it; fewer still will know precisely where to begin to look for its location."

Mr. Bennet agreed. "Mrs. Bennet will be beside herself to be assured Elizabeth is well cared for, and the girls would like a chance to visit, I am sure."

"Due to my previous acquaintance with your family, Mr. Bennet, the Darcy townhouse is at your disposal," William interjected, with a glance at his uncle. "It should help decrease speculation, if there is any." Elizabeth could not help but glance at Jane; Meryton gossip would put two and two together, and end up at five – for obviously William would only invite the Bennets to London at Bingley's behest. Jane had coloured slightly, undoubtedly arriving at a similar conclusion, but she voiced no complaints with the scheme.

Lord Matlock and Mr. Bennet agreed that seemed a fair option. Luncheon was announced, and the party settled itself around the meal. Elizabeth found herself between William and Wickham, and she asked the latter his thoughts on the scheme.

"It seems a fair one," he replied. "I cannot think of any improvements to it; that is more William's strength than mine."

She glanced towards the end of the table, where her father and Lord Matlock discussed particulars, and back at Wickham. "I know your duties to the regiment take precedence, and I do not know when the regiment is set to leave Hertfordshire, but – for as long as you can – will you help my father protect my sisters, if it seems they might need it?"

Wickham gave Elizabeth a half-smile. "Given my pristine record in safeguarding the interests of those important to me and mine, are you sure you want to be asking for my assistance?"

"My father would undoubtedly appreciate another pair of eyes, with Jane and me remaining in London – with my precise return so doubtful." Elizabeth replied.

There was little Wickham could do but consent to be of assistance, then, so long as he was not being given the responsibility. Elizabeth hoped he understood it meant she bore him no ill will, and – insofar as it might go – felt she could trust him, now as he was, when her trust would have been misplaced half a week ago.

She did not wish to see her father leave, but knew that with Mary unfamiliar and new to running the household, beyond the little Elizabeth and Jane had tried to coax her into learning (and been rebuffed, in the way younger siblings do, when they suspect the endeavour is merely an excuse for the elder ones to be bossing them about), he truly had little choice in whether he stayed or returned. Jane, at least, would remain in London with her, and they would spend the day after next in the sole company of their aunt and uncle Gardiner.

The entire conglomerate of a family gathered to see Mr. Bennet and Wickham off, but they eddied about in such a way that Elizabeth was able to speak a few words to her father in relative privacy. She was grateful for the chance, even if it may have been unintended.

"Do give Mama my love, and my sisters, as well. Tell Mama I miss her and – and –" It was not a sentence to be finished, but Mr. Bennet understood. She pressed several letters into his hands – one for each of the Bennets at Longbourn, and one for him as well.

He smiled wanly, seeing *Papa* written in her clear hand, on the uppermost letter. "I will even reply, Lizzy, if only to confirm our arrival in London." She nodded, and he searched her face, looking for she knew not what, and then was into the carriage, scant moments after Wickham had entered.

She stayed, then, as the carriage left, and watched after it. She had never believed, in her heart of hearts, she would ever be faced with the prospect of leaving her father's household, of leaving Longbourn, for more than perhaps a month or two at a time. She wondered, perhaps, if this feeling of loss is what her father would have faced, had none of this come to light, and she had been leaving on her wedding trip. She wondered if he felt his leaving her here, now, as acutely as she did at being left. Perhaps this was the final gesture needed to convince her – wholly and completely – that she had not fallen into some sort of half daydream, half nightmare state she could not rouse herself from. No matter how much she might almost wish to have never learnt the truth, for nothing now could be the same as it was.

She stayed there, some several minutes after the carriage was beyond reasonable watching distance, even if they had been in the country, with the far less obstructed views afforded by the countryside. At last, she endeavoured to shake the mood, and turned to go up the steps. She was not entirely surprised to find William had stayed to accompany her back inside. He remained silent until they found themselves standing pointlessly in the hall. "I think, perhaps, you should retire for a while, as you had intended earlier."

"You are probably correct," she replied, attempting to keep her voice sounding like her normal self. She did not believe she succeeded, after the long steady look he gave her, before offering his arm to escort her to the stairs. His last words when he released her arm showed plainly she had not – but he had understood, regardless.

"Sleep well, Miss Bennet," he said. The reminder that *he* would not forget the family that raised her eased her heart in ways she could not explain – but she hoped her grateful smile in response was sufficient.

"Thank you, Mr. Darcy. I believe I shall."

Twenty-Five

Bingley felt relieved when Caroline entered into conversation with Mrs. Gardiner – even almost amiably. Once he was assured she was at least making an attempt to be polite, he returned the majority of his attention to Miss Bennet. They spoke of this and that – nothing terribly important, but trifling details of her London and Rosings stays that he was eager to know – but Bingley felt an edge of disquiet creep under his skin as he watched how everyone in the room, excepting himself, seemed to keep one eye on Miss Elizabeth. Darcy's attention was amusing, to say the least – never had Bingley seen his friend so affected, nor so willing to _be_ affected, by a woman. He was, as always, perfectly polite and vocal as need be, in this almost-family grouping, but he always seemed to deflate the tiniest amount when someone called Miss Elizabeth's attention away from him.

Mr. Bennet, possibly an even more indolent man than he, even if neither of them could compete with Hurst, seemed far more inclined to company and action than Bingley had seen in those weeks at Netherfield. Mr. Bennet and Lady Catherine seemed to have come to some sort of truce regarding Miss Elizabeth – neither behaved as though the other was a threat, when her attention was pulled away by the other – and the expressive amusement in the shared glances when Miss Elizabeth's attention was directed towards Darcy was entirely too telling.

No, Darcy's attention was amusing, and – he hoped Lady Catherine would never hear him say such a thing – Lady Catherine's and Mr. Bennet's was endearing. He could understand Miss de

208

Bourgh's focus on Miss Elizabeth as well. He had met her a few years ago, not long after he met Darcy, when Lady Catherine had come up to London for the Season, and she had been well enough to join her mother. Her face still showed traces of her chronic problems, but his memory told him she had more colour to her complexion than before. Fitzwilliam and his mother, of course, could also be understood, if they seemed to pay more attention to Miss Elizabeth than any of their guests. Mrs. Gardiner showed a great affection for both of her nieces, but the glances she kept throwing in Miss Elizabeth's direction were puzzled and contemplative, as if she were looking for a reminder of some stray thought, and might find it in her niece's expression.

Even as he told himself that everyone in the room had valid, understandable reasons to be so focused on Miss Elizabeth, even if they were attempting to not do so, Mr. Wickham joined the party, Miss Darcy on his arm. Miss Darcy immediately went to her brother to sit quietly by his side, and Mr. Wickham followed her to that sofa. Then Bingley noticed a curious thing – even with so many valid reasons to keep an eye on Miss Elizabeth, there seemed to be a furtive desire to keep a watch on Wickham as well. Wickham, Bingley owned to himself, seemed less of the jovial officer he had known in Hertfordshire, but it was obvious the man had slept ill. He truly knew not what to make of it all.

He should not have been surprised when Caroline moved to sit beside him, and began a subtle interrogation of Miss Bennet; he did, however, wonder at the politeness of it. He was not sure if he should be dismayed that Miss Bennet – although disconcerted at Caroline's politeness – merely took it in stride and replied back with equal serenity – but, no, Miss Bennet was usually serene and calm. There could be nothing unexpected in *that,* except he had been informed by Darcy that she knew of the deceit. Only Jane could be so forgiving.

At length, a chance remark was made about the remainder of Miss Bennet's stay in London, and that prompted the reminder of Netherfield. "I have been in contact with my steward at Netherfield, about the spring planting and the like," he interjected, "but perhaps I may impose upon your father for more local advice?"

Miss Bennet smiled in reply, glancing at Mr. Bennet, who was seated closer to her sister. "I am sure he would not be adverse to exchanging ideas and experience on the topic – Lizzy has always been the one most involved in such matters – and he will probably be missing her as a sounding board."

"What are your plans for the summer?" Caroline asked.

For the first time, Bingley saw Miss Bennet look truly uneasy – but perhaps it was merely a trick of the light, for she was her happy, if serene, self again in just a blink. "Our plans are not yet fixed; I am completely at Lizzy's disposal until she has – reconciled herself with the current situation, and no longer needs my support."

"What support can she possibly need?" Caroline asked, for once in earnest. "Surely Lady Catherine and the Matlocks are sufficient – not that I do not commend you for your loyalty to her," Caroline added.

Miss Bennet actually smiled in wry amusement for a moment. "Even if she does not *need* my support, I will fret about her until I am sure she is at ease. She has experienced quite a few shocks these past few weeks. We have all felt them, but they affect *her* the most profoundly. If my father had not thought to provide what witnesses and testimony he could to her, there would have been nothing that could have persuaded her to accept the de Bourghs as family." She glanced at Miss Elizabeth, and Bingley saw the concern and remembrance of pain in those eyes. "Her world has been turned upside down," she added softly, as if she had forgotten to whom she was speaking, saying such things in public, "and I could not live with myself were I not here to help her straighten it out."

The words sounded faintly familiar to Bingley, but from his sister's expression, she knew where *she* had heard them before, and the reminder was – at best – uncomfortable. Her civility sharply increased between one moment and the next, and when Bingley made a comment on the time, he was surprised that Caroline, without prompting or even a look for approval, invited both Miss Bennet and Miss Elizabeth to tea in a few days' time.

Their carriage had followed them, and Bingley was set to hand Caroline in, but she bade him to wait a moment, for she suspected the other guest might be leaving as well, and she did not see the Gardiners' carriage. "Surely Mrs. Gardiner should not have to travel by paid carriage, if we can take her home, Charles? You would not mind, would you?"

Bingley realized he was staring at his sister in disbelief before he stammered a reply, "Of course not, if she is willing."

Caroline gave him a smile, and when Mrs. Gardiner came down the steps from the door, she made the offer of transport to the older woman, who, with only an edge of surprise and a reflexive "I should not wish to inconvenience you any," was persuaded by both Bingleys that they did not mind at all, and would be happy to be of use.

It was Caroline and Mrs. Gardiner who held conversation in the carriage; Bingley was too stunned by, and then beginning to be suspicious of, his sister's sudden, rapid change of demeanour. Mrs. Gardiner gracefully thanked them both for the assistance, and politely offered them tea. "Oh, no, we should not wish to distract you from your scheduled guests," Caroline replied.

"Perhaps tomorrow, then?"

"I have no plans," Caroline replied agreeably, "Charles?"

"I cannot say I have any plans myself," he allowed. "Tomorrow, then." And it was decided.

He waited until they arrived at their townhouse before asking Caroline to join him in his study; the noise inside of a carriage on a London street was not precisely conducive to a heart-to-heart talk.

"How long is this going to last?" he asked without preamble. "I do not wish to see you befriend Miss Bennet again, and then use that friendship as a weapon against her and her family!"

Caroline blanched. "I – I did not intend that, Charles. I just –" she looked away. "Miss Bennet's words – Do you remember when Grandpa Johnson passed away?"

It had been a difficult time on them all, Bingley remembered. His father had spent many hours consoling his mother, as had he and his sisters. It was, perhaps, what had let *him* prepare for the day he lost his own father – Caroline had been overwrought, and Louisa scarcely less so. "I remember," he agreed, confused as to what this topic change meant.

"Do you remember father's friend, Mr. – What was it? Davids, perhaps?" Caroline's brow furrowed in concentration before she shook her head. "It matters not. You had been sent on some errand or another, and I was bringing tea to papa. And father's friend stood in his study, trying to convince him he should not have to tend mother in her grief. Father's reply was almost exactly what Miss Bennet said about Miss Eliza." Caroline looked away again. "I believe Miss Bennet believes what they have been told about Miss Eliza being a de Bourgh, and – I studied *her* often enough in Hertfordshire to realize that she was not in good spirits by any means." Caroline finally looked him in the eye, and added quietly, "I always thought our inheritance came at a high price, Charles. I recognized the expression on her face, after a few minutes of watching her – it was not unlike *yours*, those weeks you pretended to the world and our sister and me, that you were recovering from our father's death. Miss Eliza may not have *known* her father, but she has abruptly discovered he is dead, and even in *our* circle, there are only a few of who would be – completely unaffected by such a thing. She is grieving."

"I thought you would be set on the belief she is only pretending to be related," Bingley raised an eyebrow at his sister.

She sighed. "I confess I was, until I saw *that.* And I – I remembered how lost I felt after the carriage accident, and –" It was rare for Caroline to show emotion, but Bingley suddenly had an armful of sniffling sister. He held her, and let her cry herself out. Four years had scarcely been long enough to recover, in his opinion. Had Darcy not reached out to the younger, grieving man, Bingley may not have recovered at all, amidst all the sly comments about his now independent fortune. *Darcy* had seen he would have traded everything to have his parents back; seen and understood.

Caroline finally pulled away, embarrassed at her display, and muttered about how she must look. "What are your plans for tomorrow, then?" he asked, before she could escape.

Caroline could not look at him, but she answered nonetheless. "To apologize for my behaviour previously," she replied. There was a wry amusement in her voice, when she added, "If naught else, if the Fitzwilliams do not have a problem inviting her to their townhouse, for Miss Bennet and Miss Eliza's sakes, I may as well get to know my future aunt," she paused, while Bingley blushed, adding slightly mischievously, "particularly given I have been informed that my future *uncle* supplies more than one of my favourite modistes, as well as at least one of the most exclusive ones I have not yet been able to patronize, but Mrs. Gardiner does. You might say that I am considering the *material advantages* the acquaintance may provide."

Bingley snorted in true amusement. "Just do not interfere with Miss Bennet and Miss Eliza, Caroline."

"I would prefer to interfere, actually, Charles," she replied, and held up a hand to silence him as her brother scowled and prepared to remind her of certain threats. "If Jane is to be my sister, and Miss Eliza – as much as I hate to admit it – is to make a match with Mr. Darcy, there are those among my acquaintance who can be ... *influenced* to make the situation easier on the de Bourghs; not that they truly need my assistance, but – I have some amends to make, of my own."

Bingley gaped at her for a moment, then asked, "Who are you, and what did you do with Caroline?"

The question caught her off-guard, and for the first time in years – in truth, since the few minutes before the constable had been admitted to their home, bearing the news of their parents' fate – Bingley heard his sister laugh – a true laugh of honest amusement. "I do not know, Charles. I simply do not know."

Twenty-Six

By the time Elizabeth returned downstairs from her nap, dressed for dinner, actually, as it was only a couple of hours away, her schedule for the next day had already been determined by her mother de Bourgh, her in-attendance-aunt, Georgiana and both of her sisters. Apparently, she was going to be shopping.

From the amused look on William's face, as well as Richard's, she had not done as good of a job suppressing the whimpering groan as she had hoped. "Are you truly sure it is necessary, *mére*?"

The other women in the room gave her a *look* eerily reminiscent of Mrs. Bennet, and she raised her hands in defeat. "I suppose, then, that I am going shopping; but I insist on Jane purchasing items as well."

"Of course she will; for she will be in attendance at the ball," Lady Catherine replied, overriding anything Jane had been about to say. "I have already settled it with her father; while Jane remains as a part of my household, *I* am responsible for her purchases."

Jane and Elizabeth both began to protest, but Anne laughed. "I think, *sisters,* that a graceful agreement is necessary. For I also sided with Mama on the subject, and your father was wise enough to let us have our way."

Jane was taken aback by Anne calling her "sister;" she glanced askance at Elizabeth, who favoured Lady Catherine and Anne with a

215

peculiar smile. "I see," Elizabeth said softly, "you were in earnest, that first night at Rosings."

"Did you ever doubt it, Elizabeth?" Lady Catherine asked.

Elizabeth smiled wryly. "I must confess I was not sure what to think then. There have been many things to consider of late."

"Then I suppose," Lady Catherine replied, "you will need to think more upon it. Your uncle," she nodded at Lord Matlock, "will be meeting with the solicitor in the morning, for advice on how to word the announcement, as well as to settle *my* will such that there can be no later disputes regarding your inheritance." She glanced between Anne and Elizabeth, "Not that I expect either of you to contest what is there at the moment, but one must always be attentive to such matters long before there can be any possible issue."

Anne and Elizabeth flicked understanding glances at each other. "Indeed, Mama," Anne replied. It would be, after all, most likely *her* future husband who would protest Elizabeth's inheritance.

The evening passed quietly, as did dinner. Each member of Elizabeth's family settled themselves near her for a quarter hour, perhaps half an hour, as they took turns satisfying their curiosity regarding her and her life since they last knew her.

Elizabeth herself endeavoured to learn everything she could about these individuals who loved her for who she had been born, not who she had grown into. She dreaded that the partiality for three-year-old Elizabeth weighed too much in the favour granted twenty-year-old Elizabeth; and, more than commonly anxious to please, she naturally suspected every power of pleasing would fail her. Jane rarely strayed from her side, and offered her unwavering support in the guise of quiet, pleasant conversation when Elizabeth and her relatives faltered for a common topic.

At length, Anne settled herself on the other side of Elizabeth from Jane, and between the two of them, they effectively ended the day's interviewing by not giving way to the other curious parties. William eventually dared to interject himself into the feminine barricade surrounding Elizabeth, and mentioned it was time for him to return to his townhouse, and that Georgiana would stay with him for the night. Georgiana, predictably, protested, but subsided when both her Aunt Matlock and brother gave her matching stern looks.

"Mrs. Annesley asked me to specifically remind you of your scheduled visits for tomorrow," William added. "Elizabeth will be well taken care of in terms of company for tomorrow's adventure; Cassandra has requested to accompany the party. I believe Aunt Matlock has agreed to her inclusion."

Georgiana flushed slightly. "I had – forgotten, in my excitement. I hope I have not offended anyone today."

William smiled slightly. "Mrs. Annesley said nothing to me of any appointments for today. Tomorrow, you will be busy, and of course there are always your studies."

"Cassandra is Alexander's wife?" Elizabeth asked.

"The same," William replied. "We should leave shortly, Georgiana."

The girl sighed and stood; the other girls rose in tandem. Georgiana impulsively hugged Elizabeth, surprising them both. "I will write to let you know if I will be free the day after tomorrow," Georgiana said.

Elizabeth nodded. "We have an invitation to the Bingleys', as well as my Aunt Gardiner's, in the coming few days. Coordinating everything may prove interesting," she added with a slight smile.

"Welcome to London," William replied in wry amusement.

After the Darcy siblings made their adieus and left, Elizabeth's sisters and mother insisted she retire. Despite the nap earlier, she found no reason to disagree, if only in the interests of being prepared for the morrow.

* * *

Mrs. Gardiner awaited her expected unexpected visitors. Most of a day had not rid her of the burning curiosity as to whether Miss Bingley's overtures were to be taken at face value. She was not blind to the advantages of a helpful Miss Bingley to her nieces. While Miss Bingley's place in Society hinged on her brother's friendship with Mr. Darcy and the Bingleys' own fortune, and she certainly was not part of the first circle, she still represented the circle that could cause Elizabeth the greatest grief. Elizabeth's own circle would accept her on the pure strength of the de Bourghs, Darcys, and Matlocks; the lesser landed gentry and the landless wealthy that brushed elbows with them would resent, if not despise, Elizabeth's unexpected rise to prosperity and influence, and do what they could to undercut her.

The guests were announced a few minutes after the appointed time; given the general commentary from Madeline's morning visitors on the state of the streets today, she was neither surprised nor offended. They settled down after the general pleasantries, tea cups in hand and crumpets close by.

"How have you fared since the winter?" Madeline asked Miss Bingley.

"Tolerably well," Miss Bingley replied. "I would apologize for the long delay between visits, as I did not last visit, but that would be at cross-purposes for *this* visit." Mr. Bingley, unusually quiet, raised an eyebrow at his sister, even as Madeline gave her a politely questioning look.

Miss Bingley did not look up from her tea cup, thus was not being prompted by Madeline's expression, but her voice and posture all showed signs of embarrassment and discomfort. "I would rather apologize for the reasons for the delay, as well as my behaviour both previous times I have been in this residence. To wit, for being unreasonably sure of my own merit."

Madeline was taken aback. Miss Bingley, being forthright, presented an unusual picture; admitting her own faults seemed utterly out of character. "I am unsure how to respond," Madeline replied. "But I thank you and accept your apology."

Miss Bingley's composure seemed to become less fragile with Madeline's reply. "Thank you; it is probably more than I deserve. But – I have amends to make to your nieces, and wanted you to be aware that I take them seriously."

Madeline eyed the younger woman for a moment. "If I may be so bold, Miss Bingley, as to ask what brought about this change of heart?"

"Miss Bennet uttered a phrase in regards to Miss Eliza's reaction to certain newly discovered facts that forcibly reminded me of something I heard my father say, in regards to my mother, once." Miss Bingley gave an elegant shrug. "Such openness convinced me of the truth of the situation."

Madeline nodded slightly, and then posed another question. "Is your intent, then, to milk the acquaintance for the purpose of your own advancement? Or for the actual acquaintance?"

Miss Bingley blushed slightly. "I have reason to believe some of the acquaintance cannot be avoided in the future. And I should reconcile myself to the new reality of the situation as well – so the acquaintance is important, in and of itself."

Madeline accepted her words at face value; for once, the multi-layered Miss Bingley was not talking in veiled comments, for all she was not saying all she was thinking. She shifted the conversation. "As

I said during your last visit, a dinner is being planned for my nieces. The date has not been set yet; would Friday of next week be acceptable for your household?"

Both Bingleys replied it would be. "My sister Louisa and her husband will be returning from his relatives' early to mid-next week. Might they be invited as well?" Mr. Bingley asked.

Madeline smiled. "Of course."

The important parts of the conversation completed, it turned to more idle conversation, and Miss Bingley became more comfortable. At length, however, the Bingleys did say they were invited to a dinner that night which they needed to prepare for, and Madeline saw them to the door.

* * *

Viscountess Cassandra Fitzwilliam was a beautiful woman, and the way she interacted with Alexander was endearing. Elizabeth felt very inclined towards affection for her in a matter of moments. She also happened to be well-dressed and displayed good taste. Placing her wardrobe in the care of the Countess' and Viscountess' knowledge of current fashion certainly afforded some measure of relief.

Elizabeth knew that the modiste they alighted at was one of the more fashionable ones that her Uncle Gardiner provided materials for, although she had personally not been to this one. The owner knew her, of course, from her London visits and the dinners attended at the Gardiners'. She wondered, in the way of those used to knowing their relatively mediocre means, if the family "discount" she often received from other modistes would be offered here – given the change of her circumstances and company.

The owner, a portly woman who had once been svelte, by the name of Mrs. Smithson, greeted them as they entered. "Lady Matlock, Viscountess, and –" a pause of startled amazement, "my dear Miss

Bennets! I knew that you were visiting, Jane, but your uncle said nothing of Elizabeth being in town!"

"It was," Jane replied sweetly, "a tad unexpected for us as well, Mrs. Smithson."

"Well, well," the lady replied. "If you will let me tend to these ladies first, my dears, I will be right with you?"

"Actually," Lady Matlock interjected, "they are with us today, Mrs. Smithson."

With an expressively startled glance at the Bennet girls, who nodded in agreement, Mrs. Smithson shook herself slightly. "Well, my dears, then you will simply have to tell me why later. What might you be looking for today?" her glance included all four women.

"The Miss Bennets will be part of the Matlock family party for most of the Season, if all goes well," Lady Matlock replied, "as well as – at minimum – at our opening ball. We wish to augment their wardrobes with this in mind."

Mrs. Smithson raised an eyebrow, and with a quick up and down appraising glance of both girls, nodded. "I understand, milady. Augment or replace?"

"Augment, if you please," Jane answered.

"At least for the time being," Elizabeth concurred. Lady Matlock gave her niece a sharp glance, but let it pass. After all, Elizabeth reasoned, if more clothing of higher quality were required later, the shop would have her measurements, and could surely fashion up a few items.

"This way then, my dears," Mrs. Smithson said to the girls. "My assistants shall get your measurements while the Countess and Viscountess sort through fabrics and patterns they deem appropriate." She glanced back over her shoulder. "That is what you intended, yes?"

The older women agreed.

Elizabeth took great care to not be caught alone with Mrs. Smithson for the duration, thus avoiding any interrogation where she might slip in her replies. Knowing what she did of the other lady, the information that she was part of the Matlock household would likely be heard by half of the *Ton* by mid-morning tomorrow. She hoped it had occurred to her aunt to drop a word about discretion into the lady's ear. She whispered this to Lady Matlock towards the end of the visit, and was given a smile.

"Already done, Elizabeth; but good thought." There was a touch of condescension to her aunt's voice, but Elizabeth tried to ignore it. She understood that Lady Matlock probably was unaware of just how long Mrs. Smithson had known her.

Perhaps Lady Matlock realized that fact when Mrs. Smithson gave her the total for the selected purchases. "Mrs. Smithson, if *I* were purchasing items, my tally would amount to significantly more than this," her aunt began.

"The girls are Mr. Gardiner's nieces, and I have known them since Miss Lizzy was waist high to me. I have wanted to fit her since then. I did her dress, a pretty yellow lace dress with red roses, for her uncle's wedding as a favour to her uncle, and have not had a chance since." The matron shrugged. "I have no girls of my own – the Bennet girls are as close to daughters as I ever had."

Lady Matlock had a peculiar expression on her face that Elizabeth could not decipher. "Very well then." No other disputes regarding the bill were to be found, once the matron gave her the percentage discount she calculated for the girls.

Elizabeth broached her aunt's reaction after they returned to the Matlock residence. "You are not – displeased with Mrs. Smithson, are you?"

Lady Matlock shook her head, and Elizabeth was startled to see tears forming. She reached out a tentative hand to touch her aunt's arm.

A forced smile and a glance away were the response, followed by a voice rough from emotion: "You made a beautiful picture in yellow lace and red roses."

Elizabeth gaped at her aunt, too stunned to reply.

"And I remember thinking, she sounds so much like our Elizabeth, but the woman – it must have been Mrs. Bennet – with you kept calling you her daughter and 'Lizzy,' as did Mrs. Smithson. And I did not recognize her, which meant she was country gentry, to be in such a shop, and it would be too much to hope you were safe and sound in such an environment. I never dared to hope for more than a kindly pastor or tenant's wife," Lady Matlock added, dabbing at her eyes with a handkerchief she had dug out of a handbag.

Elizabeth reacted in the only way she could: she stepped closer and gave her aunt a hug, and her aunt returned it with interest.

"If only I had dared hope you were safe, I would have asked questions of the woman. I nearly did as it was, but it was too much too hope for."

Elizabeth replied, "Understandably so, aunt."

Lady Matlock looked away from her. "Would you be so kind as to not tell your mothers what I just told you? There is no sense in aggravating the situation with what-might-have-beens."

"I had no intention of relaying the story." Elizabeth offered a wry smile. "After all, we do not know how many dark-haired little girls

Mrs. Smithson dressed in yellow lace and red roses at that time. Perhaps it was not me you saw."

Lady Matlock's own smile was wry as well. "Perhaps," she agreed, glancing away. "Perhaps."

Twenty-Seven

As Jane and Elizabeth alighted from the carriage in front of the Gardiners' residence, Elizabeth felt some of the tension in her shoulders dissipate. As much as she was learning to enjoy the company of Lady Catherine, her sister Anne and the Matlocks, *this* was still a place she had spent many a month in, as a growing child. When her feet itched to roam beyond the confines of Meryton, and she found herself standing in her bedroom wanting to go home, despite being there already, this was where she begged her father to send her, so she could flee those sensations for a while.

She was grateful, now, that he had never asked why she spent as much time up in London with the Gardiners as she had. He may have felt it necessary to tell her of her foundling status years ago, had he known some part of her heart knew it belonged elsewhere. The only problem was that with the information in hand, she felt even *more* adrift than she had previously.

Such were the thoughts that accompanied her as she and Jane went up the steps, were admitted, and shown to the parlour where Mrs. Gardiner entertained a friend of hers. The Bennets were to spend all morning with their aunt. Lady Catherine was proving to have self-restraint after all, and allowing her newly found daughter time away, to find solace in the well-known. Did William, perhaps, she wondered idly, have some part to play in that? She had caught a few words between him and *mère* last night that had not made sense to her, given how fragmentary they were.

"I see you made good time," Mrs. Gardiner said as she crossed the room to greet them.

"We did indeed," Jane replied. "It took us less than half the time to travel here, for nearly twice the distance, as it did to make it to the modiste yesterday."

"Oh, the roads were *terrible* yesterday," Mrs. Gardiner's friend Mrs. Baker interjected. She, like their aunt, was a well-to-do merchant's wife, and well dressed. Elizabeth's private opinion of the woman was that she could only hope Lydia came up so fortunate; the two were quite similar in disposition.

"They were," Elizabeth agreed, settling beside her aunt. "And how is your daughter?"

Mrs. Baker lit up, as she was excessively fond of her firstborn. "She is proving to have quite the talent at the pianoforte. I am in the process of selecting a master for her to study with. I believe, as does her father, that her talent merits special education."

"She is – twelve, if I recall correctly?" Jane asked.

"Twelve going on one-and-twenty!" Mrs. Bakers replied with a laugh. "I was never so serious at her age; she takes after her father like that."

"Discipline is a good talent to have, to excel at the pianoforte," Mrs. Gardiner replied. She patted Elizabeth's hand, adding, "If we could have only gotten this one to spend as much time on her playing as we could with her books, she would be one of the best."

"Aunt!" Elizabeth replied with a laugh. "I play sufficiently well."

"You do indeed, Lizzy," Jane replied, a mock-glare (for being Jane, that was as close as she got to a glare in the first place) at their aunt.

Mrs. Baker laughed; she had heard this interplay before. "If only I could get my Jane to spend as much time on her books as she does her playing!" The lady shrugged. "She does well at her studies, at least. Mr. Baker is quite proud of her."

Elizabeth smiled, "You both have reason to be proud of her; I was quite taken with her the last time I saw her."

Mrs. Baker smiled in return. "She does have that effect on people."

Another cup of tea for all parties was poured, and idle commentary about the weather resumed. Mrs. Baker suddenly commented, "It is unusual to see both you, Miss Elizabeth, *and* you, Miss Bennet, in town at the same time, particularly as I do not believe you are staying with your aunt."

"It was unexpected for us, as well, but the situation *is* unusual," Jane replied.

"We are staying with," the slightest hesitation, as Elizabeth affected searching for an appropriate term, "family friends, whose family party we are joining for the Season. Father was here for a few days; he departed the day before yesterday," Elizabeth added.

"Oh? Which friends? I did not think your father to be the kind to have many friends in London," Mrs. Baker replied.

The girls glanced at each other and then their aunt, who answered for them. "My brother-in-law tends to be very particular about who he interacts with, this is true. Given that, I have no qualms about my nieces' hosts."

Mrs. Baker looked taken-aback. "I had no intention of suggesting otherwise, Madeline. You and your Mr. Gardiner would have them here in a heartbeat if you thought otherwise." She glanced at the girls, "That is, if the girls were not here in a moment themselves." She looked back at Madeline, "They are entirely too sensible to risk their well-being."

Mrs. Gardiner smiled. "I agree with that assessment."

"But are they anyone I might know?" Mrs. Baker was not dissuaded.

Elizabeth quirked an eyebrow. "Doubtfully, Mrs. Baker. Lady Catherine de Bourgh is my cousin's patron; she requested the company of Jane and myself whilst in London with her daughter. They are visiting her brother, Lord Matlock, and thought perhaps we would enjoy exposure to some of the London festivities we do not normally have the chance to attend."

Mrs. Baker's expression became suddenly very understanding. "It is so *kind* of the first circle to take pity upon us commoners every once in a while." Her tone was not very forgiving; the pained dignity of one oft snubbed for lack of parentage and money etched her words.

"We are fortunate," Jane replied, not having heard the undercurrent to the lady's words.

"They were quite gracious to me," Mrs. Gardiner added, "when I had tea with them day before last. They seem genuinely fond of my nieces."

Mrs. Baker relaxed a little, with a strained smile. "That is good. There is nothing worse than being the recipient of false kindness."

Elizabeth felt sorry for the lady. She wondered if there was more than offended dignity behind those words. Perhaps a heart once broken because of social standing? "They have been quite kind, truly; and it is honest. If anything, they seem to be as honest as the folk of Meryton. Perhaps because they are less likely to lose everything, should they be censored."

"Indeed," the woman concurred, sounding as if her thoughts were a hundred miles away or more. She shook herself lightly and set her mostly empty cup down. "I should be leaving; I have promised to call on a few other friends."

Once she had left, Elizabeth asked Mrs. Gardiner if she knew the cause behind the bitterness. Mrs. Gardiner shook her head, but added, "She was a few years married when I met her, and her daughter had already been born. There is no telling what secrets her heart holds, and why."

Elizabeth nodded, and kept her thoughts on the subject to herself. Poor Mrs. Baker.

* * *

William read over his aunt de Bourgh's will, and shrugged as he handed it back to Lord Matlock. "I see nothing to be concerned with," he told the older man.

"Nor do I," the viscount agreed, his feet crossed and propped up on his father's desk.

"The wording was not significantly adjusted from the original version," Matlock said. "Catherine, of course, already approved the changes – which effectively removed any potential might-bes from the document. She wants it irrefutable, for Elizabeth's sake."

"It reads as such to me," Alexander replied. "A good lawyer can argue anything; there is no way to make it ironclad against *that*. We will simply have to ensure that any potential suitor of Anne's is not desirous of more than he deserves."

"Has Anne's own will been dealt with?" William asked.

"No, it has not yet been deemed necessary," Matlock replied. "Although with another heir, it should be. I will mention it to Catherine later."

William nodded. He suspected his uncle wanted his input on the will due to the assumption he would be marrying Elizabeth, although given the recent changes to Georgiana's inheritance, perhaps he just wanted the input from that side.

His uncle confirmed his suspicions a moment later. "As one who will likely be affected by that will," Matlock tapped it as it sat on his desk, "what do you think of it, William?"

"First, it is too early to tell if I *will* be affected by it," he replied mildly. For all he had hopes … he was afraid of pushing too fast, and losing what ground he had made up these past days. "Secondly, as I said, it reads well and clear. If I were to consider myself affected by it, I would certainly not find a reason to contest it. But I have more means than most – and I would take her penniless, anyhow, and be all the richer for it."

Alexander smirked at his cousin. "Funny how falling in love changes that perspective, is it not?" William blushed and muttered something – what, not even he was sure – under his breath. Alexander laughed, and reached a lanky arm over to clap his cousin on the shoulder. "Fear not, William. I will attempt to refrain from teasing you too much in front of the lady herself."

"Thankfully," William replied grumpily. It had been too many years since Alexander had teased him so unmercifully – part, he suspected, was the same restrained, not daring to relax just yet, joy that Elizabeth was found, which William heard in half the things said by the rest of the family. Part was simply that, since assuming his father's duties five years ago, even he knew he had become far more serious than had been his wont before.

"Is that true, William?" his uncle asked, carefully not looking at him. "If she were not your cousin, I mean?"

"As I told *her*, even if she only claimed the Bennet name, and did not take the portion allotted her by that family, she would be acceptable at Pemberley, and that is all *I* care about." His voice was defiant, and he knew not why. "Georgiana would side with me, in such a case, as well."

"True," Matlock replied mildly. "Georgiana is extremely taken with Elizabeth and Jane both. While I am glad that Elizabeth *is* ours, if she were not, I suspect the whole family – bar one – would have been won over in a matter of moments."

A little bit of tension in his neck and shoulders, which William had not noticed, relaxed, and he agreed. "I told her as much, that the one who would have protested her addition to the family another way, is the one who is now her most stalwart champion." He glanced aside at Alexander, who was favouring him with a peculiar expression. He raised an eyebrow at his cousin, who merely shook his head and returned his gaze to his father.

"Were there other matters to discuss, father?" Alexander asked.

"That was the only pressing issue for the moment," Matlock replied. "Although I have received a letter from Bennet – he said a letter should arrive at your household nearly at the same time, but sent two as insurance, as well as one to Elizabeth."

"Yes," William nodded. "My household is prepared. Will my aunt be – ah – interviewing my cousin's adopted sisters?"

"I believe her intention is observation for the immediate; the girls are young yet."

"They are out in Meryton society," William replied. "The suggestion that perhaps that should not hold true in London – for their sakes – should be floated by someone other than myself."

"Ah," Matlock said in understanding. "They will be here for a very short period of time, and I believe between their aunt and our households, we should be able to prevent too much social interaction."

"I have little doubt that there will be some word of Elizabeth's stay in this household circulating; Elizabeth said it likely they would have to explain why they were not staying with their aunt, to any other visitor who might be there," William added. "She thought, and I agreed, that portraying it as a kind condescension on my aunt de Bourgh's part and a wish for companionship for Anne, would be the best option for the moment."

"You – discussed this with her?" Matlock replied. "I do not recall you –" he paused and tilted his head at his nephew. "You were not just fetching a book from the library, then." He shook his head at William, who had summoned every ounce of composure he had, and gave his uncle a level look. "You are cousins; there is no reason to hide that you were speaking with her."

"No?" William queried in return. "With every member of the family intent on teasing her about my interest, when I have only recently managed to have her talking without arguing with me, I have no reason to conceal our conversations? It is the only way I can think of to shield her and not damage the fragile accord we have managed thus far."

Both his cousin and uncle had the grace to look abashed, although his uncle came back up with a glare. "Given your acknowledged interest, it would be better for her reputation, cousin or not, if they were not *concealed* conversations."

"Her sisters were aware. Anne and I had been telling her of her father. Then Jane and Anne left, so that Elizabeth and I could speak of Wic – George." Several years' habit of referring to Wickham by his family name had not yet died. "Anne is still not entirely comfortable with the topic of George."

"It will be a while before he regains the trust he had," Matlock replied, apparently choosing to pick his battles. Sometimes the older man knew when he was outsmarted.

A wry shrug, as William stood. "I have a feeling that is not precisely the issue, but only a feeling." He tilted his head at his uncle. "Anything else, before I leave to tend other business?"

"A feeling?"

"And only a feeling," William replied firmly.

Matlock eyed his recalcitrant nephew for a moment, then shook his head. "Nothing else."

* * *

"She called? And apologized?" Elizabeth's eyes were wide in surprise. "Are you quite sure we are speaking of the same Miss Bingley?"

Mrs. Gardiner hid a smile. "Indeed we are, Lizzy. She seemed in earnest, although I admit Mr. Bingley," Mrs. Gardiner shot a look at her other niece, "seemed surprised by such a frank admission on his sister's part as I was."

"I admit to some amazement; it seems quite out of character for her," Elizabeth shook her head. "If Mr. Bingley," a second, similar look at Jane, "was caught unawares by such an admission, then perhaps it is indeed in earnest. If it were not for that, I would suspect her motives to only be her allowance and its continuation."

"Perhaps she wishes to make amends in general," Jane replied. A trace of a blush lingered on her cheeks, likely from the looks her companions were giving her every time Mr. Bingley's name was mentioned.

Elizabeth gave Jane a smile. "Perhaps, for once, I shall take your view on the matter. A frank apology to my dearest aunt goes a long way towards reducing some of my dislike of her."

"Now," Mrs. Gardiner added, "I do not know if she meant for me to inform you of her apology, although I can scarcely believe she would think otherwise. Still, knowing you are to visit for tea tomorrow, I thought you should be warned ahead of time."

"So I do not disrupt a fragile attempt at peace, you mean, with my impertinent comments?" Elizabeth replied sweetly. Her voice dripped with innocence.

Mrs. Gardiner did not roll her eyes, although Jane did. Elizabeth's expression grew pensive, and Mrs. Gardiner questioned the reason.

"It seems a very Miss Bingley move, to be apologetic and wishing to make amends, after discovering that our connections are not so very low after all. Are her motives pure? Or is she hoping to be thrown into my relatives' circle?" Elizabeth replied.

"I asked her much the same," Mrs. Gardiner replied. "She said she expected some of the acquaintance would be unavoidable in the future, and that she felt she should reconcile herself to the 'new reality' of the situation."

Jane took the opportunity to tease her sister. "She meant, I suppose, William's obvious attentions to you, dearest Lizzy. He quite danced attendance on you while she was there yesterday."

Elizabeth rolled her eyes, while trying to keep from blushing. "Or her *brother's* wishes towards *you,* given he sat in easy distance of you their entire visit."

"Perhaps both," Mrs. Gardiner interjected with slight smile.

The girls glanced at each other and replied in tandem. "Perhaps."

"I should check on the children," Mrs. Gardiner added. "Do either of you wish to join me?"

Both readily assented, and followed Mrs. Gardiner to attend to their cousins.

* * *

Word that the Matlocks hosted the Bennet girls as friends to their niece spread in the hypergeometric fashion that gossip does. By the time it reached Caroline, in a parlour half way across London, she was surprised. It was a plausible reason, and she was grateful to have a chance to start her campaign early.

"Are these Miss Bennets being spoken of as staying with the Matlocks the same hoyden, country nobodies you had the misfortune to meet in Hertfordshire, Miss Bingley?" her host asked. "Scandalous, to think they would fabricate such a report."

"It is not a fabricated report. I visited Miss Bennet and Miss Elizabeth at the Matlocks' yesterday," Caroline replied. "They are to visit for tea, tomorrow."

Her host, Miss Bradshaw, arched an eyebrow. "You have been introduced to Mr. Darcy's aunt?"

"His uncle, Lord Matlock, was in attendance as well," Caroline replied. "They are quite welcoming to the Miss Bennets, and pleased to treat them as family."

"You sound far less censuring of them than you did three months ago," Miss Bradshaw replied. "Have they improved in essentials, after being exposed to such personages?"

Caroline gave a half smile. "In essentials, I believe they are much as they ever were. Miss Bennet is a good, sweet kind of girl. I look forward to knowing her better. Her sister, Miss Elizabeth, improves upon acquaintance."

Miss Bradshaw nodded. "Particularly when it allows one to make the acquaintance of Mr. Darcy's family."

Caroline hid a wince. Would that she had held her tongue better, in her relief at returning to London in late November! Her self-appointed task of easing Miss Elizabeth's entrance into Society as the younger de Bourgh sister would be off to a better start. "I am pleased with that acquaintance, indeed," she replied. "However, given the large number of guests at the time, I was unable to speak above a few words to anyone but Miss Bennet."

"Large number of guests?" Miss Bradshaw was surprised.

"Indeed. Most of the family has gathered in London, and Mr. Bennet apparently came to ensure his daughters' comfort. It was quite the merry party," Caroline replied. "I believe at least two of the guests departed in the latter part of the day."

Miss Bradshaw frowned. "Most of the family has gathered in London? Including the de Bourghs?" She gave Caroline a sideways glance. "Lady Catherine corresponds frequently with my mother, and has often told Momma about her plans for Miss de Bourgh and Mr. Darcy. Momma has long thought that perhaps she was warning me off of her nephew. Do you think it is possible Lady Catherine and Miss de Bourgh have come to London to announce her engagement to Mr. Darcy?"

Caroline shook her head. "I saw no indication of such an announcement forthcoming." *Not with the elder Miss de Bourgh, at least,* she thought with a touch of disappointment. She tilted her head. "Perhaps Lady Catherine has determined Mr. Darcy will not offer for his cousin, and intends to encourage him by giving Miss de Bourgh a London Season."

Miss Bradshaw made a noise of neither agreement nor disagreement. "With your *particular* acquaintance with their guests, are you likely to be given an invitation to their first ball of the Season?"

Knowing Miss Bradshaw as she did, Caroline suspected she was angling for an invitation herself. "The idea was not raised with me while I visited, although there is still plenty of time yet," she replied. "Perhaps your mother's own acquaintance with Lady Catherine will prove advantageous for your own attendance?"

The slightly younger girl's eyes brightened. "That is an excellent suggestion, my dear Miss Bingley. I thank you for the thought."

Another acquaintance of Miss Bradshaw's was announced, and Caroline found herself repeating much the same information about the Bennets as she had spoken previously. The first-hand confirmation of the report – and a dispelling of some of the distortions already creeping into the story – quieted some of the girl's more vicious comments. Caroline was not the only lady of the *Ton* with hopes regarding Mr. Darcy. Miss Dreyham was again distressed upon hearing of the Miss Bennets' previous acquaintance with Mr. Darcy, and there was little Caroline could do to quiet her. At length, she owned it was time to leave, and did so, hoping she had done more good than harm.

Twenty-Eight

Elizabeth knocked quietly on Anne's door, and her elder sister cracked the door to peek out. "Oh, it is you," she said, and opened the door to let Elizabeth in.

They settled on the edge of the bed. "Jane retired for the evening?" Anne asked.

"Quite. I think she wishes to meditate on the potential reversal of her fortunes in love," Elizabeth replied with a half-smile. "Miss Bingley apologized to our Aunt Gardiner, in front of her brother, and took her brother by surprise, from Aunt's retelling of it." A shrug as Elizabeth leaned back slightly onto her hands. "I think she is hopeful that, with his sister's gracious approval," a slight sarcasm she could not suppress, "Mr. Bingley will find it appropriate to finish his pursuit."

"He is a handsome man, charming and well-tempered," Anne replied. She smiled slightly. "Nor is he without fortune, which can only enhance his character."

Elizabeth laughed. "I said nearly as much to her in October." Then she sighed. "I only hope she is not due a second disappointment."

"It is in Mr. Bingley's hands, to be sure," Anne replied. "But one hopes he has more sense than to offend an Earl's extended family by disappointing one of their daughters."

A rueful laugh. "Indeed," Elizabeth replied. "Miss Bingley may find that particularly offensive herself, which should only encourage the man."

A sleepy silence reigned for a few moments, which Elizabeth tentatively broke. "Why are you so skittish about even talking about George?"

Anne's immediate reply was a heavy sigh, and to mirror Elizabeth's half-leaning back posture. She spoke after a moment, words short and somewhat halting. "I never fancied William, as a girl. He is far too clever by half for me, always was. He was -- *is* -- more brother than cousin, to be honest. Richard I adore, but his head has always been turned by women prettier than I, and I would be a fool to think at our age he is likely to change, to appreciate someone who is quieter and less enthusiastic about company than he is." She paused. "George was the only one who paid me any court, you know. I never had a Season, more because I never wished for one. But friends of Mother's and Father's, who kept up their acquaintance with our family, and all our extended family, would often visit, for Mother enjoys company. Many of them brought their sons, particularly their second sons, hoping I would fall in love with them or they me. And George ... George remains the only one who has ever paid me any court, or hinted in any way, that I might be suitable."

She leaned her head on Elizabeth's shoulder. "And then he went to university, with William, and slowly sank further and further, and then he all but disappeared from view. And then resurfaced, injuring Georgiana in the process. I know it was accident. I know what they have both said of late, but at the time, I was ... a part of me was *jealous* that he would, after all, do the same as all other men of my acquaintance, and chase after the pretty one."

Elizabeth remained silent for a moment, her head resting against her sister's. "I have always been *envious* of Jane, for she is easily five times prettier than I. I have always been reminded of it at every turn.

To be honest, I cannot understand William's interest in me, with Jane there in front of him just as often as I was."

"Men are a puzzle, are they not?" Anne replied with a half-laugh.

"Indeed. Confusing, confounding, and troublesome," Elizabeth replied, with a mix of amusement and exasperation in her voice. Another sleepy silence descended, which Elizabeth broke. "Are you at all thinking that George may be suitable, now?"

Anne sighed. "I do not know. He has been redeemed, somewhat. Only time will tell, and there are so many unknowns at the moment I barely know which way to turn." She pulled away from Elizabeth and brushed a lock of Elizabeth's hair back from her face. "I cannot even imagine how confused you are, at the moment, if I am this bewildered."

Elizabeth smiled slightly. "I am attempting to not think deeply on any given topic outside of a book or play at the moment. I fear if I give too much thought to any of it, I shall have to commit myself to Bedlam. Then what would befall us all?"

Anne giggled. "William would probably charge in on a white steed to rescue you, and be committed himself."

Elizabeth laughed. "That would be a sight to behold. I am almost tempted to see how accurate your depiction of the situation would be."

"Lizzy!" Anne cried, even as she laughed harder. "You will not!"

Elizabeth giggled. "No, indeed. *Mére* would be very put out with me, no doubt. And you have never seen Jane lose her temper."

"Dear, sweet Jane has a temper that even *you* fear?" Anne asked laughingly. "I never thought I would see our courageous Elizabeth cowed by anyone."

"We all must have our fears," Elizabeth mock-sagely replied.

"Indeed," came the laughing reply.

* * *

While Bingley did not customarily attend his sister while she welcomed guests, he would not have missed this particular tea for the world. *Jane* was to be here, after all, and Miss Elizabeth. He nearly expected Darcy to show up unannounced mid-morning for "business," but instead received a note that the Bennets had arrived at his townhouse, and he may need an escape route for tea. Bingley laughed as he penned a (for him) clear reply inviting him over.

Darcy did arrive half an hour before Jane and Miss Elizabeth, and Bingley found himself hard-pressed to keep from laughing. For a tea invitation, it was to be rather crowded: himself, Caroline, Louisa, Hurst, Darcy, Jane and Miss Elizabeth. Thankfully, Caroline never did anything by halves; there should be plenty extra even with extra guests.

Jane and Miss Elizabeth arrived a few minutes early, while Bingley and Darcy were in Bingley's study discussing a bit of news from the paper. As soon as the servant informed them of the girls' arrival, they made haste down to the parlour that Caroline had selected that morning. The girls were just settling in with Caroline and Louisa. Hurst, it appeared, would arrive shortly.

"Have my parents and sisters arrived in London yet?" Jane asked Darcy after the polite how-fare-you's were completed.

"Yes, indeed," Darcy replied. "Mrs. Bennet seems to be quite enthusiastic to be in London, and Mr. Bennet had to remind her of her plan to rest prior to dinner with the Matlocks tonight. She was quite aflutter to see you and Elizabeth."

"Yes, Mrs. Bennet does seem to be rather enthusiastic about certain topics," Bingley replied drolly as Jane thanked Darcy for the update.

Darcy laughed at Bingley's comment, and Bingley suppressed a smirk at the fact that Darcy and Miss Elizabeth glanced at each other. Jane's eyes had flicked in her sister's direction, and she seemed pleased by the interaction she saw, particularly after, a bit of teasing between the twain, Miss Elizabeth consented to play at the pianoforte. "But only," she said, "the one piece you have so *particularly* requested, William, if Miss Bingley does not mind. Tea is more about *talking* than *performing*."

Darcy affected a slightly injured air. "I was specifically tasked by Georgina to hear how you are getting on with the piece; my agreement was requisite for my leaving the house without her."

Caroline was faintly shaking her head in disbelief, but said to Miss Elizabeth, "I have no objections. We can surely not disappoint Mr. Darcy." Bingley felt a faint sense of déjà vu, and caught the measuring look between the two girls. Darcy, it seemed, was also recalling something of import. The momentary tension passed, and Caroline gave Miss Elizabeth a genuine smile. "Truly, I have no objections." Miss Elizabeth eyed Caroline a moment longer then nodded, and, with Darcy at her heels, opened the pianoforte and sorted through the music to find the piece Darcy had requested.

Jane sat facing the pianoforte, and Bingley took advantage of her sister's relocation to relocate himself. "They will do well together, I think," Bingley said quietly, for Jane's ear alone.

She glanced at him. "So I hope," she replied, just as quietly. "I have worried for her, these past days. Although I am afraid of how … rapidly their friendship has progressed. I found myself giving her similar advice as she had given me in the fall, to have patience."

Bingley suppressed the wince. It was, truly, not his fault, and yet he could not assuage the guilt he felt at having let his sister manipulate him as she had. He had suspected she wished him to reconsider Jane's suitability, and Darcy had spoken enough to lend merit to the view. But Caroline *had* injured them both by stooping to such unscrupulous behaviour to enforce the separation. "Darcy is not as eager to please his family as I am," he finally replied, under the beginning strains of Miss Elizabeth's playing. "It is not my place to say this, but he always meant to defy his family regarding her, if necessity demanded it of him. It is fortunate that such will no longer be necessary, but it would not have swayed him regardless." Bingley smiled ruefully. "He once all but said my easy-going nature was a detriment. In this case, I believe he was more correct than any of us allowed."

Jane's expression turned thoughtful, and Bingley hoped that admission would not harm his suit. "You were doing your duty to your sister, and family must come first," Jane said, even more softly. "I of anyone understand that. I do not wish to come between you and her."

"You will not," Bingley replied. It was all he had to not ask her then and there.

Jane glanced up at him, and smiled, and Bingley felt some of the anxious tension leave. She believed him, and thought no less of him. She settled ever so slightly back, relaxing a tiny amount, her attention back on her sister and Darcy. Bingley had little attention to spare for Miss Elizabeth's playing, but what he listened to -- as mirrored in Jane's delight in it -- was well played indeed. He pondered asking her before they left today, but decided against it. *I of anyone understand that.* Jane would insist on staying with Miss Elizabeth until the chaos resolved. Perhaps she would allow him to pay court, instead? Yes, that may work. Mr. Bennet currently resided in Town, it would be almost no effort at all to make such a request of him -- provided Jane allowed it.

William felt Jane's eyes on them as he assisted Elizabeth in finding the piece Georgiana had so helpfully tasked him with hearing her play. "Your sister is worried," he said in an undertone.

"She has reason to be," Elizabeth replied. She glanced at him under her eyelashes. "She gave me advice I distinctly recall giving her in the fall."

William felt hesitant at requesting clarification as to what advice that might be, and Elizabeth began to play, her eyes on the music. Mostly. "They are talking; good," she said.

William smiled at that. "No doubt about her concerns for you," he said.

"Be that as it may, I am hopeful that Mr. Bingley will not be long from the point of expressing his interest. She has waited long enough for encouragement."

"Would she accept?"

Elizabeth bit her lip, focusing on the music. "If she thought he would be willing to wait until the whirlwind I appear to be caught in has set me down on steady ground, yes."

"Ah," William said, understanding the concern. "She -- you both -- wonder if he will be persuaded to delay again?"

"Quite," Elizabeth sighed. He suppressed the desire to comfort her physically, if only because it might disrupt her playing.

"I have offered my encouragement," he replied. "From what I have seen thus far this evening, his sister has as well. I think he is only waiting for a moment of time. Would courtship, you think, be enough of a delay and an encouragement, for her? I will suggest it to him, if he has not come to that idea himself."

Elizabeth inclined her head. "Indeed, that is possible."

They fell silent for a moment, as she worked through the fingering on a trickier passage. "And how soon is too soon for me to hope?" he asked just loud enough for her to hear him.

She nearly fumbled her fingering, and did not immediately reply. "You are certainly part of the whirlwind," she said finally.

"For good or for ill?"

"I think you and Jane are the reasons I still know which way is up."

It was not a declaration of love, or even of friendship, but in a way, it was infinitely more important. She *trusted* him. "If the whirlwind seems likely to set you down askew, I will do my best to catch you."

She smiled, and did not reply for the piece was nearly finished. The occupants of the room applauded. "And your report to Georgiana?" she teased loudly enough for others to hear.

"Your progress is exemplary, of course," he smiled back.

"In truth," she said more quietly, "she had a few suggestions that, over the last few days, I have indeed practiced, when I have had time. She is quite insightful when it comes to the pianoforte."

William rose from the bench and offered her a hand up. "She has been playing since she was quite young, and there are days when she would forget her books in favour of her music."

"And I was apt to forgot my music in favour of my books," Elizabeth laughed, as she stood. William, loathe to relinquish her quite yet, escorted her to the sofa to sit across from her sister.

Miss Bingley had seated herself on the other side of her brother, and now that both Bennets were seated and talking, relayed the import of her conversation with Miss Bradshaw and Miss Dreyham the day before. William shrugged helplessly. "At least we had agreed on the story beforehand, Elizabeth, Jane," he offered.

"Indeed," Jane fretted. She glanced at Elizabeth, eyes worried.

"I do not believe there is any reason to fret, although I will pass the information on to *mére* and Lord Matlock," Elizabeth soothed. "We knew it was likely to occur, and the story is reasonable enough."

"You think we are overly paranoid," William retorted.

"Well, there is that," Elizabeth admitted. "But you have your reasons, and while I do not agree, I am pragmatic enough to agree that precautions are reasonable, perhaps necessary. Or I would not have devised a reasonable, fairly truthful, story in the first place."

Louisa and Hurst, to whom Bingley had, with William's reluctant approval, relayed the information to, under strict confidence, requested to know the story being given out for the moment, should they be placed in a position where it may be necessary. Jane filled them in, and Bingley nodded approval as he listened.

Hurst snorted his admiration. "Just enough *suggestion* of upper-class snobbery and condescension to make it believable, without actually stating anything of the sort. You are a devious one, Miss Elizabeth."

She laughed, and disclaimed any sort of praise. William simply grinned, knowing that she had experienced such firsthand, not just from himself, and that, from a simplistic viewpoint, it was a reasonably framed story. The merchant class wives and debutantes would certainly consider it valid.

Miss Bingley, however, teasingly asked about this ball she had heard mentioned. Elizabeth grimaced while Jane hid a smile. "I will be introduced as a de Bourgh then," Elizabeth replied, "although not before. And a new gown, of *course*, simply must be had."

"Poor Lizzy," Jane reached over to pat her hand. "So put upon, having to go shopping."

"The company of my cousin's wife was no issue, I hope?" William asked.

"No, indeed, I am quite taken with Cassandra. She is a lovely lady," Elizabeth replied.

Miss Bingley shook her head. "Only you, Miss Eliza, would complain however good-naturedly about a shopping trip with the Countess and Viscountess."

Elizabeth laughed. "Yes, I am certainly less *fashionable* than most, for I prefer a walk in the park to a walk down Bond Street."

William *almost* said she was perfectly welcome to do both, to the point of bankrupting him, but squelched the inclination in time.

At length, Elizabeth and Jane admitted they were needed at Matlock House prior to their family descending *en mass* on the Fitzwilliams. "Did our uncle leave a carriage with you?" William asked Elizabeth as they made their way into the entry hall. Miss Bingley had let her brother persuade her that she need not see her guests to the door personally; he and William would attend that duty. Elizabeth and William gave the other pair a bit of space.

"Yes, he did," she smiled up at him. "And you," she added, "do need to return to your townhouse to ensure my father and mother, and sisters, make it to Matlock House, rather than following me there immediately. And do not forget Georgiana!"

He grinned. "As you wish."

She glanced over her shoulder to see Bingley and Jane conversing closely. She looked back up at him, her eyes serious. "Truly, I do not need your assistance to land on my feet when stepping out of a carriage in broad daylight. I will need you, and Jane, tonight."

He nodded, and, unable to help himself, brushed a curl away from her face. She smiled. "Until later, then."

"Until later," he agreed, before leading her out the door and down the steps to the carriage that lingered in front of the Bingleys' townhouse, and bore his uncle's markings. He made sure to be as gallant as absolutely possible while handing Elizabeth into the carriage, and was still considering joining them for the trip when Bingley and Jane appeared and Bingley handed Jane into the carriage. Elizabeth rather pointedly looked at the door, and William could not help but grin in response. "As you wish," he said, shutting it, and stepping back, waved at the coachman that the girls were ready.

"So?" he asked Bingley, as they shut the front door behind them.

"She has reservations, mostly about her sister, for which I cannot fault her," Bingley replied. "But I will ask the favour of perhaps you assisting me in finding a moment to ask Mr. Bennet tonight, if I may court her, now that I have her permission."

"Excellent!" William cried. "We had thought to suggest it. Elizabeth is aware of Jane's concern, of course. *She* will be pleased."

Bingley laughed. "I am glad to know you are pleased, my friend. And you?"

William shrugged. "She trusts me, which is a treasure in its own right. There is plenty of time, and I would not wish to rush her headlong."

Bingley smiled. "Hope. I had not thought either of us would know the meaning of the word even a month ago."

"Indeed."

Twenty-Nine

"Country manners? I find them charming!" Darcy could hear
Bingley's voice echo in his ears from that first night in Meryton. The
boisterous Mrs. Bennet and her two youngest daughters descended in a
tumult from their carriage just as Darcy and Georgiana cleared the exit
of their own carriage. The staid Miss Mary glanced out of the second
carriage cautiously before she stepped down a moment later. He
wondered if she had been blocked in a carriage before by her
gregarious mother and sisters failing to clear the exit before going into
conversation with another party. Mr. Bennet, who had ridden with
Darcy and Georgiana, stepped in to move his lady and daughters along
from the second carriage and towards the entry of Matlock House.

He entered before the Bennets, as required by status and
familiarity, but with an ear on the chattering. "Lord Matlock, Lady
Matlock, may I present Mr. and Mrs. Bennet?" Mr. Bennet introduced
his daughters, as Jane and Elizabeth circled over to their father. Those
introductions made, Elizabeth tugged on Mrs. Bennet's arm, and with a
trepidatious glance at Mr. Bennet, led her to Aunt Catherine. Jane
walked along Mrs. Bennet's other side, her arm linked as well. Darcy
felt Elizabeth's worry and concern from across the room, but felt he
could not yet intrude.

"Did Lizzy not find us the handsomest cousins, Kitty?" he heard
Miss Lydia say at a volume that appeared to pass as her version of
discretion. Aunt Sarah's expression flickered in what appeared to be
more amusement than distress.

"And a Colonel, no less!" Miss Kitty replied, more muted but still audible. Darcy suppressed a smirk and the temptation to see if Richard had overheard. Aunt Sarah moved towards the girls, Cassandra in tow, and started a general discussion on fashion. Miss Lydia's attention was quite captured from discussing the 'handsomest cousins.' He noted that Miss Kitty's attention kept wandering in the direction of her next older sister, or, perhaps, that sister's conversation partners.

Richard and Alexander were currently occupied with Miss Mary. From the snippets of conversation Darcy could overhear, it appeared that she read more than the sermons she liked to quote. He wondered if this was a recent change. Still, both Fitzwilliams enjoyed discussing politics and national events, *and* had the first-hand experience and knowledge to assist Miss Mary in understanding some of the more complex issues she broached.

True, the younger Bennets lacked the refinement often found in his circle, a refinement typically grafted on during schooling. They seemed little versed in filtering their conversation based upon the company. Aside from that, however, the Bennets were not unlike his own Fitzwilliam relations, effusive and passionate under the veneer of formality. Artifice was as limited in Mrs. Bennet as it was in Elizabeth, albeit solely directed at ensuring her and her daughters' continued security.

A glance in Elizabeth's direction showed two characteristically verbose women stumbling over even the slightest of civilities. "Was it wise," Uncle Randall quietly asked, "to insist on this first meeting between the ladies occur in such an extended familial gathering?"

Mr. Bennet shrugged, a quick, almost implied gesture. "Is any of this wise?" he replied. He shook his head. "Of the options, this seemed to be the best at controlling my Fanny's response." With a slight glance at Darcy, he added, tone sardonic, "She has discretion enough to not intentionally insult the daughter of a peer." Darcy flushed at the slight scolding, perhaps only in his mind.

His uncle raised an eyebrow at the comment. "Your younger girls have not had explicit schooling, have they?"

Bennet shook his head. "None of the girls have been to school, nor did we take on a governess. I had my own intentions with education, and I endeavoured to ensure they gained at least a modicum of learning." He pursed his lips. "I confess, however, as I am not artistically or musically inclined, the girls have been taught the history of those subjects, but little in the way of execution." He frowned, apparently as a thought occurred to him, but he did not voice it.

"Your own intentions with education, sir?" Darcy asked.

"Indeed. I was a younger son, you know – or perhaps you do not." Bennet paused to muse over that point. "Not being current or particularly relevant gossip, it is unlikely to have been a topic raised during your short stay in Hertfordshire." He smiled wryly. "Country memories may be long, but they can be easily distracted when excited."

Uncle Randall shared that smile. "If what my son and nephew have relayed to me is accurate, the area was quite beside itself between the regiment and my nephew's friend moving into the area."

"Quite," Bennet agreed. "Many of the county's boys have gone to war, and not enough have returned. But my own aspirations were foiled by an elder brother who felt he was called to other duties, namely as a missionary. After my own father passed, the entail required one of us to accept that duty. My brother's work could not be as easily set aside as my own, and he disowned himself. My more advanced studies at university were set aside for the more gentlemanly pursuits of managing a small estate."

"Why not select a steward and continue those studies?" Darcy asked. He certainly had considered doing such himself. But for Georgiana's age and Aunt Catherine's manoeuvrings to take over Pemberley in the wake of his father's death, he thought it likely he would have followed through. Indeed, he considered it possible once Georgiana no longer required his chaperonage, provided Elizabeth was amendable to his pursuit of scholarly endeavours.

"Were it a larger estate, perhaps," Bennet allowed. "The cost of a decent steward, living in London, and the continual upkeep of necessary terms with university, however, would have quite prevented me from marrying and attempting to cut off the entail." He glanced at his wife. "I have maintained some of the contacts I made at the time, and keep abreast of advances in my fields of interest. My contributions, however, are limited to correspondence-driven musings with those actively engaged in furthering our knowledge of the natural world."

"And five daughters," Uncle Randall noted.

A true smile on Bennet's face, however fleeting. "Yes, five wonderful daughters. I may tease the younger three about being silly, but it is as much their age as anything, I believe."

"They will need more discretion," Uncle Randall replied. "And soon, I fear."

Bennet frowned, while Darcy winced. "For Lizzy's sake, I know. They will not have the luxury Lizzy and Jane did in that regard, for all those two did not need it."

"What of your brother?" Darcy asked.

"Malaria, around the time Mary was born," Bennet replied. "A brother missionary sent the letter along with most of his effects. The local lady he was betrothed to kept a few items for remembrance." Bennet's gaze wandered over to his middle daughter. "I have been debating giving Mary his letters, journal, and Bible. She seems the most likely to follow that path, and perhaps it would aid her decisions."

Movement caught their attention. The two mothers appeared to have come to sufficient accord to move to a settee, and Aunt Sarah gestured for minimal refreshments to be brought 'round. Bennet and Uncle Randall moved to sit opposite the ladies. Darcy could see a calculating expression on his aunt's face as she watched each member of the party in turn – not even excepting himself or her own sons. When he caught her gaze, she gave him a brief smile before moving to her next observance. Elizabeth retreated from the settee after a moment, moving to Darcy's side. Jane remained with her mother.

"How do you fare?" he asked in as much an undertone as he could manage.

"Well enough, I suppose," she replied in kind. "I left to avoid being treated to a double dose of childhood stories."

"It would be interesting to hear how you differed between households," Darcy replied.

"I know enough of Mama's stories about me," Elizabeth returned. "I need not hear their telling again. It would be any that *mère* may have which would be of interest to me." She glanced around the room, much like Aunt Sarah had. Her gaze settled on her second youngest sister. "Kitty looks quite out of her depth, and aware of it."

"I noticed she has been glancing the way of my cousins frequently."

"She is unused to Mary being more of notice than she is, and Lydia is oblivious." Elizabeth sounded almost amused. "Here is her first exposure to the idea that learning may be of more benefit than a pretty face."

"That certainly depends on the individuals involved," Darcy grumbled. "Too many of my cohort would prefer a lady who simpers thoughtless agreements, and have quite spoiled the ladies of the Ton in that regard."

Elizabeth snickered quietly. "Then my impertinent manners shall garner me as much praise as they did in Hertfordshire?"

Darcy attempted to suppress the blush. "You heard her?"

"Indeed," Elizabeth replied, half-smiling. "She did not even wait for the door to shut."

"I wonder at your tolerance earlier."

"She has apologized to my Aunt Gardiner," Elizabeth shrugged. "Jane should like to have peace if not friendship with her. Between the two, there is reason enough to allow her time to pay off arrears of civility."

"That would be twice you have granted leniency where I would be hard-pressed to do so. It is fortunate you do not possess my weakness of temperament," Darcy replied.

Elizabeth's eyes danced. "The weakness you profess to own, or the ones known to all your friends and relations?"

"I dare say the company of my most obvious and vexing weakness would render the boredom of a dreary Sunday afternoon in my own house irrelevant indeed," Darcy replied airily, but with a pointed look at his companion. Her answering blush and flummoxed expression pleased him. He enjoyed besting her occasionally, although perhaps it was a mite unfair to do so at the moment. He relented – just a smidgeon – and owned, "If we held a similar *weakness* of temper, you would not be quite so friendly with me. So it is fortunate for *me*."

Dinner was announced before Elizabeth could respond, and Darcy offered his arm to escort her in. While she was not subdued for the remainder of the evening, Darcy noted a touch of introspection in her expression which not even the lively conversation between *all* her sisters removed.

After dinner, Darcy watched as Elizabeth circulated among the various groupings which had formed and mostly held over the evening. Miss Kitty had drifted to the Fitzwilliam scions and Mary. She appeared to be asking simple, but pertinent questions. Anne and Miss Lydia settled in with Aunt Sarah and Cassandra. Darcy was amused to note that Anne had as many questions about fashion as Miss Lydia did, until he recollected that Anne's semi-self-imposed seclusion from society left her as out-of-touch with the *Ton* as Miss Lydia would be.

The evening wound down, and the guests, himself included, gathered at the door. The Bennets entered the carriage after a controlled goodbye to their hosts and a flurry of hugs and farewells to Jane and Elizabeth. Their carriage left, headed for Darcy's townhouse. Georgiana was already handed into his own, while their family returned to the house, but Darcy lingered to the side to catch Elizabeth's attention momentarily. She stepped to his side, while Jane engaged the seated Georgiana in conversation to provide them a modicum of privacy.

"Thank you," she said quietly.

"I did more to discompose you than I did to keep you upright," he replied, now a bit regretful for the flirtation earlier.

She shook her head and smiled briefly. "We do not share the same weaknesses of temperament," she replied, looking up to catch his eyes. "It is quite fortunate for *me,* as well. Good night, William." With that, she turned to the house, and Jane followed. Were he less giddy from her words, he might even think to be vexed by her leaving so quickly or Georgiana's ill-concealed smirk the entire way home.

Thirty

After a morning of being fitted for her ball gown, Elizabeth felt she was perfectly within her rights to visit the Gardiners early. She and Jane brought along clothing for the evening, as they were to dine there, as well.

The servants had taken their minimal luggage upstairs while Mrs. Gardiner led the way to the nursery to visit the children. "Was it truly so bad, Lizzy?" Mrs. Gardiner queried. She thought she was concealing her frustration better than *that*.

"Indeed, it was not," Jane replied as Elizabeth groaned theatrically.

"Perhaps not for you, dearest sister," Elizabeth grumbled. "But I felt like the prize peacock being primped for display."

Mrs. Gardiner laughed. "Well, that would not be far from the truth, either, my dear. Are you due back before dinner?"

"No," the girls replied together.

"*Mère* said we were free to spend the afternoon visiting with our family," Elizabeth expanded. "She and Anne have some legal business to review with Lord Matlock regarding Rosings."

"Fortunate for me, for I have missed my favourite nieces," replied Mrs. Gardiner, "but I do hope it is not too onerous a task."

"I believe it was a routine enough task. She did not seem troubled by it," Elizabeth shrugged.

"Mr. Bingley and Mr. Darcy are invited to dine tonight, are they not?" Jane asked, as they settled in with the children. Elizabeth was promptly swarmed for hugs and kisses, and a book produced for her to read.

"Yes, Mr. Bingley and his sister, and Mr. Darcy and *his* sister, are invited." Mrs. Gardiner asked. "Several of our friends are expected to join us."

"The usual suspects?" Elizabeth asked, between paragraphs being read off.

"Yes," Mrs. Gardiner chuckled.

The afternoon was spent in pleasant conversation and minor tasks related to preparing for the dinner. Jane and Elizabeth retired to their borrowed room to prepare with the assistance of their aunt's maid. If the maid noticed more effort on either girl's part to prepare for one of these dinners, she kindly forbore mentioning it.

Mrs. Gardiner's guests, including the Darcys and Bingleys, all arrived surprisingly promptly. Based on the *looks* Mrs. Gardiner and the girls received when their friends observed the tall form of Mr. Darcy enter with his sister, followed by the slighter Mr. Bingley and *his* sister, the gossip was already at work in their circle, as well.

With her guests announced, Mrs. Gardiner carried out the task of introducing the Darcys and Bingleys to their friends. Elizabeth noted with interest at how many faces carefully blanked as Miss Bingley was introduced to them. She was, on the whole, received with a brittle, icy politeness by all of the women, and distant wariness by the gentlemen. None of those present claimed a previous acquaintance, and Elizabeth wondered just how much damage Miss Bingley had caused the

Bingley name. She hoped that, should Jane assume the name, it was easily resolved.

As soon as the introductions were completed, William and Georgiana gravitated to Elizabeth's side. "Elizabeth," Georgiana cried, as she enthusiastically hugged her. "I had anticipated you seeing at my aunt's first."

Elizabeth laughed. "Instead of mine, indeed," she agreed. "Given I am at fault for Jane's desertion of our aunt's company this past fortnight or so, we felt it only fair she gain the temporary company of two nieces instead of one."

William's greeting of her was more circumspect than it had been of late, friendly and solicitous, but no more. Elizabeth felt the difference keenly, and chastised herself for it. She answered in kind, with a smile just for him. While they could not banter as they would in a family gathering, William remained near her and his sister. Mr. Gardiner and a friend of his, Mr. Rothschild, joined them, and the group chatted about their overlapping business pursuits and journeying abroad. Elizabeth listened attentively, asking questions to draw out better descriptions of places she had only read about.

Miss Bingley and Mr. Bingley stood with Jane near the pianoforte. Mrs. Gardiner joined that group, and what Elizabeth could overhear, they were discussing music. The glances being thrown in that direction were politely curious about, if Elizabeth had to guess, the friendliness of the conversation.

When dinner was announced, William offered to escort both Georgiana and Elizabeth to the table, and Elizabeth accepted his arm. Mrs. Gardiner had chosen to allow everyone to sit as they felt comfortable, and thus Elizabeth found herself seated with William on one side, an older couple of Mr. Gardiner's acquaintance on her other, and the Bingleys, with Jane, across. Jane sat to her uncle's side. The dinner itself was excellent, and the conversation generally jovial. Miss Bingley's behaviour was more akin to that when she had been entertaining an ill Jane in her room at Netherfield than any time Elizabeth had ever seen her. She hoped it was less studied than it had been previously.

Between courses, Miss Bingley spoke with Elizabeth. "How often did you come to London to stay here, Miss Elizabeth?"

"Generally a few fortnights at a time, sometimes during the Season, sometimes the Little Season," Elizabeth responded. "Given the varied contacts my aunt and uncle have, from their various pursuits, Jane and I often found as much to learn during these dinner parties as we could from books at home. We rarely stayed at the same time, though."

"I find I miss town when I am staying in the country," Miss Bingley said. "The society lends itself to more variation."

It was a far politer version of what she had once opined in the parlour at Netherfield, and without Mrs. Bennet to interrupt, Elizabeth felt better able to respond. "I recall you saying as much previously, yes. I still stand by my comment that, as people change and grow, the individuals themselves allow for much variation, albeit perhaps on a slower timeframe. But even in town, society is only part of the charms of a given location. Here, there are plays and museums, and gardens beyond compare. I have spent many hours in them, whenever my aunt or uncle could spare the time themselves, experiencing these."

"To be sure," Miss Bingley laughed. "There are many fashionable places to be seen at in London."

Elizabeth shook her head and smiled. "The whims of fashion have rarely held my attention. The world is simply too fascinating for me to ignore."

Miss Bingley raised an eyebrow. "I once thought you were the sort to run off with gypsies. But perhaps you would be more tempted by the bluestockings."

Elizabeth grinned in self-deprecation. "My mother often claimed that, although I only recall one incident where I tried to go with the gypsies."

"Twice," Jane replied, her expression suddenly clouded. "It was twice, as I recall, and you were insisting they had to help you find something." Elizabeth noted Mrs. Gardiner's expression flicker in surprise and then concern, even as William stiffened at her side.

She glanced at him, and he met her eyes, dark eyes worried. "It is nothing," he said in an undertone, and she nodded. *Nothing for the dinner table*, at least. Miss Bingley looked uncomfortable and lapsed into silence. Georgiana, giving curious glances at her brother and Jane, asked her about the music piece she had been working on when last they saw her. Elizabeth understood how much effort that took on Georgiana's part, and gave the younger girl an encouraging smile.

After the minor discomfort, the rest of the dinner passed peacefully and unremarkably. A delectable dessert followed the excellent spread, and before long, the dinner ended. The gentlemen broke off to her uncle's study, and she and the other ladies returned to the parlour. The separation was brief, and Mrs. Gardiner set out a few games for those interested.

William and Mr. Rothschild continued what seemed to be a potentially profitable conversation while they played a game of whist with Elizabeth and Georgiana until the latter gentleman regretfully announced he was needed at home. That gentleman's exit prompted the remaining guests, barring the Bingleys and Darcys, to depart.

Once the last uninvolved, even peripherally, party left, Elizabeth sought her aunt's attention. "What about gypsies, Aunt? Jane's comment made you think of something."

Mrs. Gardiner gave her a long look. "It was more than twice, although I am unsurprised neither of you remember that. The last time you tried to slip off with the gypsies, you were six or seven, actually, and you could not remember why you wanted to go with them."

Elizabeth frowned. "I just remember some urgency, that I had lost something and they knew where it might be."

Mrs. Gardiner nodded, looking thoughtful.

"Ma'am?" William asked, drawing Mrs. Gardiner's attention. "Do you have any ideas why that may be?"

The lady sighed. "The same thought I had a week ago, and lost in my surprise at an unexpected visit." Elizabeth noticed she did not quite glance in the Bingleys' direction. "There are several tinkers who assist with the orphanage as they can. All of them pass through briefly, but they keep tabs on their ... favourites, insofar as possible. One in particular always asks after Lizzy. I know that he lived primarily in London for a few years after Lizzy came to us, rather than traveling. He would not speak of why he did not rejoin his family. I believe he found another group to travel with, eventually, and now he typically only stops by in late August."

"You believe he may have more information?" Elizabeth asked.

"It certainly seems likely," William replied. "How soon could you ask him?" he queried.

"August," Mrs. Gardiner answered firmly. "I do not know his accustomed routes or where he may be otherwise. Even if I am traveling, I can leave correspondence for him at the orphanage. The head will ensure he gets it. He is learned enough to assist, however briefly, with the children's letters, so I have no qualms on that score. Whether he is willing to answer is another story altogether."

William nodded and Elizabeth sighed. "If he does, however, it seems unlikely he is a threat," she said. "So there is at least little to fret about in that regard."

"That does not remove the possibility," Mr. Gardiner cautioned, "that there are not others who wished, and may still wish, you harm."

"True," Elizabeth grudgingly agreed.

"Rather than end this lovely evening on a sour note," Mrs. Gardiner said, "we have three talented musicians in this room. Shall we not hear each of you perform?" Miss Bingley and Elizabeth agreed easily; Georgiana required coaxing from Elizabeth, Jane, and her brother.

It was not until they had joined William and Georgiana in the Darcy carriage to return to Matlock House that the topic came back up. "If the gypsies found me, why would they not simply return me for the reward?" Elizabeth asked.

"Fear, perhaps," William said quietly. "Fear they would be accused of things they had not done. Or perhaps they simply did not know where you had come from, and could not find anyone missing a child near where you were found. So they kept you until ... whatever happened that prompted them to take you to London."

"You do not ascribe malicious intent, then?" Elizabeth asked.

"You were delivered safe and unharmed to an orphanage that, by your aunt's description, is one of the better run, and safer orphanages in Town, with sufficient support that the children are fed and clothed regularly. That does not speak of malicious intent to me," he replied, then smiled ruefully. "Such arguments will be made to our uncle and your mother, as well, to soothe their fears."

* * *

"To ensure I am not misunderstanding: Elizabeth has no recollection of the incident, a gypsy knows to ask after her specifically, and she repeatedly attempted to leave *with* gypsies for the first few years she lived with the Bennets?" Lord Matlock queried as he leaned back in his chair.

"That appears to be the case," Darcy confirmed.

Matlock continued. "Meanwhile, the orphanage has no significant documents of her arrival, other than a date and reason. The documents themselves indicate she was a foundling for the person who delivered her to the orphanage."

"According to Mrs. Gardiner, who has offered to bring the records for us to review," Darcy agreed.

"Fragments and titbits," Matlock sighed in frustration.

"More than we had, and nothing to suggest she is in danger," Darcy replied.

"True," Matlock agreed. "Which is good, I suppose. Sarah would be quite put out if we had to remove Elizabeth from London before the introduction ball."

"Both of my aunts would be most seriously displeased," Darcy laughed.

"So there is little more to be done, then, until Mrs. Gardiner receives a response from this gypsy character, if she does. August or September is a long time."

"Not compared to seventeen years, Uncle. If he has asked after my cousin for nearly two decades, I can only imagine he would be relieved to know she found her family at long last," Darcy replied. "Sharing what he knows can only be a relief. I will, however, ensure that Mrs. Gardiner is aware of enough of that night's events to convey that *we* know he and his kin are not responsible for my cousin's disappearance and my uncle's death. That alone may be enough to gain the story from him."

"Is he literate enough to reply to a letter?" Matlock asked.

"I would assume so, if he assists in teaching children at the orphanage. Mrs. Gardiner indicated she would direct him to the Lambton inn if he preferred to communicate in person."

Matlock sighed. "Well, there is little enough we can do until that information is acquired. Thank you for letting me know. I presume you will share this conversation with Bennet when you return to your house?"

"That is my plan," Darcy confirmed. "Is the plan for the Bennets to return here tomorrow to visit, or if I should plan on guests?"

"We should check with your aunts," Matlock replied, rising from his seat. He gestured at the study door. "Let us do that now."

* * *

"I will be interviewing a few governesses with Mr. Bennet tomorrow," Lady Matlock replied to the question of locations. "One may be suitable for assisting the girls with their musical studies, among other studies, for Miss Kitty and Miss Lydia. Otherwise, we will be looking for a music tutor for Miss Mary in particular."

"So the Bennets will be in attendance here?" Matlock attempted to clarify.

"Mr. Bennet, at least, yes, and return to Darcy's later. I believe Georgiana had expressed a desire to take Miss Kitty shopping with her, pending your approval, William."

"Kitty and Georgiana?" Elizabeth asked. "I would not be opposed to joining their party if it may possibly wander past a bookshop."

William chuckled. "I will make that a conditional requirement, then. Perhaps the carriage that brings Mr. Bennet here will convey you to Darcy House for the day, then?"

Elizabeth glanced at Lady Catherine, who nodded approval. "Jane? Anne?"

Jane and Anne glanced at each other, and seemed to hold a quick, but silent conversation. Jane demurred, as did Anne. Elizabeth raised an eyebrow, but shrugging slightly, replied to William, "It seems it will be up to me alone to ensure you are not bored to tears while your sister and mine shop."

"Then I shall be well-entertained indeed," William smiled.

"As will most of High Street," Elizabeth could swear she heard Anne mutter, but when she gave Anne a sharp glance, Anne returned a look of pure innocence.

Jane gave no appearance of having heard Anne. "I do believe I would enjoy dining with Mama, Papa, and our sisters, tomorrow, if it would not be too much trouble. I could travel with Papa after his business here, and return with Elizabeth."

"That sounds perfect," Elizabeth replied. William concurred. With it settled that Elizabeth would spend most of the day at Darcy House with Georgiana and her sisters, and Jane attending for dinner, William departed to his home to share the plans, and news.

Thirty-One

Elizabeth had barely broken her fast when she heard her father's voice, speaking to the maid escorting him to the breakfast room. "Ah, Lizzy," he said, stepping into it. He made for the sideboard to fix himself a cup of tea and piling a plate himself, before settling down across from her.

"I did not expect you to arrive quite so early, Papa," she said between bites.

"When Darcy relayed the plans for you to be out with your sister and cousin today, I decided I should spend some time with my daughter before she is off to socialize," he replied. "I am surprised at you. *Volunteering* to go shopping, my dear?"

She coloured a little. "I have not been near a bookshop in weeks, Papa," she replied.

"And your assumption that Darcy would be escorting his sister, and not, say, perhaps her companion, played not a bit into it?" he needled.

Elizabeth coloured, but shook her head. "I own, I did assume he would escort his sister, but I more desired to see how Georgiana and Kitty are getting on. They both need a friend of their own."

Mr. Bennet snorted lightly before sipping at his tea. "They get along quite well, really. I am pleased with their interactions. I have provided her with some pocket money, much to Lydia's disapproval. I had to be quite stern with Lydia, though. She was most displeased to not be especially invited."

"She and Mama enjoy shopping together," Elizabeth replied. "Perhaps they can make a day of it tomorrow, with Aunt Gardiner to provide assistance."

Mr. Bennet nodded. "Excellent idea. Perhaps if you make the recommendation to them when you arrive, that will soothe the ruffled feathers."

"I shall endeavour to remember," Elizabeth replied. "Did William share the titbit from my Aunt Gardiner last night?"

"He did indeed, and your mother and I recalled those instances. I wonder that we did not put them together before this."

"So it seems reasonable that the gypsies kept me for a few months?" she asked.

"It certainly seems that way," Mr. Bennet agreed. "Although I wonder how you fared, given your dislike of horses by then."

She finished her plate. "The carriage is waiting then?"

"Indeed," Mr. Bennet replied, standing up. He opened his arms, and Elizabeth stepped in for a hug. "Be a good girl," he said quietly, pressing a kiss to her forehead. "I will see you later, either here or at Darcy house, depending on how well this endeavour today goes."

* * *

Not long after his second eldest left in the same carriage which delivered him to Matlock House this morning, Bennet's eldest appeared in the breakfast room. "Oh, good morning, Papa! I did not expect you so early," Jane said.

"Good morning, Jane. As for my timing, I expected to find Lizzy up before most of the household, as usual, and wished to spend some uninterrupted time with her," he replied.

"I heard Lizzy leaving," she half-asked.

"Indeed. She did not wish to keep the carriage waiting for long." He eyed Jane. "I admit, I expected you would accompany her in your self-appointed guardianship role."

Jane coloured slightly. "Anne and I discussed giving William and Lizzy some time apart from the rest of the family hovering over their every move. Accompanying his sister and ours seemed to be a reasonable compromise." She selected her own meal and sat down in the same seat Elizabeth had chosen this morning. "I also wished to sit in on the interviews, if you and Lady Matlock will allow it, for my own education. I have not been party to such an activity before."

Bennet pursed his lips. "Certainly, if our hostess is agreeable. We have so rarely lost staff at Longbourn there truly has been little need for such interviews. Perhaps Lady Matlock can be persuaded to share her methods for selecting candidates, as well, if you are curious?"

"That would be splendid," Jane agreed.

He smiled slightly, sensing an opportunity to tease her. "Does this mean you are considering the possibility of becoming Mrs. Bingley?"

Jane coloured deeply this time. "Perhaps," she allowed after a moment. "But if not *that* particular occurrence, I am three-and-twenty."

"And in need of your own home," Bennet finished. "While I should like to be selfish and keep you and Elizabeth with me for many more years yet, I will not stand in the way of your happiness, my dear. I have heard enough of the situation with Mr. Bingley to be assured of his character."

"I do not wish to leave Lizzy alone to face her future," Jane replied.

"The de Broughs, Fitzwilliams, Darcys, Gardiners, and Bennets support her, Jane, my love. She will be fine. She loves you very much, and would in no way wish to diminish your chances of happiness."

Jane looked pensive, an odd expression for her. "I am afraid of being ... supplanted," she said at last.

"You will always be her sister and dear friend," Bennet replied. "But when either of you marry, when, not if, your first duty and first friendship should be to your husband. I know I have not been the best of role models, there, but I have every intention of ensuring each of you are settled with a partner you and I both can respect."

Jane hesitated. "Did you ... believe you would find that friendship with my mother?"

Bennet sat back, trying to hide the wince. He had long regretted that failure of his. "A difficult question to answer," he said finally. "I should like to think on the answer, if I may, and consider it."

Jane nodded. "I should not have asked."

Bennet waved the concern away. "I all but gave you permission to ask with my statements, dear. I need to ponder over it more deeply before I can provide you, and Lizzy, a fair answer. I believe you both need one, nay, deserve one."

Sounds in the hallway indicated the *tête-à-tête* was at an end for the time being. Others in the household drifted in and out; Jane left not long after Lord Matlock sat down beside Bennet to discuss Lizzy and London politics. It seemed he appreciated a new viewpoint on some of the long-on-going arguments in Parliament, and how he might approach them for resolution. Miss de Bourgh and Lady Catherine arrived together; Miss de Bourgh asked after Jane.

"I do not know her immediate whereabouts, but she did request to sit in on the interviews later this morning," Bennet answered.

"Certainly," Lady Matlock interjected, apparently having just arrived in the room herself. "Her input may be useful. I will have a servant inform her to wait in the library in time for the first appointment."

"Thank you, Lady Matlock," Bennet replied. "Our staff at Longbourn is often fixed for long durations, so she has little experience with the process."

"All the better, then, for her to assist this time," Lord Matlock agreed. He patted his wife's hand as she sat down. "While our own staff at the estate does not frequently turn over, here in town, with so many opportunities, is quite a different story. And there are none better than Sarah for the task."

"You flatter me, my dear," Lady Matlock returned.

"Always," replied Lord Matlock. "But that does not mean I do not speak the truth as I see it. I am indeed fortunate." He sighed. "And indeed, I need to be off. Duty calls."

Those remaining in the breakfast room fare-well'd the earl and he slipped from the room. Bennet excused himself, intending to find the library. Better that he lose track of time in the location of the appointments than embarrass himself by being elsewhere.

* * *

William greeted the returning carriage and handed Elizabeth down from it. She favoured him with an amused expression. "Good morning," she said.

"An excellent morning," William replied. "Your father made it safely, then?"

"Indeed," Elizabeth agreed, "And as you see, so have I."

Elizabeth had not yet visited William's town home, and he gave a brief tour of the salient areas as he led her to the breakfast room. "I already broke my fast," Elizabeth informed him.

"So have I. However, our sisters are currently waiting there."

Indeed, when they entered, it was apparent that both Kitty and Georgiana had finished breakfast as well, and were merely waiting for Elizabeth's arrival to remove themselves from Mrs. Bennet's presence.

"Lizzy!" Mrs. Bennet cried. "You must tell me all about your stay with Lord and Lady Matlock!"

"I would not wish to delay Georgiana's errands, mama," Elizabeth replied. "Perhaps after we return from those?"

Mrs. Bennet sighed, an exasperated sound. "If you insist. So like your father you are, Lizzy."

William agreed politely. "What I remember of my uncle and what I know of Mr. Bennet, ma'am, Miss Elizabeth does take after them both."

"Elizabeth, brother," Georgiana spoke from the hallway, "Kitty and I are ready now."

"Until later, Mrs. Bennet," William excused them, still holding Elizabeth's arm.

"We will talk after we return, mama. I promise," Elizabeth called over her shoulder while William half-dragged her away. She caught a slightly disappointed look on her mother's face, and while not the first one she had ever caused, this one actually pained her.

She favoured him with a pointed look and he shook his head briefly before glancing at their sisters. Very well, she would allow him to explain himself after their sisters were distracted. They piled back into the carriage that Elizabeth had barely left, and William gave directions to the driver.

The party meandered crowded streets, full of shoppers and those out shopping to be seen. William's favourite book store was the first stop. Elizabeth acquired a few treatises on the natural sciences and mathematics for later study. Georgiana selected new sheet music, and William another volume to add to the Pemberley collection. Kitty was not left spoilless, as within a few stores, she acquired a "right smart bonnet."

Despite the generally merry outing, Elizabeth felt slightly cheated as they returned to William's town home. Little in-depth conversation could be had with William among such crowds, and she felt the loss of the opportunity keenly. As she was promised to spend a little time with Mrs. Bennet, she could not even look forward to a few moments' peace to discuss literary selections for the day.

Mrs. Bennet approved of Kitty's new bonnet even as Lydia abused it as hideous. "Perhaps," Elizabeth interjected in an attempt to head off another row between her youngest sisters, "you may find a nicer one when you go shopping with Aunt Gardiner?"

"Shopping with my sister Gardiner?" Mrs. Bennet cried. "When was that decided? For I have heard nothing of such plans!"

"It has not been decided," Elizabeth soothed. "I made the suggestion to Papa this morning, and he asked I gauge your interest. I dare say that my aunt would be pleased to take you and Lydia shopping," Elizabeth added. "She can show you her favourite warehouses."

"It is an excellent plan," Mrs. Bennet declared. "I shall write a note to Mrs. Gardiner directly."

"Please advise me when your note is completed, ma'am," William interjected. "My sister and I would like to invite Mr. and Mrs. Gardiner to dine here prior to you returning to Longbourn. Both invitations may be sent at the same time."

"Excellent!" Lydia declared even as Mary drifted over to Georgiana's side.

"May I see?" Mary asked, gesturing at the music.

Georgiana smiled as she gestured towards the door. "Actually, should you, Kitty, and I go to the pianoforte and study it there?"

Kitty voiced enthusiastic approval for the scheme, and Mary looked a bit startled but acquiesced after a glance at her sister. Kitty grabbed Mary's arm, and tugged at her to follow. Elizabeth shared a look with William at this new development. *Curious.*

"I believe," William said, "that I must leave you for the moment, Miss Elizabeth, Mrs. Bennet, Miss Lydia, if you do not mind?"

"Indeed not, Mr. Darcy," Mrs. Bennet replied. "Lizzy and Lydia will be fine company until Mr. Bennet returns."

William gave her a look which she took to be somewhat apologetic before leaving himself. Elizabeth shrugged internally, and settled down to talk lace and frippery with her mother and youngest sister, taking up a small bit of needlework to keep her hands busy. Well, *they* talked, and Elizabeth added commentary where appropriate.

Conversation turned towards the ball the Matlocks were hosting soon. "Is your gown ready?" Lydia asked.

"Not yet," Elizabeth replied. "I have another fitting in a few days, and final adjustments the day before."

"I should dearly love to see you in it," Mrs. Bennet said.

"I will see if that may be arranged, Mama. I believe you leave Friday, yes?"

"Quite," Lydia sulked. Mrs. Bennet hrmphed but did not comment.

"I dare say you would find it dreadfully dull," Elizabeth soothed. "My cousins have been telling me all about ones held in years past, and I have heard enough gossip from visitors to Matlock House to be assured it is a stuffy, pretty affair, with little entertainment by our standards. There's dancing, yes, but not like you would enjoy at the Assembly. Even William admitted to that much."

"Then how are *you* going to enjoy it, Lizzy?" Lydia asked.

She laughed. "I assure you, I have little expectations of *enjoyment* out of this ball, sister. I am fulfilling family obligations, to a most eager and anxious family. Given my druthers, I would go home with you on Friday. Still, Richard has said that despite its failings, it is still more enjoyable than most."

Mrs. Bennet shifted uncomfortably, and Lydia glanced askance at her mother before hesitantly asking, "Are you to ever come home to Longbourn again? You or Jane?"

Elizabeth knew the question would come up eventually. "We certainly have time to decide how my holidays will be split between households. Longbourn is my home; it is all I can remember. I know Jane intends to stay with me a while yet before coming home."

"But I want my sisters back!" For a moment, Elizabeth was forcibly struck by the memories of a much younger Lydia. Her distress was palpable.

Mrs. Bennet reached out to her youngest, showing more discernment and caring than Elizabeth had seen in a long time. "Come here, my dear." Lydia, still looking quite upset, moved to sit closer to their mother. "You know that my sister and my brother both visit us, and us them, dear. I write frequent letters to my brother and your Aunt Gardiner. That is an aspect of marriage and new families that you will have to learn to adjust to."

"I always thought we could stay with you," Lydia replied.

"If you think that was possible, do you *really* think Charlotte would be living in Hunsford instead of Meryton?" Elizabeth asked. "Or any of the other neighbourhood girls who have moved away with their husbands, and we only see occasionally now?"

"I wish you could, but a wife must give her first duty to her husband and any children. A rich gentleman – one who can keep you comfortably, with servants and a comfortable home – will have far more obligations to call him away. I was fortunate that my marriage to your father enabled my sister to meet Mr. Phillips, so she could marry and settle close by. Otherwise, your aunt would probably be living elsewhere, and we would see her only rarely. Indeed, by the standards of many families, we have been fortunate. My brother is successful enough to travel to Longbourn at least yearly. Many families do not have that leisure."

"But Lizzy is not marrying away, not yet," Lydia protested.

"My situation is ... unusual, yes. But Mama is saying this is a normal part of growing up and marrying away. The cause in my case is a bit different, that is all."

"What about Jane?"

Elizabeth hesitated. "I believe she will return to Longbourn before year's end. I have hopes, however, that her stay will not be for long, for the happiest of reasons."

"Mr. Bingley has renewed his addresses?" Mrs. Bennet cried.

"Will I get to be a bridesmaid?" Lydia asked eagerly.

"William and I believe he intends to, yes. He has been quite attentive and solicitous since our arriving in town. Miss Bingley has teased Jane about becoming her sister."

"Miss Bingley? Ugh," Lydia replied.

Elizabeth half-smiled. "Miss Bingley appears to be attempting to make amends, to both Jane and myself. She is certainly more pleasant and less superficially polite than she ever presented at Netherfield."

"She is a very elegant lady," Mrs. Bennet scolded.

"She is," Elizabeth conceded. "However, her company is more pleasant than I found it previously. Guarded, perhaps, but that is not necessarily uncalled for. She seems to be more ... genuine."

"As sweet as Jane is, Miss Bingley could certainly do worse for a sister," Mrs. Bennet added.

"I would not be surprised if that was one of her considerations," Elizabeth replied. "She has talked about some of her social circles' behaviours. As long as she believes she may need to live in her brother's home, certainly a sister she can tolerate would be for her best own interests."

Lydia sniffed. "Are there really so many considerations to husbands than a red coat?"

"Indeed," Elizabeth replied. "According to my cousin the Colonel, the income of the lower ranked officers is marginal at best. They certainly could not keep you in a style similar to which you have been accustomed. That is why so many of them are interested in women with more wealth than the Bennets."

"Your dowries are very modest," Mrs. Bennet agreed. "Your father's income is sufficient to be comfortable, and we would perhaps be able to supplement one of you girls' households a little, but only a little. You are worth more than that, but even handsome young men need something to live on."

"Perhaps I do not want to marry after all," huffed Lydia.

"Certainly not at fifteen," Elizabeth replied. "You have plenty of time yet."

"Fifteen is a sufficient age," their mother replied. "Lydia is well-grown."

Elizabeth responded with only an arched eyebrow and forwent comment. Lydia looked between her sister and her mother, and apparently chose to let the topic die.

Thankfully, Mr. Bennet and Jane arrived not a few moments later. "Papa!"

Elizabeth took the opportunity of Jane's arrival and their mother's desire to chat with her eldest to escape. Mr. Bennet walked her in the direction of the library. "Was it a good morning?"

"Tolerable," Elizabeth replied. "Kitty and Georgiana enjoyed it, and it was nice to be out."

"And of what your conversation with your mother and sister?"

"We discussed husband-getting considerations and the prospect of Mr. Bingley offering for Jane."

"Those seem to be popular topics among our family today," Mr. Bennet smiled. "As for Mr. Bingley, I believe that is more than a prospect."

Thirty-Two

Mr. Bennet settled across from Jane in the Matlocks' carriage. He indicated to the driver that they were ready, and the carriage jolted forward. "How do you feel about the morning?"

"Pleased," Jane replied. "I believe we selected someone Mary will be able to reach a rapport with, while still being able to exert influence and supply education for Kitty and Lydia."

"Miss McGonagall seems a bit severe, although her background seems impeccable. Your mother may find her trying."

"No more so than Lizzy or Mary try her nerves."

He chuckled. "Indeed. And if she can assist Mary's playing, she may benefit all of our nerves."

"Papa!" Jane scolded.

Mr. Bennet conceded. "I know I should not speak so, dear. She has shown improvement, with the companionship and example of Miss Darcy. She may yet develop her playing into a true skill."

"I hope she does," Jane replied.

"It seems Lizzy's cousins have her best interests at heart," Bennet shifted the conversation abruptly, now that they were on the cobbled streets.

"Yes," Jane agreed. "William and Richard have been particularly solicitous to us."

"'Us'?" Bennet questioned, tempering his concern.

"I mean, obviously, they have been far more focused on Lizzy, as they ought to be. But they have been very kind and welcoming to me as her sister, too."

"And what do you think of Colonel Fitzwilliam?" he prodded.

"He is an amiable man, well-bred as befits his station," Jane replied. Bennet thought she sounded guarded.

"What if he were to come to me, asking to court you?"

Jane's serenity fractured, for just a moment. "I would be surprised, indeed. We have not spoken closely enough for me to consider it even in passing."

Bennet kept his expression neutral if not grave. "Then I shall have to disappoint your hopes, my dear." Indeed, he noted, a shade of concern under her composure. "For it would not do, to give approval to two young men to court my eldest, and Mr. Bingley has already requested that honour. I have granted it. Unless you wish me to withdraw it?"

Jane lit up. "Yes! I mean, no. I gave him permission to ask you for a courtship. I wish very much to see if we are well suited."

Bennet smiled at her. "Very well, then. I already spoke with Matlock, as you will be living primarily under his guardianship for the expected duration. He has agreed to supervise in my stead, and I have sent a letter to your uncle Gardiner, asking him to do so as well, in tandem with Matlock."

"Thank you, Papa." Jane replied.

"You seem pleased," Bennet noted. Indeed, Jane nearly glowed. "I admit to some surprise at Bingley saying you insisted on a courtship, even though he indicated that was his intent regardless."

Jane blushed, glancing down at her hands, folded in her lap. "Two reasons. First, I was not sure he would actually speak to you or when. Second, I do not wish to further complicate Lizzy's situation with my engagement."

"I see." He did, in some fashion. Her distress at the lack of contact over the winter had been palpable. "Will Lizzy be flitting about the doorstep, then, awaiting to hear the news that I have approved the courtship, then?"

Jane shook her head slightly. "I did not tell her. I did not wish to have both our hopes dashed, if it came to that."

Bennet frowned and reached out to clasp her hands in his. "Jane, you speak too lowly of yourself. You do understand that your entire family – including Lizzy's new relations – adores you, correct? Colonel Fitzwilliam directed Bingley to me today, and I have little doubt from his disposition when doing so that he suspected the reason for Bingley's call."

Jane's diffident shrug bothered him. For not the first time, he wondered how much of her general approval of people hinged on a lack of confidence in her own worth. He hoped that Bingley was the man capable of convincing her otherwise. The sternness with which Bingley had reportedly brought his sister to heel gave Bennet hope.

"Do you wish to inform your mother of the courtship? Or should I withhold the information until you have come to a decision about an engagement?"

"The sooner my mother knows, the less her excitement later, I believe." Later, 'when' there was an engagement, not 'if,' he presumed. "I would prefer to inform her myself."

"As you wish. I shall leave you to do so when we arrive."

Darcy's staff was excellent, and Jane and Bennet were out of the carriage and into the main hall in short order. Muted sounds from the music room drifted down, with a bit of laughter around a wrong note. A question to the lass yielded the information that Miss Darcy's party had returned already, and Miss Elizabeth was seated in the parlour with Mrs. Bennet and Miss Lydia. His other daughters were accompanying Miss Darcy.

Expecting Lizzy would need the reprieve, Bennet stepped into the parlour with Jane. He pressed Jane's hand and she gave him a brief, slight smile, before moving to sit where Lizzy had vacated. Lizzy took her place with him, and he led her in the direction of the library. He prompted her slightly about her morning.

"Tolerable," Elizabeth replied. "Kitty and Georgiana enjoyed it, and it was nice to be out."

"And of what your conversation with your mother and sister?"

A fleeting look of frustration, but she answered calmly enough. "We discussed husband-getting considerations and the prospect of Mr. Bingley offering for Jane."

"Those seem to be popular topics among our family today," Bennet smiled. "As for Mr. Bingley, I believe that is more than a prospect."

Lizzy looked expressively at her father. He smiled, nodding. "Although he has only requested courtship so far, due to your situation. That was Jane's requirement. I believe she was going to inform your mother shortly."

"She said nothing to me at all!" Elizabeth protested.

"She said as much to me, after Mr. Bingley approached me for permission to court her. She said she wished to see if he would follow through with the request."

"But you all leave on Friday. Will she return with you?"

"No, she insists she will stay with you for now," Bennet replied. "I have spoken with Lord Matlock and sent a letter to your Uncle Gardiner. Matlock has agreed to act in my stead for the purpose, and I expect to hear the same agreement from your uncle. Should Bingley choose to propose, the request for permission will be forwarded to me. Assuming that Bingley does not ride down to Netherfield to submit the request himself."

Lizzy nodded. "I would expect he does so. He seems the type." She paused before adding, "Lydia is afraid of us leaving her behind. She was quite distressed earlier."

Bennet raised an eyebrow. "From the girl who has been chasing officers these past months?"

"She was quite unhappy to hear that there ought to be more considerations than if he wears a red coat," Elizabeth agreed. "She apparently thought she could marry and stay at Longbourn."

"Did your mother disabuse her of that notion?"

"I believe for the moment, yes."

Bennet sighed, shaking his head. "At least we will soon have a governess and companion for your younger sisters, to assist with all of these transitions."

"Was one of the applicants acceptable, then?"

"Quite. A young Scottish lass, a Miss McGonagall, was recommended to Lady Matlock by one of her cousins. They brought her to London to support her in gaining a position. The young lady is educationally astute, with a wide range of interest. We had quite a lively conversation."

"Someone you can tolerate, then?" Lizzy teased.

Bennet smiled. "Indeed. She even plays chess, so I will no longer be missing my evening game in the sitting room."

"I should like to meet her."

"As soon as her guardian reviews and approves of her contract, she will remove to Darcy House to meet the family and travel to Longbourn with us," Bennet replied. "I expect there to be little issue there, so you should be able to meet her."

"What is her contract like?"

"She will assist your sisters in their education, and make recommendations for specific masters if that seems reasonable. She will also act as something of a companion for your mother at times. In exchange, she will receive room and board, as part of the family, and payment. Additionally, she will be granted a reasonable allowance for the acquisition of educational materials geared towards her own pursuits. I will use my old contacts to put her in touch with the proper authorities."

"Did those contacts never have a daughter or cousin who would have suited us as a governess?" Lizzy sounded genuinely curious rather than accusatory.

"From time to time, yes, I did ask," Bennet replied with a shrug. "However, none were ever available."

They arrived at the library. Bennet noted that Lizzy looked briefly disappointed before commenting on the size of the collection to her father.

"Indeed," Mr. Bennet agreed. "A tempting lot. Darcy says that it is a paltry collection compared to the books kept at Pemberley, but I have not found it lacking yet. I have found both old friends and new on these shelves."

"Ones to add to your library?"

"Several, yes. Here," he pulled a volume from a shelf. "I finished this one but two days ago. I believe you will enjoy it."

Lizzy accepted the book and settled into a chair. He primarily recommended it because Darcy had recommended it to *him*. Bennet suspected Darcy would be quite pleased to see Lizzy engrossed in a volume he had spoken so highly of.

Darcy himself appeared not five minutes later. Bennet smiled inwardly. Yes, Darcy's staff was excellent. "Bennet," he greeted.

"Good afternoon, Darcy," Bennet replied.

"Did Bingley find you?" Darcy asked. Lizzy's head shot up from her book.

Bennet smiled. "He did indeed."

"And?"

"We spoke briefly but in-depth," Bennet said airily.

"It seems we will not need to engineer a situation where Bingley asks Jane into courtship, after all," Lizzy interjected. "Nor for Bingley to seek out my father. Not," she added, eyeing Darcy, "any more than you already seemed to have accomplished."

"Good!" Darcy's enthusiastic response felt warm and genuine.

"You seem hardly surprised at all," Bennet noted. He had not missed Lizzy's comment about engineering situations.

"If you are asking if he requested my counsel on the subject, I must report that he did not," Darcy rejoined. "He relayed the successful request, and merely asked for assistance in arranging for a moment to request your permission. He had meant to meet you here, before you left. He barely missed you."

A quiet knock on the door interrupted them. "Enter," Darcy bid.

One of the girls peaked in. "Pardons, sirs, miss, but Miss Bennet is requesting Miss de Bourgh's company."

"Certainly," Lizzy replied, setting the book aside. "Excuse me, Papa, William. If you will lead me to her?"

"This way, ma'am," the girl replied.

As the door shut, they heard Lizzy talking. "My apologies, for not knowing your name, but I do not believe we have been introduced."

Bennet noted with amusement that Darcy stared at the door for a full minute before recollecting himself. He gave Bennet a wry smile. "Sorry, sir."

"No apologies needed," the older man replied. "I have been there myself." Darcy flushed slightly. Bennet gestured to the book. "But perhaps you should make that available to her to finish at Matlock House."

Darcy picked it up. "You recommended it to her?"

"Quite."

"I suppose I should be pleased you are on my side."

"I am on *her* side," Bennet corrected. "And doing what seems best for my daughters. I may not always be right."

Darcy nodded, still holding the book. After a contemplative moment, he gestured with the book. "I have work to attend in my study. You can, if you wish, join me there, or whatever else you prefer."

"I believe I will linger here a while," Bennet replied. "This evening will be plenty of time for conversation."

"Indeed."

* * *

Elizabeth's guide took her to a small, secluded parlour, where Jane sat waiting for her. Elizabeth thanked the girl as she shut the door behind her.

"I am sorry I did not tell you," Jane started.

Elizabeth shook her head, forestalling Jane's explanation. "I am pleased for your sake, Jane. Papa told me as soon as we had gained privacy, and William knew enough to not need a detailed answer either."

"You do not blame me, then?" Jane seemed surprised and uncertain.

"*Blame* you? Heavens, no!" Elizabeth cried. "You told none of us, and I certainly believe I understand your heart enough to know why."

Jane twitched slightly. "Momma says I did it to vex her, of course."

Elizabeth snorted. "As if she did not do enough *vexing* enough for all of us? Oh, my dear Jane. I can appreciate you wishing to endure the suspense alone, without me or anyone else teasing you."

Jane looked more surprised, and then gave a – for Jane – sly smile. "Ah, has my dearest sister discovered the troubles that come from having an admirer as obvious as William?"

Elizabeth rolled her eyes, and dropped into the seat near Jane with a huff. "Verily. All of my cousins are teasing us, *Mère* asked if I had ever considered wedding colours, and any myriad of such nonsense." She glanced sidelong at Jane. "We – William and I – had quite decided to engineer a moment for Bingley to have a quiet word with you. I am pleased that such machinations were unnecessary. When did he manage it?"

"Just before we left his home after having tea with his sister," Jane replied. "Given the crush at the Matlocks' that evening, I was unsurprised to hear nothing by Saturday, and of course we spent the day out with them all. But I thought for sure -- When Papa said nothing of it yesterday, I fretted that he had lost his resolve already. I cannot express my relief that he spoke to Papa today."

"I can well imagine it, though. Did you swoon?" Elizabeth teased.

"Ha! I am not so frail as that!" Jane giggled.

"How long do you expect it to remain just courtship?"

Jane frowned slightly. "I told him I wished to wait until we had better determined your situation. Papa says that is not really necessary, but I do not want to abandon you."

Elizabeth sighed, and took Jane's hand. "Your happiness will always be welcome, regardless of my situation. I do not wish you to rush, with your concerns about his steadfastness, but do not linger on simply on my account."

Jane searched her expression, but appeared to find that Elizabeth spoke in earnest. She nodded slowly. "I will take that into consideration, then."

"Good! Aunt and Uncle Gardiner are expected here for dinner, are they not?"

"That was my understanding," Jane agreed.

"Papa said he sent a note to our uncle and spoke to mine about the courtship. So you should steel yourself for another inundation of good wishes," Elizabeth teased.

"Before or after your choice of wedding colours are discussed?"

Elizabeth mock-scowled at Jane, rejoicing at the return of her beloved sister's spirits. It had been some months since they could tease back and forth like this. "Your suitor is rather more forward than mine."

Jane suddenly gave her a serious look. "You admit, then, that William is courting you?"

"He seems in earnest, still, does he not?" Elizabeth sighed, leaning back to look at the ceiling. "As I told him, about the time you and your Bingley were discussing possibilities, that he is one of the only reasons I know which way is up. I find his presence ... soothing."

Jane was watching her intently, and tilted her head at the last. "He has quite the presence, does he not? Not like Bingley's, which is gay and chipper, and warms my heart. But more like the old oak overlooking Longbourn, the one you walk to so often. Deep and steady."

Elizabeth smiled, with a touch of wistfulness. "Aye. I had much the same thought, after this past fortnight. I cannot decide if I am more regretful for not having taken the time to actually get to know him while he stayed at Netherfield or not. If I had, I may have simply moped about until we met again at Rosings, much like you did."

"Lizzy!" protested Jane, laughing.

Elizabeth grinned and gestured at the door. "Shall we explore the home our family has been staying in?"

Jane sniffed. "You mean, you want to view your future home."

Elizabeth rolled her eyes at her sister, and refrained from further comment. That was certainly preferable to admitting that Jane was not entirely wrong.

Thirty-Three

Miss McGonagall impressed Elizabeth with her quiet composure and intelligence. She was about five and twenty, nearly six years older than Elizabeth herself, with a barely discernible Scottish accent. Their introduction was brief, but as Elizabeth and Jane were to stay to dine again this evening, it mattered little.

Miss McGonagall had relocated to William's home with the Bennets the day before. From Elizabeth's observations, and those relayed by William, she promptly set about establishing a rapport with the three Bennets she was hired to assist and guide. She even seemed to interact with Mrs. Bennet quite well.

Mary, rarely effusive, currently sat beside Miss McGonagall, speaking with surprising animation about her current reading, a book, Elizabeth gathered, the other lady had recommended yesterday afternoon, and lent to her. Lydia sat nearby, for once listening attentively rather than vying for attention. Kitty sat with Georgiana and Mrs. Annesley, discussing something that Elizabeth could not discern. William had already acquainted Elizabeth with the news that the two girls had promised to correspond at length, and that Mary also intended to correspond with his sister, ostensibly on the topic of music.

The Gardiners arrived, including the children, as they were unlikely to see their cousins again until Christmas. Lydia, surprisingly, spent most of the evening assisting in entertaining the younger ones. The dinner proceeded with less rambunctiousness than a dinner at Longbourn would have, perhaps, but it remained lively enough. The remainder of the evening passed quickly and easily. Elizabeth procured half an hour of Miss McGonagall's conversation herself, and found her initial assessment so far sound. She quite liked her, even, and requested they continue the conversation by letter. She also promised to answer any questions about Longbourn and Meryton which Miss McGonagall may have.

Still, a pleasant evening must eventually end, and when the Gardiners prepared to depart, Jane and Elizabeth regretfully did as well. The girls took several minutes to bid their family a safe trip home and pressed for a letter informing them of such as soon as possible. Lydia surprised them with a tearful group hug.

"You will promise to write to me yourself?" Lydia whispered to Elizabeth.

"I promise, if you promise to respond."

"I will. Even if I must have Miss McGonagall set it as a lesson for me," Lydia tremulously smiled.

Elizabeth smiled back. "Then you have my assurances."

"And you, Jane?" Lydia asked.

"Of course," Jane assured her. "And I will count on you for all the gossip of home!"

"Then I shall want for little to write," Lydia replied. "Even if it is only repeating Sir William's exclamations at the assembly."

Later, ensconced in her room adjoining Lady Catherine's, Elizabeth felt she ought to attend to correspondence of her own. Sleep eluded her.

My dear Charlotte,

> I have been amiss in keeping you updated on the situation here, and I am unsure how much information has been passed on to Mr. Collins by my mother de Bourgh.

> Jane has accepted a courtship from Mr. Bingley, although it is nearly a foregone conclusion that it will progress to an engagement readily. For now, his task is to reassure her of his resolve, both in his pursuit of her hand and in most tasks. He has performed miracles in bringing Miss Bingley around. I am unclear on the particulars, as William will not relay the exact situation he observed, nor what Bingley told *him*. Regardless, a decrease in animosity from Miss Bingley is a relief. Miss Bingley proves to be an entertaining, thoughtful companion when she desires to be so. She has made amends to myself, Jane, and my Aunt Gardiner. She appears to be in earnest and I am more comfortable with the thought of Jane gaining such a sister.

Elizabeth paused the letter here to consider her next words. The candlelight flickered softly, as she worried at the end of her pen.

> You will be pleasantly surprised to hear that my aunt, Lady Matlock, assisted my father in the selection of a governess-*cum*-companion for my younger sisters and mother Bennet. Miss McGonagall will do well, I believe, even among the rowdier environs of Longbourn. It seems that one of the draws for the position is that Father will provide her ready access to furthering her own education, including contacts with his former colleagues. I find I quite like the lady, myself. She is only a few years older than our Jane. I found my conversation with her to be quite stimulating, and we have agreed to continue by letter.

> Regarding the missing time which resulted in our abrupt removal from Rosings to London: A gentle tease from

Miss Bingley at dinner this past week resulted in my Aunt Gardiner's recollection of an individual who may hold some knowledge of my whereabouts for that time. However, given his livelihood, it will still be some months before contact can be made and any potential information be shared.

But for the more shocking news, which I must beg you keep close, even from Mr. Collins until Lady Catherine shares it – or does not – with him herself ...

Elizabeth faltered here. Her knowledge and suspicions were still far too fresh a memory to not hold a strong power over her moods. She took a steadying breath, and committed the broad outlines of their arrival in London, and Wickham's reveal about the night she went missing from Rosings, to the paper. His relationship to the Darcy siblings, she kept quiet, although she noted that –

Certain misunderstandings, caused by the tricks and stratagems of unscrupulous individuals, are resolved, and Wickham has been cleared of malicious intent towards Miss Darcy. Wickham is no longer considered *persona non grata* with the extended family, but he has been strongly cautioned to bring his behaviour back into line with expectations. His protestations on the topic are that he has been all bluster and no substance, which for any other situation, could not be seen in a positive light. Whether he retains his temporary grace on a more permanent basis remains to be seen. Both William and Richard appear to be disconcerted and cautiously hopeful about regaining their childhood friend.

I have been grateful for the presence of Jane, and when possible, my father or William. I am adjusting, I believe, to the idea of my birth rights being quite different than my previous understanding. My mothers have come to what appears to be an affable arrangement, and they spent some time sharing stories of my childhood with each other. I vacated the immediate vicinity, and have little knowledge of what was shared.

It has been determined that I will be presented to society at large at an annual ball hosted by the Earl of Matlock, generally marking the start of the Season. A presentation at court seems unlikely at this juncture, as Anne is disinclined to such measures. Knowing me as you do, you can well understand my relief.

Still, preparing for the ball has been trial enough, although my elder cousin's wife, the Viscountess, has been quite helpful in regards to the shopping. I am still "Miss Bennet" in general, although the staff at both Matlock House and Darcy House have been calling me by the entire mouthful. Were I inclined to take on airs of importance, surely being one of the hyphenated individuals would be a step in the correct direction.

I can hear you laugh from here, my dear friend.

Enough about us in London. I was supposed to be visiting with you, and I have absconded with most of your entertainment! How do Maria and her kitten get on? What does Mr. Collins talk about, with Anne and *Mère* not being there to drive past or visit?

Did Sir William return to Meryton as planned? I know the original plan for Maria's return included a stay overnight at the Gardiners'; I see no reason to change that. She would be more comfortable there, I believe, than staying at the Matlocks'. I am often overwhelmed. It is a very fine house, indeed, although much more in the style one may expect from William than Rosings.

Elizabeth paused, and decided to that to write more would be to court rambling. She signed off, enjoining Charlotte to write back as soon as was reasonable. She set the letter aside to be mailed in the morning, and retired.

The whirlwind of visits which accompanied the Bennets' short foray into London settled down, and Elizabeth and Jane found something like a routine among the Fitzwilliam household. Darcy and Bingley called at the Matlocks', usually with Georgiana. Even with Georgiana as an excuse, however, neither Darcy was able linger for prolonged periods. William had business to attend to, and Georgiana lessons. Elizabeth felt the loss of hi-- *their* company keenly, but dedicated her attentions to learning more about her sister Anne, mother, and extended family. Bingley stayed as long as he dared, of course, and Jane's courtship proceeded quietly and calmly under the watchful eyes of Elizabeth's family.

But not even the pleasure of seeing her dear Jane courted, and the growing comfort with her own family could keep Elizabeth from being restless. A dreary rain kept her trapped inside for more hours at a time than she liked. Her maid was kind enough to lead her to the small garden on premises, so that she could walk in the brief moments between showers.

She found some employment there, striking up a friendly rapport with one of the kitchen girls who had a good eye for selecting cuttings. Elizabeth assisted in gathering flowers, and they traded wisdom on the drying of herbs and flowers, as well as arranging displays.

She also found entertainment and solace in the library, seeking out her uncle's opinion when she finished another. He currently had her reviewing the Fitzwilliams' private history, and discussed at least some of what he was doing in Parliament. He frequently provided background necessary for her social forays, taken in the company of Lady Matlock and Anne. *Mère* had little interest in attending others any more than necessary, but did urge her girls to mingle on her behalf.

Preparation for the ball filled the background, looming ever closer, for such events took time to arrange and plan, even one as customary in timing as this. Lady Matlock relished pulling in both Anne and Elizabeth – and sometimes Jane, as well – for their comments and input on the task. Lady Catherine, naturally, had many opinions, but both de Bourghs noticed the practice with which Lady Matlock listened-but-did-not-attend her sister in law's preferences. Elizabeth felt some chagrin at how easily she picked up the trick for placating her mother – evidently, a childhood with Mrs. Bennet had served her well in that regard.

Lady Matlock discovered Elizabeth's handiwork with the flower arrangements, one afternoon, after complimenting the head housekeeper on the improvements. "Nay, milady. 'Tis Miss Elizabeth's work. She has been helping Maddy, insisted on it. She said it was a favoured task at home, and it helped chase away the grey clouds above."

Lady Matlock promptly assigned Elizabeth the task of arrangements for the ball. She provided the list of local florists for providing more than their own garden could, the colours, and a budget. She did hint at a few preferred locations, but otherwise insisted it was up to Elizabeth's preferences. The necessary activities related to that endeavour assisted in filling up the few days when even Bingley had too many business and social engagements to spend at Jane's side.

Elizabeth found herself writing many a letter, both of business and social natures. She thought back to a night at Netherfield, while Miss Bingley complimented William's hand, and felt something akin to pity for him. Still, she promised Lydia to correspond with her directly, along with several others. She ensured to keep that promise as best she could. Correspondence with Charlotte remained the most personally serious.

Dearest Lizzy,

My father did indeed return to Meryton as planned. My sister's visit has been perhaps quieter than expected originally, but she and I have spent many hours in quiet entertainment. She has taken caring for the kitten quite well, and they have become fast friends.

I lack only your company for contentment, but given the circumstances, I will relish your letters instead.

Lady Catherine has sent little information to Mr. Collins; I have relayed what seemed pertinent to his needs. I said naught of Mr. Bingley, however, for fear of jinxing Jane's chances again. I will contain my effusions until then.

Mr. Wickham is now acknowledged again? I am indeed glad that there has been reconciliation. I hope you will be able to share more details at a later time.

Thank you for your offer to maintain the plans as before. If it would not be too much trouble, perhaps I may also journey into London at that time, to return by myself, or with Lady Catherine? I would enjoy seeing the Gardiners myself, and to spend a little time with you and Jane while you remain relatively near.

Now, with all the niceties aside...

Do I detect even more of a softening of your previous dislike of Mr. Darcy? Does the gentleman maintain his pursuit? And are you, perhaps, inclined to hear his overtures? Tell me!

With all my love,

Charlotte

~~~~~

London

My dear Charlotte,

Lady Catherine and company readily agree to your proposed adjustment to the plans. Exactly with whom and when you will return to Hunsford Parsonage is still under debate, but my mother will send Mr. Collins a note herself about it, along with the invitation from the Gardiners for a short stay. She believes conveying it in such a manner will encourage Mr. Collins' agreement to the scheme.

Knowing how I left Rosings that night certainly decreases the concerns which prompted our expedited removal to London, and thus some of the stress involved. William, however, appears to be acutely aware of my distress regarding it all, and continues to tread lightly. The outstanding questions may change some of the concerns, but for now, security is being maintained without it being unbearable. I have taken to walking in the parks nearby, but I am never without company in some form, even if only a circumspect servant. Accordingly, I am looking forward to *your* company, although I warn you that Lord Matlock will undoubtedly insist on continuing the extra company.

As for your other query...

I have promised Jane I will be cautious, and not risk myself unduly. That being said, I do find comfort in William's company, and I begin to believe that it is not solely due to the fact that he is a "known face" from what I can only describe as my "old life." I do wish I had been less hasty to find reasons to dislike him in Herefordshire.

My sisters have been helpful in allowing us quiet moments to discuss weighty matters, and, before he returned to Longbourn, my father appeared to be forwarding William's interests by recommending favourite readings to the other. My father, William, and I enjoyed several discussions regarding those selections.

I expect, once we have an answer to my Aunt Gardiner's question, William will increase his attentions.

But he is not my declared suitor – at least, not in the formal manner. He has indicated his desire to be so, in the future, and certainly seems to be courting my attention. He teases, at times, and at other times is quite serious. I am finding his character just as complex as I ever expected. At least in *that* aspect of my judgement, I did not err.

His occasional forwardness has resulted in our cousins and elders taking great delight in teasing us both. Although now that I think on it, I believe he must have taken one or another to task, as the teasing has decreased. I am grateful for the reprieve. *You* know how much I *enjoy* discussions of lace and frivolities.

But anything of such a nature remains in the future, and I am no soothsayer to look ahead and know the path for sure. For now, I look forward to attending my sister as she works through *her* courtship to Mr. Bingley. I do not wish her to rush needlessly, but she is already much happier than she has been in months.

Yours,

Elizabeth

~~~~~

Hunsford

My dear, dear friend,

How sly an attempt to distract me! Do not think I did not catch it.

But for now, I will humour you.

Is Mr. Bingley as inattentive to society as he was prior to leaving Netherfield last fall? Have they progressed much past their shared preference for Vingt-un over Commerce? Has Lady Catherine insisted on you and Mr. Darcy assisting her in forming quadrille tables?

Has Miss de Bourgh found any admirers? As the heiress of Rosings and likely sister to the master of Pemberley, I would think her prospects ought not be ignored. Perhaps a different cousin would suit your mother's schemes for her. The Colonel is certainly genteel and gracious enough.

Elizabeth thought about Anne's confession about George and Richard. From a fortune's point of view, either would benefit greatly from Anne's inheritance. Anne, however, displayed no true favouritism for either. Elizabeth hoped that Anne would be well regarded at the ball, at the very least. She would encourage Anne to join them for the next trip to Mrs. Smithson's modiste, and insist she needed a new gown as well. She was dismayed to realize she had failed to think of that previously, not that Anne seemed inclined to lace and frivolities any more than she. She resolved to bring it up with their mother.

But perhaps, if her health continues to improve, her natural beauty will allow her to catch her own prospects. I have always thought she needed just a bit of joy to make her handsome.

Have you had an opportunity to take part in any of the pre-Season activities? I know how much you enjoy the parks and gardens. Please, do tell.

Yours truly,

Charlotte

Thirty-Four

Elizabeth did not respond to Charlotte's last immediately. It required thought and observation. She ensured that their mother pressed Anne into joining the next foray for her own gown. Mrs. Smithson enjoyed the challenge of bringing Anne's normal style up to current tastes.

She noticed that Richard appeared to be giving some attention to Anne, and she wondered at it. She even mentioned it to Anne, one evening. "Does Richard seem to be spending more time talking with you than normal?"

Anne considered. "Perhaps. With mother less inclined to … hover, it is difficult to tell. We are the guests here. Richard is more comfortable here than he is at Rosings, that much is obvious."

"Does he know when he will have to return to his duties?" Jane asked.

"Not yet," Anne replied. "Around now is when he and William generally visit us at Rosings for a fortnight. Usually, they leave with just enough time to prepare for the ball themselves."

Elizabeth smiled. That seemed to be one of the most consistent aspects of William's personality she had heard yet. He was quite willing to be prepared for anything, except for socializing.

Easter Sunday arrived and passed in a mostly familiar manner. Elizabeth wondered what sermon Mr. Collins was providing to the parishioners at Rosings, and how that differed from the experience at Longbourn. Here, the sermon was similar to what she expected. The trappings of the celebration were richer, but the core remained the same.

Dreary spring rains kept Elizabeth inside most of the next few days, and the last of the items for the ball were acquired strictly by delivery. She contemplated that similarity to the last ball she and Jane had attended -- the ball at Netherfield. By the morning of the ball, Elizabeth could only look forward to peace and quiet. She would have none until sometime after the last guest departed, even if she feigned a need to retire early herself.

Georgiana, still not out herself, would not be in attendance at the ball. The Darcys took tea at Matlock House, before returning home to allow William to prepare. He returned quickly.

Bingley and his party arrived earlier than most. An invitation had been extended to Mr. Bingley, his sisters, and Mr. Hurst, as a courtesy to Jane. Mr. and Mrs. Gardiner also arrived, as family to the Bennets. Elizabeth felt reassured at seeing them arrive. Elizabeth was not retained in the greeting line.

At last, the Earl stepped up to the dais where the musicians sat, and raised his hands for silence. Lady Matlock and Lady Catherine joined him. William offered his arm to Elizabeth, and they drifted closer to the stage. Anne and Richard did likewise.

"Welcome, honoured guests and dear family. Many of you have joined us in years past, and others are new faces.

Tonight's ball is unlike those we have held prior in years, for tonight, I have the pleasure to announce that my sister, Lady Catherine de Bourgh, has found her long missing daughter."

The silence broke into a sea of shocked murmurs. The Earl raised his hands for silence again. "We are pleased to present Miss Elizabeth

Bennet de Bourgh." He gestured for Elizabeth to join him and Lady Catherine, which she did reluctantly. Scattered applause could be heard. "The Fitzwilliam family wishes to extend our deepest gratitude to her adopted family, the Bennets of Longbourn, for their selfless care these past years. We know they bear no responsibility for her absence, and only credit for their treatment and raising of her.

"Tomorrow, the official announcement will appear in the papers, no doubt alongside all of those other boring details from tonight," quiet laughter met that comment, "but please assist us in welcoming Miss Elizabeth to London, along with her mother, Lady Catherine, and elder sister, Miss Anne de Bourgh, both of whom have not attended one of these balls in several years." He paused for a round of polite applause.

"With that, if the musicians would be so kind as to prepare for the first set, we shall begin tonight's amusement in earnest."

Applause and mutters answered the Earl's announcement of the ball opening, and couples drifted together. William waited patiently for Elizabeth to descend before reclaiming her for the first set.

As balls went, Elizabeth enjoyed herself. She had attended a handful with the Gardiners in previous years, although never a full London season, as well as the occasional ball held in her own Hertfordshire. She was introduced to more people than she could ever remember. William, Richard, and Bingley all hovered carefully over her sisters and her. This did not mean they did not dance -- for dance they all did. Only the bolder or less attentive single young men braved the asking the de Bourgh girls. Bingley, less formidable than either William or Richard, did not dissuade many from asking for a place on Jane's card. Fortunately, he had secured the three dances he considered most important days prior.

In between dances, Elizabeth made dutiful small talk with every individual introduced to her by one of her relatives. During the dances, she attempted to learn more about each partner. Many, she primarily learned by their questions of *her,* were chiefly concerned as to whether she would be "attaining her proper inheritance." By this, she presumed they were questioning if she had any fortune settled on her by the de Bourgh family. She simply smiled in response and changed the subject. Others wished to know of the Bennets, and she remained as circumspect as feasible. Two, both warmly introduced as friends of William and Richard, spoke to her of her cousins and how they came to know them.

She counted her dances with William -- not always talking, but enjoying the easy back and forth they had developed these past weeks -- as her favourites. Standing across from Richard and Bingley, also merited actual enjoyment. Apart from they and their friends, however, Elizabeth confessed to her sisters in an undertone that she was deriving her primary enjoyment from knowing there were plenty worse dancers she might partner, and had before. Jane looked sympathetic, and Elizabeth assumed she recalled that aspect of the Netherfield ball.

Supper met the expectations Elizabeth formed based on living in the household these past weeks, and the family conspired to sit together insofar as feasible. Good food and comfortable company made the meal pass quickly.

By halfway through the second half of the ball, however, Elizabeth wished it were over. It was pleasant, enjoyable, and all other good descriptors, but she missed Charlotte's or her father's conversation acutely. William could not speak with her quite as he normally would, Richard seemed preoccupied with deep thoughts, and Jane … well. Jane glowed in happiness whenever Bingley was in view. *She* could not be counted on for witty repartee, either. The crowd nearly overwhelmed Anne, and not for the first time, Elizabeth suspected her elder sister was quite naturally shy. She did not enjoy quite the same camaraderie with her mother, aunts, or uncles that she did with Charlotte or her father, or even William.

A few of the younger ladies, both those married and not, seemed pleasant enough acquaintances, and she could possibly look forward to furthering those relationships in the future. Among the gentlemen, William's friends she deemed pleasant enough, and a few of her uncle's set could be amusing.

In a room full of dancing, cheerful people, accompanied by splendid music and set amongst the best of decorations, she could not shake the touch of wistful homesickness for a simple Assembly in Meryton.

At length, William noticed her distraction and set about attempting to discover the cause. While she could not confess the reason to him, she agreeably entered into discussing whatever topic he brought up. Still, none of the topics could engage her well, and William paused with a half-smile. "I would ask what you thought of books, but I do recall your comment in November."

Elizabeth winced a little. "I was intolerably vexed with you that evening. But I do confess that my mind is wandering too much for a conversation like that at this moment."

He nodded, looking across the hall. "We have a monthly Assembly in one of the towns near Pemberley, and I attend those when I am in residence and as my duties allow. It is not dissimilar to the one we attended in Meryton."

"I dare hope you are in better humour, however," Elizabeth replied.

"I should hope as well," he agreed. "I was certainly in a terrible mood, and did not acquit myself favourably."

Elizabeth gave him an arch smile. "You at least accurately marked my sister as the handsomest in the room that night."

He raised an eyebrow. "No, Miss Bennet de Bourgh. Miss Bennet was -- is -- the second handsomest in that room and this one. I consider myself fortunate to be less blind than I was that night, and to have the handsomest standing beside me at the moment."

Elizabeth could do naught but flush, and William looked rather pleased with himself. "No doubt, several of your new acquaintances will visit tomorrow," he continued.

"I hope several of my older acquaintances do as well."

"I will ensure Bingley knows his sister is welcome."

Elizabeth gave him a pointed look. "My *friends* should visit, as well."

"I shall find time to escort my sister over, as well, then." Under the circumstances, that was the best answer he could provide. Given the frequency of his visits -- to his own aunt's house -- it seemed a bit odd that he would be all but asking for *her* to invite him.

Unless …

She gave him a sharp look, to find him looking at her much like he used to towards the end of his stay in Meryton. She flushed and glanced away, but did not make any attempt to dissuade him. Jane and Bingley drifted over, rescuing her from having to continue to converse under such profound confusion. They talked gamely with William while Elizabeth recovered her composure.

The evening wound down, inexplicably taking even longer than it had previously. Elizabeth danced with several others, and William once more. She knew herself to be less chatty than she had been, but the confused anticipation felt like a physical pressure on her thoughts. One part of her feared she misinterpreted his intentions, and another part feared she had not.

Not long after she had gained her room, she heard a familiar rat-tat on the door, and bid Jane to enter. Anne did not accompany her.

Jane had already changed into bedtime wear, her robe pulled tightly around her. "I thought you might appreciate some help."

"I could have called for Sally." Elizabeth allowed her sister to help.

"Indeed. She asked if you might need her assistance, but I reassured her you would be fine." Jane paused. "William left you quite flummoxed. What exactly did Bingley and I rescue you from?"

Elizabeth noted the drop of "Mr" from Jane's comment, while contemplating her answer. "He made a comment about new acquaintances visiting tomorrow, and I replied that I should hope older ones would, as well. He pressed the point slightly, and all but asked me to invite *him* -- or at least, Georgiana."

Jane's hands stilled for a brief moment. "We both know he was not asking for his sister's sake."

"It did not occur to me immediately," Elizabeth confessed, stepping into the dressing room to change into her own night wear.

"Did you rescind your invitation?" Jane asked as she stepped back out.

Elizabeth pulled her robe around her tightly, flushed, and shook her head. She could not meet Jane's eyes. Jane pulled her close, and tilted her chin up to make Elizabeth look at her. "You are, and always have been, my sister, Lizzy. I want you happy. I will still caution you to not be hasty, although I am fairly certain that 'hasty' is not a description I could ascribe to William."

Elizabeth smiled slightly. "Is this a variation of the speech I gave you last week?"

Jane smiled back. "Quite." Her expression turned a bit mischievous. "I might add, such speech went to good effect. Bingley will call at the Gardiners tomorrow, to speak to my uncle."

"Jane!"

She laughed. "He confessed he wished he could have dissuaded more partners of mine, or at least danced with me more. I told him he knew the remedy for *that*." She smirked. "He verified I was quite sure, and yes, proposed."

"Oh, Jane!" Elizabeth hugged her sister enthusiastically. "I am so happy for you!"

Jane laughed again. "Not half so happy as I am for myself!" she replied.

"Mother will be ecstatic."

"She will be beside herself when he visits my father," Jane agreed. Jane gave her a sly smile. "Perhaps I should suggest he wait a few days before riding down to Longbourn, so that he may have company?"

Elizabeth blushed but shook her head. "No, Jane. Regardless of what William's intent is, I will not have you overshadowed in this."

Thirty-Five

The paper lay open to the page of the official announcement of Elizabeth's place in the de Bourgh family. However, the early morning commotion in the Matlock breakfast room centred around a blushing Jane and a beaming Bingley.

Mr. Gardiner looked simply chuffed, but reminded the party: "All this is contingent on Mr. Bennet's final approval."

"I shall be riding down directly," Bingley replied. "Or, if J -- Miss Bennet or Miss Elizabeth would like to send a letter along, I may wait for that?" He glanced between the two.

Jane smiled. "I do indeed have a letter for my father, and one for my mother."

Elizabeth concurred. "However, mine will not be nearly so entertaining as Jane's."

Letters were collected and handed to an eager Bingley. He expressed a warm farewell to Jane, and nearly as warm a farewell to Elizabeth. The rest of the party enjoyed a more than cordial adieu. Bingley promised to be back that evening if at all feasible, preferably with Mr. Bennet's written consent in hand.

Lady Matlock glanced at Elizabeth. "Should my sister be expecting any visitors of a similar sort today?" she teased.

"Certainly, none of whom discussed such topics with me," Elizabeth replied. William's request to visit was not any kind of declaration or a request of similar magnitude. She forbore mentioning it, and Jane's happy distraction was such she missed the opportunity to join in the teasing.

Several visitors arrived at the very start of Lady Matlock's visiting hours, ostensibly to visit Lady Matlock and congratulate Lady Catherine (and Elizabeth) on the reunited family. Many of this first round of visitors had met her within the previous fortnight, as just a guest in the household. The level of attention differed, but only a few notable individuals treated her drastically better. Elizabeth noticed the matrons brought along primarily unmarried sons, some of whom obviously were more bewitched by Jane than by her own person. For once, she did not feel slighted, for Jane positively glowed. The soon-to-be-disappointed would-be suitors would know soon enough about her sister's engagement. She made note of the more amusing ones to share with Mr. Bennet in her next letter.

Elizabeth did wonder that William and Georgiana were not among the earlier guests, as they frequently did arrive quite early, when duties allowed. She left distinct relief when he – *they* were announced, and she could rise to greet Georgiana, politely escaping a rather dull would-be suitor of her own, a Mr. David Thorton.

"Now I get to call you cousin!" Georgiana cheered.

Elizabeth laughed. "Yes, but if I never hear 'Cousin Elizabeth' again in my life, it shall be too soon."

William gave her a questioning look, while greeting her in a more subdued manner than his sister, or even his own wont. Elizabeth assumed the rather crowded parlour had something to do with his reticence. She shook her head at him. "A story for later, perhaps, among family."

She realized that Lady Matlock, Lady Catherine, and both Darcys were giving her a hopeful look, while Jane briefly looked downcast even among her joy. What had she said? Perhaps for Jane, it was simply a reminder of her now temporary disappointment.

William appeared to be pondering the comment, then realization flickered across his face. "Have you had correspondence from your friend, Mrs. Collins?" he asked. The question seemed as much to verify his conclusion as genuine interest.

"Indeed, Mr. Darcy," Elizabeth agreed. "My mother has invited her to visit us in London when her sister starts her return home, given that I was *supposed* to be visiting her at this moment."

"I had forgotten that we are depriving your friend of some of her company," he replied. "When were you expecting to return, originally?"

"Saturday next week, which is the schedule that Mrs. Collins and Miss Lucas will keep," Elizabeth replied. "They expect to stay with my Aunt Gardiner, and I believe Mrs. Collins will return with *mère* to Rosings."

"Mrs. Gardiner has a lovely home," William said. "I was quite comfortable when we visited."

"Oh, yes," Georgiana agreed. "Her pianoforte is so light and responsive! I have played on others which are more sluggish to the touch."

William gave Georgianna a slight smile and shake of his head. "Not that my sister is fond of music."

Elizabeth laughed. "Oh, no, not at *all*," she agreed.

William and Georgiana stayed most of the morning, while visitors cycled in and out. Despite her intentions, Elizabeth spent most of that time conversing with William and whomever braved his presence to speak to her. Georgiana sat with Lady Catherine and Jane. A light luncheon offered a reprieve from the social barrage. "So, Elizabeth, how do you find your new social scene?" Lady Matlock teased.

Elizabeth smiled ruefully. "I recognize the necessity, Aunt."

She smiled, and turned her attention to William. "And you, nephew? Did you relish the change in being the most hunted catch in the room?"

Elizabeth almost laughed, but checked it. William looked so … William, at such a question. "I admit to being sufficiently engaged in conversation that I did not notice any behaviour out of the ordinary," he replied.

Lady Matlock raised an eyebrow, but before she could tease William further, Georgiana added, "Except for you being engaged in conversation in our Aunt Matlock's parlour, there was no particular behaviour out of the ordinary, indeed."

A hint of a smile. "Quite," he agreed. "No doubt that will also be in the gossip section tomorrow."

Lady Matlock narrowed her eyes at her nephew. "I see," she replied. Perhaps *she* did, but Elizabeth was unsure.

The conversation turned to more general comments, and Jane still glowed. Georgiana peppered Jane with questions about her hopes for a wedding, and Jane admitted she would prefer to be married from Longbourn. "With any fortune at all," she added, "the banns can be read as early as Sunday. I hope that any shopping that my mother insists must be done can be completed before Miss Lucas returns to Meryton. I expect to return then, as well."

This was the first Elizabeth had heard of that plan, and she felt a momentary alarm. From the glance William gave her, she did not suppress it as well as she ought to have. "She will be pleased, no doubt," Elizabeth agreed. "But she may press for a longer time to have the wedding."

Jane shrugged. "I am three-and-twenty. She has had seven or eight years to make her plans. She will simply have to make due. Mr. Bingley and I agreed we see no sense in waiting any longer than we must."

Elizabeth felt a touch of amazement and fierce pride that Jane was going to be set on this. She had not expected Jane would be agreeable to a long delay, however, so this was of little concern.

"And what of your plans, Elizabeth?" William asked quietly. "No doubt you would wish to stand with your sister. Would you return as well?"

"I hoped to ask both Elizabeth *and* Anne to stand with me, and our other sisters," Jane replied, apparently having heard William. Anne looked surprised and nervous. "But," she added, "I would understand if Anne and Lady Catherine feel it is not in Anne's best interest. Elizabeth's presence, I must insist on." The smile belied the almost harshness of the words.

"I think I should like that," Anne said, glancing aside at Lady Catherine.

Lady Catherine nodded. "Thank you for thinking to include Anne," Lady Catherine added. "We shall be pleased to attend."

"It seems, William, that I will indeed be standing up with my sister on her happiest day," Elizabeth smiled. "I do not know if I should return to Longbourn at the same time, however."

"Depending on Mr. Bennet's response," Lady Matlock interjected, not looking a bit like she had any concerns there herself, "you have at least a week to decide, perhaps a bit longer."

Lady Catherine announced intentions to return to Rosings, with Mrs. Collins and Anne at least, and making arrangements for attending Jane's wedding from there.

Elizabeth felt torn, and her introspection caused her to become rather quieter than her wont. She felt William watch her, but she did not move to reassure him -- or anyone else. By rights, she should leave for Rosings with *mère*, but Jane may need her at home, to cope with their mother's nerves. William would likely remain in London, and she owned in her heart that she would be happier where he was nearby. He would at least be equidistant regardless of which location she moved to. Assuming, of course, it had been decided she was safe enough at either home.

Elizabeth attempted to set aside her distraction for most of the rest of the day. Bingley returned in good time, with a positive answer, both to Uncle Gardiner and Jane. Elizabeth did not receive a reply of her own, at least from Bingley's conveyance. She did not feel troubled over *that,* however, for Jane looked radiantly happy.

It was not until later that night, when she knocked on Jane's door, and was bidden to enter, that her confusion slipped out of her control.

Jane sat brushing her hair, looking at nothing. "Anne did not accompany you?"

"She owned she felt quite worn through by all of the visitors today. It was quite a bit more excitement than she is used to participating in." Elizabeth sat beside Jane, and offered to take the brush. Jane handed it to her.

"You were quiet, after I made my plans known."

"I had, perhaps, not thought it through -- that you should be married from Longbourn, and would naturally need to return," Elizabeth replied, as she gently pulled the brush through a tangle in Jane's hair.

"And you both wish to accompany me, and not offend Lady Catherine, especially at such a time," Jane finished for her.

"I ... yes," Elizabeth sighed.

"You have your own removal, at least in part, to attend to at Longbourn, Lizzy," Jane said. "There is no reason that we cannot work on that task together, even if I am only removing five miles."

"And I, easily ten times that," Elizabeth agreed sadly.

"I suspect you will not call Rosings home, even for a season," Jane replied, and Elizabeth blushed. Jane smiled. "Bingley intends to -- or has, I am not sure -- ask William to stand up with him, and to invite the Darcys to Netherfield. I believe there is room for Lady Catherine and Anne to stay as well."

"Am I so obvious?" Elizabeth asked quietly.

"It is more that William is," Jane replied. "I heard enough surprise at his conversing with visitors in his aunt's parlour to know that to the *Ton,* he was quite out of character. That change will be attributed to you -- even if he had not spent the entire morning at your side."

"I was grateful for his company," Elizabeth shrugged. "He knew enough about each visitor to assist in conversation handily."

Jane laughed quietly. "Lady Matlock will be pleased to hear *that.* She was rather concerned, given his general detachment from the goings-on."

"I dare say, there were a few of the visitors who would have readily agreed that the sky is purple before risking a disagreement with William," Elizabeth smiled. "Lady Matlock need not worry about him garnering disapproval." She shrugged, finishing with Jane's hair. "I suspect that played into his assistance earlier."

"Combined with a subtle claim to your attention," Jane teased, taking the brush back, and the girls rearranged so she could work on Elizabeth's in turn.

Elizabeth arched an eyebrow at her sister's reflection. "I dare say that subtly will be quite ignored by some of his more ardent admirers."

Jane could not help but agree. Quiet settled while Jane worked. It occurred to Elizabeth that this may be the last time they had with just the two of them. She would simply have to accept the bittersweet loss of such quiet ease as her just desserts for encouraging her sister's happiness. Compared to the soft despondence of Jane's spirits between November and March, Elizabeth could honestly admit she would rather suffer the loss herself before seeing Jane suffer again.

"At least Mother will be happy," Jane said, as she braided the last few inches of Elizabeth's hair.

"Indeed. She has only been trying to get rid of the most deserving of her daughters since you were fifteen!"

"She only need wait for the banns and her own plans, now," Jane agreed. "Or just the banns, and hang the plans."

"Such impatience!" Elizabeth laughed. "What has become of my dear, patient and level-headed Jane?"

Jane smiled, shrugging. "I really do not know myself. Oh! Papa wrote that he will have a letter for you in the post shortly. He did not wish to delay Bingley on the road. He agreed that a short engagement would be best for *his* nerves, and offered no complaints in that regard."

Elizabeth laughed at the idea of her father's nerves being overwrought. She made to retire to her room, but paused. "I will miss you."

Jane sobered. "You are my little sister. You will always be my Lizzy. And my home will always have a place for *you*."

It was too much, and Elizabeth was sobbing on Jane's shoulder. Jane rocked her quietly, until the tears started easing. "That was not merely over my engagement."

"I do not even know any more," Elizabeth replied, her voice scratchy. "I am sorry."

"I have been expecting such a reaction for days now," Jane admitted. "You have been overwhelmed and beset at all sides. Instead, you have held together admirably. Even your tears after Wickham's story were less than I might have expected."

"Everything is cascading faster than I can think," Elizabeth said. "Every moment I believe I have a handle on it all, it comes crashing in again."

Jane frowned. "I took you at your word that you would be fine. Do *you* need me to delay the wedding? I can certainly arrange that for my dearest sister."

"No! I -- I am not trying to keep you from your happiness. I *want* you to be happily married, with a home of your own. I will be easier, knowing you are loved and cared for properly. Not like Cha -- not like others we know."

Jane searched her face, and Elizabeth did her best to make her earnestness clear. After a moment, Jane nodded slowly. "I believe you."

Thirty-Six

The gossip pages kept busy for the next week, rife with various bits of speculation around the de Bourghs, Matlocks, and Darcys. Jane's engagement to Bingley merited some natter, but it was primarily overshadowed by the hopes and expectations that Mr. Darcy's unusual sociability had created. Some hoped it meant that Mr. Darcy was finally attending to his familial duties in earnest, and that they may be the lucky choice. Others, rather clearer eyed, saw that the game was as concluded as the lady in question permitted it to be. Sly comments to Elizabeth, from more than just the extended family, became routine in the Matlocks' parlour.

In such an atmosphere, deciding to return to Longbourn with Jane became effortless. Elizabeth informed Lady Catherine of her wishes, first.

Lady Catherine nodded. "To own the truth, I expected as much," she said. "Jane needs you, and your time at Longbourn is nearing an end as well." Elizabeth could not suppress the wince, and Lady Catherine smiled. She patted Elizabeth's hand. "My girl, I did not mean a removal to Rosings, or even Brandywine."

Elizabeth huffed in frustration. "Perhaps I will turn William down, when he asks, just to spite everyone so eager to predict my future!" She blushed, and muttered an apology for the outburst.

"When?" Lady Catherine chuckled. "Your tongue betrays you. You are not unaware."

"I could not be if I wished to be, at this juncture," Elizabeth replied.

"Indeed, I do not believe there are many unaware," Lady Catherine agreed. "But he still has not asked you?"

"Not as such," Elizabeth shook her head. "If only the nips and nudges of society would be still, I would not be bothered by it. So much has changed, so fast."

"Jane's wedding will be another one."

"Yes," Elizabeth sighed. "Which is why I wish to spend the time with Jane, at ho -- Longbourn."

"Home," Lady Catherine corrected her softly. She reached out and tilted Elizabeth's chin to bring her eye to eye. "It is indeed your home, still. Rosings will not have the opportunity to gain so much of your heart's contentment. I do not resent that." She suddenly smiled mischievously. "After all, visiting my daughter at *Pemberley* will certainly be worthwhile."

"*Mère!*" Elizabeth scolded with a blush.

Lady Catherine waved the scold away. "I will send my own note to Mr. Bennet when you return with Jane. I would prefer to attend to as much as possible, as efficiently as possible."

With that, it was settled. Elizabeth would return to Longbourn with Jane and Maria Lucas.

Bingley and Jane decided on a wedding trip to the Lakes, near where his family earned their fortune. With no set schedule, they intended to be at least a fortnight, perhaps two. Miss Bingley and Jane discussed several things regarding the Bingley townhouse, and Miss Bingley made arrangements to stay with the Hursts for the duration.

A flurry of shopping and ordering items of concern took up most afternoons. The Viscountess, as the most recently married woman in the family, advised Jane on selections, with Bingley making up any shortfalls from the Bennet budget. Fortunately, Darcy remained a steady visitor whenever feasible.

Two days after her decision to return to Longbourn, Elizabeth found herself seated at the pianoforte -- not to entertain, but to practice, even if only briefly. Most of the household was engaged in other activities, and she had the room to herself. She was engrossed in studying the music in front of her, when William startled her. "May I be of assistance?" he asked.

"Oh! I did not see you come in," Elizabeth responded, looking up at him. "Certainly," she gestured at the seat. "But I am not likely to provide much entertainment, as I have not seen this piece before." She caught a glimpse of Lady Matlock at the door, looking quite nettled, before that lady realized Elizabeth had seen her. Lady Matlock shook her head slightly, and moved out of Elizabeth's sight.

"I find the process of learning a new piece to be an entertainment of its own," William replied. He caught the direction of her gaze, and glanced that way as well. He added, in a quieter tone, "Our aunt is vexed by us."

Us, Elizabeth mused. It felt … right, to be a plural with William. She did not know how else to phrase it, even in her mind. "Why?" She ghosted her fingers over keys, miming her interpretation of the fingering.

William laughed quietly. "Because we have not yet made any formal announcements."

"*Mère* has taken to teasing me daily," she replied. "Before, it was only Jane and Anne."

He frowned as he watched her fingers. "I do not wish to overshadow Bingley and Jane."

"Nor I," she agreed. She played the passage lightly, wincing as she missed a note.

"Even an informal announcement may have that effect," he added.

"Yes. Assuming there is anything to announce," she teased.

The look he gave her made her suddenly very aware they were in the parlour alone, open door or not. She blushed deeply and focused hard on the keys. "True. I have only suggested, not asked," he finally said. "Mostly for my own sake. *I* am nearly out of patience, myself."

Something in his tone, combined with that look, kept her from teasing him too much. Her stomach fluttered. "Then we are agreed that, after my sister's wedding is concluded, we will continue this discussion?" She disliked how breathless she sounded.

He inhaled sharply, and for a moment she was afraid she had upset him. She made to apologize, and he waved it off. "I am endeavouring to remember that we are only agreeing to *discuss*." She opened her mouth to tell him there was not much *to* discuss, and he put a finger to her lips. "Do not say it." His finger trailed down to along her jaw, seemingly without his input, and sent her heart racing. He pulled away, looking as affected as she felt.

After she had her own reactions under control, Elizabeth commented in amusement, "I believe we will need attentive chaperones."

William groaned, and stood up. "And lacking any at the moment, I will move to the library for both of our sakes." He paused then leaned over to whisper in her ear. "Temptress." His tone was half amusement, half the husky tone of a few moments previous.

She muttered back, "Who is tempting who? Go, before …" she would not finish that thought aloud.

William inhaled sharply again, and abruptly turned and strode out of the room. She watched him leave in relief, admiration, and disappointment. That tone of his was more intoxicating than any wine she had sampled, and she almost wished they had not agreed to wait until after Jane's wedding. But she knew her mother, and Jane deserved to have all of the attention that would be removed by the announcement of Elizabeth's engagement.

Because if Elizabeth had doubted her answer to the question William had been hinting at for weeks before, that ended the moment he admitted to his patience being nearly gone. She realized hers was, too.

* * *

Darcy settled into his uncle's library, but found he could not focus on the book in his hands at all. After a few minutes, he set it aside and moved to look out the window. He daydreamed about how he wished that conversation with Elizabeth could have gone. Not that he would have done *that,* but daydreams can have a mind of their own. He would have time to arrange a proper amount of solitude for the idea at Pemberley. *After.*

Lady Catherine's voice interrupted him. "I was expecting you to seek me out, perhaps with a question," she said.

Darcy suppressed his irritation at being disturbed, and looked to see both of his aunts staring at him. It would not do to antagonize either of them *now.* "Forgive me, madam, but I have not the foggiest clue why you would have such an expectation at this moment," he replied dryly.

Lady Matlock glowered. "I did not leave you alone with Elizabeth in the parlour for *nothing* to happen."

He raised an eyebrow. "My dear *cousin* is still there, I believe, practicing a new piece on the pianoforte. We did converse on important topics, but agreed the conclusion must be delayed until after her sister's wedding."

Lady Catherine huffed, but Lady Matlock stilled her. "The delay is about Jane and Bingley?" He nodded. "Then ask her already! There is no need to delay the engagement itself."

Darcy laughed. "I assure you there is a need. Should my application be successful, however, I dare say that any arrangements will need to be completed rapidly." He knew Elizabeth was accurate about their requirement for attentive chaperones.

Lady Catherine narrowed her eyes at him, and he met her gaze squarely. "Do you believe there may be any other answer than a positive?"

He shook his head. "I do not, but it would be imprudent of me to assume otherwise. I have worked far too hard on cultivating her good opinion to simply throw it away in pride and arrogance."

"But you have agreed to discuss an engagement?"

"Without those exact words," Darcy agreed.

Lady Catherine pursed her lips, and strode out of the room. Darcy looked askance at Lady Matlock, who shrugged and seated herself with a book. Several moments later, Lady Catherine returned with Elizabeth in tow. Elizabeth saw Darcy and flushed, looking away. He wrenched his attention back to the current situation before his mind could start meandering again.

"Elizabeth, Darcy, this has gone on long enough. Agree to *something* formal, for propriety's sake. Sister, let us leave them for a few minutes." She gave Darcy a stern look. "We will be just outside."

Lady Matlock smirked and rose to join Lady Catherine. She made little waving motions with her hand at Darcy and Elizabeth.

Elizabeth just watched as the door closed behind her aunt and mother, waiting until it was fully closed before giving Darcy a rueful look. "I fear I was unable to dissuade *Mère* of this being necessary."

Darcy remained where he was, trying valiantly to not think about the curve of her neck … or anything else. He gestured at nearby chair. "I hope you understand why I am keeping my distance at the moment."

She laughed. "Quite." She sobered as she sat. "I do not understand what has come over them."

"Perhaps they have heard enough speculation. Perhaps your mother has been as desperate as Mrs. Bennet to arrange a wedding." He shrugged, before giving her a long look. "Perhaps it is because they wish to see some of the activity before you remove to Longbourn, and I follow to Netherfield?"

"It is settled you will remove to Netherfield as well?"

"Indeed," Darcy agreed. "Georgiana will not follow immediately, as some of her studies are best managed in the London house or at Pemberley proper."

Elizabeth nodded, before rising to join him near the window. He allowed himself the pleasure of watching the sunlight play down her features. She glanced up, and blushed. "What makes you blush?" he asked.

"Your expression," she replied, fidgeting a little. "I feel … exposed, somehow."

He smirked slightly. "I do hope that I am not leering."

She laughed, startled. "Oh, no. Just intent."

"Enthralled would be more accurate," Darcy replied. *Much more than enthralled,* he admitted to himself.

"And what would your enthrallment entail?"

He firmly suppressed the immediate image of his daydream involving the pianoforte. "Would a courtship be acceptable?" He watched her suppress a reaction, and added, "It may appease to our relatives, without *too* overshadowing your sister and my friend?"

"I would be pleased with a courtship," Elizabeth agreed. She gave him a sidelong glance. "Provided the conclusion of our earlier discussion remains scheduled for after Jane's wedding."

He stepped close to her, and bent to her ear. "How long should I wait? Immediately upon exiting the church?" He did not follow through on his impulses, and knew he would pay for such control later today.

She shivered, and replied with a shaky, husky voice. "Who is tempting who again?"

He laughed softly. "I am only grateful you are suffering now, as well."

"You look entirely too pleased with yourself for *suffering* to be the term I would choose," she rejoined.

"When I first realized your, ah, *distaste* for my company, I suffered, I assure you," he admitted. "I do own my current mood is closer to elation."

"I still have not a clue why or how I caught your attention, particularly given our," she gave him an arch look, "*stellar* introduction at the Assembly."

He smiled. "That exact look, I believe. Challenge and teasing all in one, followed by a refusal to be cowed." He smirked. "Excellent qualities for the lady of such an estate holding such as Pemberley. *We* cannot be so easy-going and complying as the Bingleys, no matter how sweet and generous your sister may be."

Her expression turned softer than he had ever seen it. "When you joined me at the pianoforte earlier, I thought about how right *us* sounded." She looked out the window. "Hearing Jane and Bingley referred to in plural gives my heart a contentment I did not know I could feel again." She looked back up at him. "But *'we'* is comfort and joy."

Darcy did not quite recall kissing Elizabeth until the lack of air pushed them to break. She looked very pretty, prettier than normal, with her lips parted and cheeks flushed. She shook her head as if to clear it, and gave him a smile. "I will suppose," she said, "that means you agree with such a sentiment." He laughed, and made to kiss her again. She pressed a finger to his lips instead. "I believe our *elders* would like to know we have come to an agreement," she paused. "Also, I dare say we should stop *tempting* each other for the moment."

Darcy had not truly understood the experience of being giddy, but that seemed to be the only appropriate description for what bubbled in his chest. "Whatever my lady requests," he replied. He stepped back and offered her his arm with a silly flourish.

She took it, with a slight smile. "Facing dragons, my dear knight, is best be done together."

Thirty-Seven

"Well?" demanded Jane, not seconds after Anne shut the door to Elizabeth's room that evening.

"Well?" Elizabeth queried with as much wide-eyed innocence as she could conjure. She knew, of course, what was being asked.

Anne rolled her eyes, poking her sister in the side as she sat down. "You and William, of course. Do not think it was not obvious that some kind of agreement was made earlier today."

"Quite," Jane agreed, sitting down on Elizabeth's other side. "I may be eager to wed Bingley, but you and William act like newlyweds at the bruncheon!"

Elizabeth blushed. "Courtship, and courtship only," Elizabeth admitted. She gave Anne a sidelong look. "For which you can only blame our mother. William and I had already agreed we would come to a conclusion after Jane's wedding," she nodded at her sister, "but that was deemed insufficient by our female elders."

"Finally!" Anne exclaimed. "You will do wonders for William."

"You complement each other quite well," Jane agreed. "Now I can wed Bingley without a fret of concern about your future happiness. It shall only be second to my own."

Elizabeth laughed. "I do not have your goodness, Jane. I cannot have *your* happiness, but I do seem to have escaped a need to wait for another Mr. Collins."

Jane laughed, and Anne looked askance. "I did think I understood that, but … *Mr. Collins?* Did he really?"

Elizabeth nodded vigorously. "Oh, indeed, and," she winced, "not even the threat of my mother, sisters, and myself being left to the hedgerows should my father predecease him could persuade me to accept him." She gave Anne a long glance. "I know my hesitancy won some respect from our family, but no amount of loyalty could force me to join my life to *him*."

Anne nodded slowly. "Having been in his company several times, I cannot fault you there. He seems a relatively decent person, but he is … uncomfortable company for Mrs. Collins. I can only imagine how much more so he would have been for you."

Elizabeth bit her lip. "It was a prudent match for Charlotte. It would have been a prudent match for me. But I … could not."

"And for my cousin's sake," Anne replied hotly, "I am glad you did not! For *my* sake." She shuddered. "Had you come to us, and he presented you as his wife … I do not know what would have become of our mother."

Jane looked pensive, and Elizabeth asked her why. Jane pursed her lips as she thought. "Secure in Bingley's affections as I was at that moment, I do not think I would have accepted Mr. Collins either, had he offered for me. A month later, I was despondent enough to have accepted him simply to never hear 'Oh, sister! Oh, Mr. Bingley!' from our mother again. A month before?" Jane shrugged. "I may have decided that Mr. Collins was acceptable enough, for our mother and my dearest sisters' sake, and that my wish to marry for love was immature."

"I am glad," Elizabeth replied softly, "that timing fell in our favour, there. For you are happy, Jane, and I would not want to see you any other way. I would have indeed attempted to dissuade you, much like I did Charlotte. I would not wish you to sacrifice your happiness for the rest of us."

Jane suddenly shook herself and smiled. "Fortunate, then, we fools in love, that we need not forsake one happiness for another."

"Quite," Elizabeth agreed.

Jane kissed her sister on the cheek and made to leave. She paused. "Are we to keep this from mother?"

"Until your wedding is completed," Elizabeth affirmed. "Although I believe there will be *some* sort of official notice, the banns will not be read until after you are Mrs. Bingley."

"Very well," Jane replied. "I shall let Bingley know our timeline for our wedding trip, then. I will not miss *your* wedding, either, Lizzy!"

"How can you be sure of how long you will have?" Anne asked, although Elizabeth suspected she was teasing.

"I dare say William will ensure a proper engagement before Bingley and I leave for our trip," Jane replied.

Elizabeth, remembering William's suggestions of the steps just outside, blushed but did not give her sisters that satisfaction. Who knew what might change betwixt now and then?

* * *

Darcy felt relieved that Georgiana's enthusiasm for gaining *six* sisters all in one fell swoop was just as much as she had hinted it might be, when nudging him to ask Elizabeth. She was disappointed that they were not yet engaged.

"Six weeks? You must wait six weeks?" she asked.

"Perhaps a bit more," Darcy shrugged. "She will want Jane to stand with her, and I intend to ask Bingley stand with me, as well."

Georgiana made to pout, but sighed instead at her companion's pointed but quiet cough. "Yes, Mrs. Annesley." She focused back on Darcy. "You do have every intention of ensuring she becomes my sister at the earliest possible time?"

Darcy firmly squashed his wayward imagination again. "Yes, my dear sister. At the earliest *appropriate* time, in the *appropriate* manner, following all of the proper proprieties and sundry."

Georgiana laughed, and even a shadow of a smile flickered across Mrs. Annesley's expression. "The gossip pages will be *so* disappointed, I am sure," she replied.

Mrs. Annesley smiled. "I have little doubt the gossip pages will concoct their own amusements with no assistance from reality."

Darcy chuckled. "Quite, Mrs. Annesley. The writers exercise their wild flights of fantasy as often as they report on public activities."

Thirty-Eight

The initial questions of arrival asked and answered, and a mild refreshment offered and consumed, Mrs. Collins and Miss Lucas made themselves comfortable in Mrs. Gardiner's parlour. Congratulations in person were extended to Jane and accepted cheerfully. All in all, they made a happy gathering.

Plans for the afternoon and next few days were discussed, then -- "You will be returning to Longbourn as well, Lizzy?" Charlotte asked, perplexed. "Mr. Collins and I presumed you would return to Rosings with Lady Catherine."

"*Mère* understands my reasoning, and supports it," Elizabeth replied. "She and Anne still intend to return to Rosings, and still expect to escort you as well. They anticipate attending Jane's wedding in Hertfordshire."

"What a merry party we will be going home!" Maria cheered.

"Yes," Jane replied, far more sedately. "Mr. Bingley anticipates opening Netherfield just a day or two after we return to Longbourn. Mr. Darcy expects to join Bingley at the same time."

Charlotte gave Elizabeth a significant look at that news. "Does he indeed?" she replied, her tone deceptively mild.

"He *is* standing up with Bingley," Elizabeth replied. "It can be of little wonder that he joins his friend at such a time."

"And what of Miss Bingley and the Hursts?"

"Miss Bingley has indicated she will travel to Netherfield with the Hursts a few days later." Jane shrugged, seemingly at complete ease.

"And you can think of no other cause for Mr. Darcy to join Mr. Bingley before Mr. Bingley's own family?"

"Bingley has owned he considers Mr. Darcy as good as a brother," Jane said, although Elizabeth suspected she caught a teasing note in the comment.

Mrs. Gardiner smiled slightly, *her* tone quite teasing. "How fortunate for your Mr. Bingley, then, that Elizabeth has agreed to consider Mr. Darcy's suit."

Exclamations overlapped from the Lucas sisters, and Elizabeth bid they lower their voices. "Yes, I have agreed to a *courtship* with Mr. Darcy. I only presume my aunt shared that information with you to prevent any … misunderstandings." Elizabeth shot a slightly irritated look at her aunt, who simply smiled back.

"Only a courtship?" Charlotte nearly pouted in disappointment.

"We agreed we do not wish to overshadow Jane's wedding," Elizabeth shrugged. "We all know what my mother Bennet would do should I also return properly engaged."

Charlotte and Maria both winced slightly. "Quite," Charlotte agreed after a moment. "But that sounds much like you intend to accept."

Elizabeth shrugged again. "I would not have agreed if I did not."

Mrs. Gardiner turned the subject to the schedule for the next few days, and then rose to tend to the children. Elizabeth opted to leave for a walk, and Charlotte joined her, as did the groom.

Charlotte glanced back at the groom, sedately following behind several paces. "Are there still concerns?"

Elizabeth nodded. "Fewer than there were, but concerns remain."

"Does that play into your relocation?"

"Not at the moment. It was deemed safe enough," Elizabeth replied.

"I will not be able to attend both your wedding and Jane's, if they are separate."

"*Mère* may be able to assist in transport, if that is the concern," Elizabeth replied.

"Travel so far, twice, may be too much for me *and* ... well," Charlotte started to clarify, but ended with a vague gesture at her middle.

Elizabeth gave her friend a sharp look. "Are you sure?"

Charlotte nodded. "It is early yet. I have not even told Mr. Collins or Maria."

"And early is as risky as very late," Elizabeth frowned. "I hope all goes well, and *of course* do not risk yourself needlessly." She smiled. "I know you approve, and that is more than sufficient."

Charlotte laughed. "Approve is a mild word for it, but yes." She sobered. "I expected to talk to you at Rosings, but I may not see you again for some time."

"We did not expect to see each other for some time once I left Hunsford," Elizabeth replied.

Charlotte gave her a rueful smile. "I own, I had raised my hopes that you would, at least temporarily, take up residence at Rosings." She shook her head, and laughed slightly. "But the change of plans pleases me greatly, for your sake."

Elizabeth eyed her friend. There seemed a sense of regret in Charlotte's air. "Charlotte, please be honest. Are you happy?"

Charlotte glanced away, frowning. "I find myself melancholy, but that may be the," she gestured at her middle again rather than setting a word to her condition. "I recall my mother doing likewise at this stage. Otherwise, I am … as content as I could be, in my situation. I am certainly better off than some of our friends in Hertfordshire." She looked back at Elizabeth, with a slight smile. "Any hope I had of *romance* ended long before Mr. Collins became a prospect. I have all that I ever dared truly hope for. This," the gesture again, "is the last piece, assuming all goes well, although I certainly would welcome more than one."

Elizabeth nodded, but not being sure what comfort -- if any -- she could give her friend, she remained silent, and they walked companionably. After a few moments, they turned back to the Gardiners' road, and ended back at the doorstep.

"Strange, is it not, how much has changed since you stood here on the way to my home?" Charlotte asked, looking up at the façade.

Elizabeth looked as well, her mind going back to the thoughts of three fortnights ago: Jane's health and happiness, her own discomfort at being in Mr. Collins' presence, her curiosity regarding Lady Catherine. William barely impinged on her thoughts, except as a vague source of discomfort in entering Kent. "So many stories have been told, these past few weeks," Elizabeth agreed. "So many still yet unknown."

"You will have to write them all down, some day," Charlotte opined as they gained the door and the groom disappeared to his duties. "You have the flare that the rest of us lack."

"Perhaps," Elizabeth temporized. "Once I know more of the stories myself, perhaps."

* * *

Richard found Darcy in his library, tending to correspondence. The door had barely shut when he spoke. "My mother tells me that you formalized your courtship with our Elizabeth."

Darcy, who looked up as soon as he heard Richard's voice, laid his pen down. "I have, although I persuaded both of my aunts that there need not be any public disclosure of that change."

Richard smirked, settling himself into a chair across from Darcy. "You know there will be quite the outcry when you announce the wedding."

"Undoubtedly," Darcy agreed. "But, while the only opinion I truly care about on this topic is Elizabeth's, I doubt you came to share your disapproval."

"Not a shred of disapproval here," Richard concurred. "I came to be pleased with you."

"And, perhaps, escape your mother's commentary about your lack of progress in the same field?"

Richard snorted. "She reminded me that I am yet another year older, and 'even *Darcy* is finding someone to settle down with'." He mimicked his mother's voice, accurately enough that Darcy looked quite amused.

"She is, of course, correct," Darcy observed, smirking at him.

"'Tis your fault for finding the Bennets first," Richard huffed at him.

Darcy leaned back, suddenly intent. "Jane seems a bit … sweet, for your tastes, Richard."

"And Elizabeth, before becoming a de Bourgh, rather too poor for my habits of expense," he sighed.

"Ah. Which diminishes the potential interest of the younger girls."

"Miss Mary asked intelligent questions, and Miss Catherine seemed quite empathetic."

Darcy nodded slowly. "What of Anne?"

"I do not know," Richard replied. "It is not that she is not pretty of her own accord, in her own way, but she … lacks something I do not know how to describe."

"Elizabeth, for all her innate sweetness, is unafraid to challenge all and sundry," Darcy said.

"That may be it." Richard gestured in the general direction of the street. "Too many lasses interested in agreeing the sky is purple, or perhaps green, if only it means I take a fancy to them. My career allows me plenty of opportunity to see how such a mentality can wreak havoc on a battalion. I cannot imagine that such refusal to make the most miniscule of objections can improve the health and financial prospects of an estate, even if only a borrowed one."

"Alexander still offering you the use of one of the smaller estates?"

"Provided I find a lass to tolerate," Richard affirmed. "For now, he is content to let me manage the horses in exchange for a percentage."

"You do have an eye for them." Darcy leaned forward. "Perhaps, with your brother's support, fortune is less of an issue than you believe. I think you require a different metric to consider."

"And what might that be?" Richard retorted.

"Can she learn what is necessary to breed and raise horses of a quality fit for nobility? Can she enjoy your favourite pastime -- riding -- easily enough, or learn to? Or will she be content to accept you have a deep love for them, and not hinder those pursuits?" Darcy leaned back. "A gentleman's daughter -- not brought up too high -- would not need quite as many expenses as you have a habit for, but may also have the understanding of all the concerns of husbandry."

Richard rested his head on his hand. "What you mean, of course, is to find a lass with her head on straight, knowledge enough to be economical, fond of horses -- or at least knowledgeable of livestock, and a desire to better our circumstances."

"Not in so many words, but yes."

"That is not Anne."

Darcy shrugged. "It may not be Anne. But you mentioned two prospects who may fit, and I dare say if you look for someone willing to challenge you, you may find others."

Richard nodded slowly. "It may be worth looking at the field from a different vantage point."

* * *

Wickham took the mail at roll call in a bit of surprise. Apart from the unanticipated summons from Lord Matlock, Wickham had not had a letter at this posting yet. He tucked them away, to pursue later, although the two letters weighed on his thoughts most of the day.

Miss Lydia even teased him, when he and the rest of the officers joined the Bennets for dinner. "So distracted you are today, Wickham!"

"Forgive me, Miss Lydia. I have had much to think about these past few weeks," he replied with what he hoped was a disarming smile. "I shall attempt to concentrate more assiduously."

He did try, and Miss Lydia did not broach his distractedness again. Therefore, he appeared to do so tolerably well.

Mr. Bennet, however, was not fooled. During the separation of the sexes, Mr. Bennet asked him in an undertone if there were any concerns which should be shared.

"No, sir. I simply received two letters, earlier, and have not had the opportunity to peruse them."

Bennet glanced around the room, before nodding. "I can understand hesitancy. Please do let me know if there are any concerns to share."

"Of course, sir."

The carriages returning the officers to the barracks had left over an hour previous, and most of his fellows had retired for the evening. Wickham continued to dawdle, until the remainders offered to deal him into their current round. "I thank you, but no. I have other business to attend," he excused himself. He had promised William, after all.

His room looked no different than it had when the express from Lord Matlock arrived, upending his already topsy-turvy world. He took the letters out, and stared at them for a moment longer, before deciding to open the one with a more masculine hand. He expected it was William's, although another page slipped out from the middle, in a more feminine hand.

Brother,

Georgiana professed a wish to communicate with you, and I felt it appropriate to enable her desires in this regard.

The staff at the London house have been informed that communications from you to her are approved, although they are not yet aware of the relationship. I have informed them that you are considered family, and will be treated as such.

Wickham took several minutes to digest this, before turning back to the letter. William noted that he had likely already heard the news of Bingley and Miss Bennet, and communicated his own current understanding with Miss Elizabeth, such as it was. It was brief, and to the point, but their communications had been strained or worse for so long, Wickham could not expect more. He had not even expected this much. To be given permission to write Georgiana was an unexpected windfall.

He opened her letter next, and read her excitement at William agreeing.

> Mostly, brother, I wished to be able to tell you that you are not entirely alone in the world, as you used to believe. William has not shared all of the details of your estrangement's start; I will leave it to you to decide if you wish to share them with me. I know he is concerned about your influence on *me* but I am more concerned on *our* influence on *you*.
>
> Not knowing all, or even most, of the details means I cannot provide advice on how to, if it is even possible to, make amends for past deeds. Knowing the truth of your intent behind our previous interactions has placed them in a proper light. While, perhaps, manners were not as proper as they were meant to be, an explanation to William of whatever disagreement lies between you may help? Or perhaps, if you believe that will not bring some measure of understanding, simply *asking* what you need to do to set things correct?
>
> The letter shifted again, and ended on a trivial note, with an affectionate adieu.

Wickham sighed. He knew, of course, one of the causes of the estrangement, even before the misunderstanding about Georgiana. Certainly, given his previous failings, Darcy had been entirely correct to be concerned about Georgiana's safety.

A waterfall of blonde hair, cascading in his hands … rain drops pattering on the small dual headstone …

Emma.

He shook the memories away, and focused his attention on the other letter. Miss de Bourgh?

Wickham shrugged and opened the letter. Anne confided her confusion about Elizabeth -- joy, but also disconcertion at so much change so fast. She noted she could not truly confide that emotion to anyone else in the family, for they all were focused on softening the changes for Elizabeth. From here, she segued into what Wickham initially felt was gossip -- Lady Catherine's long-time steward was starting to feel his age, and mentioning the idea of retiring. What, Wickham wondered, did that have to do with him?

Her next paragraph explained thusly:

> … I have reminded Mother that you were in training to take on the Stewardship, either Rosings or at Pemberley. She has expressed reservations, given what we know of your gambling habits from the debts William has discharged over the years.
>
> I have countered that I believe it is a habit borne of a form of nihilism, especially in light of recent divulgences.
>
> She does not know all of your circumstances for such a malaise; William only shared that information in close confidence to Richard and myself.
>
> Did you love her? William says that he believed you did, for you talked about her often, speaking of a desire to ask for her hand. But I suppose you anticipated your vows, and when her family realized it, her family refused to allow any contact. They wanted only Pemberley money. He told us he only agreed because he was going to bring you personally to her after the babe was born, so you could follow through. He made them quite cross when he told

you of their death. I am so very sorry; child birth can be so risky.

From what William says, she at least knew you did not abandon her by choice.

You truly have just had poorly dealt hand after poorly dealt hand, have you not?

Take a few months to settle down from the recent upheavals, and consider the possibility of at least training with Mother's Steward. It is not a dishonourable profession for a second son.

Yours, etc,

Anne

Wickham set the letter down, undone in multiple directions. His Emma had not cut *him* off, and William had intended to bring them together despite her family's displeasure. His grief came over him afresh, the loss of his beloved, his betrothed, and the loss of his unexpected but wanted firstborn.

The grief storm raged for a while before Wickham was spent. He did sleep, but it was not a sleep of refreshment.

Thirty-Nine

A week with good friends seemed to set Mrs. Collins into a better mood, and Elizabeth endeavoured over that same week to further a closer relationship between her dear friend and her oldest sister. She hoped it was enough to ease Charlotte's concerns about her condition.

"Until we meet again in Hertfordshire," Anne said, embracing Elizabeth a last time before entering the carriage.

"I will miss you, sister," Elizabeth replied.

"And I you," said Anne. She ducked into the carriage to sit beside their mother.

Lady Catherine smiled slightly from the carriage, and Elizabeth fancied she saw a shimmer of tears. She forwent comment, believing that her first thought for a joke about misplacing either Anne or Charlotte would be rather misplaced itself. She turned to Charlotte, and the friends hugged fiercely. "If you must avoid travel, Jane will not hold it against you any more than I would," Elizabeth whispered.

Charlotte nodded. "You will write to me, Lizzy?"

"Always, Charlotte," agreed Elizabeth as they stood back. The groom assisted Charlotte into the carriage.

A last round of farewells, and then Lady Catherine directed the coachman to start off. Elizabeth felt a pang of separation she had not entirely anticipated, not only for Charlotte. She could not linger over it long, however, as their last week in London remained busy with the details of socializing with friends old and new, along with preparations for Jane's wedding. Some items, Elizabeth also looked at, with an eye towards ordering by mail if possible.

It was the second week of May, in which the three young ladies set out together from Gracechurch Street. For Jane and Elizabeth, the morning had already been busy as farewells occurred first at ------ House, with both Darcys in attendance as well as the Fitzwilliams. Thence, the carriage brought Jane and Elizabeth to Gracechurch Street, where another round of affectionate farewells took place.

By the time they reached the town where Mr. Bennet's carriage was to meet them at the inn, the older girls were far from refreshed, while Maria still chattered intermittently about kittens. Still, upon seeing their younger sisters waiting for them, Jane and Elizabeth shared a smile, and sought out their father's coachman to arrange moving their luggage to the Bennet carriage.

The younger girls came down to meet the elder and Maria, and they adjourned to the dining room which had been secured. News about the militia being sent to Brighton and Lydia's despair of such was shared, and then Lydia broached *other* news. Elizabeth dismissed the waiter, and Jane shook her head at Lydia's antics.

Wickham, by Lydia's report, had lost interest in Mary King, and the girl had been removed to Liverpool to live with her uncle. Lydia cried triumph over the other girl, but Elizabeth and Jane shared a glance. "How has Mr. Wickham fared these last weeks?" Jane asked.

"Oh, aye," Kitty replied, "fair well enough. *Lydia* insists he flirts with her constantly, but I have seen none of it."

"Lies!" cried Lydia.

"Perspective, perhaps," Elizabeth corrected. "He is quite a few years older than you, Lydia. He may be unaware of how you perceive his actions."

"But," Kitty continued as if Lydia had not interrupted her, "I believe he has been melancholy since his abrupt visit to London. Denny and the others have mentioned he no longer joins them for cards, at the very least."

"I hope he rallies his spirits soon," Jane answered mildly, although the half not-glance at Elizabeth showed her concern.

Lydia, however, caught the look, and cried, "Perhaps Lizzy gained a beau and Wickham is pining for her!"

Elizabeth dismissed such nonsense promptly. "Mr. Wickham was called to London by Lord Matlock, my maternal uncle, to discuss various business concerns." A truth, without elaborating on the type of concerns. "I only encountered Mr. Wickham but two days before he returned to Hertfordshire at the same time as *our* father."

"Truly," Jane added, "such conjectures are problematic, Lydia. Dreadful rumours have been caused by far less such comments."

"Oh!" Lydia huffed. "Maria and Kitty will side with me on this. It is simply silliness."

Maria shook her head briskly. "Do not draw *me* into that quarrel, Lydia. I know what happened to Charlotte, long before Mr. Collins married her. She fancied someone, a long time ago, when I was little. I remember he was very nice. But a rumour started up that he was responsible for one of the tavern maid's … situation. He left for the Navy, I think. And she later admitted she had lied to protect someone else." Maria shrugged sadly. "But a while later, word came from *his* family that he had died while at sea. And Charlotte married Mr. Collins."

Elizabeth wondered if she had known that story and forgotten it, or if perhaps it occurred before she was an age to have been aware. Mrs. Bennet certainly never mentioned it. Lydia made a moue of disgust, before grudgingly agreeing to be a *little* bit less silly for the sake of simply being silly. No one wanted to be stuck with a Mr. Collins.

"It does lessen the fun, however," Kitty sighed. "We did have many good jokes to share with you."

"Perhaps in the carriage," Elizabeth replied.

"And as long as there are far fewer in the future," agreed Jane.

"Barely engaged, and already nagging me like an old lady," Lydia laughed.

"But I *am* engaged, and I do not wish to lose my fiancé over a frivolous rumour," Jane replied.

"True!" Kitty agreed.

"And you shall not turn out an old maid after all!" Lydia exclaimed, diverted to a new topic already. "I know my Mother and my aunt Phillips had begun to despair you might!"

"Ah, yes," Elizabeth sighed dramatically, with a slight smile. "The hedgerows. I nearly thought I would take up residence there myself, after Charlotte's engagement."

The other girls laughed, and the conversation settled into lesser news. Before long, the entire party was cozy in Mr. Bennet's carriage, with every spare space stuffed with a bandbox or small bag. The stories and jokes soon flowed, and Elizabeth attempted to suppress her wince. She noted how often certain names came up -- Wickham, Denny. Her own situation appeared to have not yet made the rounds of gossip -- at least, not from Lydia's recounts. No mention of militia officers arriving at Longbourn to ask after her health, or any such various instances.

They were welcomed by a large party, for the Lucases arrived to collect Maria, ask after Charlotte, and warmly congratulate Miss Bennet. Mrs. Bennet's pleasure with her eldest, however, eclipsed all else. Mr. Bennet's pleasure *for* his eldest, while palpable, was far more contained. Elizabeth watched it all, feeling reassured she and William had been correct to delay their own agreement.

After the Lucases left, Lydia attempted to convince her sisters they should walk to Meryton. Elizabeth steadfastly opposed such a scheme, and Jane supported her. "After all," Jane said sweetly, "I shall not have much longer to spend with you here. I should like to visit with my sisters for a while, before I must turn my attention to the matter of preparing for my wedding. But perhaps tomorrow? I do have a list of items to look for at the milliner's."

Mrs. Bennet overheard the comment, and chastised Jane. "You were in London! You did not need to leave anything for Meryton."

Jane shrugged slightly. "I had my reasons, Mama. Mr. Bingley particularly requested a few items be selected from the milliner's here, as this is where we met."

It did not go unnoticed how easily the words "Mr. Bingley" soothed over any of Mrs. Bennet's concerns or complaints. Elizabeth wondered if, over the next few weeks, Jane would occasionally run dangerously close to *over*using that method of reprieve.

Forty

Lydia brought up a scheme to join the militia in Brighton the next morning. "For it will all be so dreary here," she complained. "The parties will be so less interesting."

"We have far too much to do," Mrs. Bennet replied sharply. "Jane is getting married!"

Lydia looked surprised at this source of refusal, and subsided. Not that anyone else could bring up a word sideways over Mrs. Bennet's exultations and plans.

The girls only extracted themselves from Mrs. Bennet's effusions by Jane's well timed "Mr. Bingley would like" comment, and all five of them nearly fled their mother's presence. Even Mary looked harried, and agreed to join her sisters for the walk to Meryton. Mr. Bennet took pity on them, and his pocketbook, and conveyed a much pared down of items which Mrs. Bennet insisted would be necessary to celebrate her Jane's handsome catch.

The banns were to be read this week Sunday, which provided Jane three entire weeks and a few days more to prepare any items not already ordered and to pack. Bingley, according to Jane and barring any misfortunes, intended to arrive at Netherfield sometime late today.

"Then," Kitty teased, "we should not dally long with the officers. We should not keep you from your intended!"

"Oh, aye!" agreed Lydia. "But perhaps we can convince one or two to join us for the walk home."

"Perhaps," Elizabeth allowed. She remembered Wickham's hints about some of his fellow officers.

Kitty and Lydia voiced disappointment upon not seeing any of their preferred officers when entering Meryton. Elizabeth hushed them both, reminding them of the discussion at the inn just the day before. Lydia huffed a little but desisted. Kitty looked properly subdued. However, the Miss Bennets were shortly joined by some of the same officers which Lydia and Kitty despaired so vocally about, and another.

"Miss Bennet, Miss Elizabeth," Mr. Wickham greeted them both warmly, in his own turn. Elizabeth felt the difference of *this* warmth to his prior greetings, lo not that many months ago now. Lydia certainly caught the slight change, even if she did not know the meaning of it.

"Do not forget me, Wickham!" she cried, before he could even turn his head to do just so.

He smiled gamely at the youngest Bennet. "My apologies, Miss Lydia, but I could hardly forget you! Propriety, however, does indicate I greet your elder sisters first." He glanced at Mary and Kitty as well. "I hope this day finds you all well?"

"It does indeed," agreed Jane, and Mary murmured an assent.

Lydia gave Wickham a reproachful glare, and attached herself to Denny's arm. Elizabeth gave Wickham a sharp glance, and from the look he gave her, he was agreeing to stay close at hand. "I mostly wished," Wickham continued as if this little byplay were not going on, "to give my sincere congratulations to you, Miss Bennet. I have it on the best of authorities that Mr. Bingley has been granted the favour of a living angel to be his wife."

Jane coloured. "I know nothing about *that,* Mr. Wickham, but I am engaged to Mr. Bingley."

The other officers looked calculating at Jane and a little more so at Lydia. Elizabeth felt her ire rising, and felt compelled to ward off a predatory intent. "It is indeed fortunate for our Jane. She has found love *and* fortune, and, as we all know, even the very beautiful must have something to live upon. It is pity that our lot is so very *small*." A frown flittered across Denny's face.

"Quite," Jane assented. "I am fortunate."

"It is my studied opinion, my dear ladies, that it is *Bingley* who is the blessed one, but I quite understand your position," Wickham agreed easily.

Horses were heard and the party moved towards the shopfronts to clear the way. "Miss Bennet!" cried Bingley, and the riders -- for William was with Bingley -- directed their steeds to join the party directly.

Elizabeth felt a wave of *déjà vu* upon seeing William while speaking easily with Wickham. Both men also appeared to be recalling that particular instance. This time, however, William dismounted beside Wickham and Elizabeth. The men shook hands cordially enough, and muted gasps could be heard from the curious nearby. "Miss Elizabeth," William greeted her, before glancing in the direction of Bingley and Jane, already in close conversation. "Miss Mary, Miss Kitty, Miss Lydia, sirs."

"It is obvious what brought Mr. Bingley to town," Elizabeth said laughingly. "Did he allow you to wake at a reasonable time before riding to Longbourn?"

William chuckled. "I normally wake before Bingley, but not this morning. We were in fact on the way to your home." He glanced at his friend, then nodded at the horses. "I suspect Bingley will wish to assist your sister. Let me tend to setting the horses, so that it is easier to join you." Wickham offered to assist.

Lydia had already dragged Denny further from the party, nattering on about bonnets. Denny's attention, however, remained on Wickham and William. When William and Wickham rejoined Elizabeth and her sisters, Mary posed a question to William. "Mr. Darcy, I recall what your cousin noted about his duties and how ofttimes he is not available for his mother's social engagements. How does that compare to what you have seen from our militia officers in Meryton?"

William tilted his head as he considered the question. Wickham answered, "I suspect, Miss Mary, that the differences you allude to at this moment comes to a difference in experience. Darcy's cousin has nigh twenty years in the Army, and I believe he has served on the Continent several times. This militia, however, has seen little action, and those newly joined such as myself, none-at-all."

William nodded at Wickham. "What Wickham says is true. My cousin has suffered enough injuries on the field that he has been retired to service on this side of the channel, pending an heir from his elder brother."

"But he remains in the Army? He mentioned nothing of injuries," she added, looking disconcerted. "They do not trouble him?"

"His insight to battlefield operations assists the home office in making wiser decisions," William replied. "Or, so he has described his current posting to me. He does not make the most patient of patients, and does not relish recounting when he has been put into that position."

"Meanwhile, Miss Mary," Wickham picked up, "Most of us in the militia have not such heavy loads on our shoulders, and thus find ourselves free to escort such lovely ladies as you and your sisters."

Mary blushed faintly at any such praise, and Kitty snorted. Elizabeth noticed William's careful not-study of Mary, and saw a flicker of something in his expression, for just a moment.

Jane and Bingley entered the milliner's, following Lydia and Denny. Kitty opted to join them, while the rest of the party went across to the bookstore. When Mary turned down Wickham's game offer of assistance with book shopping, the other three retreated to the music section, "for Georgiana is always keen for something new," William said.

Once they were out of ear shot from her next-younger sister, William spoke in an undertone. "Promise me, Miss Elizabeth, you will assist Miss Mary in her preparations for my friend's wedding?" She shot him a questioning look, just as Wickham breathed out an "Ah ha!"

"If you insist," Elizabeth agreed as she looked from one to the other, and William and Wickham shared a triumphal smile.

"And then there was one," Wickham muttered under his breath.

Forty-One

The last week of the militia's stay in Meryton drew to a close with several parties, hosted in turn by the Bingleys, the Bennets, and the Lucases. Miss Bingley proved herself quite the capable hostess for her last event before turning over such household requirements to her new sister the next week.

While perhaps the youngest Miss Bennets attempted to throw a pall over the mood of the household in their dejection, the manic energy of Mrs. Bennet more than compensated for the youngest. Indeed, *she* brooked absolutely no displays of distress, not now, not so close to her crowning achievement of marrying Jane off to a young man of good family and fortune. The young ladies of the neighbourhood certainly drooped, but most came back to hope when reminded that many of Mr. Bingley's still single and eligible gentleman friends had been invited to witness his felicity personally.

The two weeks of comradeship between Wickham and William in full view of the neighbourhood soon put paid to some of the hatred Wickham previously stirred up. Wickham owned to a few 'friends', such as he had among the officers, that he had previously spoken twisted words, and admitted his fault. In doing so, however, the protection William had previously enjoyed from feminine attention as the formidable Mr. Darcy, not even tempted by the Miss Eliza Bennet, evaporated as soon as the last redcoat left the area.

The week of the wedding it became apparent that only Elizabeth's company could purchase William a moment of peace outside of

Netherfield or Longbourn. Mrs. Bennet remained so overjoyed by Jane's good fortunes that she barely even noticed Mr. Darcy *existed,* and he found this a pleasant, albeit unusual, state of affairs. Netherfield hosted several of Bingley's friends at this point. Lady Catherine and Anne were expected to stay at Longbourn, and due in just a day's time.

Fortunately for both William and Elizabeth, their younger sisters were quite happy to entertain themselves. Additionally, between Elizabeth's gentle encouragements and Georgiana's praise, Mary showed sufficiently promising improvement that even Lydia did not scold her for (as much) for her music choices. Whenever Jane's presence was required, Bingley attached himself to William and Elizabeth, and she did likewise. Today, however, the men were obliged to be good neighbours and attend a dinner elsewhere.

Elizabeth watched as Jane sorted the last of her belongings, leaving only two days' worth left, and a few less important trinkets for her room. "At least you will not need to fret if you forget to pack something," Elizabeth observed. "Five miles is easy travel enough for something misplaced."

"Certainly better than Derbyshire," Jane agreed. "You will need to be more thorough than I am."

"What is in Derbyshire, pray tell?" asked Mary. Jane and Elizabeth both started, as they had not heard her approach the room. She slipped in quietly, shutting the door firmly behind her. "I only know of my aunt, Miss Darcy, and Mr. Darcy as of importance from there," she continued.

Elizabeth coloured slightly, and looked askance at Jane. Jane tilted her head in encouragement. Looking back at Mary, she shrugged. "Mr. Darcy."

Mary nodded, not a slip of surprise in her expression or tone. "Are you engaged?"

"A courtship. Our father has agreed, as has my mother. *Our* mother does not know."

"Congratulations. Why -- because Jane, of course," Mary sighed.

"Quite," Elizabeth agreed readily.

"He has been as good as a brother to Kitty, Lydia, and myself, even in our stay in his townhouse, " Mary offered. "I quite like this version of him."

Jane nodded. "We are given to understand he was quite distressed when he arrived with Bingley in the autumn."

"Georgiana shared a bit of her troubles," Mary said quietly. "I understand his … mood." She glanced between the elder girls. "Is Lydia at risk of something similar?"

Elizabeth bit her lip and Jane winced ever so slightly. "I certainly hope not," Jane sighed. "But -- "

"But ever since the militia came, there has been nothing but love, flirtation, and officers in her head!" cried Elizabeth, however quietly.

"Nor has that been improved by Jane's engagement," Mary replied. "Lydia will not be allowed to go to Brighton, will she?"

"I am certainly unaware of there being an intention of her going," Elizabeth replied, brows furrowing. "She certainly cannot go without family."

Mary seemed concerned. "Did you not know Mrs. Forster had written a letter, offering to let her join her after Jane's wedding?"

"No!" cried both elder girls. "Does our father know?" Elizabeth demanded.

"I would hope so, but I have only heard Lydia speak of it to Kitty. She seemed quite certain she was to go."

"The militia has left; the Forsters with them. *How* was she planning on traveling?" Elizabeth questioned.

"I believe the discussion was that Captain Denny had offered to escort her."

Jane and Elizabeth shared concerned glances, and Elizabeth rose to the door. "You will go to father?" Jane asked.

"Yes. Can you send a note to Bingley and William?"

"Of course."

Forty-Two

With an express sent to Brighton moments before, Bennet poured a stout drink for each Bingley and Darcy, as they conferred on the next steps. He leaned back with a sigh.

"Elizabeth had mentioned that Wickham had expressed concerns about Denny," he said.

"He did mention he considered some of his fellows to be of ... questionable motives," Darcy agreed, "but he did not single Denny out as one to me."

A knock interrupted their conversation, and Bennet called, "Enter."

Miss McGonagall peered through the door, Mrs. Hill and Elizabeth with her.

"You called for me, sir?" the governess queried.

"Yes." He rose, gesturing at all three. "Please come in." Elizabeth closed the door behind her at his direction.

"How would you say you and Miss Lydia are getting along?"

Miss McGonagall glanced at the entire group assembled, and answered with a cautious air. "I have not been disappointed in her efforts, but the novelty of the situation has not yet worn off, I suspect."

"Would you consider yourself in her confidences?" Bennet did not expect that to be the case, of course. Mrs. Forster was much more the personality to gain Lydia's confidences quickly.

"Not at all, sir. I am entirely too new to her for that. Any remarks or comments she has made have certainly been of a general nature, rather than confidential."

"Had she mentioned any correspondence at all?"

"None." She paused; her expression became more disconcerted. "She and Miss Catherine appear to be close; she may know." She glanced between the others in the room. "Is she safe?"

"She has not left this house, and she is in fact safe," Bennet assured her. "Has she spoken about any particular friends, perhaps among the recently departed militia?"

"Not any particular one, no," Miss McGonagall frowned. "When the militia were shortly to depart, she spoke of her disappointment in Lieutenant Wickham's attentions towards herself, and alluded to it being due to Miss Elizabeth. She did remark on a Captain Denny as being a fine dancer, and a few others. The captain was mentioned several times, which is the primary reason I recall him. I presumed that it was a fancy which would fade with his departure."

Bennet nodded. "Thank you for being candid, Miss McGonagall. I wished to cover all angles, but I did not expect you would have any further insight."

She nodded slowly. "What may I anticipate on the morrow?"

"I have not yet spoken with her myself. We are attempting to … dissuade her by more politic means. With any luck, it will not be an issue for tomorrow."

Miss McGonagall shewed a questioning look, and Bennet half-smiled. "Best you know as little as possible, ma'am, so as to not show our cards."

* * *

The reply from the Forsters arrived late the next day, with an additional letter from Wickham to Bennet.

The acknowledgement from Colonel Forster was terse, but complete. It seemed that Denny had not been difficult to get to confess to his plans, with a little help from Wickham, and the end result was that Denny would not be free for quite some time. *"To so treacherously plan to use my wife's name to betray my wife's friend and your daughter – I could not let such a situation stand."*

The letter from Mrs. Forster to Lydia, which Bennet perused prior to admitting its existence, put paid to any notion which Lydia may have had about absconding to Brighton with Captain Denny.

> My dearest Lydia,
>
> Such horrid news I have to share! My dear Colonel discovered that Denny – yes, *that* Denny – had designs to gain his fortune – by kidnapping *you.* Such ludicrous ideas he had for his goal! Most of Meryton knows that you and your sisters have little money to offer a husband, yet he thought he could ransom you for a princely sum! Perhaps he ought read fewer novels, although he may have little else to do in the brig, where my dear Colonel, quite incensed he would threaten a friend of mine so, has put him for many weeks.
>
> I never would have suggested he bring you to Brighton to visit after you recounted your mother's refusal, and certainly not alone and unchaperoned! Not when you suspect your other elder sister will be engaged soon as well! Weddings are such fun, and so important to a family, I would not countenance you being gone. No, my dear

friend, I will miss your company, but it is best for you to stay there for the moment.

When it is better timing for a visit, I shall certainly let you know, *and* direct an invitation to your parents, so that they know all is above board. I am grateful that my dear Colonel discovered Denny's plot before you could be injured by it! To think we thought so well of him!

I pray to hear that you are tolerably well in your reply. I know you must be disappointed, but you are safe, and that is no little thing! Please let me know how Miss McGonagall is treating you! Is she still showing you interesting things?

All my love,

Harriet

Wickham's letter elaborated on the Colonel's:

...

After the Colonel shared the information you provided to him, I offered my services to assist in resolving the situation. He questioned *my* motives, but I believe I persuaded him that the Bennets are, by round about ways, good as my family. (I hope I have not offended you, sir, but Miss Elizabeth *is* part of my extended family, and thus you-all are as well.) He consented.

It did not take long to ease Denny's guard, and straight into his cups. He was rather self-congratulatory about his intended tricks on Miss Lydia, and once he confessed that, I worked to tricking him into drinking himself into a stupor as I had a few times previously.

I did not relay this to the Colonel, to decrease the risk it might get bandied about, but Denny made a few comments which lead me to believe he intended to do more than just *ransom* your youngest. She certainly would not have been delivered in pristine condition. Not even in my most caddest of moments have I ever *forced* such upon a woman. His comments lead me to believe it is possible there is at least one in Meryton so injured by Denny, but I do not know who it may be. He kept enough wits to not be more explicit. He also did not share who assisted in mimicking Mrs. Forester's hand sufficient to trick your daughter.

I am grateful for whatever interference granted you awareness in time to preserve her from such. I only wish I had known he was of such proclivities in time to protect others. I hope that my easy rapport with he and the other officers did not lull some unsuspecting soul into unguardedness around such a creature.

…

Bennet poured a stronger drink than he normally preferred as he digested the meaning of Wickham's words. His little girl, so close to not just ruin but worse, from thoughtless naivete. Right now, he could only picture her as the babe-in-arms she once was and feel nauseous. He would put a word to his brother-in-law in Meryton to gather gossip. If there was an injured girl, he was fairly certain the good Colonel would be quite helpful in gaining justice for her.

After letting the drink temper his racing pulse, he resolved to share some of the information with Darcy and Bingley, but perhaps not *all* of the concerns even with Elizabeth. He reckoned he would be dissuading Darcy from taking responsibility for Denny's assumption of a ransom payment, as well.

He resolved that, governess or not, he would try to exert himself for the younger girls' benefit. His laziness and disappointment should not leave her – any of them – at such risk.

* * *

After the servants left the breakfast room, Bennet produced the letter from Mrs. Forster to Lydia. "As Colonel Forster and Mrs. Forster indicated I should review this prior to it being delivered, I have done so." Mrs. Bennet, thankfully, had kept to her rooms this morning with little hinting on Mrs. Hill's part.

Lydia glared at him, but took her letter with artificial graciousness. Jane and Lizzy both gave him concerned glances, and he shook his head slightly. Lydia opened it, and scanned the first paragraph. She looked up at him, shock in her expression. "Papa?"

"Do you see why they wished I review it?"

She swallowed hard and nodded. "Yes, papa."

"If you wish to talk further about it, later, I will be in my library. Miss McGonagall may be able to assist you, as well."

Lydia nodded, and, biting her lip, slipped the letter under her plate. She did not eat much more, picking at her plate. Elizabeth kept shooting glances at Lydia then to Jane. Once Jane was ready, Elizabeth set her plate aside. "May we be excused, papa?"

"Of course, my dears."

"Come, Lydia," Elizabeth coaxed her, and Jane echoed. Lydia pulled the letter out and left with her eldest sisters. Kitty and Mary watched worriedly.

"Papa?" Mary asked quietly.

"She will be fine in a day or a few. She may be mightily angry in a few days, or she may be despondent. But she will be fine." *I hope.*

Later, Elizabeth slipped into his library, looking worn.

"She will be fine," Elizabeth reported after a few moments of quiet. "She is resting, and Jane is still with her."

"I presume there was a storm of tears and fury?"

"Rightfully so," Elizabeth agreed. "Particularly after we set the letters side-by-side. The hand was similar, but not the same. Close enough that it must have been modelled off of Mrs. Forester's own letters. To learn of the deception before any other risk to her person or reputation ..." she trailed off, shaking her head. "George did well in protecting one of us, this time."

Bennet raised an eyebrow at the use of Wickham's given name. She tilted her head. "He *is* family, Papa. I dare say, in saving my little sister, he has earned that much."

"He expressed regret that he had not realized Denny would sink so low."

"It is shocking to believe that any of our acquaintance would make such falsehoods -- using the name of his superior's wife, no less. Let alone that he would do so for mere farthings!" Elizabeth rejoined. "I cannot blame him for a failure to foresee *that*."

"No, and when I reply, I will reiterate that myself. We are fortunate indeed that he volunteered to assist in the matter."

"He has not been, perhaps, the best of men, even by his own accounting. He seems to have been given good principles, and then left to follow them with little guidance." Elizabeth sighed. "Good meanings and wishes, and all of that."

"At least his appearance of goodness was not entirely false," Bennet replied. "With such an expression, he could have inflicted much harm on your family."

"Our family, papa."

Bennet smiled at the correction. "Yes, Lady Catherine did write me to share her consent for courtship, in detail. Four pages, front and back, were not enough to contain her approval and attentiveness. I do wonder how my cousin will respond to this when he finds out."

Elizabeth snorted. "He was quite confused, that first afternoon. He was all in favour of me throwing out my entire life to be Lady Catherine's daughter, until Charlotte and I both scolded him for being so mean of character."

Bennet owned he wished he could be more surprised. "He certainly has a unique perspective of a pastor's solemn duties."

Forty-Three

June dawned. The tumult of the last three days, from Lydia's ultimately fruitless scheme, to the arrival of *mère* and Anne, as well as the Gardiners, at Longbourn, had not prompted Elizabeth to forget her agreement to ensure extra care on Mary's toilette and dress.

Mary touched the more elaborate styling with significant self-consciousness, and tugged at the dress -- one of Jane's, for she was more like Jane in stature than she typically allowed. "I know it is her wedding, and I should be well turned out, but this seems ... excessive, Lizzy."

"You look *lovely,* Mary," replied Elizabeth. She lightly swatted her little sister's hand from her hair. "Do not fuss with it, or you will ruin all of Sarah's hard work."

"There is something more," Mary accused her. "What are you scheming?"

"Me?" laughed Elizabeth. "Nothing at all. But I do believe that *you* caught someone's eye, and his friends wish to ensure it stays caught."

"By me?" Mary looked positively frightened at the concept.

Elizabeth gave Mary a long look, and pulled her into an embrace. "By your wits and questioning mind, I believe. There is no harm in being as pretty as you can be just as encouragement."

Mary pulled away after returning the hug. "Is he a friend of Mr. Darcy's?"

"I believe so. William is being quite tight lipped about it."

"Or just using them for other purposes," Mary teased.

"Oh, you!" Elizabeth blushed. "*Once.*"

"An hour?"

"Insufferable!" Elizabeth cried. "You know full well Mama has not given anyone much time to themselves."

Mary laughed, the tension slipping away. "Quite. And we have a sister to marry off now." She gave Elizabeth a side long glance. "*You* are quite well turned out, too."

"I am standing up with Jane," Elizabeth replied, attempting to not colour.

"Of course," Mary smirked at her. "Time to enter the fray again, I believe, sister."

"Indeed," Elizabeth agreed.

* * *

Elizabeth took careful note of scenes, tiny moments to keep as paintings in her mind. The enraptured expression of her brother-to-be as his bride walked down the aisle. Jane simply glowed with joy, while their father looked as proud as could be. Miss Bingley appeared pleased for her brother, as did the Hursts.

The subdued but *expressive* look from William which made her feel undone. A glance at Anne, sitting with *mère* as part of Jane's family, showed her other elder sister enjoying the show at her expense.

Lydia's mood was palpable from here, despite her attempts to mask it, for Jane's sake.

The agog look of Richard towards Mary, which aligned with her suspicions. Richard's admiration of Jane at Rosings had not gone unnoticed -- and Mary, right now, looked every inch the little sister of Jane without being her replica. Mary's conversations with him in London were extensive, and she had occasionally asked questions explicitly about him since. Elizabeth felt few qualms at such a match for her sister.

In a breath of eternity, Mrs. Bennet's greatest ambition became fulfilled. Jane Bingley signed her name and the wedding party dispersed to Longbourn to celebrate. Elizabeth felt a loss, a tugging at her heart, when Jane left not only before her, but *without* her. The emotion warred with her deep joy for Jane. No such battles had taken place when Charlotte assumed the mantle of Mrs. Collins, even when she counted her friend was mostly lost to her by such a choice.

Her emotions continued to flutter about, as the party's removal increased her own anticipation.

"Shall we walk back to the house?" William asked, offering his arm.

She could not recall her exact words, but knew she assented. They walked *slowly,* and with Longbourn in sight, William turned her towards the hermitage.

For a moment, the only sounds were the rustling of the branches in the breeze, their footsteps, and their breathing. William pulled her towards one of the more secluded paths before speaking. "I believe we had a discussion to continue."

His tone was much as it had been at the pianoforte at Matlock House. She nodded, not trusting herself to speak. They continued walking, however slowly, until he halted her. "I must confess -- I have thought of a thousand little pretty speeches for right now, and I cannot recall a single one of them. All I can think of is your comment about *us* and how desperately I want that to be reality."

A ghost of a laugh, borne of amusement and nerves. "Ask, then, William. *Ask me.*"

"Will you marry me, Elizabeth?"

"Ye -- mmph."

Several pleasant moments later, Elizabeth pressed a finger to his lips. "I believe it is certainly time to return to Longbourn and *chaperones.*"

William chuckled, before agreeing with a sigh. "As wise as you are beautiful, my love."

They walked to her home quietly, with only a few comments about their intentions for the remainder of the day. They joined the festivities; her arm still entwined with William's. Jane spotted her, for the newlyweds had not yet adjourned to Netherfield, and cried for them to join her and Bingley. "I hope you enjoyed your *walk*," Jane teased Elizabeth quietly.

"*We* did," William replied with a faint smile. "And now I leave your sister in your capable hands for a moment." He clapped Bingley's shoulder with a congratulations, before heading to Mr. Bennet's side. Based on the sharp look that Mr. Bennet gave her, Elizabeth was certain that her father had been expecting this approach. She hoped that meant the progression from courting to engagement would not be unwelcome to her father. The two disappeared from the room.

Jane gave her a matching sharp look as their father left with William, to which Elizabeth just smiled. Lightly played strains on the pianoforte drew her attention to see Mary with Richard sitting beside her. Lydia's laughter, the first since the militia left just over a week ago, echoed as Anne smiled, and she spied Kitty and Georgiana in close conference.

Right here, right now, Elizabeth felt more at peace than she had in weeks. She would miss Jane's constant presence, but she would gain William's. Her family would be safe and hale.

A light touch on her arm drew her attention. "Go to your father, he wants you in the library," William whispered. In a moment, Elizabeth was seating herself across from her father.

"Mr. Darcy appears to have changed his mind about you being handsome enough to tempt him," Mr. Bennet observed after a moment of quiet.

Elizabeth blushed, and nodded. "I suppose so, sir."

"I know your opinion of him has improved, Lizzy, but I need your assurances. I cannot bear the thought that you might not have a true partner in your marriage."

"Even when I thought I hated him, he treated me as an equal. Apart from that overheard comment, he has been perfectly respectful. When I cared for Jane at Netherfield, he solicited my opinion several times, although there was certainly no requirement that he do so. We have lively discussions, even if we do not agree. I could go on," Elizabeth offered.

Mr. Bennet nodded slowly, his eyes fixed on some indeterminate point. "That fits with my observations," he agreed. His attention focused back on her as he leaned back in his chair. "You will have more than sufficient pin money certainly. Will you be *happy*?"

Elizabeth hesitated, searching for the words to reassure her father. "When I agreed to the courtship, it was only not an engagement because I did not wish to overshadow Jane's happiness. William sat with me at the pianoforte at Matlock House, and he made a comment that our aunt was unhappy with *us*. I realized that I found comfort in he and I being 'us.' "

Mr. Bennet smiled slightly at that, his eyes looking suspiciously bright. "I find comfort in the idea that someone worthy will treasure you. I believe he may be the only man I could have allowed to take you from me." He rose from his seat and offered a hand to Elizabeth. "Come. We should announce this. Your mothers will be pleased, as will Jane."

"Now?"

"Jane has had her moment, and perhaps this will permit her and Bingley to escape quietly." Mr. Bennet shrugged. "Darcy suggested it, in fact."

Elizabeth tried valiantly to not blush, knowing full well why William suggested it. She found no issues with the plan, however.

By the time they returned, a few neighbours and many of Bingley's friends had already taken their leave. Mrs. Bennet and Lady Catherine monopolized the remaining conversation, effectively detaining the newlyweds. William was carefully attempting to distract the elder ladies to give his friend a respite. Into this, Mr. Bennet and Elizabeth stepped into the room. Mr. Bennet loudly cleared his throat, and beckoned Darcy over. The conversation in the parlour stilled.

"It is my great pleasure to announce, on a day already filled with joy, the engagement of Elizabeth Bennet de Bourgh to Mr. Fitzwilliam Darcy."

"Finally!" Lady Catherine cried. Jane and Bingley immediately were at their side, congratulating them, and taking leave. Neighbours followed, departing before the presumed outbursts from Mrs. Bennet. All had experienced her nerves at some point or another.

Mrs. Bennet, however, was so shocked she did not even twitch for a full minute.

By the time Mrs. Bennet began to recover, only family, excepting the Bingleys, remained. "Is it true?" she finally asked.

"Yes, Mama."

Mrs. Bennet blinked and nodded, before looking at Lady Catherine with disconcertion. "And … and … will you be married from Rosings?"

"Nay," Lady Catherine answered even as Elizabeth started to do so. "I believe it is best if she is married from here, where most of her friends will be. If, of course, you are willing to plan and host another such event so soon?"

"For so great a family? I do not --" Mrs. Bennet started.

"My dear Mrs. Bennet," Lady Catherine interrupted, "my brother the Earl, myself, and all of our Elizabeth's relations will be happy to simply enjoy her wedding. We only dared dream of such an occurrence, not three months ago." She paused. "I will, of course, cover the expense."

"Much appreciated, of course," Mr. Bennet replied, seeing his wife still mostly dumbstruck. "But only *some* of the expense. She is our daughter, as well."

A little playful back and forth ensued between Mr. Bennet and Lady Catherine about which family should supply the greatest support for their daughter's wedding. Despite the peace of barely an hour ago, Elizabeth abruptly felt overwhelmed, and excused herself. William followed, quiet concern in his expression.

She collected the bonnet and gloves she had set aside when they returned from the wedding. "Elizabeth?"

"Half an hour ought to be enough," she said.

William blinked, before nodding slowly. "Would you prefer to walk out alone? It would not be quite the same as being sent to fetch you by your cousin, but I can wait until your father asks for your presence."

Elizabeth half-smiled, remembering the quiet little pond at Rosings. "No, not the same." She tugged the gloves on and fastened the bonnet. "I just need time to think."

When she finally met his gaze, she took in the depth of the uncertainty in those eyes. "You are not ..." he did not finish the question, for she had pressed a gloved finger to his lips.

"I am not." She tilted her head to the side. "I simply need time to think. And you, my dearest William, make that quite difficult."

He nodded, before pulling her finger away and kissing her exposed wrist. She shivered. "Half an hour," he agreed.

A moment later, after he ascertained her intended direction, she felt him watch her from the front steps of her childhood home.

Here, in Hertfordshire, it had not been deemed necessary to assign anyone to walk with her, provided she kept to known paths. Indeed, until this moment, she had not actually walked out on her own since her return, for she had been accompanied by at least one sister, William, or Bingley at all times.

The solitude she had been bereft since that day at Rosings wrapped itself around her like a shawl borrowed from an old friend. One could not be properly alone inside a home, even in a library full of books, for human thought swirled around in such places. Inside, in all directions, human touch and thought were on display. Here, however, the rustling of the leaves and the call of birds and insects coloured the air. The road, worn from carriage wheels and horse hooves, shewd the only significant imprint of humans just now. No doubt, in a few moments, a carriage or rider would turn around a corner and into her sight or hearing, or perhaps William would come up from Longbourn to fetch her.

She did not reflect on any serious thoughts, no pressing concerns, no mysteries of life. She simply *was* for an entire, glorious, half hour.

At length, she found herself near the small rise where she had stood the morning her mother had come home aflutter with news about the new tenant at Netherfield. Such high hopes Mrs. Bennet had professed! And lo! her dearest Jane was now Mrs. Bingley, fulfilling both Mrs. Bennet *and* Elizabeth's hopes for her future.

And she … she was no longer Lizzy Bennet.

The realization was abrupt, and for a moment, it nearly snatched her breath away.

Oh, she had rationally come to terms with being the lost de Bourgh daughter. She had accepted that her frequent yearnings for *elsewhere* were, in fact, the faintest memories of another life, and the need to find her family. She recognized her easy trust of Wickham had been that same faint memory, and her reaction to William's dismissal at the assembly likely found its roots there, as well.

The realization, as she looked out over that familiar landscape, that shook her so was that *home* was no longer Longbourn. Even when her heart wished to wander and look for her first home, Longbourn had been her *home*. The distress that overcame her in the parlour while her parents bandied about which household held more responsibility for her wedding found its source. Neither was her home.

She was not quite sure where "home" was, now, although she suspected her heart's allegiances had declared it to be wherever William was. This sensation was more than just the comfort of 'us', and she wondered if this is what fuelled Jane's declarations about "hang the plans" in London.

She caught sight of William, in his pursuit of her, and called to him. He paused and raised his hand to acknowledge, and she gestured for him to join her.

A few moments later, and he was by her side. She watched as he took in the view. "I see why you chose this spot for today," he said after a moment.

"Oh?" she asked.

"Distant enough to soothe the restlessness, near enough to still be comfortable, and," he added as he smiled at her, "a lovely view does not hurt."

"It has been a momentous day," she replied.

"I certainly am not going to disagree with that description. A friend I love as much as I could a brother has gained a happiness he has long wished for, and the most handsome, most brilliant, most talented woman I have ever met has consented to be my wife."

"I am not," she protested.

William smiled, before glancing back out over the view. "You are to *me*." She flushed, and he continued, "I will, of course, allow that Bingley may think the same of Jane, and suitors that come to call on *our* other sisters, including Anne and Georgiana, have the same courtesy. It would be dreadful to think otherwise."

How quickly the man, one who had expressed such visible distaste for her family, adopted all of the Bennets. "Such fine condescension!" she teased. "Next you will tell me that you will be *excessively attentive* to all of those suitors!"

William barked a laugh and then affected a grave mien. "But of course, my dear. They will need to understand the worthiness of their chosen lady." He paused ever so briefly. "After all, I do hope to need to put the fear of *father* into a lad, in a score of years or so, when he comes to beg for my *daughter's* hand."

A brief image of a curly haired little girl, peering over William's shoulder at her, flashed across Elizabeth's imagination. Her heart clenched. "Only *a* daughter?" she asked, trying to sound still playful. She failed.

"As many sons and daughters as we can reasonably hope to have," William replied. Elizabeth decided then and there that Jane was eminently correct about "post the banns and hang the plans," and that her wedding day could not come soon enough.

Forty-Four

Elizabeth fretted about everything left to accomplish, and felt that perhaps her wedding *could* come too soon.

Letters, sometimes accompanied by parcels, flew from Longbourn and back. Elizabeth was quite certain the post's horses would soon refuse to make the turn to Longbourn House proper. Thankfully, they only had to tolerate quite *this* level of correspondence for less than another fortnight.

Jane and Bingley were due back in a week's time, Mrs. Bennet was in a predictable flutter, and Lady Catherine would be arriving in the next few hours. Lady Catherine and the Gardiners intended to travel in an entourage to Longbourn, as Anne had spent the previous se'enday with her sister's aunt and uncle. The Matlocks were quite busy with the social requirements of the season, and Anne had simply wanted to spend time with friends in town. The Gardiners, young, fashionable, and intelligent, as well as quite astute about people in general, obliged readily.

The latest news from Brighton indicated that Wickham's duties were not so strenuous that Colonel Forster could not spare him for a few days. He was expected to arrive a day prior, and stay in the Meryton inn. Mr. and Mrs. Collins travelled with Lady Catherine, but were to stay with the Lucases. Darcy opted to invite primarily family and close friends. Accordingly, a majority of the invitees had been in the locality just a fortnight ago.

According to Lady Matlock's letter yesterday, Richard would be spared from his duties as well, and arrive with his parents. Comments regarding Mary's need for tutelage to befit her future station solidified Elizabeth's suspicions. Her mother Bennet's ill-considered boasting at the Netherfield ball about "throwing the other girls into the paths of *other* rich men!" seemed to be at least a little fruitful. Jane and Bingley had graciously offered the use of Netherfield for the family which would overfill Longbourn, including a few other Darcy relations.

Having those details worked out set Elizabeth's mind at ease. Her mother could attend to the rest herself, and probably more happily so than if Elizabeth's more sedate and practical wishes were strictly followed. *She* however still had to attend to her own personal items. Her notes about items and fabrics taken while shopping with Jane assisted immeasurably, and the items from Mrs. Smithson's modiste arrived in good time. Those items which she needed to pack were being sorted and some already sent ahead to her uncle's London house.

The settlement papers were deemed completed pending a final review when *mère* arrived in a few hours' time. The primary settlement came from the de Bourgh family, much as Lady Catherine had described that beautiful but tumultuous morning nearly three months previous, but Mr. Bennet did settle some of Mrs. Bennet's and his personal assets on Elizabeth. They were, necessarily, items not included in the entail. William's side of the settlement fulfilled Mrs. Bennet's hopes for Elizabeth's pin-money and jewels, and then some.

It – most importantly for Mrs. Bennet – ensured that she and the other Bennet daughters would not be turned out into the hedgerows when Mr. Collins inherited. The Pemberley dowerage cottage, used only by family guests and occasionally rented for large parties over the past many years, would become available for Mrs. Bennet and any unmarried children upon Mr. Bennet's death. Lady Catherine did not require such reassurances, as she retained lifetime residency to Rosings as long as she lived, so William had insisted that Mrs. Bennet receive that due. As Elizabeth's inheritance of Brandywine remained separate from the Darcy estates by both Lady Catherine's will and the marriage settlement terms, it was not, strictly, a necessary offer. Elizabeth could ensure her family remained comfortable regardless.

Lady Catherine sided with William, when the particulars were discussed one last time. "*Of course*, you could let Fanny and the girls live at Brandywine should the entail come into effect! None of us would think meanly of that at all, my girl. But this is about more than just a home in sad circumstances, is not it, Darcy?"

William nodded. "It is. It is ensuring that Mr. and Mrs. Bennet's selflessness in taking on a foundling is repaid in the only way I can do so, beyond ensuring their daughter's – *your* –happiness insofar as I can. As *they* took you in under their roof, so – in not dissimilar circumstances – I, and by extension, the rest of the Fitzwilliams, can take them under *our* roof."

Elizabeth barely controlled the tears at having the reasoning laid out in such a way, and Mr. Bennet did not look unaffected himself. "I should protest that the honour of raising Elizabeth offsets any need for repayment – but I will not be so proud as to turn down a future home for my wife and children, either."

"Because you are not a simpleton, Bennet," Lady Catherine rejoined. "I told you we would find *some* way to ensure you were repaid for saving her." She paused to smile at the betrothed. "We are just fortunate that such an easy path for that presented itself."

"I suspect it would be the first time *either* of these two took the easy path in anything, and likely the last," Bennet teased.

"Papa!" overlapped with a sardonic "A first time for everything, sir."

Lady Catherine chuckled. "Were there any other concerns *you* had, Elizabeth?"

Elizabeth shook her head. "I have gone over it a few times, with Papa, with William, and again with Uncle Phillips. He may only be a country lawyer, but he has experience in this field. That was my remaining concern, to be sure it was fully considered."

Lady Catherine asked, "Should I sign it fully, then?"

Elizabeth nodded. Mr. Bennet had already affixed his signature for the Bennet side of the agreement, and William his for the Darcy side. Once Lady Catherine put ink to paper, the contract would be in force the moment the wedding was formalized. Elizabeth's own will ensured that, even if she should predecease her mother, even without issue of her own, her mother would not be rendered homeless. She had done her best, and her dear friend would not need to fret about turning her friend's family out of their home with nowhere else to go, either.

All that remained now was a se'nnight of patience, and she would be at William's London house for their wedding night. In a month's time, her Aunt and Uncle Gardiner would join them at Pemberley, for the tour of the countryside which had been discussed that day that Elizabeth's world changed.

In the meantime, Elizabeth divided her time between spending a last few half-hours with each sister. She listened to how Mary continued to improve with Georgina's encouragement, sometimes joining in for duets at their request. She listened in to Lydia's and Kitty's lessons, and assisted Miss McGonagall where she could. She assisted Mrs. Bennet wherever their mutual tolerance for shared tasks overlapped.

Also importantly, she ensured that she and William had diligent *enough* chaperones. Mr. Bennet had shared his elder brother's journals with Mary, and when the betrothed were not too unsociable for conversation with her, she would share highlights with them both. One passage, she simply blushed as she handed the journal over to William, and asked how much was accurate. Elizabeth noted that he flushed quite charmingly, before he handed it over to *her* to read as well. It was of, er, significant immodesty, from a male perspective. "Did Papa read this before he gave it to you?" she asked Mary.

Mary nodded. "He said he wondered if I would be brave enough to *ask* about it, but that perhaps a brother may be better to answer."

William flushed again, and sighed. "I would say that even the most self-controlled gentleman may find his mind … wanders … at the best of times. And sometimes our *anatomy* is definitely not under our control. That does *not* mean that our *actions* are not, of course." He smiled slightly. "That is, of course, why some fashions are as ridiculous as they are."

"To maintain your discretion?" Mary asked.

"Indeed," William replied, and Elizabeth felt rather than saw him glance at her, so swift was the action. "I do recall your father mentioning the journals, and that he thought you may find it useful, depending on your intentions." It was very clearly an attempt to change the subject, and the girls obliged.

Mary nodded slowly. "I confess, I had long considered the possibility of a similar course for my life. I have never felt *called* the way that my uncle describes, however, and I do not know if I could handle such hardships for so little reward."

William nodded slightly. "Longbourn may not be as large an estate as Pemberley, but it is still quite different than the life of a missionary."

"And," Mary replied softly, "that of a soldier."

"Aye," William concurred. "I have only my cousin's stories, and no experience. He said that, once in the field, many of the illusions of society are stripped away, in ways he cannot quite express."

"He has tried, certainly," Mary replied.

"Oh?" Elizabeth knew they had spoken long and close, several times now.

Mary placed her bookmark in the journal, and closed it, holding it close to her chest. She did not answer directly. "I am grateful for the opportunity to read, with my own eyes, some similar hardships. I believe it helps frame what the Colonel tried to express." A long pause fell as the trio walked along.

"He seems ready to find another choice of employment," William finally offered.

"Yes," Mary agreed. "He mentioned that Lizzy's cousin the Viscount and the Earl both have offered use of a smaller estate, and horses."

"And what think *you* of horses?" William asked.

Mary glanced at Elizabeth with a slight smile. "I am certainly fonder of them than *she* is, but we have few, and they are often wanted on the farm proper. I can ride."

"And better than I, true! Fortunately, I believe there are ponies and a chaise at Pemberley that I can use," Elizabeth laughed. "I will not need to come much of a horsewoman."

William smiled. "Even if there were not today, that could be easily resolved."

"Good!" Mary rejoined. "Our aunt would be terribly disappointed, for she has long wished to walk the grounds."

"Convincing her niece to let me marry her is certainly an elaborate method of ensuring the chance to indulge such a wish!" William teased.

"I am such a *dutiful* niece and daughter," Elizabeth replied as solemnly as she could muster.

The trio's composure lasted barely a moment, and then it was quite lost. It was a merry party indeed that returned to Longbourn's steps. Perhaps those who witnessed the stolid Mr. Darcy laughing with his fiancée and her sister were amazed, or perhaps they simply shrugged it off as the minor miracles of courtship.

Forty-Five

The morning dawned. Elizabeth recalled, not quite a month ago, finding Jane watching the sun rise, and part of her was mildly amused at her doing the same. Watching the sun rise *this* morning, however, came with the awareness that her world was about to change all over again. This time, by her own choices, of course, but it would be another up-ending. She refused to dwell too closely. For all of her other concerns, none centred around William himself.

Jane stirred on the bed, as she had elected to spend the night at Longbourn to ensure she would be available to help Elizabeth prepare. With the house so crowded, and Jane's old room housing guests, the sisters had shared a room as they had many times over the years.

Jane settled in beside her at the window. They had spoken late and long, the last three days, and there seemed little to say which would not be a repetition. Elizabeth leaned her head on her sister's shoulder, as the pink greys faded into blue.

"We should start getting you ready," Jane finally said.

Elizabeth half-reluctantly agreed, and rose. "Into the whirlwind, then."

Elizabeth barely recalled her own wedding, caught between anticipation and trepidation. Bits and flashes of the preparations – her hair refusing to be entirely contained – Lydia abruptly turning into a waterworks – Mrs. Bennet's exultations and Lady Catherine's dabbing at her eyes. The ceremony itself – she remembered William's *expressive* look at her as she joined him at the altar – the matrimony vows – and then signing her name as Elizabeth Darcy.

Time slowed back down after that, perhaps unnaturally slowly, although Elizabeth still barely tracked most of the goings on. The congratulations from cousins, new and old, rang around the wedding breakfast. *Their* sisters, all six of them, were quite effusive. Jane, very much in the role of *Mrs. Bingley*, ensured that Elizabeth and William were able to actually take to the coach awaiting them, assisted by the understanding and obliging Charles.

Jane's face – most beloved of those not in the carriage with her right then – was the last one she saw before leaving Longbourn. Jane's smile seemed to be both radiantly happy for her, and deeply wistful. The clip-clop of hooves on the road filled the carriage for a moment.

"Well, Mrs. Darcy. How are you feeling?" William asked, with a teasing note.

Elizabeth smiled up at him, and snuggled in closer. "Well enough," she allowed. "And you, Mr. Darcy?"

"Impatient is the most accurate term," William chuckled. "I have been quite irritated by the presence of *chaperones* the last few days."

"You poor, poor man! Such torments to befall you! How – mmph!" William silenced her teasing rather effectively, and it was some minutes before they spoke again.

"A few hours to London," she reminded him.

"Too long," he sighed, before desisting, reluctance written in every line on his face.

"I shall refrain from tempting you until tonight," Elizabeth promised.

William laughed. "My love, you tempt me just by *existing*." She blushed, and he smiled at her. "But I shall restrain myself from tempting you into tempting me *more*."

It was her turn to laugh, and she shook her head at him. "Books?"

"Books," he agreed, and he rummaged under the bench for their trip provisions. He handed her the selection she had made the night previous, and they settled in together to read for a while.

Elizabeth never doubted the competency of William's staff at the townhouse, but she was mildly amused at how *carefully* they gave the newlyweds space that first night. They spent two nights in London, then they were on the road to Pemberley. William ensured that Elizabeth had plenty of opportunity to sight-see on the road north, and they did not arrive at Pemberley by the most direct route or the fastest time.

Nearly a week after leaving Longbourn, William announced, "We are nearly to the turn for Pemberley." Yet it was several more minutes before William directed the driver to slow.

Elizabeth paid close attention as the carriage rounded the turn to the house. The carriage paused, even without William's direction. She thought she might have gasped; she could not be sure. She understood then, why William and Georgiana loved their home so much, beyond the normal affection for one's familiar surroundings. When she tore her eyes away from the sight, she found William gazing at her with a slight smile.

"I hope, very much, that the house meets with your approval?" he asked, in a tone between jest and apprehension.

"I dare say there are few in the world who would *not* approve, and I would hope I am not such a simpleton," she rejoined. He chuckled.

She glanced back at the house, still as handsome as it had been at first sight. The carriage started moving again, and the jolt made her aware of how very large the house was. Trepidation crept to her awareness again, and she leaned into him. He wrapped his arm around her. "I do hope," she continued, "that I am up to the task of being her mistress."

William snorted, and tightened his embrace. "I remember the first day I came home from Cambridge after several months, with greater awareness of what tasks would face me when I would take over the guardianship of the estate from my father. It was awe-inspiring, to think that I could ever be entrusted so." He breathed into her hair slightly. "And, a few days after his death, frightening, that I could ever be entrusted so." A sigh, and she gripped his hand tightly in comfort. "You will be a fine mistress for Pemberley. She has been without one for many years."

At the door, William assisted her out of the carriage, and introduced her to the head housekeeper, Mrs. Reynolds. She was a respectable-looking elderly woman, quite civil and not very fine, with a warm manner. "Welcome home, Mrs. Darcy," the lady said with a smile.

The words wrapped themselves around her heart, and whispered comfort, belonging, life.

Home.

Forty-Six

A fortnight later, Elizabeth stood beside William as the Matlock carriage, carrying Georgiana, her companion, and the Matlocks themselves, followed by a touring carriage. Elizabeth spied her Aunt and Uncle Gardiner admiring the view, much as she had even that first morning.

Once all of the flurry of arrivals and welcomes subsided, Elizabeth found herself settling down on a chair in the room set aside for her Aunt and Uncle Gardiner, while her husband absconded with her uncles for fishing. Elizabeth had discovered she enjoyed the sport herself, but knew her Aunt Gardiner – and perhaps Aunt Matlock – would wish to check on her, beyond what letters had already been shared.

"Marriage seems to suit you well," Mrs. Gardiner noted after the servant left the room.

"We are still adjusting, of course," Elizabeth replied. "I only imagine that would be true of any newlyweds. But I am happy, and William seems to be as well."

"And what of other concerns?"

Elizabeth considered her answer. "It is early yet, but I feel that I will not shame the shades of Pemberley."

Mrs. Gardiner, obviously recalling the sharing of *that* story, chuckled. "You are fortunate Lady Catherine is such a staunch supporter of your decisions."

"You know that my courage always rises in the face of intimidation," Elizabeth laughed. "While I am grateful that *Mère* is supportive, I dare say I would have weathered her displeasure in any other circumstance, as well. How is she, and Anne, truly?"

"Have you had letters?"

"Of course. But I feel a faint concern, still."

"Lady Catherine seemed melancholy when we saw her last, just before she and Miss de Bourgh left Longbourn for Rosings. Miss de Bourgh has written, and her spirits do not seem to be particularly affected. Of course, I have no knowledge of how she presented prior to her staying with us in London. Her companion, Mrs. Jenkins, seems a genteel enough lady, but I do not know how compatible she is with Lady Catherine. Miss de Bourgh did not hint at any concerns regarding her mother."

"I am given to understand that *mère* enjoys society, and that visitors are not infrequent at Rosings," Elizabeth replied. "It seems that a companion is less necessary for her than my sister. And Mama? Lydia?"

"Lydia volunteered to help Miss McGonagall with the children, Kitty as well. When Mary can spare time from her piano, studies, and letter-writing, your father is teaching her more about estate management, particularly the household side, than she has yet learnt. She did well, the few days he was at Rosings with you. Your mother – " Mrs. Gardiner shrugged. "If you assumed she was boasting to all of the county about the wedding they attended, you may be reassured it is, thus far, only about *half* of the county." Elizabeth burst out in laughter as Mrs. Gardiner added, "After all, she still had not finished boasting about Mrs. Bingley, before she could boast about Mrs. Darcy."

"Indeed, I think she had not!" Elizabeth eyed her aunt. "But Mary? Letter-writing?"

"Ostensibly to Lady Matlock and Miss de Bourgh. If she has other correspondents apart from yourself, or perhaps Mrs. Collins, she would not share. It does not seem likely that she would be writing Jane when Netherfield is a mere five miles away."

"Perhaps not," Elizabeth allowed. "Any other news from London?"

"Especially from Mr. Boswell, the gypsy?" Mrs. Gardiner replied. "None yet. I left directions. We can but hope he chooses to share what he knows."

"Indeed," Elizabeth rose. "Would you like a brief tour? Mrs. Reynolds is more familiar with the history of the house itself, of course, but I can certainly show you the salient points."

"Perhaps when your uncle returns," Mrs. Gardiner replied. "I would not be displeased to see your favourite spots, though."

Elizabeth guided her aunt to her personal study. Mrs. Gardiner took in the room before settling in the chair across from Elizabeth's desk. "I notice you have the room arranged much like your father's. How have you taken to the management of the household?"

Elizabeth tilted her head as she considered her answer. She leaned forward to tap the household ledger. "My experience with Longbourn's books has been beneficial, of course. Naturally, there are differences, beyond Pemberley's tenants being more numerous. Pemberley has many more sheep than Longbourn, although we are fortunate to have enough flats to have some cereal and row crops. The needs of the tenants reflect that difference." She leaned back. "Mrs. Reynolds has managed the role of mistress since William's mother passed, and she has been supportive in my learning the differences."

"How did she react, discovering you had been keeping such books for years?"

"Surprised, certainly. It is apparently not as common in the upper circles of the gentry as one may believe." Elizabeth shrugged. "I suppose being able to afford a Steward, and needing to attend to multiple estates and responsibilities, changes that viewpoint."

"I would certainly prefer to be able to tell when my Steward was cheating me!" replied Mrs. Gardiner in surprise.

"I readily agree. But Lady Matlock, for instance, cannot be auditing the books while she is managing the London house during Parliament's active season."

"Has Georgiana learnt much, then?"

"Not as much as Mary, I believe. Among many other things, that is one area I will endeavour to encourage them both." A knock at the door. "Come in," Elizabeth called.

"Ah, there you are." Lady Matlock stepped into the room, gesturing for the women to stay seated. She glanced around. "I approve of the rearrangements, not that you need such approval. It is certainly your space now." She settled herself in the chair beside Mrs. Gardiner.

"This was Lady Anne's study before?"

"Yes," Elizabeth replied. She gestured at a door to the side. "The master's study – William's study, now – is through that door. I saw no reason to rearrange *that* aspect of it." She paused, with a quick glance at Mrs. Gardiner. "I am told that my sister Mary has been writing letters to you?"

Lady Matlock smiled. "Indeed, although perhaps not all of the letters have been *meant* for me, regardless of how they have been addressed."

Elizabeth arched an eyebrow, and Lady Matlock shook her head. "No, no clandestine communiqués, rather many a comment for me to pass on to Richard."

Elizabeth half-smiled. "Does my cousin seem inclined to listen for such comments?"

Lady Matlock laughed. "I dare say I see him more often when there may be a letter from Miss Bennet to share titbits than I did the entire time that you and Mrs. Bingley were in residence!"

Mrs. Gardiner chuckled. "Is that not the way?"

"So it seems," Lady Matlock agreed. "I, of course, do my proper maternal duty and relay such comments from *him* to *her* as are appropriate." She paused. "I rather like Miss Mary. Miss McGonagall has been a fine influence for her already, and I suspect she will have sufficient composure to brave the wilds of London society whenever we need her attendance. I hope that Richard makes the right choice sooner rather than later."

Elizabeth nodded agreement, before shifting the subject. "Anne wrote that she has suggested that Wickham study under our mother's steward, as had been suggested years ago. The steward is apparently making noises about retiring."

Lady Matlock pursed her lips and glanced between the other two. "I have my reservations about that idea, of course."

"William mentioned that perhaps Anne is trying to bring Wickham into her sphere to determine if he might be suited to another role."

Mrs. Gardiner blinked in surprise, and Lady Matlock suppressed a start. "He certainly seemed genteel and gallant enough when he was in London," Mrs. Gardiner replied cautiously.

"And a Darcy, a gentleman's son, without the concerns of being a Fitzwilliam," Lady Matlock allowed. "I know that Anne has voiced concerns related to her own weaknesses, that 'outbreeding' would be better for the de Bourghs." She looked at Elizabeth. "Is there a reason you shared this possibility?"

Elizabeth sighed. "She is my sister, but I know her only a little. I know my mother even less. I know Wickham as he was before his absolution, but I do not know if or how long any changes may last." She paused, searching for words. "I do not know whether to encourage or discourage her – in either the spoken scheme or the unspoken one." She smiled slightly at her aunts. "I suppose I need advice."

Lady Matlock shook her head. "I have little to none to offer myself immediately. Watchful observation would be best."

"Is there likely to be *harm* should he take up a stewardship?" Mrs. Gardiner queried.

"All else aside, he has been less than sterling in his personal management of money over the years," Lady Matlock replied.

"William has provided reasons why he may have been less than attentive to such matters, in at least two situations. My understanding is that Wickham has rather more sensibility than sense when under emotional duress." Elizabeth paused, sighing. "Although, under similar circumstances, I suspect I would be hard pressed to be sensible, as well. Losing loved ones is quite difficult."

Lady Matlock looked surprised. "I knew about Wickham's parents, of course, the elder Mr. Wickham and *her*." A decided note of distaste at even referencing Wickham's mother. Elizabeth presumed that her aunt had her reasons. "But they were both quite alive when Wickham first had debts which William discharged."

"I am given to understand that George had an intended, and the family strongly disapproved. The girl did not live another year, to her maturity. Anne knows of this, as well." William, of course, had shared more, but Elizabeth did not want to share Wickham's heartbreak any more widely than necessary.

"Oh," Mrs. Gardiner replied, a voice full of sympathy. "I can well understand how that might cause disarray, especially after your disappearance several years before."

Elizabeth nodded, and Lady Matlock expressed agreement. "Such was our thought." Elizabeth glanced between the older women.

After a moment, Lady Matlock slowly nodded. "Catherine may be not inclined towards bringing Wickham into her home as steward, but it would be reasonable to see if he might be agreeable." She paused a moment. "Randall has expressed concern about his health, certainly, as it does not seem as robust as it ought. A more stable situation under the excessively attentive eyes of your mother may be beneficial. I may suggest that to her myself in my next letter. We would be willing to buy out his commission if necessary."

"Should I communicate a willingness to assist to Anne, then?" Elizabeth asked.

Lady Matlock agreed. "I will work on your mother, if your husband is willing to work on convincing Wickham."

Elizabeth smiled slightly. "I believe William already planned that action, but I will share your support for the scheme."

With the most pressing schemes of supporting the unmarried in their pursuit of resolving that problem discussed as thoroughly as the women could do at the moment, Elizabeth and her aunts adjourned to the parlour to await her husband's and uncles' return to the house. Georgiana had already opened the piano, and Mrs. Annesley sat serenely enjoying her charge's performance. Georgiana's fingers stilled with the end of the music, and she was startled by the sudden applause.

"Oh!" she cried. "I had not seen you all enter. My apologies! I was practicing."

"If that is practicing, my dear," Lady Matlock replied, "then I doubly look forward to hearing you perform in earnest!"

Georgiana flushed from the praise before rising. "Has my brother come back to the house yet?"

"Not that I am aware," Elizabeth replied. "But I expect he will soon. They have been out for a few hours now."

Forty-Seven

Madeline Gardiner _nee_ Hollsworth spent the first few days rekindling old friendships in her old town of Lambton, while introducing her husband and her niece, the new Mrs. Darcy, to those friends. Miss Darcy sometimes accompanied her sister. Lambton merchants exerted themselves to garner favour with Mrs. Darcy, in the hopes of attracting her business.

A few days were spent at Brandywine, reviewing the estate in person. Lady Matlock shared stories of _her_ courtship, while the Earl shared stories of his late sister's. Elizabeth found the estate to be larger than Longbourn, but certainly comfortable. She noted that it was not above thirty miles from Pemberley, an eminently comfortable distance for, say, offering Jane and Charles use of the estate until one could be purchased outright, "should Netherfield lose its charm," as she phrased it. Madeline understood her meaning and concurred.

A week into the Gardiners' stay, a messenger arrived at Pemberley, looking for Mrs. Gardiner. He was shown into the study where she sat with Elizabeth and Lady Matlock, as they discussed tenant issues. Elizabeth and Madeline recognized him as the White Hart's groom, and briefly introduced him to Lady Matlock. He moved straight to his message.

"Ma'am," he said, "We have a guest who has arrived from London looking for you. He indicated that he believed you would wish to see him soon, but he looked tired enough from the road that the Missus insisted he rest."

Madeline glanced sharply at Elizabeth, who drew in a harsh breath. "Please return to the inn, good sir. I will be there shortly." The groom nodded and withdrew. Madeline continued, to Elizabeth, "Mr. Gardiner and I will see to the visitor. *You* will stay here. "

"I should —" Elizabeth started.

"You shall not," Madeline overrode her, for the first time in many years. "You will have to trust me and your uncle."

"However, I will also go," Lady Matlock added quietly, placing a light hand on Elizabeth's arm. "Trust us. We have no reason to believe he is hostile, but it is too late in this game to take the chance."

Elizabeth wilted slightly. "I … want to know, too."

"And whatever I learn, my love, I *will* tell you," Madeline promised, drawing her niece into her arms for reassurance, as if she were a child. Right then, she nearly was.

After a moment, where Madeline felt Elizabeth trying to regain her composure, she felt the nodded agreement. "Let me send a letter with you," Elizabeth said, "for the innkeeper. If it indeed be Mr. Boswell, or someone bringing news on his behalf, all of the customary expenses for his stay ought to be covered by Pemberley." She moved to her desk to draft the letter.

Madeline agreed and Lady Matlock gave a rueful but approving smile at her niece. "Heart of gold, that one," she said in an undertone to Madeline. "We all are better for her."

"Indeed," Madeline concurred.

Elizabeth blotted the page, and waved it a moment to dry the ink before sealing it. She offered it to Madeline, her expression still vulnerable and wary. "I will send for my uncles – do you think Lord Matlock would wish to join you as well?"

Lady Matlock shook her head. "Even if he should wish it, he will listen to me that it is better if we do not make *too* much spectacle of this. Mrs. Gardiner *was* telling me about some lovely lace she saw at the milliner's just a few shops down from The White Hart."

Elizabeth smiled, albeit weakly. "As good a reason to go to town as any," she agreed. She led the way out of the study and directed her staff to inform her uncles that her aunts were bound for Lambton for "lace and gossip," and to request they meet the ladies at the carriage, in no more than half an hour.

All three husbands were in attendance by the time the ladies made their own way, Darcy's expression worried and guarded. Lady Matlock apparently understood his expression and moved to reassure him quietly. "Not so much gossip, William, as information," she said in an undertone before more loudly sharing, " Mrs. Gardiner assures me that there is some lovely lace at the milliner's. It is a beautiful afternoon for an outing."

He nodded, taking in Elizabeth's expression. "Enjoy your shopping, then, Aunt Gardiner, Aunt Matlock. We look forward to hearing about your shopping later." Lord Matlock evidently caught the meaning of his wife's own pointed look, for he professed a desire to remain and attend an urgent round of billiards. Thus, Madeline, Mr. Gardiner, and Lady Matlock alone alighted the carriage.

It was only five miles to Lambton as the carriage rides, and Pemberley's carriage rode easily in most weather. Any discomfort was due purely to the anticipation that weighed upon them all. Mr. Gardiner knew what little Madeline knew already, and all three were keen to know all that there could be.

When they arrived, the groom was quick to move to assist the driver. "The Missus said to send you in as soon as may be," he told Mrs. Gardiner.

She nodded, and Lady Matlock led the way. In just a moment, they were led to one of the smaller let rooms, where Mr. Boswell indeed waited. "Mrs. Gardiner!" he exclaimed upon seeing her. "You look well."

She remembered how much she liked the man, for he was warm and genuine. He was near her age, but looked a little older due to a harder life. "Thank you, Mr. Boswell. It is good to see you again. This is Mr. Gardiner, my husband, and Lady Matlock."

Mr. Boswell's eyes went wide, even as he gestured for them all to sit. "I am pleased to meet you both, but especially you, ma'am," he said to Lady Matlock. "I read in the papers that Elizabeth Bennet is your niece."

"Indeed," Lady Matlock agreed. She paused as a servant set tea down on the small table, and was politely dismissed. "And I am given to understand that *you* may know some of how she came to be with the Bennets."

His head dropped for a moment, as he took what seemed to be a steadying breath, before meeting her eyes straight on. "Aye, ma'am. Mrs. Gardiner asked as much in her letter, which is why I am here. I swear to ye, if we had known she were yours, we would have brought her straight to ye. But *she* did not know. Did she join you? I wish her to know."

"We will share the information with her," Madeline promised. "She has been through many shocks these last few months, and she is now Mrs. Darcy, as well. But I promise I will relay it all."

"Perhaps you could start at the beginning?" Mr. Gardiner prompted.

"It has been nigh on twenty years, has it not?" Mr. Boswell returned. "I may not recall everything *exactly* but I shall endeavour." He sipped at the tea he currently cradled, and faltered.

"Seventeen and a half," Lady Matlock replied. "Pray, continue."

"Seventeen years," the man murmured. "Seventeen years, I have done what I could to keep tabs on her, to make sure she was still safe. Pa gave me a task, and I have done my best." He shook himself lightly, and straightened, setting the cup down.

"We were traveling, as we do, from Southborough to Crawley," he began. "Now-a-days, I do not quite recall where we bedded down for the night, but it was nearer Crawley than Southborough. East Grinstead perhaps?"

More than twenty miles? Madeline thought. *Good heavens!*

"Middle of the night, the watch heard a ruckus, and went to investigate. Pa was with them. They found a little girl, crying for her mama. They asked her where her mama was, and she said she was lost, her pony had run away from George, and *she* had fallen off the pony some time later." The Gardiners shared a glance with Lady Matlock, but they did not move to interrupt.

"Pa brought her back, because what else could they do in the middle of the night? Of all the watch, he was the only one with littles, so he brought her to our wagon to feed her and get her cleaned up.

"I remember Ma waking me to help. She was a tiny little thing, same as my sister Mary. She could tell us her name was Elizabeth, but she could not remember her parents' names. She had bruises all over, probably from falling off the pony, and a terrible lump on her head. I have seen grown men die from hits to the temple like that; she was right lucky. But she could not remember much, just 'big house' and George taking her for a pony ride, and wanting her mama. But she could not tell us what her mama even looked like."

"How long did she stay with you?" Lady Matlock probed.

"Well, we had someone's child, right? So we had meant to be in Crawley for a faire by Lady's Day with our usual stops along the way for work, but we could not just *take* her. Most of the clan went ahead, but Pa and us, we stayed there a few days, looking and asking. Parish clergy had no knowledge or mention of a missing child, and she was so badly shaken Ma would not simply leave her. We did give the parish directions to one of our regular stops to get a letter to us if anyone came looking for her, but the next year we checked again, and no one ever did."

Another sip of tea, seemingly more for gathering his thoughts than any thirst. "We took her along with us, to Crawley, but as she healed up over the next while, it became apparent that she had developed a terrible fear of horses. She had a few memories come back, here and there, asking for *her* sister Anne. She was terribly distraught and kept trying to go find her. But the horses terrified her, and I reckon that if *I* had my pony bolt and throw me far from home, I might have done the same.

"In between her nightmares and her terrors, she was the sweetest little girl, and she and Mary got along wonderfully. I would have been pleased to keep her as a little sister. Ma thought to keep her, too, but Pa insisted that the fineness of her dress meant she had to be the daughter of someone important. Clan tried, but could not find anyone missing a daughter. We all asked everywhere we went. We even sent a rider to Westerham, but he heard no such news.

"But the fear of horses – well, that cannot be for a gypsy child. Ma cried when Pa said we needed to take her somewhere else, where she might be found by her family, or at least a family that did not live and die by their horses. The clan agreed and Ma accepted it. Pa tasked me with taking her to London and keeping her safe, because by his reckoning, that is where all the fine folk go at least some time of the year. We also had work dealings with a couple of orphanages there, and on occasion we would take in an orphan who seemed to be gypsy.

"We were nearer Reading by then. I took her by post coach. Hated leaving my own horse with the family, but there was no way she would stay calm enough to ride. Even the coach was difficult, I had to cover her eyes to get her inside. She was terrified." He paused again.

"I thought she might feel … betrayed, abandoned by being taken to London. I promised her that we were only trying to help her find her mama and her papa, but that she needed to stay in a place with other children missing *their* mamas and papas for that to happen.

"I swear that I did not know about the fever, though. The orphanage did not say anything of it, although I learnt later that they knew. Else, I would have taken her back with me to Reading, to catch up with the family from there. I only found out about the fever when I went back a few weeks later to check on her, like I promised her and Pa. That is when I learned that she had left London with Mr. Bennet, and been taken on after he lost his own children to the fever." He paused, glancing at Mrs. Gardiner. "I cannot tell you how grateful I was to know she had been spared and found a family to live with, a proper family. We still asked around whenever we went through there, but we never heard of someone *missing* a daughter. Plenty o' young ones lost to fever and sickness, but not just *lost.*"

Silence hung over the little gathering for a few moments, while each digested the story. Madeline spoke up first. "Why did you never share that story with me until now? We spoke about her every time you came 'round."

Mr. Boswell grimaced. "Would it have done any good?" he returned. "For all you knew and I knew, her entire family was lost and her life with the Bennets was all she had. I never gave up *hope* and I am grateful she has found her kin at last. But why complicate things more than needful?" He shrugged helplessly. "I meant to tell *her,* one day, by letter if need be. I am telling *you* because you promise to share it with her. I …" he faltered again, before rising to rummage in a bag to the side. He returned with an unsealed letter, handing it to Madeline. "I wrote this for Miss Elizabeth, a few years ago when my own eldest was about the age she was when we found her. Being a father has added a whole different level to my recollections of it all. But I never quite had the courage to give it to her. I did not wish to disturb her if it was needless."

Madeline took the letter, and nodded. "I will, of course, review it before giving it to her," she replied.

"I expect nothing less, ma'am," he agreed. "But that is why I came myself, I … wanted to *see her* with her kin, at long last. I should like to know my promise to Pa, to her, is finally fulfilled."

Lady Matlock glanced at the Gardiners. "We will return to Pemberley soon, although there was a discussion of a brief shopping detour prior to returning," she replied. "I can well understand wanting to see your promise fulfilled, although her mother and sister are not currently visiting. Would seeing her with myself and her uncle, Lord Matlock, and her husband, Mr. Darcy, suffice for now?"

"It would ease my heart greatly, ma'am," Mr. Boswell replied.

"Then rest now," Mr. Gardiner said, standing in preparation to take leave. "We will call for you to join us in a few half-hours' time."

Forty-Eight

Madeline reviewed the letter on the return, while Mr. Boswell rode his rested horse alongside the carriage. It was indeed dated a few years ago, and contained much of the same information he had spoken, with only a few minor details included. It concluded with an apology for not being able to find her family, and hoping that she would forgive them for having abandoned her to an orphanage, even if it seemed it turned out for the best.

She passed the letter to her husband, and he to Lady Matlock. Lady Matlock's lips tightened as she read it, undoubtedly from renewed distress. Indeed, Madeline suspected she saw a shimmer of tears in Lady Matlock's eyes.

"Her story is almost complete," Lady Matlock murmured, handing the letter back to Madeline.

"No," Madeline corrected. "Her _story_ is not almost complete. This _chapter_ is. Her _story_ continues – as Mrs. Darcy, with hopefully many children to brighten the shades of Pemberley, and all the laughter and joy that Elizabeth brings with her."

Lady Matlock smiled at the correction. "You are, of course, accurate as always, Madeline." She glanced out the window at the rider alongside the carriage. "My sister will be pleased to know that her daughter is safe after all, and that she was cared for and loved every moment possible."

"Is Lady Catherine likely to wish to honour Elizabeth's saviours?" Mr. Gardiner queried.

"Entirely possible," Lady Matlock agreed. "And will that not be quite the sight? Gypsies, being honoured at Rosings!"

The house came into sight, and Mr. Boswell paused, falling behind. He caught up a moment later, asking through the window. "Miss Elizabeth – pardon me, Mrs. Darcy – is the mistress of *that?*" he asked in awe.

"She is indeed," Lady Matlock replied with a laugh.

"Ma will be thrilled," he replied. "I wish Pa were still here to tell."

The meeting of Mr. Boswell and the Darcys was brief, with Mr. Boswell conveying his entire family's well-wishes on her marriage and reunited family. He took his leave, declaiming any need for hospitality. "My own family beckons, Mrs. Darcy. I will rest at the White Hart – thank you for covering the expense, ma'am. But perhaps when we journey this way, we shall call upon the house?"

"Please do," Mr. Darcy agreed, with Elizabeth echoing him. With that, Mr. Boswell remounted his horse, and turned up the drive for Lambton.

"One *chapter* closed," Lady Matlock murmured with a glance at Madeline.

"And an entire *story* to continue," Madeline agreed.

~ The End ~

www.ingramcontent.com/pod-product-compliance
Lightning Source LLC
Chambersburg PA
CBHW070618260626
47161CB00007B/2480